JULEBORD
(THE HOLIDAY PARTY)
Book II: A Story About Recent Events
Correlations Trilogy

GUERNICA WORLD EDITIONS 68

JULEBORD

(THE HOLIDAY PARTY)

BOOK II: A Story About Recent Events

DAVID ØYBO

GUERNICA
World
EDITIONS

TORONTO—CHICAGO—BUFFALO—LANCASTER (U.K.)
2023

The world described in this story—although it is affected by events
that have happened in ours—is a world of fiction.
Therefore names, characters, places, and incidents
are either the products of the author's imagination
or are used fictitiously. With the exception of real public figures,
institutions or places, any resemblance to actual persons,
living or dead, as well as businesses, companies, events,
or locales is entirely coincidental and never intended or implied.

The contents of this book are the sole responsibility of the author
and do not reflect the views, opinions or policies of the U.S. Air Force,
the Department of Defense, or the U.S. Government.
Mention of trade names, commercial products, or organizations
does not imply endorsement by the U.S. Government.

Guernica Editions Founder: Antonio D'Alfonso

Michael Mirolla, editor
Cover design: Allen Jomoc Jr.
Interior layout: Jill Ronsley, suneditwrite.com
Front cover photo of a female surfer
riding a winter wave somewhere in Norway: Mats Grimseth

Guernica Editions Inc.
287 Templemead Drive, Hamilton (ON), Canada L8W 2W4
2250 Military Road, Tonawanda, N.Y. 14150-6000 U.S.A.
www.guernicaeditions.com

Distributors:
Independent Publishers Group (IPG)
600 North Pulaski Road, Chicago IL 60624
University of Toronto Press Distribution (UTP)
5201 Dufferin Street, Toronto (ON), Canada M3H 5T8

First edition.
Printed in Canada.

Legal Deposit—Third Quarter
Library of Congress Catalog Card Number: 2023935409
Library and Archives Canada Cataloguing in Publication
Title: Julebord (the holiday party): a story about recent events / David Øybo.
Names: Øybo, David, author.
Series: Guernica world editions (Series) ; 68.
Description: Series statement: Guernica world editions ; 68 | Book II in the
Correlations trilogy.
Identifiers: Canadiana (print) 20230204074 | Canadiana (ebook)
20230204317 | ISBN 9781771838337 (softcover) | ISBN 9781771838344 (EPUB)
Classification: LCC PS3615.Y26 J85 2023 | DDC 813/.6—dc23

For my Family.
But especially for Zino—Dad will always love you.

Joachim: Sorry for being responsible
for the time you almost broke your neck.

For the patients I was allowed to treat,
and for all members of the healthcare team with
whom I have had and have the privilege to work.

CONTENTS

Warning

Philanthropic Pledge

A share of any financial proceeds from this story will be donated in equal parts to organizations that fight against Female Genital Mutilation (FGM) and study the so-called caregiver-child relationship problem providing support to victims of these two atrocities.

Author's Note

Parts of this story are based on true events. In other words, the author has, from time to time, taken the real, the documented, the observed and the recounted as a starting point, and let his imagination take over, fill in, and expand. Certain names and locales have been changed, while others have not. Certain situations have been added, while others have been taken away. Therefore, any similarities between what is described in this story and reality are—at best—coincidental.

* * *

The opinions expressed in this story belong to the fictional characters and should not be confused with those of the author.

* * *

Most of the events described take place in Norway and other countries in Europe, which use the metric system to measure distances and mass, the 24-hour clock convention (also known as 'military time') for time-keeping, and degrees Celsius for measuring temperature. In keeping with its setting, the author has opted to use the metric system, the 24-hour clock, and degrees Celsius in this story.

A Guide for the Reader of this Book

TURN or FLICK?

Dear Reader,

My daughter interrupted me one night. "But Daddy! I don't want you to tell me what's going to happen next to the princess, I want to know what's happening in the castle now!"

* * *

The question: eBooks and books published online offer the ability to jump from one section to another through the use of hypertext links and other amazing ways to avoid a strictly linear reading. So why not offer something similar for physical books? In today's small world, with its amazing complexity and wonderful diversity, and where at times it may be just simply wrong to follow our somewhat archaic human instincts, should the paradigm that a story can be read in only one way predetermined by the author still be followed at all times?

In this story you—the reader—are empowered to abandon the normal reading strategy of a paper book and you have, for parts of this story, a choice of how to engage with it.

Chapters One to Six follow the lives of six doctors working at Godshus General Hospital in 2019 and cover the period between August 26th, 1960 and the early evening hours of December 20th, 2019. How did the doctors end up in Godshus General Hospital? What dreams in their lives were shattered by subsequent events?

What personal traumas did they bring with them? What were the consequences of their actions for themselves and for others? What were the things that connect them, knowingly and unknowingly? How were they affected by the events that shape our world?

You—the reader—can engage with the stories of the doctors' lives in many ways, but perhaps in two ways above all:

TURN

The first option is to read the story the same way as you would read any other book made from paper; just continue to TURN the pages. You will follow the story of one doctor's life prior to moving on to the next doctor in a sequential fashion, eventually reaching Chapter Seven, which will answer the question of what exactly happened the night of the Julebord.

Or you can:

FLICK

The second way to experience the sequence of events which make up the story is to do some 'hopscotching'. Starting with Section One in Chapter One you will find a field similar to this at the end of each section:

←··· 56 ○◎○ 322 ···→

The number on the right (i.e. 322) is the page number of the section covering the next point in time in the overall time period covered by the story (i.e., as already mentioned, between August 26th, 1960 and the early evening hours on December 20th, 2019). With the exception of its endpoint, December 20th, 2019, the story follows a linear timeline, so that if you choose to FLICK you will be taken to the event in any of the six doctors' lives which occurred immediately after the section you have just finished reading. Most of the time—but not always—you will land in another doctor's mind than the one you have just been in. Eventually you will reach Chapter Seven as you would have if you had been turning the pages in a regular way through the book. To explore the story in this alternate way, you need to FLICK ahead to the page indicated on the right side of the field provided at the end of each section. For your convenience—to make it easier for you to go back in time to the section you just came from—the number on the left side (i.e. 56 in the example above) is the page number of the section you just read.

So what will be different?

Rarely in today's world do we encounter situations where the problem is a lack of information. Most of the time we are faced with the opposite—too much info—making it difficult for our minds to discern what is really important. Whether you TURN or FLICK, you will have gained the same information about the six doctors' lives by the time you reach Chapter Seven. What will differ at times is the order in which you, the reader, will acquire that information. This may or may not change how you interpret the words you read next and consequently how you interpret some of the actions happening in the lives of the six doctors.

* * *

"But Dad! It makes no sense at all for the princess to go back to the castle. It's just ruins now. You told me it burned down! Silly daddy!" This was my daughter's second interruption that night. Obliging her earlier wish to hear what was happening at the castle, I had told her that the princess's castle had burned to the ground after it had been struck by lightning—the result of the summers in the kingdom getting hotter and drier every year and the thunderstorms stronger. Of course, the princess was unaware of this, as she was busy saving the prince from the dragon. I then continued with the story.

After your initial decision to TURN or FLICK you can always opt to FLICK or TURN or TURN or FLICK at any time at the end of any section, choosing your own unique reading path through the narrative, diverging from the two ways suggested above. If you opt for that approach, just be aware that you might end up at Chapter Seven having skipped over some of the information provided, which may or may not be relevant.

Also be aware that of course you will meet the doctors in the book for the first time only once in your life. Even if you choose to read the story again in a different way, first impressions count and are remembered, are they not? Therefore, choose wisely.

Have fun

turning
or
flicking
or
turning and then flicking
or
flicking and then turning.

Well, whatever you do, just start reading the book already!

Yours,
David Øybo
P.S.:

57 ⋯→

FLICK to page 57 if you got here from Chapter One, Section One: Dr. Alessandro Gianetti – August 26th, 1960 – Friday and want to get back to where you came from in the story.

Julebord

As some of us know, a Julebord (translated—politically correct—as 'The Holiday Party') is an important and lively event to socialize once a year on a December evening with your colleagues, deeply rooted in the working culture of organizations and employers in Norway.

Occasionally, people even call it *'the event of the year'*.
For those of us, who don't know:

It means:
skirts and blouses,
suits and ties,
high heels and smart shoes,
mascara and cufflinks.

It means:
pinnekjøt and ribbe,
julepølse and potatoes,
and—rarely nowadays—lutefisk
followed by riskrem. Always riskrem.

It means:
mugs full of gløgg and glasses filled with wine.

It often means:
bubbly champagne and colorful cocktails,
and sometimes—only sometimes—a little too much akvavit.

It's always the damn akvavit.

It means:
celebration and speeches,
laughter,
music and dance.

It means:
releasing pent up frustrations and, for some:
fulfilling romance.

It has only ONE rule:
What happens at the Julebord stays at the Julebord.
Forever.
Just like Vegas.
But it's freezing cold and pitch-dark outside.

This is Norway.
In winter.

In the middle of winter.

December 21st, 2019 – SATURDAY
Godshus – Norway

It would be the darkest day of the year.

* * *

09:36

The ice-cold of the salty water in his face finally awakened him fully. His headache was gone. He still felt strange. The sky just had started to turn from a pinkish-purple-violet to deep blue. It was the time of the year when the days start way too late and end too early. The sky was unusually clear, with only a few thin, high, white clouds—not the usual heavy boring gray of the long weeks before.

The lull was over. The next one looked like it would be a heavy bomb. He was right in the impact zone. He had to start charging or he would end up getting caught inside.

He turned around and felt the light, crisp wind in his face. It was blowing away from the faint sun that was barely rising above the glittering white of the glacier peaks.

He lowered his body.

Earlier, he had woken up confused, much later than usual, to a bedroom filled with the artificial rays of his wake-up lamp. Yes, he had drunk two glasses of the French merlot at the Julebord the previous night and then some akvavit. After that, everything blurred. He usually did not drink akvavit. He had no clue how he had got home. His mouth tasted awful. He was naked. The bed smelled of a perfume that he knew did not belong to Maria. He had smelled it yesterday, but never before. His head hurt.

He heard the tone announcing a new message on his phone. The phone was still in the front pocket of his suit pants, which were in a pile next to the dresser, as if someone had dropped them there, sandwiched between his white shirt and the wrinkled dark blue dress jacket below. His boxer shorts and socks lay to one side. When he moved his pants, he noticed that some buttons on his shirt were missing. There was a faint red stain next to the breast pocket. His dress shoes were lying at the foot of the bed. The sole of one of them was facing upward—covered with a thin layer of dried whitish-gray mud.

It was still almost pitch-dark outside. The phone screen showed 08:41.

The message read:

Morning! Wake up!!! G-Point in 30 minutes????

He had to be at work by 12:45. He noticed his second pillow lying on the floor, next to two buttons from his shirt. Nothing made sense. He had promised Erik he would join him. Should he go? He went to the bathroom. His eyes were burning, but he could see clearly—he had not taken out his contacts at night.

The red pigment on his face was staring at him in the mirror. As if someone had rubbed it around. Frightened, he quickly filled the palms of his hands with the warm water and lowered his face. He felt ashamed.

He brushed his teeth. His body urged him to shower. The hot water felt good on his skin. The black wetsuit was hanging on the bathroom wall—still damp from the last quick session after he got off work yesterday. After all, surfing was the reason he had chosen to live here. He craved the security of the familiar. He took the wetsuit off the hanger and squeezed himself into the thick rubber, as was his routine. The neoprene felt safe against his skin.

In the hallway, there was an array of whitish-gray, muddy footsteps on the brown tiles. The clock on the wall showed 09:12.

His key-chain was lying dropped carelessly on the floor. His light gray winter coat was hanging in its usual place, but in an unusual way. The yellowish stain on it smelled like puke.

He put on his neoprene booties and gloves. Outside—after pulling the neoprene hood over his head—he could feel the cold air only on his face. He locked the door and hid the key. He walked down the outside stairs of the small modern building with its six apartments. His Tesla Model 3 was still plugged in, standing in the covered carport where he had left it the day before. He wished he could forget trying to remember. He loosened the straps and lifted his board from the roof-rack. The parking stalls were not paved, and the gravel was whitish-gray, muddy, and loose, as if it had not frozen the night before. He recalled the mud on the hallway tiles and his shoes. Just a hint of snow coated the yellow-green grass. He took his board under his arm and started running toward the sea. As soon as he turned the corner of the house, he could see the waves through the rows of crosses.

The sailors' graveyard stood next to the beach as a reminder that you should never forget to fear what you live for.

Lacking imagination, but capturing the essence, they had named the surf spot 'THE GRAVEYARD' or simply 'G POINT'. Erik was surfing already. He quickly attached his surfboard leash to his right leg. He felt warm. The waves were just right. He needed to feel the power of the ocean. He skipped his warmup and jumped right into the waves. Erik waved at him. As the icy water seeped into the wetsuit, he felt the short, sharp sting of cold. The familiar reaction of his body calmed his mind. He paddled out to his spot.

"You're late, dude. Too much party last night?"

Per sat down on his board, nodded to his best friend, and stared westward to wait for his first wave.

09:37

Dude! Silence? Only a nod for your best friend whom you have not seen for ages?

Erik could not even remember exactly when they had last surfed together.

But, of course, he would never forget what was yelled when they first met in the ocean years ago.

"Skitstövel!"[1]

"Unnskyld."[2]

"Hey, Norwegian! Stop dreaming," Per had said, in an older bro reprimanding younger bro type of way.

Perhaps he should have waited for Per at the beach to paddle out together, but today the waves were just too good.

Erik saw the deep-greenish-blue wall of water rolling towards his friend. Per had already turned around and the wave just started to form a whitecap slightly to his left.

The lull was over. The wave was a heavy bomb[3]. It was good that Per started charging[4]. He was right in the wave's impact zone and otherwise would have gotten caught inside[5].

---

1 **Skitstövel** – *Swedish*: Profanity that is similar in offensiveness to 'motherfucker', 'asshole' or 'bastard'. Although its literary translation is 'shit-boot'. Originally a derogatory expression for peasants, implying that their boots are stained with manure.

2 **Unnskyld** – *Norwegian*: Sorry.

3 **Bomb** – Surf slang word for a massive wave.

4 **Charging** – Surf slang word for aggressively trying to catch a wave.

5 **Caught inside** – Surf slang word describing the situation where a surfer is trapped between the shoreline and the breaking wave.

JULEBORD (The Holiday Party)

For an amateur surfer, Per's pop-up[1] was not bad. When they had first met, it was he—Erik—who was still a total kook[2], and Per had every reason to yell when he dropped in[3] on him on that wave in Morocco. Things had changed a lot since that January 5th, 2010. Erik remembered the date—his older brother had been killed exactly a year earlier.

He could tell that Per's first wave this morning would soon form into a small barrel[4]. Then suddenly his friend's ride came to an abrupt stop, as if Per's board had hit something in the water. Per wiped out immediately. Seconds after emerging next to his board, it appeared that Per was holding on to a dark floating object.

"Erik! Come here!"

---

1 **Pop-up** – Surf slang word for the movement a surfer makes to get from lying on the surfboard to standing up to start surfing.

2 **Kook** – Surf slang word for a rookie surfer who is not very good at surfing.

3 **to drop in** – Surf slang word used to describe the action to catch a wave in front of another surfer who was going for it first and was closer to it. This effectively means that the surfer who 'drops in' steals the wave from the other surfer. Considered the worst violation of surfing etiquette.

4 **Barrel** – Surf slang word synonymous to a 'tube', which is the hollow part of a wave under its curl when it is breaking. It is considered one of the most sought after things in surfing.

10:46

There were some things in the world James would just never, ever understand. One of them was that if a woman decides to work as a flight attendant, she is expected to dress in an elegant feminine uniform. If, however, she becomes a police officer she is made to wear the same light-blue shirt and black tie as her male counterparts. To make things even worse for his young colleague, who just had picked him up from his home, Maria's light-blue shirt had very large breast pockets on both sides. Given the size of her breasts, Maria was certainly in no need of highlighting them with oversized pockets, which—in her case—lacked any practical application whatsoever.

He estimated that Maria was about the same age as his wife Eva had been when they met that late evening more than thirty-five years ago. It was late February, and he was driving. His Eva—despite what she had been through earlier that afternoon—looked more than stunning in her torn dark-blue flight attendant uniform, with the white blouse and white scarf with the Scandinavian Airlines logo. She was missing some gold-colored buttons and had a large bandage on her knee. He had volunteered to drive her. The nurses and doctors in the emergency room were still overexcited and nervous after the disaster plan had been activated in response to the plane crash. Although—luckily—it proved not to be such a big deal, they had forgotten to give her crutches after she was cleared to go. This, of course, had given James the opportunity to help her get into the light-blue Dodge Diplomat, as well as out of the car at her hotel, and then to assist her up to the room. They started kissing passionately even before the hotel room door swung shut.

Who knows, perhaps if the nurses and doctors had done their job properly back then, he would not be sitting in this car today being driven through the rugged winter fjord landscape of Godshus.

What James knew was that everyone at Godshus General Hospital had done everything they could for his Eva over the years. The breast cancer had still killed her just a little over nine lonely years ago. He had missed her every day and night since.

Maria appeared excited but scared at the same time as she drove down the winding road to the beach. Although there was no clear need for it—they were the only ones on the road—she had turned on the blue flashing lights. She kept the siren off, so James decided not to say anything. They had rarely worked together before. He had just gotten out of bed when she called him and told him about the situation. She spoke with his Eva's Vestnorsk accent. A true local fjord country girl—deeply rooted in Godshus, just as his Eva had been.

He only had time to eat a slice of bread with a piece of ham on it and put some coffee into his travel mug before Maria arrived at his house in the white Volkswagen Passat station wagon with POLITI—police—written on it. James had noticed the insecurity in her grey-blue eyes. Mostly they sat in silence for the twenty-minute drive.

He glanced at his watch: 10:48. The road now led straight down to the beach. Two people were standing on the beach. One of them started walking and met them as the car stopped in the small parking lot next to a beachside cemetery. A VW Type 2 Transporter painted in psychedelically vivid colors was parked to the left. Maria opened her door first.

"I totally forgot that you were working today," Per said. He was clad in a black whole-body wetsuit which revealed only a small oval of his face.

James got out of the car and could now see the body lying in the sand on the beach. It was clear to the chief investigator of the Norwegian police even from a distance that most of the dead man's left leg was missing.

11:07

The picture in a silver frame stood next to the phone on his nightstand. The phone rang. This was a rare occurrence these days. Werner lay in bed, awake already. He had slept little. He felt very weak and very, very thirsty. The nausea had finally stopped. So far it did not feel like the water that he had sipped about fifteen minutes ago would cause him to vomit again. The last time he'd had diarrhea was around five in the morning, but he had lost track of time. It must have been just before seven when he finally fell asleep. The red numbers on the small clock in front of the picture in the silver frame showed 11:08 when he picked up the phone.

"Dr. Bjerknes speaking."

A female voice answered:

"I'm sorry to disturb you. This is officer Maria Michelson of the Godshus police department."

For the briefest of moments, Werner found it hard to breathe. "Yes."

"Dr. Bjerknes—my senior colleague Mr. Redding gave me your number and asked me to call."

"Yes." He recognized the name. He had known chief investigator Redding even before he had volunteered his home phone number during one of their many meetings in the late summer of 2011. He wanted to make sure Redding knew how to reach him. Just in case. Just in case something like what had happened on Utøya were to happen one day in Godshus.

"Is it correct that there was a Julebord at the Dypthav restaurant last evening for the doctors working in the medical department of Godshus General Hospital?"

"Yes. That's correct."

"Mr. Redding will need to talk to all those who participated. I can't share any details of the nature of the investigation with you right now, but he would like to meet with the doctors at the hospital as soon as possible. He suggests meeting in the conference room next to the Intensive Care Unit."

"Okay." Werner knew that the chief investigator likely remembered his way around Godshus General Hospital very well. Redding's wife had been their patient for many years. A very sad case. Aggressive breast cancer. She was only in her early forties when they found it. Right at diagnosis, it was clear that the cancer had already spread to her lymph nodes. They immediately referred her to the Radiumhospitalet in Oslo for treatment. She had a young son. She was determined to live as long as possible for the sake of her family. For several years it seemed like the cancer was gone. Until it came back. She died with her husband and son at her bedside. He had rushed to the hospital straight from work when she suddenly got worse. Still in his black Norwegian police uniform, he sat next to her bed—crying.

"Mr. Redding suggests that you activate the Nødnett Pager system to notify the physicians who were at the restaurant. He'll be at the hospital at 12:30."

"Okay."

"There are two more things."

"Yes."

"Please don't mention to anyone that this is a police investigation. Mr. Redding suggests that for now, this is just an unannounced test of the Nødnett system."

"Okay." Of course, the chief investigator knew everything about Nødnett and surely was carrying one of the pagers himself, as all the doctors who worked in a hospital in Norway did. Werner had occasionally taken part in the many discussions over the years about whether it still made sense for the country to keep this analog technical communication dinosaur alive in a time when everyone, everywhere, had cell phones. In the end, the government always opted to continue with it and had just recently upgraded it. They deemed the old technology to work better in all the deep fjords, along the rugged coastline, and up on the glacier peaks. Just more reliable. Requiring far fewer antennas to cover the entire country.

In addition—reportedly—nobody could hack it. As one presenter had once said during a committee meeting, the simple archaic code used to program it was the 'equivalent of Egyptian hieroglyphs'. Werner vaguely remembered when the first heavy, clunky pagers had arrived in the late 1970s, just after he started working in Godshus. Back then they just beeped. Now, after the modernization, short messages could even be sent. No emojis though—just alphanumeric.

He recalled the last true alarm. It was when they were sure that a big cruise ship, whose engines had failed in the huge North Sea waves off Godshus, was going to crash into the cliffs with all its passengers still on board. Luckily, some skillful mechanic was able to fix things at the last moment. Before that, it was during Utøya—like everywhere in the country. Since the ship incident, it had been just test alarms—about twice a year—which made the pagers vibrate and start the nonstop beep with its characteristic piercing high-pitched sound. He always got a headache from that sound before he could silence it. It just took too much time for him to remember how to turn off the now lightweight sleek pager, whose buttons had gotten too small for his hands, which were turning clumsy.

"The second thing is that Dr. Nystrom-Miller will be late for his shift today."

"Okay." What happened flashed through Werner's mind. It surprised him to hear the name of the young, talented, and reliable junior doctor mentioned by a police officer.

There could be no way he had anything to do with last night's event.

"Any questions?"

"No."

He immediately regretted his decision to sit up on the edge of the bed. The dizziness made him almost pass out. He must have become severely dehydrated.

Finally, the room looked less blurry, but only after he had closed his eyes for a long while. His fingers dialed the number without the need for him to think.

The phone rang a little bit longer than it would have been necessary, unless, of course, they were busy.

"Godshus General Hospital. Intensive Care Unit. Nurse Louise speaking," said the familiar voice with her typical Vestnorsk accent.

"Why are you at work just before Christmas?"

"Not only today, Dr. Bjerknes. I'll also be working the next three days. Tomorrow, Monday, and then on Christmas Eve. After I'm done on Christmas Eve I will go home, lie down under the Christmas tree and just pretend I'm a gift."

Werner knew that Louise did not need to pretend at all.

She was a gift, and not just under that Christmas tree, but to the entire universe. Although he was unaware of it when they first met, he now knew very well that in the end, it was nurses like Louise who would save the patients' lives. Not him.

Although, unjustly—it was he who received all the credit most of the time. He knew he would miss her tremendously after she retired in February.

"Louise, I need to ask you for something."

"Yes."

"Could you please activate Nødnett?"

"Why? What happened?"

"Nothing, just an unannounced test."

"Dr. Bjerknes. They are gonna hate you. It's just before Christmas. People are busy."

"I know. But, we have to do it."

"I mean ... whatever ... everyone?"

"Actually, only the doctors from the medical department."

"Well. That's a bit better. At least nobody with small children. Or? Dr. Nystrom-Miller. He doesn't have kids yet? Correct? I don't know him that well. Is he married?"

"No children and not married."

"That's good to know. You know, one of the young nurses who works in the operating room says ..."

Werner interrupted her, "So, Louise." He ignored his passing thought about all the chatter that would start echoing off the walls of the hospital after the police officer showed up about an hour from now. News always seemed to travel way too quickly. He did not know if this was just the case in Godshus General Hospital or if it held true for all hospitals. "I need you to notify Dr. Gianetti, Dr. Noor, Dr. Andersen, Dr. Rønneberg, Dr. Nystrom-Miller, and myself."

"What about Dr. Boisen-Jensen?"

"Of course. Of course. Dr. Boisen-Jensen as well," Werner answered with a barely noticeable change in his voice.

"Okay. I'm logging into the Nødnett portal here now." Louise paused briefly. He knew that this required a couple of clicks with the mouse.

"So let me count. One. Two. Three. Four. Five. Six. Seven doctors selected. Confirm name selection. Andersen. Bjerknes. Boisen-Jensen. Gianetti. Noor. Nystrom-Miller. Rønneberg. Is this a test activation? Yes. Okay. What message should I send?"

"Let's do: Sorry. Required pager check. 12:30. Conference Room."

"Will do."

"One more thing, Louise."

"What?"

"I forgot his name, but could you let the locum doctor from Bergen who was covering for everyone last night know that he might have to stay a bit longer. Dr. Nystrom-Miller will be late a bit."

"Werner! What have you done to that poor young Swedish boy! Have you no morals?"

Werner knew she was joking, but deep, deep down he was still just a bit put off and simply answered: "Julebord."

He put down the phone and started to stand up from his bed very, very slowly and carefully. He glanced at the sparkling, almost black, eyes full of light of the person who looked at him from the picture in the silver frame, on the nightstand next to the phone.

Then a piercing high-pitched sound started coming from somewhere.

11:23

She needed to pee. Maria decided to stay in the warmth of the police car after she had made the two phone calls. The full awkwardness of the situation was making her more and more uncomfortable—to a point where it was getting to be too much. And not just because of how badly mutilated the body was.

Of course, they had tried to prepare her for something like this during her training. But finding mangled bodies anywhere in Norway was very, very rare. In contrast to the books she liked to read, which gave the impression that this happened every other day; or every week at least.

In real life? Perhaps in the big city, Oslo. Sometimes. Once, twice a year max.

But Godshus!

There had been a reason why she went up north to Bodø for her training and not Oslo. Big cities were not for her. She did not like them.

That Erik and, especially, Per had to be involved in all of this just added to the bizarreness of the whole situation.

Erik—not so much. Everyone knew Erik. Everyone in Godshus at least. But after the recent ad-campaign by a life insurance company, she suspected that everyone in Norway did.

"For jeg vil ikke bekymre meg mer for: HAIER,"[1] were the words he said in the TV spot with a baby in his arms and a big grin that showed off his perfect teeth. It was funny, very well designed marketing. She ended up buying life insurance for herself because of the spots.

She briefly envisioned tonight's lead story on the local news:

'First Scandinavian Pro Surfer, who doesn't worry about sharks, drags half-eaten body onto shore. Was it a shark or something else?'

---

1 **For jeg vil ikke bekymre meg mer for: HAIER** – *Norwegian*: Because I don't want to worry anymore about: SHARKS.

But Per in the midst of all of this. Why Per? How embarrassing!

But what really started making everything unbearable was the feeling she got while she was taking pictures of the dead man's body. She had not dared to log into the national driver's license database to confirm her strong suspicion as to his identity by checking the name Per had given them. The electronic driver's license records would show her a picture of the living face that belonged to the remains still lying on the sandy beach.

Maria turned around to reach for the bag on the back seat. She took out the rugged official Norwegian Police tablet with its built-in SIM card and turned it on to log in remotely. The signal out here was awfully weak, and because of the encryption, this always took forever.

She noticed that her senior colleague had stopped talking to Erik and Per and was walking toward the car. Maria was glad that he had been on backup duty this weekend. She had heard the stories people told about him in the station. Redding must have loved his wife very much to give up his job as a homicide detective with the New York Police Department and move to Godshus. Surely he had seen similarly mutilated bodies in New York back in the 1980s. Likely all the time. Or at least with a frequency similar to the Norway she read about in books by her favorite Scandinavian crime authors.

James got into the car and closed the door so it would stay warm inside.

"So. How did the calls go?"

"The doctors should be in the conference room at 12:30. I didn't provide him with any details, as you said." She vaguely remembered the former chief physician of the hospital she had been born in. Her grandma had been sick in the intensive care unit. He had been very kind and caring, but then the phone rang one morning and he told her that Grandma had died.

"And the forensic team?"

"Once everyone gets in, they'll start driving here. They estimated they'd be here in about two-and-a-half hours."

The big van with all the equipment required to do the work on the beach was based in Volda. Although Volda was only about sixty kilometers away as the crow flies, because of the fjords and all the high mountains, the team would need to drive more than twice that distance on the small, winding, and at times single-lane roads. After they got done on the beach, it would be their job to transport the body to the morgue where a forensic pathologist would perform an autopsy. Of course, that would not be in Volda but all the way in Ålesund. Now, with the new bridge and the tunnel under the fjord, at least only one ferry ride was involved. It would still take at least three hours to get there from the beach. Maria was relieved that she would not need to go with them. It would be a long drive through darkness.

She realized that it would already be getting dark by the time the big van even made it to the beach.

"They'll have to use the lights. The van has a generator," was the comment of the experienced colleague sitting next to her.

Maria realized that somehow lights were never mentioned in her crime novels when forensic teams were summoned to a mutilated body. Even in the middle of winter and even when a body was found much farther north.

"So to give you an update on what your ..."—James paused briefly as if hunting for the correct word—"friend just told me."

The mention of her relationship with Per created an expression on her face that clearly conveyed her discomfort with the entire situation. They had met at the beginning of the summer. She loved resting her head in the crook of his muscular left shoulder after he had fallen asleep next to her and tracing the blue lines of the abstract tattoo that formed multiple interlocking waves on his chest. Lately, she had started dreamily rationalizing that he might be the one. However, she was not at all sure if the feeling was mutual. They had not talked about it yet.

"Of course, he's been extremely helpful with identifying the body and with all the information about yesterday evening," James said. "The thing which is, let's say, unusual and which he just let slip, is that he claims not being able to remember how he got back home last night. Basically, he has no recollection of anything from when he drank some akvavit at the party until he woke up in his bed this morning. I mean, everyone will get drunk at a Julebord. But so wasted that you can't remember anything? He's not a teenager. He's a doctor. Does he drink a lot?"

This did not sound like Per at all.

"No," she said before pausing briefly. "But I guess you know! Julebord."

She made a mental note to talk to Per about it later.

"You got all the necessary pictures of the body?" James asked, changing the subject.

That had been the first thing he had asked her to do. She remembered how she retrieved the camera. Erik and Per had dragged the body of the man onto the beach. His age was difficult to estimate—except that he was clearly no longer twenty but not sixty yet either. The man's torso lay roughly in parallel to the shoreline, with his right side facing the ocean.

The trauma to the head and face was significant. Given that and the bluish discoloration, it surprised her that Per was so sure about his identity. But he was still wearing the same clothes as he had on the night before.

Well, at least in part. The man's left leg was missing from just above where his knee should have been. In addition, whatever had caused the missing leg was also likely responsible for a large gash on the left side of his pelvis, about where his black pants must have ended and a belt had likely held them in place. The combination of the two wounds had caused significant defects to the man's clothes. Whereas the remnants of his black pants still covered the right leg entirely, the left pant leg was completely missing and what remained of his left thigh was fully exposed. Besides, whatever had caused the upper wound on the man's pelvis had also managed to totally tear apart the bridge of fabric that would have connected the front side of the low-rise briefs the victim was wearing to their backside. The thick waistband of the briefs, thanks to its elasticity, had caused the remaining crimson fabric of the briefs to recoil to the right.

The end result was—in short—a postmortem wardrobe malfunction.

Simply no textile remained to cover the dead men's genitals. His penis, testicles, and carefully trimmed pubic hair were on full display.

Not just a little exposed. But entirely, completely, fully, totally, not-leaving-any-doubt, and in toto exposed. Not even the tiniest bit left to the imagination.

But what raised Maria's level of anguish to the point of becoming unbearable wasn't that she had to take pictures of a dead man with his private parts uncovered, as he lay on fine sand, so white and powdery that it could be mistaken for snow.

Looking through the camera's viewfinder, Maria zoomed in on the dead man's genitals for the required picture. She noticed, despite all the deadness, an unusually large vein running down the shaft of the dead man's penis.

Suddenly it became very difficult for her to press the shutter release button. Her finger started shaking in the black glove she wore. Eventually, her finger did push the button.

And the next thing she did?

Of course, she took another picture—the application on her phone with its purplish-red logo had taught her well.

Moments like this needed to be captured—moments, like spotting an unusually large vein on a dead man's penis that she remembered very well.

"Yes. I got all the necessary pictures of the victim."

"Body for now. Not victim. I actually don't think this is a crime. Looks like an accident or suicide to me. Likely fell or jumped off a cliff and then drowned."

"Why are we calling the forensic team then?"

"One can only draw valid conclusions if one has all the information. Did you verify the driver's license picture?"

"I should be able to log into the system any second now."

The screen on the tablet indicated that a secure connection to the national driver's license database had been established. She typed in the name Per had given them. Several names appeared on a list, but only one with an address in Godshus. After a brief instant of hesitation, she pushed on that name. Wanting to delay the confirmation of what she already knew, she closed her eyes for a moment. Then she opened them.

The picture showed the face of a middle-aged man. Yes, it was definitively him. He had introduced himself as Klaus. New Year's Eve less than a year ago. At the hotel. The Leonkulen Glacier ski resort. She had gone there to celebrate. As a single. She bit her lower lip. Her left ear registered a knocking sound. The memories of that night caused a warm pleasurable feeling, paired with a tingly twitching sensation deep in her pelvis. The knocking sounds returned. She became aware of a pleasurable feeling of warmth and tension under her bra. More knocks.

She felt a rush of shame when she looked up and saw Per's face as he knocked on the side window.

"Well, he has a really smashed up face now!" James said next to her, examining the picture when she handed him the tablet.

She opened the car door just a bit. The rush of the incoming cold felt good on her face.

"Just wanted to let you know. It was low tide when we dragged Dr. Boisen-Jensen out of the water. The tide will start coming in soon. Depending on how long all this is going to take, Erik and I think we might need to get him to higher ground so that the tide doesn't carry him out to sea again," Per said, in his adorable Scandinavian amalgam of Swedish and Norwegian. But the somber expression on his face was just so not him. She realized that she now had an even more urgent need to pee.

"Okay," James said. "I would suggest we do the following then: Let's first move the body further up on the beach as you proposed. We must make another set of pictures to document that. You, Dr. Nystrom-Miller and myself will have to start heading to the hospital soon, so I can talk to the other doctors who were at the Julebord yesterday. That way the hospital will also know what happened. You said that he was the new chief physician, correct?"

Per briefly nodded. "Yes. He started back in January. Same day as myself actually."

"Maria. If you could wait here with Erik until the forensic team arrives. I guess you will have to hang out in the cold a bit to keep an eye on things until the van gets here. When they're done, they'll drop you off at the police station. I'll join you there once I am finished at the hospital."

"I'm sure you can wait in Erik's van. He can turn on the heating for you. Also, he usually brings some hot tea when he goes surfing," Per said, having clearly misinterpreted the concerned expression in her face. It actually had nothing at all to do with the prospect of standing out in the cold for some time, but rather the continued feeling of warmth in her pelvis, caused by memories of someone other than Per.

Not that her current boyfriend lacked experience in bed, but that night at the ski resort with Klaus had been in a class of its own. She realized that it might be more appropriate to remember the dead man under the name displayed in the driver's license database as Dr. Anders Boisen-Jensen—and not as Klaus.

"Sorry you have to work after all this, Doc. I would have offered to drive you, but I think it's better if you take your own car to the hospital."

Having clarified this remaining logistical detail, James started to get out of the car.

Maria now really needed to pee.

"Sorry, but can I just quickly use the bathroom in your apartment, Per, while you guys move the body?"

Per broke eye contact with her and glanced at James.

"Okay. You go to the toilet and I'll start taking the pictures of the body after we move him," James said, and got out of the car.

"The key is where I always put it when I go surfing. You remember?"

"Under the doormat?"

"Yep."

The moment Maria entered the familiar apartment she smelled something was not right. The immense feeling of relief she experienced when stepping out of the bathroom was suddenly replaced by overwhelming anger when she saw the unusual way the sheets had been left in disarray on the bed. She was breathing heavily now and realized that the scent of the perfume in the room was not her Son Venïn-Le Voleur, which she had discovered in an expensive perfume store on her weekend trip to Oslo the previous spring. Chance from Chanel perhaps, but she was not sure.

She stepped into the hallway. Her anger had risen to a pitch even higher than that of the annoying beep, which sounded the same as her Nødnett pager and appeared to come from a light-gray winter coat.

And just when she decided to leave this apartment forever, she saw the entrance door slowly swing open.

11:41

Per pulled the neoprene hood off his head. He saw that Maria had left the door open just a bit so he could get in. A high-pitched beep was coming from inside the apartment.

The forceful blow to his face came unexpectedly, just as he stepped through the door. He staggered back, unable to keep his balance on the slipperiness created by his still wet neoprene booties and the thin film of whitish-gray mud left behind on the brown hallway tiles by the footsteps of the night before. He tried to roll into the fall, but the blow had left him dizzy. As he fell, the side of his face slammed against the sharp metallic handle of the front door, causing a deep cut from just above the outer corner of his eyebrow down to his cheekbone. The thin subcutaneous tissues around his eye started swelling immediately.

"Asshole. Fucking asshole. Can't remember? Yah! Can't remember who you fucked last night!"

From his position on the floor, Per saw how Maria now had fully opened the front door and tried to squeeze out by the side of his curled-up body, which partially blocked her exit.

She took two steps. Then paused. She turned briefly toward him. He could see her angry eyes.

She appeared to hesitate for a split second. But then she lifted her leg decisively and—with full force—used her foot, enclosed in her heavy black police winter boots, to brutishly kick him in the balls.

Because of the excruciatingly immediate, stingingly sharp, nausea-inducing pain Per could barely follow her words:

"Fucking asshole. And I was dreaming about having kids with you!" After Maria stepped out the door, he could no longer understand what she kept on shouting.

He lay there, even more tightly curled up now, eyes closed, his entire body wincing. After his mouth had initially produced a sound of his misery, which was something between a shriek and a

33

wail, he lay in silence, just pressing the palms of both hands against the black neoprene covering his groin.

Per felt the nausea caused by the pain. He didn't know how much time had passed when he first realized that the high-pitched sound was still filling the room.

He opened his eyes and saw his blood mixing with the gray-ish-white mud into a surreal hue of pink on the brown tile in front of him.

He slowly lifted himself up from the floor and went to the bathroom.

The motions required to get out of his wetsuit had made the bleeding start again. He repeatedly applied pressure with the white towel, now adorned with spots of his blood, creating an irregular psychedelic pattern of innovative red polka dot design.

Per knew he was late. Naked, he walked back to the hallway. Pain still radiated outward from his groin. His junk was a red, swollen, painful mess. The clock on the wall showed 11:52. He wouldn't have the time to shower off his blood and the ocean's salt from his skin. He returned to the bathroom after finally silencing his Nødnett pager.

The red pigment of the dried blood on his face was staring at him in the mirror. He had rubbed it around with the towel. He quickly filled the palms of his hands with the warm water and lowered his face. He did not feel shame this time.

Per got dressed.

The little bit of freshly dried blood around the scab forming on the cut on the side of his face was the only hint of color against all the black, white, and shades of gray that surrounded him. The lingering smell of recent newness coming from the white seat of his Tesla mixed with the faint stench of vomit spreading from the yellowish stain on his light-gray winter coat after he got back in. In his rush, he had initially forgotten to unplug the car. The large screen in the middle had reminded him to do so. He now pushed the virtual button which turned on the autopilot and set the destination to work. Of course, he had agreed to be a beta-tester for the full self-driving version of the autopilot when the email with the offer had come.

The estimated arrival time at Godshus General Hospital showing on the screen was 12:27.

Perhaps he would just arrive in time for the meeting. The car started moving. He leaned his body back deep into the seat. He parted his legs to make more space for his still-tender testicles. After the Tesla had taken the turn out of the parking lot, his hands let go of the steering wheel completely.

Just for a short while.

To take a deep breath. Relax a bit.

He knew he would have to put one hand back on the wheel in a minute. A loud beep would let him know. Per closed his eyes. He felt the Tesla's gradual acceleration. His mind had just started drifting back to the events of the day when he suddenly heard a noise coming from the roof of the car just above his head.

Per was immediately fully awake once he realized what was happening.

"Shit."

The car's autopilot—not programmed to understand the sudden anguish of its human occupant—continued speeding up as normal.

"Shit. Shit. Shit."

He sat bolt upright in the seat. All the muscles in his body tensed up, ignoring the sharp pain coming from his groin after he pushed his legs back together too quickly. He had grabbed the steering wheel, but before his foot could touch the brake pedal, he heard another noise from the back of the car's roof.

It was too late. And it was all his fault.

As two beeps signaled that the autopilot had turned off, he observed the short aerial performance unfolding in the rearview mirror.

His 6'3" Tamba HP Tri Fin Surfboard had become airborne as the car sped up. Earlier, when he had rushed back from the beach, he had just hastily laid the board on the roof-rack without attaching the straps—an omission which he had failed to correct prior to getting into the car for the drive to the hospital. His short-board—a gift from Erik—flew straight up in the air, before flipping one hundred and eighty degrees and then crashing nose first into the dark-gray asphalt of the narrow single-lane road. After a small final bounce and another ninety-degree spin, it skidded down the road, its deck facing the sky, its fins not elegantly gliding forward through salty water, but scratching backward against the hard mixture of stone, sand, and bitumen.

Per stopped the car and got out.

"Fuck!" The damage was much worse than expected. When he picked up the board, he could feel that below its fiberglass skin the polyurethane core of the surfboard had split in two, snapped by the impact.

Carefully assembled on Kaua'i in the warmth of a tropical paradise where it belonged, his board had been broken beyond repair in a most undignified way because of his stupid mistake: not in the ocean by the force of a mighty wave, but on a gray, cold single-lane road close to where a deep fjord meets the North Sea in Norway.

He felt:

SHOCK
GRIEF
SURPRISE
SORROW
AMAZEMENT
MOURNING

and

GUILT

all at the same time.

Tenderly he laid the surfboard to rest on a chilly patch of yellowish grass next to the road.

Back in the car, the estimated arrival time now showed 12:31.

Except for a single moment of pressing the backs of his index fingers against his eyeballs to suppress the formation of tears, he sat in the car in contemplative silence for the rest of the drive.

As the Tesla entered the hospital's parking lot, he could see the sliding entrance doors just closing behind the chief investigator.

It was only when he got out that he noticed the small smears of blood on the white seat. Blood was slowly dripping again from the cut on his face.

The small motion with his finger to hold back his tears must have caused the wound to re-open. He looked down and saw blood highlighted against the light-gray of his winter coat. Per pressed the base of his thumb against the wound and with quick, almost running steps made it to the entrance. He saw the surprise on the face of the emergency room triage nurse sitting behind her white desk.

"Dr. Nystrom-Miller ..." he could not hear the rest of her words as he briskly walked through the staircase door next to the elevator. He took two steps at a time until he reached the second floor. He walked hurriedly through the short hallway.

The high-pitched cries of a baby came from one of the rooms on his right.

He reached the locked door and quickly took the ID card from his pocket and held it against the reader. After a click, the door swung open.

Louise was standing there. The alarmed expression in her face became even more so when she saw him.

"What's going on? A police officer just walked into the conference room. They're all in there. Why do you have blood all over you?" he heard Louise almost scream, as he quickly passed by her into the short hallway.

His right hand pushed down the handle of the conference room door.

"... found dead," the chief investigator said, just as Per entered the room.

Whereas Chief Investigator Redding was standing with his back to him, he saw that his colleagues—except for one—were all sitting at their regular places around the rectangular table.

As they did in all the morning meetings. Almost like yesterday morning. Dr. Rønneberg was at the short side of the table to his left, her back facing the fire escape door. Next to her at the long side of the table were—from left to right—Dr. Andersen, Dr. Gianetti, and Dr. Noor—their backs facing the balcony window. Dr. Bjerknes had taken his seat opposite Dr. Rønneberg on the right short side of the table, with his back toward the interior glass wall that divided the room from the small office reserved for the chief physician. The three places closest to Per were empty—his, the one on the left, on the side of Dr. Rønneberg, and also the one next to Dr. Bjerknes, where Dr. Boisen-Jensen always used to sit. He had never seen anybody sit in the middle chair.

From his position in the doorway, Per could clearly see the faces of his colleagues, all of whom were looking at the police officer standing in front of him.

And for just the briefest of moments, he saw the same expression on all their faces:

Not

SHOCK

Not

GRIEF

Not

SURPRISE

Not

SORROW

Not

AMAZEMENT

Not

MOURNING

What he saw was just

one

common expression:

GUILT

Nothing and nothing but expressions of guilt in the faces of his five colleagues, as the first reaction to the news that Dr. Boisen-Jensen was dead. A man—as he well knew—nobody really liked, and some of the doctors perhaps even hated.

Once they realized that Per was standing in the doorway with blood on his face and coat, the expression of guilt in their faces didn't linger and was quickly replaced by:

SHOCK

SURPRISE

and

AMAZEMENT

Dr. Gianetti was the first one to break the silence, "Mamma Mia, Per! What happened?"

Godshus General Hospital

The architecture of the building indicated that it was a solid place.
In other words:

IT WAS UGLY.
A three-story structure—hastily planned and raised using the first batch of the sudden, unexpected money received in exchange for the oil found under the ocean floor off the coast a couple of years prior.

The exterior was red brick alternating with bands of windows, separated by brown pillars. The top of the boxy structure just a flat roof, covered with small black stones in summer and white snow in winter. A little tower, housing the staircase and the two elevators, rose just to the left of the only entrance, where everyone would

ENTER

&

EXIT.

A constant *IN* and *OUT* of —
— the sick & the healthy —
—the old & the young—
— the pregnant women with contractions &
the newborn babies in their car seats —
— the hopeful & the desperate —
— the sane & the crazy —
— those who could be healed & those for whom there was no more help —
— the ones that walked & the ones lying on the ambulance stretchers —
— the visitors —

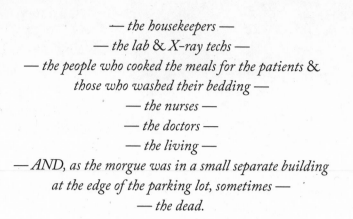

— the housekeepers —
— the lab & X-ray techs —
— the people who cooked the meals for the patients &
those who washed their bedding —
— the nurses —
— the doctors —
— the living —
— AND, as the morgue was in a small separate building
at the edge of the parking lot, sometimes —
— the dead.

Once the sliding entrance doors closed, the elevators—or the stairs, if one preferred to climb—were to the left.

Straight ahead a hallway led to a small detached separate single-story box of a building where all the meals were cooked and all the linen washed.

To the right was a white counter with a nurse sitting behind it
— 24 hours a day —
— 7 days a week —
&
— 365 (or every 4 years 366) *days a year —*
titled the *'triage nurse'*. Her—or occasionally his—experienced eyes carefully scanning each person in front of them from head to toe, and back, to make the initial decision about which bed in the emergency room would be the best and which of the four kinds of doctors should be summoned:

The **internist**—most of the time. One of them would always be in the building.

Or it could be one of the two **surgeons**, often busy in the operating room during the day, but if awakened at home around midnight, grumpily trying to find every reason not to get into the car before morning.

Rarely, the one ancient-looking **obstetrician/gynecologist** who had, during her lifetime, delivered at least half of the population of Godshus and therefore could no longer sleep well at night.

On very, very uncommon occasions, the one young **pediatrician**, who would always be there immediately from home.

Only one of the wife and husband pair of **anesthesiologists**, with the three small children, would ever show up—seemingly out of nowhere—if called directly by one of the other doctors for help.

The shy superwoman and superman disappeared as quickly as she or he had come, once the situation was either under control, or the patient dead.

When originally built, the ground floor only contained the operating rooms beyond the emergency room. A simple X-ray machine was all that existed. Technology advanced over time, and therefore at some point in the mid-1990s, another box-like single-story building was constructed, quite comparable to the kitchen/laundry annex right next to it. Reachable through a short enclosed hallway with floor to ceiling windows, which allowed for a brief glimpse of the stunning landscape outside. It housed the CT-scanner as well as a changing room for those outpatients who would only have their scan done and then go home. It also contained a small, dark office with large screens to examine the films, and an additional room. This space was similar in size to the room housing the CT-scanner but was completely empty—an area reserved for an MRI-scanner, which had yet to be bought.

Back in the main building just past the emergency room were the two operating rooms. The "BIG" one was called number '1' and the "SMALL" one called number '2', although both of them were exactly the same size.

It was more about the kind of operations that were performed in each. Operating room number '1' was where the 'real' operations were done.

Two kinds.

The vast majority were the ones that both surgeons would routinely perform at Godshus General Hospital: taking out an appendix or uncomplicated gallbladder, the small bowel obstruction, or the abscess which needed to be drained. The hemorrhoids requiring removal and the infected diabetic toe that had to be cut off. Operations any general surgeon would do if she or he was really a surgeon.

The other kind of operations performed in operating room '1'—luckily only done on rare occasions—were those where if the surgeons did not act immediately the patient would be dead. Those patients were just too sick to be quickly wheeled outside to the heliport at the edge of the parking lot and then briskly loaded into the rescue helicopter and hastily flown away—either to Ålesund where the regional hospital was, or straight to the University Hospital in Bergen or, at times, even all the way to Oslo. Emergencies like a rapidly expanding epidural hematoma, a badly mangled lower leg with an open artery which no longer could be fixed and which required urgent amputation. Or part of a stomach, which needed to be removed due to a large bleeding ulcer. Most of the time the heroics performed did not help and the patient would die in operating room '1'.

But on occasion, a life would be saved.

If what was being done to the patient deserved the more appropriate name of *procedure* rather than *operation*, these were performed in operating room number '2':

Most of all, the endoscopies: Stomach—colon—and—occasionally—lung.

But also some minor procedures done by the gynecologist—like a dilatation and curettage.

Eventually, it was also here, where a modest cardiac interventional suite was installed, where Dr. Boisen-Jensen—while still alive—would fix hearts, by putting small expanding cages called stents into the clogged arteries supplying blood to this vital organ.

This, however, led to some crowding of the space and tensions.

Not to be forgotten, at the end of the two operating rooms was a second set of stairs. In the entire history of the hospital, it had only ever served as a secret passageway between floors.

It had never, ever—except for the occasional drill—actually served as the fire escape, which it had been marked as in the hospital plans.

Compared to the somewhat confusing layout of the ground floor, the first floor was simple. It housed thirty-five of the hospital's total of forty-four inpatient beds. Arranged in nine double rooms on each side of a long hallway with an open nursing station at the end and a single isolation room which was located in the space just across from the elevator and stairs.

When in 1998 Godshus General Hospital received its one dialysis machine, the room next to the isolation room, originally containing two patient beds, was converted into a dialysis room, reducing the number of beds on the floor from thirty-seven to thirty-five and the overall number of beds in the hospital from forty-six to forty-four.

On stepping out of the elevator on the second floor—or perhaps arriving just a little short of breath if one opted to take the stairs—one would initially find a hallway that looked just like the one on the first floor.

Otherwise, the architectural and human drama the second floor contained was a world apart from the much more structured and quiet flow on the floor just below.

Occupying the same space as the isolation room one floor beneath—just opposite the elevator and stairs—was the hospital's laboratory.

Its quite unusual location, a direct result of the solid Norwegian granite which was unexpectedly found just below the construction site of the hospital.

Efforts to construct a below-the-ground basement floor, as initially planned, had to be quickly abandoned.

The desperate architect who had originally placed the laboratory—as in most hospitals in the world—in the basement had no other option than to place it right there. With a stroke of his pen, he permanently evicted the hospital's director, whose office was meant to occupy that space on the original plan, into a small detached structure at the opposite end of the hospital's parking lot. The architect did the 'separate little annex building trick' with the kitchen, laundry, and the morgue as well.

That the structure housing the morgue was located right next to the office of the hospital director led in the early years to a constant stream of inevitable insider jokes whenever somebody was called for a meeting with management.

In the later years, these jokes stopped, as it was decided that the hospital could be very well administered even more remotely than from across the parking lot—via telephone, email, and the occasional in-person site visits—by a management team based at Ålesund Regional Hospital.

The little building now no longer housing any executive authority therein became the home of the computer server, which was connected to all the electronic workstations that had appeared on all floors of the hospital.

The building's sole human occupant was now a tall Norwegian, who over time turned old and grew a long white beard. Him being responsible for maintaining all the electronic medical equipment which had started invading the hospital: the pagers the doctors carried, the infusion pumps, the ventilators, the telemetry monitors, the beds in the ICU which would tilt the patient by themselves, the ECG machine that would send a digital copy directly to the patient's electronic chart and many more of such gadgets, all of which had an occasional breakdown and then needed rest and tender-loving-care in a small hospital of their own.

Back on the second floor, if one were to walk down the hallway from the elevator, the first thing one would hear was very often screaming coming from the rooms.

Either from one of the laboring women, followed days, hours, minutes, *or* seconds *later* by the scream of a baby.

Or occasionally two.

The small microcosmos of the four-bed maternity ward even had a separate little nursery with a single 'certified' neonatal bed, reserved for the baby who needed some extra help upon arriving in this world. Babies able to remain with their moms in the rooms after being born were—strangely enough—not counted as new occupants of the hospital.

Originally the maternity ward was much bigger. But all this changed at the beginning of the 1980s, when about half of its space was converted into the then-brand-new intensive care unit. This made sense, as at that time a Norwegian mother gave birth to about a 0.84 of a child less than in the year the hospital was opened. No longer exactly 2.51 children per woman, but now 1.67—and therefore the rooms in the big maternity ward frequently remained empty. Unused.

The conversion was a year filled with nervous breakdowns, dust, delays, cost overruns, and constant hammering construction sounds mixing with cries of moms and babies.

This caused lifelong traumas for several soon-to-be mothers, who were disturbed by rugged construction workers who—in error—opened the wrong door and ended up being eyewitnesses to the women's very naked attempts to push a child into this world.

Near the end of the revamp misery, they installed a door, interrupting the hallway. In hindsight, it was obvious that the installation of that door should have clearly been the first thing done in the entire construction process.

Behind this door, which was always locked and where either a small buzzer needed to be pushed to be let inside or a hospital ID card placed on a reader to open it, were four beds in which the sickest patients would receive treatment. In contrast to the maternity ward for the most of times, it was a world of eerie quietness, for even if alarms started beeping they would quickly be silenced by the two ever-present nurses charged with guarding the ICU patients.

The perpetual rhythmical blowing sounds of the ventilators were almost always the last thing a patient there would hear before having a breathing tube inserted through her or his mouth into the windpipe, prior to being connected to a ventilator. Of course, by then the patient had already been drugged unconscious, or, in other words—'*placed into a medically induced coma*'—by the exquisitely balanced mixture of pharmacodynamically active molecules, which were being infused into the patient's veins.

It was a world of tubes, urine collected in bags, infusion pumps, devices with euphemistic names such as: *'fecal management system'*, cables, monitors, and other life-saving machines.

Given how sick these patients were, death was a frequent visitor. It was the place where the most experienced nurses in the hospital worked, carefully adjusting the medications and machines that labored to save the patients' lives. Of course, for those patients in imminent danger of their lives ending soon who were still awake when they were wheeled into this unit, it was a reminder of the circle of life to hear crying babies, before the hallway door locked and before the drugs started working. Drugs, which would ensure they remembered as little as possible about their stay in this unit—if they ever made it out alive.

Just past the intensive care unit: Five more doors. Two on each side off the hallway and one upfront.

On the left were two offices, one reserved and shared among the junior physicians and the other for the senior physicians. Little sanctuaries where the doctors could retreat to complete required paperwork, refresh their memories by looking up diseases and treatments—in the early years in thick books and later on internet websites—have a quick cup of coffee or an undisturbed chat with colleagues about things the nurses shouldn't hear. These rooms were also used to make phone calls to the bigger hospitals to convince an overworked colleague there to accept the sick patient who could no longer be adequately treated in Godshus.

It was also there where most of the doctors updated their resumes when they felt like it was time to move on from Godshus General Hospital.

Opposite these offices were two rooms with a simple bed and an ensuite bathroom with a shower. These were the 'on-call' rooms. One of them was reserved for the internists, who on quiet nights could use it to try to catch a couple of seconds, minutes, or hours of sleep and take a brief refreshing shower, once the overnight call was close to its end.

As Dr. Boisen-Jensen had brought his habit to Godshus of cycling to work regardless of the weather outside, one would encounter him there taking a quick shower and changing every weekday shortly before the start of the morning meeting.

The other room was basically the second bedroom of the old obstetrician, who would retreat there for a short time if it looked like a birth was progressing but would take another couple of hours at least.

If one entered through the door at the end of the hallway, one would reach the conference room. While it was available for everyone in the hospital to use for meetings, in practice, the internists mostly used it for their morning meeting.

This meeting had forever started at 7:30 every weekday until, as one of the first things he did, Dr. Boisen-Jensen moved it to 7:15.

It was here that the overnight admissions and any events which occurred would be shared by the doctor who had been on call with the rest of the doctors who would take over caring for the patients during the day.

It was also a forum where news was reported and, although this had never been the case before, heated discussions took place, which became ever more agitated the longer Dr. Boisen-Jensen was the chief physician of Godshus General Hospital.

The conference room was spacious, spanning almost the entire width of the building. On its left side was the chief physician's office, which was separated from it by a glass partition wall and a glass door—glass chosen by the architect to signal transparent, accountable leadership. On the right was a similar glass wall next to the fire escape door—selected to illuminate the fire escape stairway during the day with light from the large windows that spanned the entire width of the room. The furnishings were simple, consisting of a sturdy rectangular table surrounded by eight chairs. In addition, a small refrigerator stood to the left of the entrance door under a small table on which a coffee machine was placed for general use.

The very last part of the building was the long balcony which spanned the entire width of the second floor. Reached through a door in the middle of the row of conference room windows, it had been envisioned by the architect in an act of creative desperation after he had drunk not only one, but two bottles of Bordeaux—all by himself—one afternoon in the midst of the Norwegian winter, while thinking about sunny summer weather somewhere south.

Although it had no proper function, did not make any sense at all, and could have easily been scrapped during one of the subsequent reviews of the building plans, it prevailed and was built. Stepping outside, a most stunning view would open up. From one side one could see out onto the mostly stormy North Sea with frequently more than house-high white-capped waves, whereas from the other side one could observe the calm deep blue waters of the fjord headed inland, flanked by the dramatic shades of gray of towering rock. On a clear day—which was rare—one could glimpse the white of the glacier peaks in the distance.

As constant exposure over time often renders the human eye undiscerning of the beauty right in front of it, these surroundings did not seem especially impressive for the people who had worked at Godshus General Hospital for long.

But to everyone else, they most certainly were.

Given the climate, the balcony was impractical most of the year, but it was sometimes needed for smoking either cigarettes or pipes. It also— occasionally—was used for the performance of other acts that might be deemed

IMMORAL.

Organogram
Department of Medicine
Godshus General Hospital
(as of January 2nd, 2019)

Chief Physician:
Dr. Anders Boisen-Jensen – *Cardiology*
Senior Physicians:
Dr. Pia Andersen – *Gastroenterology*
Dr. Alessandro Gianetti – *Gastroenterology*
Dr. Hana Rønneberg – *Nephrology*
Junior Physicians:
Dr. Faiza Abdi Noor
Dr. Per Nystrom-Miller
Part-time:
Dr. Werner Bjerknes *(Emeritus Chief Physician)*

TURN or FLICK
Chapters (1 – 6)

Chapter 1

Dr. Alessandro Gianetti

August 26th, 1960
Dr. Alessandro Gianetti
Brindisi – Italy

Friday

The familiar noises and vibrations Alessandro had gotten used to during the last days and nights suddenly stopped. Papà lifted him up over white metal bars out into the sun.

"Alessandro. Look. Italy. Home," Mamma said with excitement in her voice.

What Mamma was talking about made no sense to him at all. He just saw several of the things which he liked looking at in his book so much. But these were real, driving around, not like those in the book.

"Mamma. Papà. BRUM—BRUM" Alessandro was wildly shaking his right hand at his discovery so that Mamma and Papà would notice.

* * *

Sophia and Mario Gianetti—Alessandro's parents—were looking forward to disembarking from the M/V Africa. The lengthy train ride from Brindisi to Borgo a Buggiano was still ahead of them, but it felt good to finally be back home in Italy after having been away for so long. Most of the reporting in the newspapers they bought at the train station was about the Summer Olympic Games, which had just begun in Rome the day before.

* * *

TURN or FLICK?

YOUR CHOICE AS A READER:

If you want to engage with the story by exploring what happened next in the life of Dr. Alessandro Gianetti, just continue to TURN the pages.

If, however you prefer to 'hopscotch' and read what happened next to any of the other doctors working at Godshus General Hospital in the overall timeline of the narrative, i.e. between August 26th, 1960 and the early evening hours on December 20th, 2019, then FLICK ahead to page 128 of the book as indicated below (128 ⋯→). This will take you to February 20th, 1964. Please refer to 'A Guide for the Reader of this Book' on page 7 in the beginning if you require further information.

* * *

128 ⋯→

July 15th, 1977
Dr. Alessandro Gianetti
Borgo a Buggiano – Italy

Friday

"Tanti Auguri, Alessandro."

It felt bittersweet realizing what was inside the box he had just unwrapped.

"And what do you think you'll be able to do later in life? Sit under an umbrella on the Piazza Della Signoria in summer and sell portrait sketches to badly dressed American tourists in white tennis shoes?" Papà was no longer the diplomat when it concerned Alessandro's further education.

Two choices: LAW or MEDICINE.

Alessandro thought he would be able to use his hands more in medicine. That way he could also send at least a small sign of rebellion by diverting from Papà's footsteps.

"You can always continue to do what you like, but as a hobby. Your father is right," Mamma said, as he inspected the contents of the box.

Later in the evening, he went back up to his room, which overlooked gentle green hills covered with olive trees. He put down his new set of stone-carving tools next to the half-finished marble sculpture of a girl's face, which he had hoped to send to the Accademia Di Belle Arti Di Firenze as part of his application.

* * *

←··· 141 ○◎○ 144 ···→

May 27th, 1983
Dr. Alessandro Gianetti
Florence – Italy

Friday

Billie Jean ...
Alessandro's torso swayed slightly to the pop music which was traveling out of the corner gelateria catering to the tourists on the Piazza del Duomo.

It was the moment his eyes spotted her. She was sitting on a bench in the distance—the front of her body facing Giotto's bell tower, her long straight hair facing him.

Finally, Alessandro was on his way home for the weekend. He had selected the Ospedale di Santa Maria Nuova in the old center—a hospital founded even before the Medici family came to power and left their marks on the city—for the anesthesiology clerkship. His other clinical rotations took place in the modern Carreggi Hospital—north of the historic center. It had been a quiet, regular, sunny Friday until around 11:30, and Alessandro had hoped to leave the hospital early and get to the villa to spend the weekend with his parents. He and the supervising anesthesiologist had just started with the last checks on a woman who would have general anesthesia for a minor arthroscopic knee surgery. She was the last scheduled case for the day.

Suddenly, the chief physician of the anesthesia department rushed into the small room next to operating room BETA and asked him to join, as a patient required urgent intubation downstairs. They hurried down the medieval stairway. A not-so-small American tourist had walked into the small emergency facility of the hospital about ten minutes earlier. The triage nurse's English was limited. What they knew was that he had slipped on the sidewalk in front of the nearby Palazzo Medici. Unfortunately, instead of landing just on the pavement, he had crashed face-first into one of the marble stone benches, which—in some places—lined the perimeter of the palazzo.

He was bleeding profusely from his nose and mouth and was missing some of his upper teeth. The welt on the left side of his forehead was a near-perfect straight line. He was conscious after the fall. His wife had—with the help of several bystanders—quickly dragged the bleeding man down the roughly three blocks to Santa Maria Nuova's small 'guardia medica' department, which was better suited to handle patients presenting with migraine headaches, dehydration, or sprained ankles. Nobody had thought about calling the emergency ambulance services, which would have otherwise stabilized him on the street and transported him to the trauma unit at Carreggi Hospital.

A path of blood drops marked the route the man had taken from the entrance door to one of the stretchers. The internist who was staffing the department that late morning had grabbed some gauze and applied pressure to the nose and upper mouth and had urgently summoned the surgeon to come. Now, he was just standing in the middle of the room with a somewhat helpless expression, from time to time grimacing at his blood-soaked hands. An IV had been started and labs were drawn. Shortly after the surgeon arrived, the patient, who had been awake and trying to say something to them in English, suddenly rolled up his eyes and started seizing. His trauma was clearly more extensive than just the massive bleeding from his nose and mouth, and it was then they had called the chief anesthesiologist to help. A breathing tube needed to be put down into the patient's windpipe to assure that his airway stayed open. With all the blood coming from his mouth and throat, this would be a difficult task.

"Does your husband have any medical problems?" As it definitely was not up to a medical student to try to intubate this patient, the internist with the blood-soaked hands, who was in his mid-fifties and spoke only some German apart from Italian, had signaled Alessandro to help him talk to the patient's wife.

"He had rheumatic fever as a child," his wife, whose white summer dress, speckled with splatters of her husband's blood, now resembled a Jackson Pollock painting, said to Alessandro, after complimenting him on his English. "So last spring he had to have a heart valve replaced because it was so damaged. We went to Cedars-Sinai. I think they call it a Björk-Shiley valve, or something like that. You, of course, know more about heart valves than me. Is he going to be okay?"

Alessandro spoke English quite fluently because of his father's insistence and thanks to several British and American women who had fallen in love with Tuscany and had served as his tutors through the years.

"So, is he taking any medications?"

"Well, he's been on a blood thinner since his surgery. Warfarin[1]. You know, the rat poison. To make sure that no blood clots form on that valve. So he doesn't get a stroke. Is he going to be okay?"

The blood thinner explained why the American was bleeding from his mouth and nose so profusely. Alessandro quickly informed the surgeon and anesthesiologist about what the wife just told him. After great difficulty, they had inserted a breathing tube into the patient's trachea and were now using an Ambu bag to regularly press air into the patient's lungs. The patient's blood-soaked light blue Lacoste tennis shirt had been cut away by a nurse exposing a long, well-healed

---

1 **Warfarin** – Medication used as a blood thinner. It is known under many different brand names worldwide (e.g. Coumadin, Marevan, Aldocumar). Warfarin is used to treat blood clots such as deep vein thromboses and pulmonary embolisms. It is also prescribed to prevent strokes in people with atrial fibrillation, valvular heart disease, or artificial heart valves. Its discovery is linked to outbreaks of a disease in cattle in the northern United States of America and Canada in the 1920s, which caused cows to bleed to death after ingesting moldy silage made from sweet clover. This led to further research by *Karl Paul Link* at the University of Wisconsin and to the isolation of 'dicoumarol', which proved to be the molecule responsible for the blood-thinning effect. Subsequently, warfarin, which is similar to dicoumarol, was developed and initially registered for use as a rodenticide in the USA in 1948. It was approved for human use in 1954.

61

scar down the middle of his chest. He continued to have intermittent jerking movements, mostly of his right arm and leg, blood dripping from his face onto the already blood-soaked white linen on the stretcher. The anesthesiologist asked Alessandro to bring vials with diazepam—a sedative—as well as some morphine—a strong pain killer—from the hospital's small intensive care unit. He ran down the hallway and, under the watchful eyes of the senior intensive care unit nurse, quickly retrieved the requested vials, which, being controlled substances, were only stored there and not in the small 'guardia medica' department. At about the same time he made it back, one of the laboratory technicians arrived, announcing critical results of the patient's bloodwork. Considering all the blood around them, it was not a surprise that his blood counts were low. But it was another very abnormal number that was much more alarming.

"Are you sure about this? This isn't a lab error?" the surgeon harshly asked the laboratory technician.

"Yes. His prothrombin time is 118 seconds. We ran the test twice."

"That's why he's bleeding like a pig. Is that like ten times longer than normal?"

"Yes, about that. Our upper limit of normal for prothrombin time is twelve seconds," the laboratory technician said.

The Warfarin was thinning the American's blood way too much. Warfarin being a difficult medication to dose; its effects differing not only from one human to another but also often quite variable for an individual patient, depending on what she or he would eat. Patients on this medication therefore required frequent lab draws. The blood of one patient could be ideally thinned with just one milligram of the medication, whereas another patient might require ten times more to achieve the same result. Ideally the time it would take for blood to clot in patients with a mechanical heart valve, like the seizing and bleeding American visitor had, should have been lengthened from the normal around twelve seconds to a value of about thirty seconds, but never the almost two minutes they had just measured. Another methodology to report the prothrombin time was not in seconds but as INR (International Normalized Ratio). The value in a person not on Warfarin would be around 1. The goal in a patient with a mechanical heart valve would be somewhere between 2.5 and 3.5, but not the unlucky number of 13, which the 118 seconds were roughly equivalent to.

What they discovered during the patient's physical exam was even more concerning than all the surrounding blood. Shortly after the diazepam and morphine had been injected into his vein, the jerking movements stopped, and the American finally appeared to be resting.

When the doctors opened his eyelids, they found a significant difference between the right and the left eye. His right eye revealed a normal-looking rim of green iris—and the green rim got even larger when they shone a flashlight into it. In contrast, the pupil on the left stared at them like a large black full moon, surrounded only by a thin green rim of iris and its size did not change even with the brightest light.

Considering what had happened, this likely meant that the fall had also caused major bleeding around the left side of the brain, with the blood pressing and displacing brain tissue. Standing within the massive stone walls of the Ospedale di Santa Maria Nuova, some of which still dated from the Renaissance, they could not verify their suspicion. The only CT scanner in Florence had just been installed at Carreggie Hospital. Given how rapidly he had deteriorated, there was no chance that the American would survive long enough to be transferred in an ambulance to Carreggie. The pressure from the blood on his brain would be too big by then. The anesthesiologist and the surgeon talked briefly and then asked Alessandro to quickly pick up some units of blood and especially plasma from the blood bank, while they whisked the patient to the elevator leading to the operating rooms.

The blood Alessandro was picking up would replete the American with blood. The plasma would supply additional clotting factors which the patient's liver had stopped producing due to the effect of the Warfarin, and hopefully help to stop further external and, more importantly, the internal bleeding around his brain. However—to save the patient's life—the surgeon would need to bore a hole in his skull through which the blood could be drained from the brain surface and the mounting pressure on the patient's brain relieved. In contrast to his nose and mouth, the blood in the patient's brain had nowhere to go and was building up more pressure in the tight skull with every passing minute.

The patient's wife had been forgotten in her grief, left standing in her no longer white summer dress together with a helpless-looking internist, whose hands were still soaked with her husband's blood. She kept repeating the same question over and over, which the internist would not have been able to answer, even if both of them had been able to exchange words in a common language: Is he going to be okay?

Unfortunately, they could not save him. Shortly after the surgeon had drilled the hole through the patient's skull, which had confirmed their suspicion of a large bleed around the brain, the patient's heart rate slowed down. Alarmed, the anesthesiologist injected medications to try to counteract this. However, this did not help. Although they had been successful in draining out the blood from around the patient's brain, the pressure on the brain had become too massive and had crushed his brainstem. The epidural hematoma which he had suffered from the fall had expanded too rapidly.

The sixty-seven-year-old American visitor from Los Angeles who had traveled to enjoy the artistic wonders of Florence with his wife died at 12:39 on a table made of cold stainless steel in operating room ALFA of a hospital founded long before an Italian had sailed to the New World.

He was still wearing the white tennis shoes he had put on that morning.

The Michael Jackson song faded away with several mentions of *Billie Jean*.

Alessandro walked up to the woman with the long straight hair, stopping at her right and peeking over her shoulder. She was making a pencil sketch of Giotto's bell tower. He realized that it was not just a sketch. She had to be an artist. He just stood and watched how the fingers of her fine hands were swiftly recreating the beauty of the tower on a blank piece of paper. Suddenly her hand stopped drawing. He looked to his left and met two light blue eyes and a smile.

"You know, I actually prefer sculpture. I'm Charlotte. What's your name?"

She was wearing brown leather sandals.

* * *

←··· 146 ○◎○ 148 ···→

March 13th, 1985
Dr. Alessandro Gianetti
Copenhagen – Denmark

Wednesday

Seeing the small black cross on top of the greenish dome of Marmorkirken with its golden stripes in the distance made Alessandro remember how Papà's black coffin with the golden cross on it was lowered into the ground.

The ship's horn sounded.

From the height, he could see the strict geometry of the palace in front of the church. He also saw how flat everything was. Not the gentle, rolling green hills of Tuscany, nor the dramatic grey mountain cliffs around Godshus. Just a flat city made up of old houses with mostly dark grey roofs, with a light grey March sky above. The cold in his face caused Alessandro to shiver just a bit. His body had gotten used to the warm spring breeze. So quickly. The thought of someone ever swimming in the ship's empty outside pool behind him, completely displaced, made him freeze even more. They would be in Oslo in the morning and hopefully make the drive back home to Godshus before sunset the following night.

They had stayed in Borgo a Buggiano for only ten days. After Mamma had called that afternoon and a sleepless overnight drive, they had taken the plane from Oslo via Linate. A desperate race to try to be there in time. But they still arrived too late. Of course, it was not unexpected.

Now, on their way back, they traveled as they had always in the past almost two years. But this time they had tears in their eyes when they said their farewell on platform sixteen of Santa Maria Novella, over twenty-four hours ago. Mamma seemed a bit lost but tough at the same time. She would continue to rent the rooms in the villa to the tourists, as she had done before. Of course, she had help. She could not have managed alone with Papà over the last years.

They used up all the Deutsche Mark bills Mamma had given them on dinner in the large drafty hall of a train station in Munich before boarding the overnight train, leaving them with just a couple of Pfennig coins.

Surprisingly, Alessandro could sleep. He felt the crisp spring cold in his face when he opened the train door around lunch the next day. The commission they had to pay at the small kiosk to have enough Danish kroner to cover lunch and the expensive taxi for the short ride through the city was outrageous. It was too early in the year for their usual quick stop in Tivoli, and therefore they picked one of the small touristy places in Nyhavn after they had left the suitcases in their cabin. Alessandro was still a bit surprised that the waiter had no problem at all understanding his Norwegian when he ordered the smørrebrød for himself. Of course, the other way around, he could not understand the man at all when the confusion arose about the two hundred Italian Lira coin, which he had mistaken for a five Danish Kroner coin when he tried to pay. Luckily Charlotte was there to sort things out.

A man had pushed a woman in a wheelchair out onto the deck. They were looking at the pier below. Occasionally the man waved at someone on the pier.

The wheelchair made him remember Papà and the wedding. He was glad that Papà was still part of it last spring. Of course, he needed the wheelchair. Because of the Parkinson's, in the pictures, it seemed, that he wasn't smiling. Charlotte looked even more beautiful that day. Papà was so happy for him and Charlotte. He also liked the idea of him moving to Norway. Papà said that he had been there. A long time ago. Once. During the war. The move was much easier than expected. The oddly melodic language appeared difficult at first, but with Charlotte's help, it became easy over time. He got the job right away, and they paid him for it. Not like in Italy, where he would likely have to make money on the side somehow, in the beginning, while working at a hospital. Charlotte enjoyed teaching the kids at the local school.

The change in the noises and vibrations coming from the ship followed by a gentle jolt made the memories vanish.

"Farvel Pia! Vi ses på søndag!"[1] the man next to him shouted and both the woman and he waved frantically.

Alessandro decided to go back into the warmth.

"Far, kan jeg få vaniljeis?"[2]

"Anders, jeg ved ikke om de har nogle på færgen her. Måske kan vi få nogle i Oslo. Ellers får vi nogle, når vi kommer tilbage til Hirtshals."[3]

Then, the announcement started.

"Welcome aboard DFDS Seaways! We're now leaving 'Wonderful Copenhagen' to bring you to Oslo. First, we would like to review some of the safety procedures aboard the MS Scandinavia ..."

Charlotte lay in a deep sleep of exhaustion in her bed already. She never could fall asleep on the train. Her face was relaxed, just with a hint of a tan from the warm Italian sun. Alessandro wanted to snuggle next to her, but the cabin had two separate single beds.

He carefully opened the suitcase that held the books.

At times, he missed Italian.

The melody of the language. The drama. The passion. The charm. The seductiveness. The odder-sounding words.

Mamma would occasionally send him some books. On the evening, when he packed the suitcase, she had given him as many as would fit. The books she had read already, as now she did not need to hold on to them because of Papà. He selected Umberto Eco's *Il nome della rosa*. Of course, he had heard about it but hadn't had the time to read it.

Alessandro also took the last of the newspapers he had not read so far from his leather shoulder bag. He had bought them at the

---

1 **Farvel Pia! Vi ses på søndag!** – *Danish:* Bye Pia! See you on Sunday!

2 **Far, kan jeg få vaniljeis?** – *Danish:* Dad, can I have some vanilla ice cream?

3 **Anders, jeg ved ikke om de har nogle på færgen her. Måske kan vi få nogle i Oslo. Ellers får vi nogle, når vi kommer tilbage til Hirtshals.** – *Danish:* Anders, I don't know if they have some on the ferry here. Perhaps we can get some in Oslo. Otherwise we'll have some when we get back to Hirtshals.

Santa Maria Novella train station the morning before. Carefully he closed the door of the cabin so he would not wake up Charlotte. He found a red lounge chair.

The music had not started playing yet.

It was time to read the newspaper before yesterday's news became even older than it already was. The bold headline in *La Repubblica* announced:

Comincia l'era Gorbaciov

above a picture showing a man with an interestingly shaped birthmark covering the right side of his bald forehead.

* * *

←··· 148 ○◎○ 254 ···→

June 14th, 1985
Dr. Alessandro Gianetti
Godshus – Norway

Friday

"But are you sure we shouldn't just complete everything at once?" Alessandro said while he was loading the first set of sample tubes into the centrifuge. "It'll take us only thirty minutes longer and everything will be done."

"No, no. I'll come back tomorrow and run the rest of the samples. It's Friday, and it has been a long week for you and I'm sure you want to go home. And it's sunny outside. I have no plans for tomorrow anyhow," Dr. Bjerknes said, although this did not make any sense to Alessandro.

Earlier that day, his senior colleague had asked him to assist in the laboratory. It was one of the many things done a bit differently at Godshus General Hospital because of it being so small. The doctors themselves ran the laboratory outside the regular working hours of the laboratory technician, known as the 'lab lady', a tall woman with short hair who wore a lot of make-up.

Initially—just after he had started working—regular hours had been set aside with the 'lab lady' until he could run the basic testing of blood samples by himself. She was there during weekdays from 6 until 14:30. If an urgent analysis was required outside these hours, on weekends, or when she was on vacation, it was the doctors who had to run the samples. Given the recently installed quite new automation equipment, all had become much less complicated over the years.

Of course, the test kit delivered by post the day before had arrived in the middle of the laboratory technician's two-week holiday. The parcel contained the Abbott HTLV III EIA—mailed to all

Norwegian Hospitals earlier that week—urging them to test all blood products they stored.

Norway's blood supply should be declared HIV free.

At the latest by Monday, June 17th, 1985.

The centralized blood banks located in the country's three large university hospitals in Oslo, Bergen, and Trondheim would from now on perform this test on all the blood before sending it out to the smaller hospitals. But given that PRBC units, which contained concentrated red blood cells, could be stored up to a month and a half in the smaller hospitals, it would have been an enormous hassle to send all the blood back and forth just to run a quick test. Doing the testing locally on the blood they already had in storage totally made sense.

Alessandro assumed that Dr. Bjerknes had asked him for help because of his recent training on the newer equipment required to run this somewhat non-standard test.

They both carefully read the instructions of the test twice and it was actually quite straightforward. After quickly collecting the needed supplies, they transferred samples from the blood to be tested into tubes. The singular roadblock they encountered was that their small laboratory centrifuge could only spin twelve samples at a time, and therefore they would need to do two rounds of spinning to process all the seventeen units of blood of the various blood types the hospital had in storage.

"So can we offer the test to patients now?"

"No. They're very clear that this is just for the blood products. The letter they sent with it states that so far it's not approved for testing patients. We actually have to send back the unused reagents once we're done with the testing."

Alessandro did not really care. AIDS was a problem in America and big cities, but not something which had any relevance in their small fjord community.

With concentration, they both worked at completing all the steps described in the test instruction material.

DAVID ØYBO

At the end none of the samples turned yellow, meaning that no antibodies against the virus which caused AIDS were detected in the twelve tested blood units stored at Godshus General Hospital.

The news on the radio, which Alessandro had turned on to play some music in the background while they were working, announced that a TWA jet was hijacked while flying from Athens to Rome and that some European countries were envisioning to abolish all border controls in Europe.

He had never heard the name of the town where the agreement had been signed before: *Schengen.*

* * *

←⋯ 254 ○◎○ 150 ⋯→

72

April 28th, 1986
Dr. Alessandro Gianetti
Godshus – Norway

Monday

Alessandro had picked up the fresh salmon at the local salmon farm. The farfalle were now al dente and just a couple of minutes later he served Charlotte his special version of farfalle al salmone. When they were done eating, they turned on the TV and snuggled on the sofa a bit. About in the middle of NRK[1] Dagsrevyen,[2] a television reporter was asking a bald mature gentleman who was standing on a rooftop outside, with a grayish rainy Oslo in the background:

"For you, as the director of the National Institute for Radiation Hygiene, does this mean that large parts of the country have been covered by a dangerous radioactive cloud?"

"I wouldn't call this cloud dangerously radioactive, because after all there has been a relatively small increase in the radioactivity we find everywhere in nature around us. But still, there's an increase, an artificial increase, in the radiation that can get on people, and we must try to avoid such things. The first thing we've done is to intensify our readings, but we've not yet had these readings analyzed, so it's too early to say what this radioactivity consists of."

"So there's no cause for alarm?"

"Absolutely no cause for alarm, no."

When the program switched back to the news announcer, who was wearing a dark purple shirt under his dress jacket, he said:

---

1 **NRK** – Norsk Rikskringkasting – Norwegian Broadcasting Corporation

2 **Dagsrevyen** – *Norwegian*: *The Daily Review*. Daily evening television news program by NRK.

"We've just received a message that the Soviet Union has announced that there has been an accident in one of their nuclear power plants."

Later that night, while in their bed making love, Alessandro suddenly stopped.

"Are you okay?" Charlotte asked.

"You know—perhaps we should use condoms. Just for a while. Until this whole radioactive cloud thing is sorted out."

* * *

←··· 332 ○◎○ 335 ···→

July 10th, 1989
Dr. Alessandro Gianetti
Stockholm – Sweden

Monday

He was humming the song mentioning an alien, albeit a legal one when he finally found a parking spot for the 3-door Saab 900.

Alessandro could not get Sting's lyrics out of his ear since the song had played on the radio somewhere between Karlstad and Örebro early the previous night—but, of course, as an Italian in Norway he would drink coffee and not tea like an *Englishman in New York*. Charlotte had fallen asleep in the passenger seat by then.

Being pregnant always exhausted her.

The drive from Godshus to Stockholm was long. Very long. With lots and lots and lots of trees.

The entire reason for their trip still felt completely bizarre to him. But there had been no way around it.

The Norwegian Immigration Office had no issues with processing all the paperwork needed for granting him his citizenship by just presenting his valid Italian passport.

It was a sentence in a letter from the Norwegian Medical Association which he had received back in March which ultimately had made them make the long drive:

"Unfortunately, according to our internal rules, we cannot accept a *'Baptism Certificate'* as a substitute for a *'Birth Certificate'* to allow you to register to take your internal medicine specialty board exam in Norway when you will be eligible to do so."

Both he and Charlotte had called them numerous times trying to explain. They talked to the department head. What followed were repeated excuses, but in the end, it was always:

"We're sorry, but we have to *follow the rules*."

NO EXCEPTIONS

The Italian embassy in Oslo was also not helpful:

"Of course, you are Italian. But we cannot issue birth certificates to Italians who are not born in Italy. I also do not understand the problem they are making you. You have your passport. That just has to be enough for them. If they absolutely insist, contact the embassy of the country you were born in. They should be able to help you."

Helplessly stuck between a totally illogical clash of Norwegian and Italian bureaucracies, it was the small office on the second floor of a simple building in Norrmalm, with a deep orange façade and red windows that appeared to be his last hope.

Charlotte had opted to wait in the car. She had been too nauseous to eat breakfast in the hotel.

A woman opened the door. After starting their conversation in Norwegian—on Alessandro's part—and Swedish—on part of the woman—they ultimately settled on English to make sure similarly sounding words, which however could mean something slightly—or totally—different, would not add to the already confusing situation.

"Honestly, I've never heard about something similar before. Let me see if the ambassador can help you in some way."

She took the original of the baptism certificate—a small atypical-sized piece of paper which had become slightly yellow over the years—and left the room, closing the door behind her. A couple of minutes later she emerged with a tall skinny elderly gentleman in a light blue suit.

He smiled at him.

"I think I know your father! How is he?" was the unexpected greeting Alessandro received in fluent Italian.

The gentleman in the suit seemed genuinely sad when he heard the news that Papà had died over five years ago. He asked him to sit in the chair across the desk in his office. He talked about how things had changed since the time Papà had been the 'vice amministratore'.

How everything started to slowly but surely descend into chaos.

How he had just received the news that the man to whom the signature on Alessandro's yellowish 'baptism certificate' belonged had been murdered in the cathedral the evening before. He shared that he was afraid that the worst was yet to come.

That a war might start.

About thirty minutes later Alessandro opened the door of the Saab where Charlotte was waiting for him with a concerned expression on her face.

He had been given a piece of paper, which—as it contained several stamps and an eloquently long signature—was very official-looking.

It had the following information written in three languages on it:

Shahaadada dhalashada / Certificato di nascita / Birth Certificate

Magaca / Nome / Name:
Alessandro Gianetti

Taariikhda Dhalashada / Data di nascita / Date of Birth:
Julaay 15 aad 1959 / 15 luglio 1959 / July 15th, 1959

Goobta dhalashada magaalada / Luogo di nascita / Place of Birth:
Muqdisho / Mogadiscio / Mogadishu

Alessandro felt confident that the administrators of the Norwegian Medical Association would be fully satisfied when the paper would lie in front of them on their desk in Oslo. Nobody would ever know that only one such document existed, typed up on the embassy's green IBM Selectric II typewriter and stamped and signed by the Ambassador of Somalia to Sweden, Norway, and Denmark himself. A man whose country was failing but who did not want to fail the son of the man he had worked with many years before in an atmosphere of hope and big dreams.

But all stopped to matter completely the moment Charlotte told him with a shaky voice:

"Alessandro—I started cramping fifteen minutes ago."

She started bleeding even before he found the way to the Karolinska Sjukhuset, the leading teaching hospital in Stockholm.

That morning was the fifth time they lost the hope of having a baby.

* * *

←·· 335 ○◎○ 192 ··→

November 9th, 1989
Dr. Alessandro Gianetti
Godshus – Norway

Thursday

When Alessandro saw the blood oozing out from the bottom of the large ulcer in the patient's stomach, he knew he should have come as soon as Hana had called him the first time.

"Hey. You're not picking up the phone! Dr. Rønneberg sent me to ask if you think she should cross-type some more blood for the patient and also if he needs to go to the Intensive Care Unit after you're done?" Nurse Louise said as she poked her head through the door of operating room number '2'. It was she who had rushed to the patient earlier, just after she had helped to collect the dinner trays on the first floor. He had suddenly started vomiting a lot of blood again. Now he was lying on the stretcher in front of Alessandro and fighting the unpleasant feeling of the endoscope down his throat, despite all the medications Alessandro had given him to relax. The nurse assisting him therefore had her hands full of holding him down. Neither of them had been able to answer the phone on the wall, which had been ringing several minutes before.

"Yes. Two more units of PRBCs and please tell her to unfreeze two FFPs. And yes, he definitely must go to the ICU. He's really bleeding quite a lot. I'll have to inject that ulcer. Can you give him another two point five milligrams of valium please?"

Alessandro was argumentative with Hana when she first called.

"Just fluid resuscitate him. Give him some blood if necessary and keep him NPO.[1] He'll be fine until the morning and we'll do the endoscopy then."

---

1 **NPO** – *Nil per os* (Latin) – Nothing by mouth is an instruction not to provide a patient with any food and fluids by mouth.

He really had not wanted to leave Charlotte alone at home and drive to the hospital.

"Hana. He'll be fine. Yes, I understand that it was about a cup full of fresh red blood. But you know this always looks worse than it actually is. If he has any black stools, then call me, okay? Have a good night."

Hana started her internship one month early, back in June. She was smart and caring, but of course, if somebody needed an endoscopy over night she would have to call one of the more experienced doctors to do it. He was the person to call from Thursday to Sunday this week.

"Did you know? She had number four. Number four! She basically could have picked any place in the country. And she comes to Godshus General Hospital!" Dr. Bjerknes had told him all excited one day. It was a Norwegian medical student thing he never really fully understood. This whole 'number thing'.

About fifteen minutes after he put down the receiver, the phone rang again.

"So he just had a toilet bowl full of black stool with some fresh blood clots in it. He's super pale and sweaty. His heart rate is up to one hundred forty-five and the best systolic blood pressure I can get is eighty. I have two IVs in him and I am pushing in the fluids wide open. He's on the stretcher already and Louise and I are going to wheel him down to operating room number '2' now and I'll then prepare four units of blood." She hung up on him before he could say anything.

"Go Alessandro. Go. I'm fine. I'm fine. Really." He kissed Charlotte and quickly grabbed his coat. They had just arrived home the night before from Oslo after they had admitted Charlotte for all the testing on Monday and Tuesday. She had spent one night at the Kvinneklinikken,[1] the women's Clinic, at the Rikshospitalet.[2] He was not able to drive back on Tuesday

---

1 **Kvinneklinikken** – *Norwegian*: Women's Clinic.

2 **Rikshospitalet** – *Norwegian*: 'The National Hospital' is one of the three hospitals in Oslo, which together form the University Hospital

already, as he had initially wanted, after what the professor and one of the senior physicians had told them.

"Charlotte. Alessandro. I'm very sorry. You know, the hysteroscopy Dr. Kjekshus did this morning shows that Charlotte has a condition called Asherman Syndrome. Unfortunately, yours is very, very severe. It's honestly the worst I have seen in my entire career. If it were a lot milder, doing a procedure might help. But you have to understand that in your case it will just not work."

"Have you considered adopting?"

Asherman syndrome. He had never heard of it. They explained everything in detail. His mind understood the message back in Oslo, but his heart only really started feeling it when they had opened the door of their house the night before. It was the first time he cried since Papà's funeral.

The valium had made the patient in front of him finally relax.

"Could you please get some epinephrine so we can inject around the ulcer?" Alessandro asked the nurse.

"How much?"

"Thirty milliliters, please. One to ten thousand dilution."

If he could not stop the bleeding by injecting the epinephrine around the ulcer, he would need to call the surgeon and ask him to take out the patient's stomach. The patient would of course be ideal for the endoclips like they had in Japan. The ones that the professor from Oslo had talked about during the last meeting he went to in Bergen. But for now, they did not have these in Norway or at Godshus General Hospital. But soon, perhaps.

He enjoyed working with the black endoscopes. Transforming the flat picture showing the interior of the stomach or colon, which he saw on the monitor screen in front of him, into a three-dimensional image in his mind. The alteration between the crude motions necessary to insert the flexible skinny black polymer coated metallic rods through the patient's mouth or anus and then the fine movements with the deflection knob to move the bending section of the

---

in Oslo. Originally established in 1826 as the nation's teaching hospital, it was located in the center of Oslo until 2000, when the current building was finished in the Gaustad neighborhood.

endoscope's tip around in the examined body cavity. The play of his fingers between pushing down either on the suction or irrigation valve to get a better view. And now the delicate exercise to inject the epinephrine around this patient's ulcer with the small needle tip which appeared on the monitor—attached to a long thin tube of plastic, which the nurse had just threaded in through one of the channels on the endoscope. Not too little and not too far away from the ulcer as then the bleeding would not stop, but also not too much or too deep as he could otherwise rupture the thin wall of the stomach. In some ways, it reminded him of using his hands and fingers to sculpt the face of a girl in a piece of marble. One small wrong movement and all the work would be ruined. Only that marble was white and not the hue of grayish pink like the mucosa of the stomach.

"We'll watch him in the Intensive Care Unit overnight. He'll get more blood. I was able to stop the bleeding now, but it can restart. If that happens, I'll try to stop it again with the endoscope, but we'll also have to call the surgeon as he might need to operate to stop it."

Alessandro told the patient's wife whose eyes were big after they had brought the patient into the ICU. He then walked over to the lab to check how Hana was doing with the blood.

"No problem. No need to apologize. Could you take the blood to the ICU for the patient for me? I'll be right back up. Just have to tell the one patient who is left in the ER that surprise, surprise she's pregnant. Guess that explains her nausea. Otherwise, I would have admitted her, but all her labs look fine."

The memories of the sparingly decorated office in Oslo came back. He put his right hand over his face, pushing his thumb against his right eye and his index finger against his left.

"Alessandro, are you okay?"

"I'm sorry, Hana. You know they told us in Oslo that Charlotte has Asherman's syndrome."

"Oh gosh. Alessandro, I'm so sorry!"

"You know what Asherman's syndrome is?"

"Of course I do."

Alessandro decided to wait in the office a bit before driving home. It was 19:31. He was a minute late when he turned on the TV. He had just missed how the red 'N' logo turned around the stylized globe. The first thing on the TV screen was an enormous explosion in the ocean. Did he miss that a war had started? Oh, no—just a lengthy report that a Norwegian shipbuilder had been awarded a contract to build some mine searching boats. Four hundred people would have work for a couple of years. The second news-block showed, as so often in the past couple of weeks, a group of Eastern Germans protesting against their communist government. There was definitely a lot happening on the continent these days. All of this felt quite distant when viewed from the senior physician's office in Godshus General Hospital.

A brief part of the report sounded interesting and novel: apparently, it had been announced at a press conference in East Berlin just about thirty minutes ago that the Eastern German communist regime had decided to open the border immediately and allow Eastern Germans to travel freely. It was interesting to hear that type of news, however, it seemed a bit bizarre—likely something had been misinterpreted in the NRK newsroom.

If it were really that important, it would have surely been in the news first, prior to a report about some shipbuilding contract. One would see what would come out of this. After the reporter had started talking about how the West German chancellor was visiting Poland for the last couple of days, Alessandro concluded that nothing really important happened in the world on November 9th, 1989 and switched off the TV. He would quickly check in the ICU how the patient was doing and if Hana needed any help and then would drive back home.

A home that Charlotte and he now knew would never be filled with the crying sounds of a baby.

* * *

←··· 192 o◉o 336 ···→

December 21st, 1990
Dr. Alessandro Gianetti
Godshus – Norway

Friday

Alessandro parked the Saab 900 in the usual spot. How could this have happened? He and Hana had always enjoyed talking, and this evening was no different. They discussed the patient who died in the morning. They danced a bit to the mediocre band the restaurant hired for the Julebord, which this year for the first time mixed nurses and doctors from the hospital with the workers from the local fish factory. There was lots of food. The wine tasted cheap. Hana definitely had too much to drink. They left early. He still was sober enough to drive her home. She grabbed his forearm when the moose suddenly appeared amid the light snow in the headlights in front of them. He stopped the car at the very last moment.

He should have never agreed to try a glass of the expensive wine the team had given to her as a farewell gift that morning.

She shared her frustration about going to Oslo and not back to Trondheim as she had hoped.

He was sympathetic towards her.

Their lips met.

Their tongues followed, and from there it was all animalistic impulse, haste, and confusion.

The sex was short, but given the lack of any reproductive intent, oddly releasing for him.

It was as if the sex organ, which distinguished humans from the other mammals on earth—the frontal lobes of their brains—had taken a temporary time out. An act of unchecked animalistic instinct, fueled solely by the estrogen and testosterone in them, making them in no way different from two *gatti randagi*[1] uniting at night on a medieval red tile roof in Florence.

He left quickly in the awkwardness which followed.

Charlotte was asleep already.

He undressed for the second time that night and put the cufflinks that had been Papà's back into their box. He tried not to wake Charlotte but failed.

"How was the party?" she asked.

"Nothing special," Alessandro said.

And then he tried to fall asleep next to the woman who was the love of his life.

* * *

←·· 153 ○◎○ 342 ··→

---

1 **gatti randagi** – *Italian:* Stray cats.

January 5th, 2009
Dr. Alessandro Gianetti
Godshus – Norway

Monday

He was so deeply asleep he did not hear the phone. It had been ringing repeatedly for at least ten minutes. Luckily Charlotte had come home directly from school.

"Alessandro! Wake up! Wake up!" She was shaking him. "The hospital is calling."

There was still a hint of light outside, and he guessed it must have been between 14:00 and 15:00. He had hoped to sleep until the morning and then go straight to work at 7. He had worked more than twelve hours the previous night and the same on Saturday night. And more or less every single day since Christmas Day before that.

As almost every year the hospital had filled up with patients just after Christmas, sending a clear signal that the more quiet time which usually started around mid-December had come to a sudden halt. People, no longer busy with their Christmas preparation, all of the sudden found the time to be sick. But in reality Christmas never really healed anyone or made somebody less sick. It just meant that everyone just stayed too long at home during the holidays, allowing minor problems to explode into big ones.

All the beds on the first floor were occupied. In the ICU every single patient was on a ventilator. Alessandro had spent a large part of the previous night trying to find a bed in any hospital in Norway for a recent grandmother whose kidneys—for reasons which were not entirely clear—decided to take a winter holiday as well and whose potassium now was 7.2 millimoles per liter and who therefore needed urgent dialysis, which they could not do during the night at Godshus General Hospital. What made everything worse this year was that they had an unprecedented doctor staffing crisis. Rarely did they ever have the full staff of six doctors in the first place. Besides Werner, who was chief physician, but who also worked the same hours as everyone else, it currently was Hana and he as the two senior physicians. The third senior physician position was still unfilled after the guy from Oslo left, after less than three months.

"Too rural. Too isolated. Think that Oslo is a better fit for me."—not the first time Alessandro had heard somebody say these words.

But things would have been okay with five doctors in the department.

The current problems only started on January 1st. The contract for the doctor from Poland who had been working as a junior physician with them was up on December 31st. His father in Warsaw had been diagnosed with ALS the previous summer and very understandably he had decided to return to be with his family. The Polish doctor liked it at Godshus General Hospital, and everybody liked him. He technically worked even longer than he should have, as he covered the night of New Year's Eve. Alessandro, therefore, was able to have a quick toast with a glass of champagne with Charlotte that evening. The Polish doctor promised he would let them know when he was ready to come back. Alessandro just hoped he would not hear from him in a very, very long time because he knew a phone call meant that the Polish doctor's father would be dead. They had found a replacement for the Polish doctor. Someone from somewhere up north in Sweden. But she would only arrive on January 12—being in Thailand until then, curing her 'pan-Scandinavian lack of sunlight winter depression syndrome' which affected her the same way as everyone else.

So it was only four of them.

Well, four until the afternoon three days ago. That was the day when anything that would have vaguely resembled an overworked but not self-destructive schedule completely fell apart.

The occasionally difficult doctor from Bergen, who was doing her internship with them since the summer, had been coughing for a while. She started having fevers already on December 28th but continued to work despite her influenza test being positive. The Tamiflu, Panodil, hot tea, and generous amounts of freshly squeezed lemon juice had appeared to help her—well, at least until Friday afternoon, when she suddenly began shaking while attending to a patient on the first floor. After the nurses measured a fever of 40.5 degrees Celsius, she reluctantly agreed to his and Werner's recommendation to get a chest X-ray. Some fifteen minutes later, Alessandro admitted her to room 133, with quite a large bilateral pneumonia.

Of course, room 133 happened to be the room where she had seen her last patient.

The old lady who had been her last patient that day and with whom she now shared the room was joking about this a little.

The junior doctor from Bergen had taken the last bed in the house. Clearly, she could not work until at least the following Wednesday.

That left three doctors to cover the hospital, with no realistic chance at all to get a locum to come to help out on a Friday afternoon.

So Hana, Werner, and Alessandro were faced with caring for 39 patients, four were on ventilators and one was a colleague with a severe pneumonia.

In every other place of employment which could be entered through a door with a lock, a situation like this would have led to somebody finding: a piece of paper, a pen, some tape and a key.

That somebody would then proceed to hastily take the pen—preferably a thick marker—and write six capital letters on the said piece of paper.

The somebody would then take the piece of paper as well as four short—previously prepared—pieces of tape and attach the said piece of paper to the outside of the entrance door of said place of employment so it could be seen by everyone passing by and then use the key to lock the door.

The six capital letters written on the piece of paper would read:

CLOSED.

But Godshus General Hospital—like every other building which calls itself a hospital on planet Earth—was a special place of employment and Hana, Werner and Alessandro somehow quickly came up with a plan to make things work.

It was Werner who was on the phone.

"Alessandro, I need you to work tonight."

Although Alessandro was still very, very far from being fully awake, he immediately sensed a very unusual tone of alarm in Werner's voice.

"But Hana's supposed to work."

"Alessandro, It'll be just the two of us for the next couple of days."

"What! Are you crazy! That's impossible! Crazy and impossible. I'm exhausted. I cannot do that! Somebody will get killed!"

"Alessandro, Hana's son got killed this morning."

Alessandro suddenly felt ice cold and goosebumps appeared, first on his back and then on his arms and legs.

"Oh, Santo Cielo![1] What happened?"

"I don't know. She hung up crying before I had the courage to ask."

"When do you need me to be there?"

"Get some more sleep and come in around 22:00."

He hung up and told Charlotte who, by watching his face, already knew that something was terribly wrong.

"But he was in my art class today."

"It must be her older son. The one who went to Israel."

* * *

←··· 203 ○◎○ 208 ···→

---

1 **Santo Cielo** – *Italian:* For the holy heaven's sake.

December 17th, 2010
Dr. Alessandro Gianetti
Godshus – Norway

Friday

"Dr. Gianetti, could you please come to evaluate the patient in bed three? After I gave her her morning bath, it seems like her left pupil is much wider than her right." Nurse Louise from the intensive care unit had called him on the call room phone, waking him up.

"On my way."

The night shift was almost over. It had been a quiet call. It was 6:15. Alessandro had even managed to sleep for three hours. He slipped into his white sandals and walked over to the ICU.

Everyone knew the patient very well. She was about his age. A very sad case. Aggressive breast cancer, diagnosed in her early forties. She went to Oslo for all her treatment. It seemed to have worked. Until a couple of months ago when she developed back pain. The CT showed that the cancer had now reappeared in her spine. They again referred her to Oslo. She opted for more chemotherapy. Had two rounds. Tolerated them surprisingly well. The plan was to continue the regimen in Godshus General Hospital. Ten days earlier, after suffering through bouts of nausea, she vomited everything, could not even keep water down. Eight days ago, they admitted her. Her laboratory work showed what one would expect from a dehydrated patient after chemotherapy. They gave her medications against the nausea and hydrated her. She started to feel a bit better, but then six nights ago she started running a high fever. It was not clear if the sepsis came from her urine or the lungs, but they had to send her to the ICU. Her breathing became more labored and her blood pressure was low. They had to intubate her and put a central line in to give her vasopressors, antibiotics, and all the other drugs. She had been deeply sedated

90

since then. Her husband was there all the time, except when he was at work or at home to catch some sleep. Her son stayed for several hours every day after school. The last two days she had improved. It looked like they could remove the breathing tube. That was the plan.

He took the small flashlight and shone it into her pupils. Louise of course was right. Her left pupil was wide and did not get smaller at all when he shone the light into her. The right one was mid-size and became smaller with light. It was hard to evaluate anything else as she was getting all the medications sedating her.

"I guess we have to do a CT scan of her brain."

"Before shift change?" Louise asked.

"Yes."

They immediately called the X-ray technician and got things prepared for the trip to the CT scanner. Alessandro logged into her electronic record. She did not have a CT scan of the brain done during her current admission.

After the X-ray technician came up to help with the transport, he, Louise, and Alessandro quickly wheeled her through the maternity ward to the elevators, the patient now connected to the much smaller portable ventilator. They took her two floors down and through the emergency department through the hallway with floor to ceiling windows looking out into the night. She was a tall woman but skinny, so it was easy to transfer her fifty or so kilograms from the bed onto the patient table of the CT scanner. Once they had her settled, all three of them left the room and sat down in the control room where they could watch how the table automatically moved her into the gantry of the CT scanner, which looked like a very oversized sugar iced doughnut. After the CT technician punched some buttons on the control panel, a characteristic 'zzzzzzzzzzzzzzz' sound as well as the red blinking light reading 'X-ray in use' indicated that the scan was in progress. It took a couple of seconds, after the sound and the blinking had stopped, that the image made out of black, white, and different shades of grey showing what was inside of the patient's skull started appearing in front of Alessandro's eyes on the screen.

"O Dio!" was what Alessandro said when he saw all the white pixels lighting up in a place where only grey pixels belonged. He did not need to wait for a radiologist to look at the scan to know what this meant. The time stamp on the screen next to the patient's name read 6:37.

"Will you two be okay getting her back upstairs by yourself? I'll have to call her husband." Alessandro asked.

"Think we'll be fine."

"Thanks."

He took the elevator to the second floor and walked over to the physician's office and sat down. He dialed the cell phone number listed in the patient's electronic chart. It rang three times before a male voice answered:

"Good morning. This is Dr. Gianetti from Godshus General Hospital. I was the doctor working tonight. Unfortunately, I have to call you because Eva is not doing well."

"What happened? I thought she was doing better and you wanted to take the breathing tube out today. Is she dead?"

"No. But it's very serious. We just had to do a CT scan of her brain. I don't have the final report back yet, but it looks like she has a very serious bleed in her brain."

"Oh my god! How did this happen?"

"Will you be able to come to the hospital?"

"I'm just starting my shift at work. I was planning to come in the afternoon. But let me talk to my colleagues here. I'll be there as soon as possible."

"Okay. You should also bring your son."

He hung up and went back to the ICU. Louise and the X-ray technician just were wheeling the patient through the door.

"Dr. Gianetti. The radiologist from Bergen is on the phone for you."

Alessandro picked up the phone.

"So you know she has a very large cerebellar bleed. There's quite a lot of edema, which is compressing the fourth ventricle and the brainstem."

"Yes, I saw the large bleed."

"Is she a cancer patient?"

"Yes. Recurrent breast cancer."

"Okay. I see some other abnormalities in both hemispheres. With what you just told me, these are likely diffuse metastasis from her breast cancer. I also think that she likely had a metastatic lesion in her cerebellum which bled and that this isn't a spontaneous bleed. Of course, an MRI could tell us more here, but I don't think this would make any difference for the patient."

"We don't have an MRI scanner in Godshus. I agree with you, nothing is going to make any difference for her."

Alessandro hung up the phone. Nurse Louise was looking at him but asked nothing. The expression on his face must have told her what she wanted to know.

The door to the ICU opened and Dr. Bjerknes walked in at a quick pace. Alessandro's and Louise's faces must have given away the most important information to him, as he only asked:

"What happened?"

"Mrs. Redding. Huge cerebellar bleed. Likely from diffuse brain mets," Alessandro said.

"Ah, no. That's why she was so nauseated when she came in ten days ago. It wasn't the chemotherapy, but brain metastasis. The poor husband and the son. Have you called him?"

"He's at work, but will come as soon as possible."

After the morning meeting was over, Alessandro walked over to the Intensive Care Unit with Werner. Louise was still there and Alessandro saw that the husband and the teenage son of the patient in bed 3 were sitting next to her on two chairs. The husband was still wearing his black Norwegian police officer uniform.

"I'll take them to the conference room," Werner said and took over what needed to be done so that Alessandro could go home and sleep.

* * *

←⋯ 208 ○◎○ 210 ⋯→

July 22nd, 2011
Dr. Alessandro Gianetti
Godshus – Norway

Friday

Alessandro very carefully pushed the fine point chisel against the round, flat piece of aluminium. He was sitting at the work desk in the small, red barn building that Charlotte and he had converted into their art studio.

The summer sun was shining through the large windows. The grass outside was deep green against the sparkling blue of the water of the fjord in the distance and the towering grey of the surrounding rock cliffs. One could see three brown cows grazing on the neighbor's property.

His hobby definitively evolved over time. He had taken his stone carving tools with him from Italy when he had moved to Norway. However, working with Norwegian granite proved to be much more difficult compared to using marble from Carrara.

For a while, he therefore did wood carvings—inspired after he had seen the intricate carvings of the famous wooden Urnes stave church. Then, while they were preparing for Christmas one year, he suddenly felt inspired when he saw the old krumkake iron which had been passed down in Charlotte's family. He always enjoyed eating the cone-shaped cookies.

Of course, as with most of the food consumed for pleasure and not just for the intake of calories, the krumkake cookies had Italian roots.

In principle, a krumkake cookie was nothing else than an Italian pizzelle, or farratelle or cancelle—depending on where in Italy one would put the batter formed from flour, butter, sugar, eggs, and water into a pizzelle iron. By not using the iron and just adding a little bit less water one then could cut the resulting dough into disks and roll it around a pipe and subsequently fry instead of bake it. In this case, one would end up with a cannolo. Depending on the overall size once filled with the sweet creamy filling, a cannolo would turn into a small cannulicchi or sigaretta or full-size cannolo or cannula in Sicily. Of course, in Norway, one would never fry the dough, but only press the batter—made from the same basic ingredients used to create a pizzelle, farratelle, cancelle, or cannolo in Italy—in a special decorative iron and then, just after removing the flat hot waffle cookie from the iron, shape it using a conical wooden rolling pin. The resulting tubular shape not open on both sides like a Sicilian cannolo, but open on one and closed on the other. A cone-shaped delicacy. Although it had been the tradition in Charlotte's family to eat krumkaker plain, with no filling around Christmas, Alessandro realized very early on that this smart little Scandinavian design modification in shape would be perfect for stuffing krumkaker with a ricotta based cream. Whereas when eating traditional Sicilian cannoli by hand one would always risk the creamy filling spilling out of the open other end and creating a little—or big—mess, this hazard was greatly reduced by the cone shape of the Krumkake-Cannolo, which was how Alessandro named his treat.

And so it happened that the Krumkake-Cannolo Christmas tradition was created.

And whereas on December 23rd, if he did not need to work that night, he would celebrate 'Lille Julaften'[1] with Charlotte's family by cleaning the house, hanging ornaments onto a fresh cut tree from the forest, and decorating a pepperkakehus,[2] all while watching a more and more drunk James celebrating Miss Sophie's

---

1 **Lille Julaften** – *Norwegian*: Little Christmas Eve, i.e. December 23rd.

2 **Pepperkakehus** – *Norwegian*: Gingerbread house.

90th birthday—performed in 'Grevinnen og Hovmesteren'[1]—on Norwegian national television.

The same procedure as every year.

On December 24th then—again if he was not scheduled to work—he would celebrate 'Julaften'[2] the same way as Charlotte's family had forever, by eating a heavy meat-based dinner and dancing around the tree singing 'Så går vi rundt om en enebærbusk'.[3]

The same procedure as every year.

On December 25th it would finally be his turn. For all the years he had always managed not to work that day to prepare a 'Cenone di Natale'[4] for all the visiting family. As it was difficult to get a traditional panettone in Norway, he would substitute his Krumkake-Cannolo as a dessert that day. The highlight of the entire Christmas

---

1 **Grevinnen og Hovmesteren** – *Norwegian*: The countess and the butler. Also known as '**Dinner for One**' or '**The 90th Birthday**' is a two-hander comedy sketch written by British author Lauri Wylie (1880–1951) for theatre. The German TV station Norddeutscher Rundfunk (NDR) recorded it in 1963—in the original English—with a brief introduction in German. It is an 18-minute black-and-white short film, performed by British comedians Freddie Frinton (1909–1968) and Mary Warden (1891–1978). The film is now broadcast annually during the December holiday season on many national TV stations across Northern Europe and Scandinavia, as well as Austria and South Africa. Despite its popularity in many countries, the film remains mostly unknown in the United Kingdom, with its first national broadcast occurring only on New Year's Eve 2018. Apart from a few satires, 'Dinner for One' is virtually unknown in North America.

2 **Julaften** – *Norwegian*: Christmas Eve.

3 **Så går vi rundt om en enebærbusk** – *Norwegian*: *So We Go around the Juniper Bush* – Norwegian Christmas Carol.

4 **Cenone di Natale** – *Italian:* Christmas supper. Traditionally no meat is eaten on Christmas Eve in Italy, but—instead—in parts of Italy, the 'Feast of the Seven Fishes' is celebrated. Meat-based dishes are consumed on Christmas Day.

celebration. In order to preserve the crispiness of the confection, he would bake them in the morning on the 25th, but only stuff them with their creamy filling directly before serving them. Alessandro's little edible pieces of art. His Krumkake-Cannoli.

The same procedure as every year.

Initially, he would only fill his Krumkake-Connoli's with the ricotta-based cream. Unadorned. But a couple of years ago—on a trip back to Italy—Alessandro had one day stumbled upon a store called 'c.u.c.i.n.a.' in the Via Mario de'Fiori in Rome. This changed everything. This special little shop, located amid all the touristy restaurants and the chain stores that displayed the same clothes like they sold everywhere else in the world, was a demonstration of the true soul of Italy.

Amid all the pasta pots, pans, knives in various length, garlic presses, colanders, spoons made of plastic or wood, flat or tower-shaped Parmigiano cheese graters, different-sized setacci[5] and griglie di raffreddamento,[6] Alessandro found what would turn his Krumkake-Connoli into even more ad hoc pieces of art: An entire collection of wonderful decorations made of sugar.

Little snow stars in silver or gold, red or white 'stelle di natale',[7] small bearded Santas, and, yes, even reindeer faces, and large white and silver pearls—all of this made of sugar and perfectly safe to be consumed. In addition, unique edible ink markers allowed for even more variation. The name of the little company producing all of this just south of Napoli was simply 'Decora'. Since then on December 25th he would spend most of his time putting these decorations on his Krumkake-Connoli once he had filled them with the cream.

---

5 **setaccio** – *Italian*: Sieve used in Italy to sift wheat meal flour to avoid clumps.

6 **griglia di raffreddamento** – *Italian*: Cooling grid on which cakes and other desserts are placed to cool them in a refrigerator.

7 **stelle di natale** – *Italian*: 'Star of Christmas' Poinsettia plant (*Euphorbia pulcherrima*).

But of course, all of this was only to be done on December 25th and not in the middle of summer.

In contrast to its Italian relatives, where the pizzelle iron only had a simple pattern, the Norwegian krumkake irons had elaborate patterns on them, resulting in a fine decorative pattern on the outside of the krumkake. And it was this part of his little ephemeral pieces of art, where he centered his creativity on throughout the rest of the year.

Whenever time allowed he carved krumkake irons. Two round pieces of aluminium into which he would carve elaborate designs which would then serve as the very transient decoration on the outside of the cookies. He had done hundreds throughout the years—from a coat of arms, to superhero figures, to landscapes.

Today he was carving one with the Florentine coat of arms—a Florentine lily. He would use the red edible ink marker this Christmas to color the lily red on the outside of the cookie, and he was carefully shaping the right side of the flower in the soft aluminum in front of him.

He heard a car arriving outside. He looked at his watch. It was 18:23. Charlotte must have changed her plans. On the little note he had found on the kitchen table when he woke up just before 17:00 after his overnight call, she wrote she would be back only after dinnertime. She had driven to Volda to have coffee with a friend.

The noise of the car door closing was followed by steps in the gravel, which were unusually quick.

"Alessandro?" he heard Charlotte calling in the main house.

"Alessandro?" with an unusual tone of nervousness in her voice. He paused his work on the carving of the krumkake iron, got up, and walked to the door of their art studio. He stepped outside. Charlotte had left the door to the main house open.

The summer sun felt warm on his face. The deep green of the grass outside contrasted against the sparkling blue of the water of the fjord in the distance and the towering grey of the surrounding rock cliffs. From the door, he could see the glittering white of the glacier peaks in the distance, and many more brown cows grazing on the neighbor's property.

"I'm here. Working on a krumkake iron."

Charlotte appeared in the doorway of their home.

"Alessandro. There has been a bombing in Oslo."

And then a piercing high-pitch sound started coming from inside their house.

* * *

←⋯ 210 ○◎○ 167 ⋯→

March 25th, 2019
Dr. Alessandro Gianetti
Godshus – Norway

Monday

"I really don't see what you don't understand here, Alessandro."

The discussion with Dr. Boisen-Jensen was going absolutely nowhere. His position had not changed even a bit since they had talked last Monday, or the Monday before.

"Listen. I have been working in this hospital for more than thirty-five years now, and that's the way we have been doing things here."

This was his last and final argument. Always when he could, Alessandro wanted to talk to the patients first before doing the exam. Without doubt, things had changed over the years. Back when they started doing colonoscopies at Godshus General Hospital, they considered it a big deal. The patient would be admitted the night before so she or he could spend a sleepless night mostly on a hospital toilet after they had consumed the liquid to clean them out totally. Then, once the procedure was performed the next morning, sometimes they would even keep the patient one more night in the hospital to make sure they completely recovered after all the sedating medications they had received for the colonoscopy. Clearly, it was much more comfortable for most of the patients to sit on their own toilet during the night before and to get the little sleep they would get in their own bed. And the focus of the procedure also shifted. Whereas in the beginning it was mostly done only if a patient had some form of symptoms already, over the years it had become more a screening procedure for colon cancer.

Now that the government decided that every woman and man in Norway should get a screening colonoscopy at age 55. This meant many more procedures. But was it really fair to the patient to just show up in the morning and meet a physician—she or he had never seen before—who would put a black flexible tube up their anus?

"Well, then, it's about time to change things a bit. Isn't it? And also Pia has no issue at all doing it the way we suggested. This is a simple mathematical problem. Now that they have launched the national colon cancer screening program, we have to do a lot more procedures. Godshus General Hospital—as you know—is the primary hospital for about half of all inhabitants of Nordre Bergenhus, meaning roughly 55,000 people. We currently have I think 731 people who will turn 55 this year in our catchment area. There are approximately 250 working days per year in Norway. So simple, isn't it? 731 divided by 250 is what? Hmm? Yes, Alessandro. Three. Of course, there are the other non-screening colonoscopies and EGD's that need to be done as well, which means we need to have at least five endoscopy slots available per working day going forward."

It was not only the discussion which made Alessandro upset. It was also, that instead of having a focused talk with him, Dr. Boisen-Jensen was more concerned about filling a black pill organizer. He had done the same two weeks ago when Pia had been there as well for the meeting. And of course, he again had his morning snack on the table—two slices of crispbread with brunost.[1] Dr. Boisen-Jensen was the only non-Norwegian he knew who would actually eat that stuff.

"But ..." Alessandro said.

"Alessandro. I honestly don't care what you think about this. This is simply how it will be done here in the future. At least as long as I'm the chief physician."

It must have been when he saw the angry expression on Alessandro's face that Dr. Boisen-Jensen started slightly raising his voice.

"There is absolutely no reason that you have to see the patient twice. One of the nurses will go over everything with them a week

---

1 **Brunost** – Typical Norwegian brown cheese made from caramelized whey, with a sharp, sweet-savory dulce de leche taste.

prior, give them the canister with the prep solution, and only—and only—if any concern pops up when the nurse completes the check-list the patient will be seen by a physician prior to the morning of the test. The only thing you'll do is show up in the morning and stick the fucking colonoscope up the patient's ass. Is that under-stood? No more little socializing with patients a week before. That way you can do four colonoscopies a day instead of the two you are doing now."

Okay. It was time to give up.

"And how are we going to split up operating room once the cardiac catheterization equipment is installed?"

"Well, of course, the patients scheduled for an elective cardiac catheterization will be the first in the morning. And once I'm done with the procedures, the endoscopies take place."

"So we'll have the people sit around and wait for their colonoscopies?"

"Well, I don't really see another option. Do you? Whereas the procedures I do are sterile—you deal with shit, don't you? Therefore, it doesn't really work to do a deep clean of the operating room once you are done so I can do my procedures. Simple as that," Dr. Boisen-Jensen said and then bit into the crisp bread with brunost.

* * *

←⋯ 386 ○◎○ 288 ⋯→

July 15th, 2019
Dr. Alessandro Gianetti
Pescia – Italy

Monday

Alessandro's phone vibrated. The little red circle with a one in it in the right upper corner of the AIRBNB icon indicated that someone had sent a new message. He pushed on the icon with his thumb. The last guests had left their review:

The villa is set atop a hill, overlooking the valley, and offers spectacular sundowner views. The gardens are stunning. This is the stuff of Tuscan dreams. Unfortunately, while we were here Sophia was taken to the hospital. Shewit told us she had a stroke ☹. So sad. Please get well soon Sophia!! We would love to come back!
Aleš—June 2019

He decided to read some of the other recent reviews while he had the app open. He did not want to wake up Mamma yet. She was resting comfortably.

Semplicemente perfetto, just perfect, einfach perfekt, JUSTE PARFAIT. Thank you so much, Sophia and Shewit!
Natacha—May 2019

To say this place was exquisite would be the understatement of the year. The views are breathtaking. Everything we saw online was 100% accurate. Sophia is such a fabulous host. You will enjoy having interesting discussions with her over a glass of red wine on the terrace. We will DEFINITELY be back!
Steen—May 2019

我们喜欢这个地方！
毛泽东—2019年4月

This place was the best Airbnb we have ever stayed at! AMAZING accommodations in a villa from the 16th century. We enjoyed the pool very much. Overall everywhere you went this place had amazing views and our family already wants to go back next year! And of course Sophia. All the history of the villa and local tips she shared with us. And all the stories from her life! In addition, Shewit was so nice to pick us up at night at the train station when our train was delayed. Thank you so much for everything!!

Megan—March 2019

"Alessandro?"

"Oh, Mamma. You woke up. You should still sleep."

"When will I be able to go back home?"

"They said they would deliver the hospital bed today. Shewit is there to let them in. So hopefully tomorrow once everything is ready."

"But why do I need to wait for this stupid bed? I want to sleep in my old bed."

"Mamma, but we talked about this. The new bed is electric. So it will be much easier for you to get out of bed. You know that your left leg is still giving you a lot of trouble."

In contrast to Papà, who over the period of the final ten years of his life had because of his Parkinson's disease become gradually weaker and more and more dependent, Mamma still had trouble accepting that things would be different since that morning nine days ago when she woke up not being able to move her left side at all. Of course, Alessandro knew that at her age something like this could have happened much earlier, but over the last five years everything had gone so smooth and easy that he simply had not allowed himself to think about such things. He remembered how in the early spring of 2014 everything looked like it would fall apart. After she slipped and broke her right hip.

She was determined to go back to the villa, although he had argued that it was too big for her and she was getting too old to manage all of it. Also the visitors—mostly from England and Germany, who she had hosted repeatedly over the last forty years, and who had by word-of-mouth shared the stays in the villa with others, came less and less. Of course, the financial crisis was partly to blame, but also they were simply members of a generation who were becoming too aged to travel. Therefore Mamma was all by herself in the villa most of the time. Until Charlotte spent a month in the villa, while he was back working in Godshus, to help Mamma after the hip fracture and convinced her to give Airbnb a try; and also found Shewit.

Suddenly younger people started coming to the villa from all over the world, not only British and Germans. A lot of Americans, French, Swedes, Danes—the occasional Kiwi or Aussie, Japanese, and more and more Chinese. Mamma loved this breath of fresh air in the villa. Sharing her stories with the visitors if they wanted, and keenly listening to theirs.

But all of this would not have worked without Shewit. Alessandro did not remember how Charlotte had found him. He had made it to Lampedusa on a boat which for him was a better option than the military service in Eritrea. He learned Italian very quickly and already spoke English. Without his help with everything, it would just not have worked out at all.

Alessandro's phone vibrated again. It was a WHATSAPP message from Shewit:

They just delivered the bed. Mamma can come home now.

* * *

August 29th, 2019
Dr. Alessandro Gianetti
Godshus – Norway

Thursday

"Dr. Gianetti, are you able to take a phone call?" Louise's head popped in through the door. He was sitting at his workstation in the office, clicking through the lab results in the electronic medical records on the patients he had just rounded on earlier. "It's Dr. Boisen-Jensen. He's on the ICU phone. He wants to talk to one of you doctors."

"Sure. Just put him through."

Shortly after, the phone on his desk rang.

"Yes, Anders. It's Alessandro. What's up?" He knew that the new boss was off for the rest of the week and the next week. He was glad he did not need to see his face for some time.

"Hey, Alessandro. Thanks for taking the call." Dr. Boisen-Jensen's voice sounded slightly muffled.

"Are you at a computer now, Alessandro?"

"Yes."

"Great. Listen, could I ask you for a favor?"

"Okay."

"The situation is—I'm actually unfortunately at my dentist's office in Copenhagen right now. I stopped in Malmö on my way to the conference in Paris. My left second lower molar started hurting like crazy yesterday on the plane from Oslo to Copenhagen. So I went in today."

"I'm very sorry to hear that." Alessandro was not sure how he could remotely help his boss with his dental pain. But given how he overall felt about him, the thought of Dr. Boisen-Jensen having a bad toothache gave him a certain degree of satisfaction.

"It turns out that I have an apical abscess there and the tooth needs to come out. My plane to Paris leaves in the afternoon."

"Okay." Alessandro still did not understand how doing any kind of favor could help.

"So. I don't think you know. I'm actually on Warfarin because of my heart valve. Been on it for years." This was definitively new information for Alessandro.

"Of course, the dentist wants to have a fresh INR before she pulls that tooth to make sure I don't start bleeding like crazy. I actually did my routine draw in the lab yesterday before I left. I rarely check them. Luckily, I'm one of those people who is predictably stable by just taking 2 mg of Warfarin a day. I've always been therapeutic on the 2 mg. The result wasn't back by the time I had to leave for the airport. Could you please look up my medical record and check what it was? That way she can pull the tooth now and I can make it to Paris."

Yes—Alessandro knew that the system would not allow Anders to remotely access his record if it detected an IP address outside of Norway. He used the mouse to move the white arrow on the screen in front of him to the appropriate field. He typed in Anders and then Boisen-Jensen. Given that Norway had several years ago linked all the different health records into a single national medical records database, a total of six Anders Boisen-Jensen popped up.

"What's your birthday?"

"December 15th, 1972."

He clicked on the name of the boss he had learned to hate so much since the late spring. As expected, a threatening red warning screen popped up immediately.

"The computer asks me to BREAK THE GLASS." Somehow, somewhere and without Alessandro ever fully able to understand, an algorithm in the system knew that he was trying to look up confidential information of someone who he was working with. Of course, there was an override function. He had used it a couple of times. The last time was when he admitted the overweight chef from the hospital's kitchen, who was smoking too much.

"That's okay. Just select 'at patient's request'."

Alessandro clicked the mouse so that a checkmark would fill the appropriate box, then pressed ENTER and a screen with a lot of information appeared. He also knew that in the same instant the system had automatically sent a message addressed to his boss's e-mail with the following long subject line:

POSSIBLE BREACH OF YOUR CONFIDENTIAL HEALTH RECORD BY USER: Dr. A. Gianetti, LOCATION: Godshus General Hospital

The body of the e-mail would contain instructions of what to do if the recipient indeed believed that the access was unauthorized. The feeling of being Ali Baba quickly passed and Alessandro clicked on the sub-folder, where he knew he would find the information his boss wanted to know.

"Your INR yesterday was 2.6."

"Thanks so much, Alessandro."

"Well, good luck with your tooth. And enjoy Paris."

The little white arrow on the screen had already moved over to the box with the little black X, but then the index finger of Alessandro's hand paused just before pushing down on the button of the black mouse. Instead, the little white arrow on the screen slowly wandered over to a field labelled MEDICAL AND SURGICAL HISTORY. It did so gradually, not taking the direct and shortest line over the screen, but more in a zig-zag movement, occasionally pausing as if the little white arrow hesitated whether that was the right direction. The screen that followed after the field had been clicked displayed the following:

Chronic Anticoagulation with Warfarin due to Presence of Mechanical Aortic Valve

Chronic Atrial fibrillation

Hypercholesterolemia

Mild Chronic Systolic Heart Failure (EF 45%)

h/o Life-Threatening Bleeding (Genital) due to suprathera-peutic INR requiring blood transfusions—July 2000—UMAS[1] Malmö, Sweden

h/o Anaphylactic Shock—December 1990—Rigshospitalet,[2] København Ø, Denmark

h/o Circumcision—March 1990—Regional Hospital North Jutland, Hjørring, Denmark

h/o Mechanical Aortic Valve Replacement (Carbomedics bi-leaflet mechanical prosthesis)—December 1989—Odense University Hospital, Odense, Denmark

The little white arrow subsequently moved over to a field labelled MEDICATIONS. This time in a more direct movement, not zig-zag, but with a very brief stop about halfway. A click made the previous screen change to the following:

Warfarin tablet 2 mg once a day

Diltiazem capsule 90 mg once a day (Do Not Substitute: ADIZEM-SR)

Rosuvastatin 20 mg tablet once a day

Omega-3 Fish Oil capsule once a day

Furosemide tablet 20 mg once a day if needed

Potassium Chloride CR tablet 20mEq once a day if needed

There was one allergy listed:

VANILLA (Severe—Anaphylaxis)

---

1 **UMAS** – *Swedish*: Universitetssjukhuset MAS (Malmö Allmänna Sjukhus). University Hospital—Malmö General Hospital. Leading teaching hospital in center of Malmö. Renamed Skånes Universitetssjukhus (Skåne University Hospital) in 2010 after merging with the Universitetssjukhus i Lund (University Hospital in Lund).

2 **Rigshospitalet** – *Danish*: The Kingdom Hospital. Leading teaching hospital in Copenhagen, located just west of the city center. Lars von Trier's Danish 'The Kingdom' is set at the Rigshospitalet and this thriller TV mini-series served as the inspiration for the author Stephen King to develop 'Kingdom Hospital'.

555555555

After pausing for a while the little white arrow then moved back to where it had originally come from, that is to the box with the little black X.

* * *

←··· 294 ○◎○ 393 ···→

November 18th, 2019
Dr. Alessandro Gianetti
Godshus – Norway

Monday

"So where should I drop off this thing exactly?" Alessandro was standing in the emergency room next to Dr. Boisen-Jensen.

"If you just put it on my desk in my office, that would be great. The door's open. I actually never lock it."

"Okay."

"Thanks a lot. That way I can start getting home and don't have to run upstairs again. Oh, yes, and for the patient. His defibrillator shocked him appropriately. Just admit him overnight. Finish giving him the amiodarone drip and then just watch him on the monitors. If he gives you any trouble, call me."

Dr. Boisen-Jensen had been clearly ready to go home when Alessandro called him about a fisherman, who had had a large heart attack only a little more than a month before and who—due to recurrent episodes of Ventricular Tachycardia—had a defibrillator implanted just ten days ago. The device had shocked him three times while he was withdrawing money from the ATM in the bank in town.

He arrived in the emergency room with the pacemaker programmer already having put on his black Loffler biking overpants and neon yellow NORTH 66° Polartec sports jacket. Alessandro had never thought Dr. Boisen-Jensen would keep up the biking to the hospital thing, even in winter in Norway—but he seemed clearly determined to do so.

Of course, never wearing a helmet.

There was so much wrong about this man in general that the fact that he biked to work was the least of them.

Bicycling in Norway, over hills, up and down!

He must have lived in Copenhagen for way too long.

Alessandro had the feeling it would be a busy night and took the elevator up to the second floor. He opened the door to the chief physician's office. The place where he had all the fruitless discussions. The desk was empty except for the black pill organizer. An unusual design for a simple pillbox. Must be designed in Denmark. After putting the pacemaker programmer on the desk as instructed, he decided to take a look. Fancy black plastic. Alessandro opened the lid. Interesting. Fourteen spaces for pills. Enough space for two weeks of pills. He opened one of the small plastic subdividers. Two tablets, two capsules. He recognized the light blue warfarin tablet as being the same one they started Mamma on in Italy. The other tablet looked the same as the cholesterol pill he was taking himself—rosuvastatin. And given the yellow-golden clear color of the one capsule, it must be fish oil. He did not recognize the last capsule, but remembering Dr. Boisen-Jensen's medical record, it must have been the diltiazem. Carefully he closed the pillbox and put it back in the spot on the desk where it had been before and left the room.

Later that night when Alessandro checked the news on the RAI NEWS App on his phone, the major headlines were about ongoing protests in Hong Kong.

* * *

←··· 400 ○◎○ 235 ···→

November 28th, 2019
Dr. Alessandro Gianetti
Godshus – Norway

Thursday

The waiter put down the plate in front of him.

"So what's this?" Alessandro asked.

"Seared brown crab head, on koji induced buckwheat topped with local soft, slightly acidic, fresh Nýr cheese."

Seafood mixed with cheese. Okay …???

As soon as the server left, he looked at Charlotte.

His surprise must have been clear to her from the expression in his face as she started laughing after she had taken a careful bite of the dish in front of her.

"Alessandro. It actually doesn't taste as bad as it sounds."

He took a small sip of the Pinot Grigio which had been the only familiar taste in his mouth for the entire evening. Charlotte would be driving them home so she was drinking a non-alcoholic concoction, that the restaurant had named 'juice', created from white currant, pickled turnips, and black currant leaves, whose color was a bit more golden than his wine. He liked it, as he had all the other dishes they ate so far as part of the gastronomic 'Gifts of the Norwegian Ocean' tasting menu experience.

Among others, the albueskjell[1] made into a parfait with butter and onion reduced in white currant juice. The confit of cod loin cooked in birch bark oil with a sauce prepared from birch and oak leaves. The sea cucumber cooked sous vide in butter and then barbecued and glazed. The langoustines presented with pickled plums on top, which the chef added to break their sweetness. The raw

---

1 **Albueskjell** – *Norwegian*: Limpets (Latin: Patella Vulgata); type of snail that attaches itself to rocks along the coastline.

Mahogany clams served with just a few silverberries and preserved tomato water.

But mixing seafood with cheese?

Alessandro very much appreciated the taste as well as the philosophy behind the New Nordic Cuisine movement. Using fresh locally and sustainably sourced ingredients. Unexpected innovative combinations of pure, naked flavors.

A couple of years ago Charlotte and he had gone to Copenhagen just to dine at Noma, nominated at the best restaurant in the world. He enjoyed the meal a lot.

So when the spectacular new restaurant in town opened in March this year, of course, they needed to make a reservation. The earliest date they could get was this night—November 28th. He was still surprised the owner had opened this one-of-a-kind architectural and culinary experience in Godshus and not in a more convenient place on planet Earth.

But not only the dishes were special about the place. So was the entire concept and its architecture. Charlotte and he had witnessed the building's construction. A giant minimalist concrete monolith that now jugged out from the rough shoreline with its one end tipping into the cold and rugged waters of the ocean. Like an oversized periscope submerged from the coastline into the bluish-grey North Sea below.

After they crossed over the small metal bridge from the parking lot, the first striking thing they saw when they stepped through the entrance door was the emerald-greenish light rising from the depth of the restaurant. In the narrow hushed oak wood-clad foyer the maître d' freed them of their winter coats, and after they quickly washed hands in their respective restrooms, ushered them down a long, straight oak stairway into the dining room below. It was sparse, soaked in the emerald-greenish light, which entered the room through its principal attraction: a massive window where outside the underwater of the North Atlantic Ocean took centre stage. At about five meters below the ocean's surface—now that it was dark already outside—illuminated by a circle of powerful lights, the tone of the water appeared emerald green and one had an un-obstructed panoramic view of the ever-changing live aquatic show; while eating some of its inhabitants. A forest of kelp in which cod, pollock, and jellyfish swam past and where lobsters paraded on the seabed which was gradually vanishing into unknown depths in the distance.

They had a non-alcoholic apéritif at a small bar at the back of the room, before they were seated directly beside the window at a simple wooden round table, unadorned with any tablecloth, in very comfortable wooden chairs.

For a restaurant where one could experience the submerged universe of the ocean in such a unique way, the name Dypthav, or deep ocean was more than appropriate.

But mixing seafood with cheese?

This was something that definitely took the Italian in Alessandro beyond his comfort zone. Of course, the cuisine of Italy had the advantage of being shaped by countless generations of chefs, creating a culinary tradition in which the demarcation line between products of the sea and cheese would never, ever be crossed.

Clearly, the chefs of the Nordics were free of such a limiting tradition.

"So, will they serve a similar menu for the Julebord?" Charlotte asked, while a jellyfish swam outside in the ocean just beside her.

"No, I don't think so. Should be regular traditional Norwegian Julebord food. At least that's what was announced." Alessandro was using his fork to carefully move around the soft whitish cheesy cream which sat on top of the crabmeat, not entirely sure yet what he should do next.

"Do you have your schedule already?"

"We're really quite well staffed this year. Looks good. Faiza is only leaving at the end of the year, and as I agreed to work on New Year's Eve, the Christmas week actually looks really good. Just working on the 28th."

"So you are not on call for Christmas at all?"

"No. Pia took vacation over Christmas so I will have to take over all the screening colonoscopies that week. I still cannot believe Dr. Boisen-Jensen is insisting on us doing them even in the Christmas week. Imagine getting a colonoscopy as an early Christmas gift on the 24th of December in the morning." He saw how Charlotte smiled. She had definitively become used to discussing such matters over dinner.

"I mean, that's ridiculous."

"I fully agree, but that's what we supposedly need to be in compliance with the new national colon cancer screening program."

"So because you're doing all the screening colonoscopies, you can't be on call that week?"

"Yes. There are colonoscopies scheduled for the 23rd, 24th, and 27th. So the only day I could work would be Christmas day."

"Well, you never worked on Natale in your entire life! Oh, it's going to be so nice. You'll be busy making all those Krumkake-Cannoli. How many will you make for the nine of us?"

Finally, Alessandro decided to be Italian and put his fork down.

"Well, guess I will start off with four per person? It will be fun having your entire sisters' family over!"

"You know what? You should talk to the chef here, perhaps they can add your Krumkake-Cannolo to their menu?"

He smiled and took another sip of his Pinot Grigio. The waiter came and removed Charlotte's empty plate and Alessandro's plate with a completely uneaten mixture of crab and cheese. Shortly after, he returned with two more plates.

"So this is the last course. Our special dessert," the server said.

"What is it?" Charlotte asked.

"Pinnebrød glazed and brushed with seaweed jam made from five different kinds of seaweed."

* * *

←··· 235 ○◎○ 118 ···→

December 2nd, 2019
Dr. Alessandro Gianetti
Godshus – Norway

Monday

Alessandro was staring in disbelief at the updated call schedule for week 51 and 52 in front of him.

WEEK 51	Sunday 15.12.	Monday 16.12.	Tuesday 17.12.	Wednesday 18.12.	Thursday 19.12.	Friday 20.12.	Saturday 21.12.
NIGHT	Rønneberg	Gianetti	Boisen-Jensen	Abdi Noor	Nystrom-Miller	LOCUM*	Nystrom-Miller
EARLY	Bjerknes						LOCUM
Colonoscopy		Andersen	Andersen	Gianetti	Gianetti	Andersen	
Vacation / Off		Rønneberg	Gianetti	Boisen-Jensen	Abdi Noor	Nystrom-Miller	

WEEK 52	Sunday 22.12.	Monday 23.12.	Tuesday 24.12.	Wednesday 25.12.	Thursday 26.12.	Friday 27.12.	Saturday 28.12.
NIGHT	Andersen	Nystrom-Miller	Rønneberg	Gianetti	Nystrom-Miller	Rønneberg	Gianetti
EARLY	Abdi Noor			Bjerknes	Bjerknes		Boisen-Jensen
Colonoscopy		Gianetti	Gianetti			Gianetti	
Vacation / Off		Andersen; Boisen-Jensen	Andersen; Boisen-Jensen; Nystrom-Miller	Andersen; Boisen-Jensen; Rønneberg	Andersen; Boisen-Jensen; Gianetti	Andersen; Boisen-Jensen; Nystrom-Miller	Andersen; Rønneberg

* Friday 20.12. - Abdi Noor will cover 12:45 until 17:45 - LOCUM will start at 17:30 and cover both the Friday NIGHT and also the Saturday EARLY shift.

NIGHT:

Monday, Tuesday, Wednesday, Thursday - 16:00 until 08:00 next day

Friday and Saturday - 12:45 until 01:00 next day

Sunday - 12:45 until 08:00 next day

EARLY:

Saturday and Sunday - 00:45 until 13:00

"But I thought Faiza's last day would be on December 27th," Hana said.

"Yes. That was the plan. Until the payroll department sent me an e-mail on Friday. She has some overtime accumulated and as she will no longer be employed in Norway, she has to be compensated for that and her last day at work will therefore be on the 22nd of December," Dr. Boisen-Jensen answered.

"I mean, we need to get a locum in this case. This schedule is crazy now," Werner said.

"Again. I'm sorry. Nobody had considered that upfront. She actually offered to still work the two shifts on the 25th and on the 27th of December for free. But unfortunately, they will cancel her malpractice insurance on the 23rd, so we just cannot do this."

"You have to try to get a locum."

"There's no budget for that."

Werner, Hana, and Dr. Boisen-Jensen's voices were becoming louder and angrier. Alessandro said nothing. It would be useless saying anything. For the very first time in the thirty-five years he had worked in Godshus General Hospital, he thought about perhaps quitting. He still needed to work a couple of years to be eligible for his retirement benefits. But what if he would just start working around Norway as a locum? Fly up somewhere north for two weeks and then be off for a while. But it would mean leaving Werner and Hana alone in this.

"At least the screening colonoscopies should be cancelled."

"We'll not meet the target otherwise. Sorry. We have to do them."

"So why don't you just cancel your meeting in Copenhagen?"

"I'm sorry—I didn't know that there are no flights back to Godshus before December 27th."

"Anders. Everybody who lives in Godshus knows that the airport is closed on exactly three days every year. That is the 24th, 25th, and 26th of December. It must have been like that since they opened that airport."

"Well, if you didn't notice, I'm new here. And I didn't know that. I mean, how do you want me to get back from Copenhagen. Take a train? Swim?"

"I'm sorry, but you are really putting the entire team in a terrible position here. As a chief physician, it's your role to pitch in in such a situation, and again I think you should cancel your meeting on the 23th of December and cover one of those shifts."

"That's not going to happen."

"You should be a little bit more respectful to the people who have worked in this place their entire life, you know."

"I mean, it's not like any one of you has small kids, which would make it important to be home for Christmas. All this schedule drama just because it's Christmas!"

What an *ebete*![1] Drama just because it is Christmas, said by someone who had no children, likely because of his own choice and not because of nature's choice. Someone who was off anyhow because of some meeting he could not postpone.

"Well, you know, perhaps some people value being with family during those days."

"Okay. That's it. Get out of my office now. There's nothing I can do about this. I have to sort my pills."

Alessandro saw how Dr. Boisen-Jensen took his fancy designed black pill organizer, opened it, and began his every-other Monday pill sorting ritual. He started with the light blue 2 mg Warfarin tablets. A plate with two slices of crispbread covered with brunost was—as usual—on the table as well. As the three of them left the office, Alessandro had an idea, just as Hana whispered to him:

"Alessandro. Let's see. Hopefully, we will somehow find a way to get you off for the 25th. I know how important that day is for you. We three—Werner, myself, and you—need to sit together outside of the hospital at some point this week and make a plan, what we should do with this dummkopf going forward."

* * *

←⋯ 113 ○◎○ 364 ⋯→

---

1 **Ebete** – *Italian:* Moron, idiot. Used as an insult in the region around Florence.

December 16th, 2019
Dr. Alessandro Gianetti
Godshus – Norway

Monday

He was careful not to make any noise when he closed the door to Dr. Boisen-Jensen's office behind him. Alessandro felt that his hands were sweaty under the blue exam gloves. He could take them off now and throw them away into one of the wastebaskets in the ICU when nobody was watching. It was close to midnight. His call had been very quiet. He was the only doctor in the hospital. Everything had gone exactly the way he planned after he had the idea two weeks ago. He made the decision the moment he had stepped out of that same door following Hana and Werner. The door he just closed.

At that time, he was not sure if it would work.

Later that Monday afternoon, just before going home, he had stopped by the ICU.

"Louise, I have a terrible headache. I'll just get two Panodil tablets," he said before stepping into the small room in the ICU where all the medications were stored. He took his time taking the two 325 mg tablets out of their blister pack and watched how Louise and the other nurse had stepped into the patients' rooms, away from the nursing counter where they would otherwise sit. He then quickly took just one light blue 2 mg Warfarin tablet still in its blister-pack with him and put it into the pocket of his lab coat. As soon as he was home, he went over to the art studio and placed the tablet into the drawer of his work desk.

The next two days he did nothing.

"I'm just going to work a bit on another Krumkake iron, have an idea for a new motive," he told Charlotte on Thursday evening and went to the art studio while she was watching TV. On his way, he stopped in the kitchen and grabbed the packaging with the Decora sugar pearls as well as the edible ink markers, both of which he had bought in the small shop in the center of Rome. These—as all the other years—had been intended to decorate the Krumkake Cannoli, which he had planned to prepare for the Cenone on December 25th. Of course this tradition, for the first time ever, would not happen this year due to the excellent planning skills of the new chief physician. He took one of the white sugar pearls and compared its diameter to the size of the Warfarin tablet. The sugar pearl was just a little bit larger. This would work. Using one of the fine engraving tools to make his Krumkake irons, his fingers carefully sculptured an exact replica of the blue Warfarin tablet. Apart from it being white and not blue, it looked exactly the same. The last step then was to take the blue pen of the edible ink markers and paint the little sugar tablet blue. The hues matched exactly. The resemblance was exact. This would definitively work. That was all he did that Thursday.

Over the next ten nights, he then gradually formed a total of fourteen small blue tablets out of the sugar pearls which were originally intended to serve as decorations of his very special Christmas pastry, storing them in an old round metallic *snus* (smokeless tobacco) box left over by his father-in-law, which, of course, he had thoroughly washed.

Today then, after the emergency room had completely emptied out, and after making sure nothing was urgently needed either on the first floor or in the ICU, he went to his office and took the snus[1] box from his shoulder bag. He turned the key in the lock of the conference room door after he stepped in. It was then that he put on the pair of blue exam gloves. Just out of precaution. The door to Dr. Boisen-Jensen's office was unlocked, like it had been the other night about one month ago. The black pillbox organizer was

---

1 **Snus** – *Swedish*: Moist powder smokeless tobacco, that originated from a variant of dry snuff in early 18th-century Sweden.

in the same spot on Dr. Boisen-Jensen's desk as it had been during every single time he had sat in that office. When he opened it, it contained—as expected—the precisely arranged pill supply for the next fourteen days, which Dr. Boisen-Jensen had prepared as was his Monday habit every two weeks. The only thing different was that it did not contain any of the diltiazem capsules. Dr. Boisen-Jensen must have run out of them. Alessandro carefully removed the fourteen blue Warfarin tablets from the black pillbox organizer. It was then that he felt that his hands started to sweat. For just a second, he paused. But then he thought back to the words Dr. Boisen-Jensen had spoken the last time Alessandro had been in this room: 'It's not like anyone of you has small kids, which would make it important to be home for Christmas.'

He quickly replaced the blue Warfarin tablets he had just removed with fourteen tablets which thanks to his skillful hands looked exactly alike, but contained nothing but sugar.

Alessandro knew nothing would happen immediately. Over the next three or four days Dr. Boisen-Jensen's liver would start producing the clotting factors again, which it had not done for years as the Warfarin had constantly blocked their production. Perhaps as early as Friday this week, Dr. Boisen-Jensen's blood would clot normally. Then it was just a matter of time until a blood clot would form on the metallic valve in his heart. It was unpredictable what would happen. A stroke, like Mamma had earlier this year? A blood clot going to the gut, the kidneys, or an artery of his leg? Or would the clot just block the metallic heart valve entirely?

Alessandro did not know. He knew he potentially might need to repeat the exchange a couple of times before something would happen.

But, eventually, something would happen, something that would either harm or kill Dr. Boisen-Jensen, but most importantly get him out of his life. The man who—on top of everything—had reminded him of the pain that Alessandro, deep down, had felt every year at Christmas, when he saw the sparkle in the eyes of all the kids, who were not his.

He took off the exam gloves, put them into his lab coat pocket, and carefully turned the key in the lock of the door of the conference room.

Satisfied.

His action had assured that, while Dr. Boisen-Jensen would assume he was taking his regular 2 mg dose of Warfarin, he—in reality—would be taking none.

* * *

←⋯ 407 ○◎○ 314 ⋯→

December 20th, 2019
Dr. Alessandro Gianetti
Godshus – Norway

Friday – 18:55

Clumsily, Alessandro collapsed the umbrella under the small awning. There was a bike leaned against the railing opposite the entrance door. He had not been prepared at all for the words Hana had just shared with him in her car. They completely made him forget what happened in the morning. She had picked him up from home. It began drizzling outside as they drove closer to the fancy underwater restaurant.

"No, that cannot be true! Did you double-check?" His first words in disbelief.

"All is okay. All is okay." The lie she told to both of them. He had the urge to put his hand onto her forearm—but then the memory of that night so long ago intervened. She parked the car. He got out and went to the driver's side, carefully holding the umbrella over her; as if this somehow could protect her from her future and not only from the light rain. They walked side by side in silence. The melody of Hana's heels changed their tone as they reached the small metal bridge. The grey concrete façade of the Dypthav restaurant appeared to their left, slowly disappearing into the stormy sea up front. She grabbed the entrance door. It should have been him— the Italian—holding the door, but he was busy with the umbrella.

The moment Alessandro stepped into the emerald-greenish light which rose from the depth of the restaurant, he heard her voice from behind, "Alessandro. There is one more thing you need to know."

* * *

←·· 245 ○◎○ 189 ··→

Chapter 2

Dr. Werner Bjerknes

February 20th, 1964
Dr. Werner Bjerknes
Tinnsjå – Norway

Thursday

Dad stopped the car. It was something his mom insisted they do every year. Werner was no longer the boy he had been, almost a young man, and he clumsily moved his still-unfamiliar long legs out of the back seat of the Volvo PV544. The air felt crisp after the two-and-a-half hour drive from Oslo. Snow had begun to cover the wreaths which were left over from the ceremony that had happened earlier in the day.

They would always go by themselves. One time he asked his mother why they never went in the morning. She told him that she did not want to look the people who were responsible for it in the eyes. For her they were not resistance heroes, but murderers. The wreck of the SF Hydro lay somewhere at the bottom of the icy waters of the deep blue lake in front of them, together with the barrels full of heavy water the Nazis needed to build an atomic bomb for the German Reich.

Werner saw the names of the people who should have been his grandparents and aunt written in the middle of the bronze oval plaque.

* * *

←··· 56 ○◎○ 322 ···→

April 5th, 1973
Dr. Werner Bjerknes
Oslo – Norway

Thursday

"They failed you because of what?" Werner was still in total disbelief. In contrast to him, Max actually seemed to have found his calling in the one-month obstetrics and gynecology rotation they had just finished together. At least in the obstetrics part. His friend had realized that helping the process of new life find its way into the world was what he wanted to spend doing the rest of his life. After Werner observed his first birth, it was clear that this would definitely not be the case for him.

For him obstetrics was all about constant screaming:

First, the soon to be mother, then—hopefully—the child, and in case neither of the two did, it would be either the obstetrician or the pediatrician, who would take over. And if things occasionally went really, really bad, the two specialists would even perform a little duet between themselves.

"Asherman syndrome."

"You didn't know what Asherman syndrome is?"

"I mean, come on. Don't tell me you know about Asherman syndrome!"

Thanks to the old senior physician Werner had spent a lot of time with during the last three weeks, Asherman syndrome was about the only named obstetrical and gynecologic pathology Werner was sure he would still remember on his deathbed. The old doctor who was Werner's mentor for most of the month had been relegated to do the procedures, which were necessary but not glorious and nobody else really wanted to do. Together they were mostly performing dilatations and curettages of women who had miscarriages, but whose bodies had failed to expel all the remaining

129

dead fetal tissue. Werner, under his supervision and with his guiding hand next to him, had performed several of them by himself. Not that he enjoyed doing this work, but it was much better than being in the delivery room.

Almost every single time his mentor reminded him:

"Always be very gentle with the curette. Never harsh. That's really the only time you can end up with complications. You have to be a real brute to perforate the uterus, but you also do not want to traumatize the endometrial lining of the uterus too much. Some women will then develop Asherman syndrome. Scar tissue will form within the uterus, and the uterine cavity will be obliterated to a varying degree. In severe cases, the entire front and back wall of the uterus could fuse together. The woman will still be able to become pregnant, but the developing fetus will have no place to grow, leading to a miscarriage."

Of course, basically, the same procedure could be done to abort a fetus if the pregnancy was not desired—however, this was not something legally allowed in Norway and the old doctor had shared his position on this with Werner several times:

"I really do not know why Stortinget[1] is dragging their feet on the abortion legislation. Look at Denmark and Sweden, they're so much further along with this discussion already."

Depending on who the anesthesiologist was during the procedure, a passionate discussion on occasion followed these remarks.

In order for Max to have a better chance to pass his repeat oral obstetrics and gynecology exam, Werner shared with him what he knew about Asherman syndrome and then decided to head home from Max's modest studio apartment on Sofies plass, after a quick peek through the round window in the round little room assured him that the rain had stopped. He had gotten to know the small place well over the last four years since he met Max, who had been assigned to the same study group as himself in the first semester at the Medical University in Oslo.

---

1 **Stortinget** – Parliament of Norway ("The Great Assembly")

The room at the same time served as Max's bedroom, living room, and kitchen. Occasionally, when they went out to one of the bars in Grünerløkka,[1] he would sleep on Max's sofa, avoiding the long way back home to his parents' house. Of course, this would only happen if his friend did not have a female guest that night—something Werner felt Max was definitively more skilled at achieving than himself.

Just before leaving Werner realized that he still had the *Playboy* magazine in his leather shoulder bag that Max had loaned him two weeks earlier. Reading the interview with Milton Friedman had been the most interesting part. Although Werner really did not understand why it would not be good to require paying people a minimum wage in the United States. He took out the issue with a sitting woman on its cover—dressed only in long red stockings which reached about halfway up her graceful thighs—and handed it back to Max.

He exited the house, which faced Bislett stadion,[2] and walked down the streets lined with mostly three-story buildings, built at the beginning of the century, until he arrived at the Historisk museum. It was no longer far from there. Once Werner could see the Royal Palace appear on his right, he would sneak through the two rows of trees and enter the Nationaltheatret station opposite the building after which it had been named. He had to wait a bit until the rattling teak tram car arrived. He boarded and, as always, selected a seat on the left side of the tram facing the direction of travel. Slowly the tram rattled uphill, until it turned and he could no longer see the blue of the Oslo fjord shimmer in the distance.

Werner got off at Skogen station. The deciduous trees were still naked after the long winter, but small tips of green heralded the

---

1 **Grünerløkka** – Part of the city of Oslo, which was traditionally a working-class district—until it became more gentrified in the late 20th century. It is now known for its street art, stylish bars, indie boutiques, dance clubs, cafes, and weekend markets.

2 **Bislett stadion** – Sports stadium in Oslo.

soon to be spring. He walked up the small hill to the house which had been built by the father of his mom and entered. His mom and dad were not back home from work yet. He got a glass of milk from the fridge and sat down in the big recliner in the living room. He started reading the day's edition of *Vårt Land*, a Christian publication that his parents subscribed to and that had been lying on the side table next to his dad's bible. On one of the pages, he saw the image of two slim towers rising to the sky. The highest building in the world had just officially been opened in New York City the day before. He realized that the height of the twin towers at 417 meters had to be approximately the same height he was sitting at above sea level right now. He glanced out of the window and saw nothing but forests with the occasional blue dots of lakes in the distance, and wondered what the view from that building would be like.

It would be nice to visit it one day.

* * *

←⋯ 325 ○◎○ 327 ⋯→

April 28th, 1976
Dr. Werner Bjerknes
Oslo – Norway

Monday

374

Werner was just not able to get the number out of his head. He sat almost at the same place as a week earlier. Max and he had opened their letters that day. They wanted to know what their numbers were, which would directly influence where they would end up for their internships. A long time ago, they had agreed that they would open the letters sent to them by the Norwegian Registration Authority for Health Personnel sitting in Justisen Bar in Møllergata together over a glass of Ringnes[1] Pilsner. The letter contained the randomly assigned candidate number, which indicated the order in which they could choose the hospital they would do their internship in. It was a simple process: The medical student who got assigned number 1 could choose any post in the country, while the student with the year's highest number had to accept the post that was left over after everyone else had made their choice. There were 374 medical students graduating in Norway this year. 374! Max—who had opened his letter first and whose number was an acceptable 57—started laughing so hard that he almost fell from his chair once he realized that it was his friend sitting at the table across from him who was the one without any choice at all. Of course, it was only for eighteen months,

---

1 **Ringnes** – Largest brewer in Norway. Originally founded in 1876, it remained a family-owned business until 1978. Since 2004, the brewer has been fully owned by the Danish drinks giant Carlsberg.

but whereas Max's number 57 meant that he had a very good chance of being able to stay in Oslo as almost everybody wanted, Werner's 374 with certainty meant spending eighteen months somewhere in the sticks—of course beautiful Norwegian sticks, as all of Norway is beautiful—but still the sticks. There was no point for Werner to attend today's meeting in the grand auditorium of the university, where all those who had a choice would make theirs, so he just asked Max to take his confirmation letter with him after all of his 373 classmates had made their choice. Max now walked in with a large grin. A reggae song started playing in the background:

I shot the sheriff ...

"You know—it's just for eighteen months. I mean, you'll have a blast. All the lonely women whose fishermen husbands are at sea all day and night. The long nights. Being snowed in the hospital for like a week or longer."

Teasingly Max was waving the white envelope, which had clearly already been opened, in front of his face. Werner ripped it out of his hand.

I shot the sheriff ...

"No worries—when you come to Oslo in your time off, you can always crash at my place. Or we just meet in Skeikampen[1] or Trysil[2] for some skiing."

"Just stop it."

I shot the sheriff ...

"And, well, how's your Vestnorsk accent? And, and, and better get used to writing all your notes in Nynorsk instead of Bokmål!"[3]

---

1 **Skeikampen** – Ski area located north of Oslo in the Gausdal municipality in the county of Innlandet.

2 **Trysil** – Ski area and municipality located north of Oslo in the county of Innlandet.

3 The Norwegian language can be written in two written standards: **Nynorsk** (which translates to 'New Norwegian') and **Bokmål** (which translates to 'Book Tongue'). Overall Bokmål is the preferred written

Somehow, before the previous week—although of course, he knew that there was a chance that he would need to leave Oslo—Werner had actually never thought about this in detail. That he might have to move away from the city where he was born.

I shot the sheriff …

He took out the official-looking letter from the envelope:

Your mandatory internship from 1.7.1976 until 31.12.1977 will be at: **Godshus General Hospital.**

Werner tried to remember his Norway geography lessons from middle school.

"Godshus? Godshus—isn't that the place with the shittiest weather in Norway the weatherman makes fun of so often on television?"

Max in the meantime had opened his briefcase and taken out a map with 'Norway' written on it.

I shot the sheriff …

"I got you a little gift for the occasion," Max said with an even bigger grin than before.

The reggae song in the background stopped.

The map was quickly laid out on the table between them. Well, it could have been worse, but not much worse. He did not end up way up north beyond the polar circle at least, although only three hospitals offered internship places north of Trondheim that year. He guessed that somehow numbers 371, 372, and 373 really liked either the endless nights in winter or endless days in summer.

Godshus was way more south. Actually, more or less in the middle between Bergen and Trondheim.

A long large peninsula with a fjord on its south and another one on the north, with then another much smaller peninsula about in the middle sticking out at the end into the almost always stormy and cold North Atlantic Ocean.

---

standard of Norwegian for 85%–95% of the population, and it is used throughout Norway except for the south-west of Norway, where Nynorsk is preferred.

Basically, like an arm with a hand made into a fist with the middle finger stretched out.

The closest contours on a map could get to a visual:

FUCK YOU WERNER!

* * *

←⋯ 327 ○◎○ 137 ⋯→

June 30th, 1976
Dr. Werner Bjerknes
Oslo – Norway ⊳ Godshus – Norway

Monday

His parents had lent Werner the money to buy the used red 1972 Saab 96 V4. He had squeezed his skis into the passenger compartment the evening before by lowering the passenger seat next to the driver's. The trip would take him a minimum of nine hours, he had been warned.

At least it was summer, so he would be able to drive the entire way and not have to take the two ferries. He would need to do that when the road over the Strynefjellet would be closed, which was usually the case until around mid-June and then again from mid-October, but some years even in September—depending on the first snowfall of the season.

He had an early breakfast with Mom and Dad and he walked with them to the Skogen station, where they said their goodbyes before his parents got on the tram to go to work.

When he returned to the empty house, he finished packing the last things into his suitcase and loaded them into the trunk of the Saab. Mom had prepared him a matpakke,[1] and he put that, as well as a thermos filled with coffee, on the floor in front of the passenger seat.

He drove down into town and made his way through downtown Oslo and started heading north. The road until north of Lillehammer was quite familiar to him from all the ski trips to Skeikampen. He reached Tretten shortly after noontime and decided to stop in a parking lot overlooking the false lake called Losna.[2] Werner took

---

1 **Matpakke** – Norwegian packed lunch.

2 **Losna** – The 'false lake' (also called 'river-lake') Losna is formed by the Gudbrandsdalslågen River between the municipalities of Ringebu

out the matpakke and ate four of the five slices of brown bread covered with his favorite brunost and drank two cups of the black coffee. He packed the four squares of mellomleggspapir[1] and put them into the Saab, as there was no garbage bin. Refreshed, he continued his drive north until Otta, where he filled up the gas in the car. It was also there that it was time to leave the E6 road, which continued to Trondheim, and start driving westwards.

Traffic all of the sudden became much thinner. He continued until a sign with 'Godshus' on it indicated that it was time to take a left turn. A large poster had been erected on the right side of the road at the turnoff. It read:

Grasdalstunnelen
expected completion date late summer 1977
The way to get you to Godshus even in winter!

The road number changed and it became a single-lane road quickly. He could see the glacier-topped peaks rising in front of him. The road started climbing uphill gently, with only low bushes on both sides, now covered with fresh green leaves and only interrupted by clear lakes with greenish-blue water, in which the white fluffy clouds from the skies were reflected.

There were small turnouts on both sides of the road at an irregular distance from each other, just in case one would encounter another car, which so far had not been the case. As the road rose higher, he started encountering the first remnants of snow, and the shining white of the glaciers came closer. The road passed a long lake on the left, which became narrower and slimmer. The bushes had now completely disappeared, being replaced with just flat scrub. Gently, the road inched a little bit higher until it was

---

and Øyer, where the river widens out and runs so slowly that this stretch appears to be a lake.

1 **Mellomleggspapir** – *Norwegian*: Between-layer paper. Thin sheets of paper used to separate the bread slices in a matpakke.

almost flat, passing through a landscape of snow, ice, blue water, grey rocks, and the occasional brownish-green fern determined to make a living here.

The ridge on his left was now fully covered in ice. The mountains from both sides were coming closer, as if planning to squish his car between them. He started to feel how the road now began to go downwards, and after a gentle left turn the peaks on both sides all of the sudden opened themselves up, revealing a gentle round valley shaped by the ice of glaciers, in the middle of which the road was winding down to the blue ocean water of the fjord, shimmering in the distance.

He would find Godshus at the end of this fjord. Faced with the undeniable beauty which surrounded him, Werner stopped the car at the next turnout and got out.

Yes, it was the end of the world, where he would be, but it for sure was the most beautiful end of the world in the world.

He ate the last slice of brown bread with brunost and finished the coffee. He realized that he needed to pee and looked around for a couple of seconds, understanding that it was just him in the middle of nowhere with no bushes or rocks behind which one could hide in any conceivable way. With no car or person in sight, he decided to relieve himself unhidden at the edge of the road, directing the yellow stream onto a green-brownish-yellow low scrub, away from the remnant of old snow at its side.

Once he was done pissing and had pulled up the zipper, he briefly thought about how it would feel to have sex here. Outdoors. In the middle of majestic nature. He stiffened.

It took him almost another about three hours to cover the remaining way to Godshus. After the road reached the fjord, it continued to hug it all the way along until the waves of the North Sea started appearing. There was a short up and down over a coastal cliff of a mountain until he reached the town, which was located at the neck of the small peninsula. He drove through town, passing the harbor with the large fish factory on his left, and already could see the modern building of the hospital in the distance.

Werner could feel the wind blowing from the North Sea and smell the salt in the air when he got out. They had placed the hospital on a flat lot on the tip of the peninsula, against the North Atlantic Ocean with the fjords in the back.

He walked to the entrance and the sliding doors opened.

Except for a young nurse sitting behind a white counter, he was the only one in the lobby.

"Hello! Can I help you?" she said in an unfamiliar accent, while scanning him from the top of his head to his toes and back.

"Good evening. I'm Dr. Bjerknes. I'm here for my internship."

"Oh, hello Dr. Bjerknes. I'm Louise. One second. They left an envelope with a key so you can get into the room for the night."

* * *

←··· 133 ○◎○ 330 ···→

January 23rd, 1977
Dr. Werner Bjerknes
Leonkulen Glacier – Norway

Sunday

White – Blue – Grey – White – Blue

The fresh white snow covering the frozen water of the fjord and the cloudless, blue, morning winter sky made the trees at the bottom of the mountains shimmer in a bluish tint against the grey rock walls above them, topped by the always-white icy glacier caps. Werner's skis had taken him towards the edge of the mountain, and the plunge down to the frozen fjord some thousand meters below was just ahead. He was alone. His mind drifted back to the insecurity which had woken up his naked body next to the woman in the bed in the hotel below. He realized that he had done something irresponsible to both of them. This had not been the plan. He had arrived in the early darkness of the Friday afternoon. Max was happy to see him. The cable car which would whisk them up the mountain had just been completed the summer before. It was the closest where people went to ski if they lived in Godshus. So it made sense to go, while he was stuck here. Fresh snow had fallen. Max and he would share a room in the old hotel and ski together as they had in Trysil in the years before. That was the plan. Then the two Americans from Stockholm appeared—an early birthday trip. Both of them would turn twenty-five on the same day. Two girls from Godshus, who just had turned eighteen and nineteen the year before, soon joined. The ski trip had grown from two to six.

"Being born on January 25th, 1952 as an American was just not a lucky number in August 1971," the soon-to-be birthday boy with the dark brown-black eyes and stocky, muscular energy explained.

"You would surely get a 'greeting' from the president, and Stockholm was definitely a better destination than Saigon if you had to be 'leavin' on a jet plane'," his companion with green-hazel eyes—who had traded the Rocky Mountain peaks of Jackson, Wyoming for five years in Sweden—added, while putting his arm around the other's toned waist. Max really liked one of the girls, and she liked Max as well. All six of them skied together on Saturday. When the early winter darkness started to appear, their group took one last ride up the mountain. They ordered the expensive beer in the bar that had been opened where the cable car ends—for the 'après-ski'—while the sun in the west added gold to the white–blue–grey–white–blue for some time.

"You know, your president just pardoned you two guys. You can go back to America now," the bartender said.

"What?" the former Wyomingite questioned in disbelief. A TV was quickly turned on. NRK Dagsrevyen at 19:04 that night confirmed that President Carter, during his first full day in office, had granted unconditional pardons to those who evaded the draft during the Vietnam War. The two soon-to-be birthday boys fell into each other's arms and hugged for a long time.

"You can finally meet my 'Ohana[1] in Hawai'i," the young man with the dark brown-black eyes said.

"Yes, yes. Well, unfortunately, Wyoming isn't a place where we could live. But it's still beautiful." More of the expensive beer was ordered. Vodka soon followed. They all started dancing. ABBA's *Fernando* was playing.

The joy coming from the bodies of the two dancing Americans made Werner look at the girl. Her light blue eyes lacked the dark brown-black endlessness of those belonging to the man from Hawai'i. She was a nice girl. Long, straight hair. She told him that

---

1 **'Ohana** – *'Ōlelo Hawai'i*: ( ) Term for 'family' used mostly in an extended-sense meaning, which includes adoptive and intentional family members and not only blood-related relatives.

she loved art—sculpture especially—and was hoping to get accepted at the Academy in Oslo in the fall.

"Also, one day I'll likely just end up as the art teacher at the Godshus Upper School," she judged, realistically. Max and the girl who liked each other soon disappeared. The vodka did what it was supposed to do. He exchanged a drunken kiss with the girl. The last cable car was racing through the night back to the bottom of the fjord with just the four of them. The two men, whose Swedish exile was coming to an end, were kissing passionately, exchanging wet saliva, their bodies firmly pressed against each other in the metal cabin.

"Have fun" was the advice they had for Werner and the girl back at the old hotel before quickly vanishing. The sounds coming from the room he had shared with Max the night before made it clear that he needed to find a different bed. The alcohol made things progress swiftly once they entered the girl's room. They kissed. Stripped. They moved purposefully—Werner gliding smoothly into her. For a brief moment, he sensed a feeling of pleasure, but it was false. Realizing the girl's desire to just get it over with, he obliged and quickly emptied himself inside her. They fell asleep with their backs facing each other.

A "Good Morning!" was shouted from a distance. The insecurity in his mind immediately decided. He pushed his body over the edge of the mountain and he started skiing towards the fjord—all the while pretending he had not heard the American with his dark brown-black eyes who would soon return to Hawai'i.

* * *

← 330 ○◎○ 58 →

October 13th, 1977
Dr. Werner Bjerknes
Airspace over the Mediterranean Ocean
close to Perpignan – France

Thursday

"Kann ich bitte ihr Tablet haben?" Werner's eyes turned away
from the Pyrenees which had appeared in the distance and looked
at the woman in the yellow dress. "Oh, sorry! Can I please have
your tray?" the Lufthansa flight attendant insisted, now in a language he could fully understand. He obeyed.

He had not expected to hear so much German during the
last twelve days as he did. In a couple of hours, after changing in
Frankfurt, he would land in Oslo Fornebu. He would stay in Oslo
with his parents until Sunday and then start out his final trip back
to Godshus General Hospital on Sunday morning. The drive was
considerably shorter now that the tunnels under the Strynefjellet
were complete. It was surprising how quickly time had passed in
Godshus. He did not know what would be next, but he had grown
quite fond of the hospital and its people at the end of the world.

He turned his eyes back out of the window. Sitting in the last
row, he saw the coastline appear to the left under the wing of the
737.

He had planned the trip to Mallorca early on after starting in
Godshus as a thing to look forward to, which would signify that his
time at the end of the world was almost over.

He never imagined things would turn out the way they did.

The sparkle of the almost-black eyes full of light blinded Werner
at breakfast the first morning.

"We moved to Britain when I was seven," Akira explained later
in the evening over a glass of heavy red wine. They shared the next
couple of days, dipping into the now refreshing water off the sandy

beach, laughing after getting lost among medieval walls, and soaking up the weakening October sun amid all the invading German package tour tourists at the pool. The afternoon four days before, it was just the two of them standing at the windswept Cap Punta De N'Amer gazing out over the dark blue ocean in front of them. Their first kiss felt clumsy but was passionate. The next morning, after Werner woke up in the disarray of white sheets, his disbelieving hand started to gently caress the cheeks of the sleeping man next to him, feeling something he had never felt before.

The plane jolted slightly. Werner reached into his jeans pocket and took out the business card:

Akira Kaku
Junior Legal Counsel
Japanese-British Chamber of Commerce – London

The smell of freshly brewed coffee filled the cabin. He heard noises coming from the front of the aircraft. Although his body knew better—his mind decided no. He realized then and there that he was not ready to admit this. Not to himself. Not to anyone else. And he also knew that he would never be ready.

Werner's fingers were about to rip the card in two when the noises became screams. He looked up, and saw the hatred in the brown eyes of the young woman with the black dress, who was standing in the aisle and holding a hand grenade. Then the announcement came:

"This is Captain Martyr Mahmud. This plane is now under my command. Who doesn't follow my instructions will be shot immediately."

* * *

←⋯ 58 ○◎○ 331 ⋯→

May 23rd, 1980
Dr. Werner Bjerknes
London – United Kingdom

Friday

No. I am your father.

That was unexpected. Werner had slipped into the heavy grey bathrobe and stepped out onto the balcony. The dome of St. Paul's cathedral lay lit in the distance under the yellowish-black sky, which had become so familiar to him. The construction cranes—now halted—stood in the deep to his left.

It took a little effort to light his pipe in the early summer breeze. He had only started smoking after he had returned to Godshus General Hospital. Before it had helped with the anxiety, if it occasionally hit him; nowadays he just enjoyed.

He could still sense the surprise.

No. I am your father

—said by a man with a black mask and a deep mechanical voice.

No. No. That's not true! That's impossible.

His mind counted that the kid would have been around two and a half by now.

He remembered Charlotte's determined light-blue eyes after she suddenly had found him in the hospital on that snowy March afternoon. There was never even a hint of accusation in her words. She talked to him as a patient asking for help. Giving him the feeling that he was the solution and not someone with responsibility for their situation.

"Can I somehow get this done here, Dr. Bjerknes?" she asked, after he had suggested the necessary long trip to Sweden.

Norway hadn't given the right to her women to make such decisions about their own bodies yet.

He talked to her about the risks for almost an hour. She still wanted to go through with it, so he agreed.

It was the Saturday her parents had taken the boat to Bergen with her younger sister. Charlotte and he had carried the coffee table from the living room into her bedroom together, and he draped it in the borrowed blue sterile towels. The instruments which were temporarily borrowed from operating room number '2' of Godshus General Hospital much earlier that morning were carefully arranged. She was lying in the bed she grew up in. Her body and mind relaxed after the injection. Werner had removed the morphine and diazepam from the hospital's stock earlier in the week. The necessary steps followed: sterile speculum, sponge forceps, Hegar dilators.

It was only when he started the scraping movement with the curette that his hands in the sterile gloves began to tremble.

"What's my big Viking doing out there?"

"Thinking about Darth Vader and smoking my pipe."

Werner knew that he would not be standing here if Charlotte had not made the decision for them.

He took one more deep inhale through his pipe, stepped back into the bedroom, and lay down next to Akira in their bed.

It was just the two of them now.

* * *

←⋯ 331 ○◎○ 59 ⋯→

June 18th, 1984
Dr. Werner Bjerknes
Godshus – Norway

Monday

"So, should I pick him up next to the morgue?"

"Yes, Werner. The director wanted to talk to him first. If you could just show him around a bit. I really have no clue why a freshly graduated medical student from Tuscany wants to work at our wonderful hospital." The chief physician of the medical department had asked him to stay after all the others had left the conference room when the morning meeting was over.

"They don't have a mandatory internship in Italy?"

"Apparently not. When I called the Ministry of Health, they said that they could issue him a license to work as he already has all the paperwork in place. We would also get permission to give him one of the two internship slots outside the lottery. Clearly, they know, that we're, well, not the most attractive hospital in Norway to work at."

"Interesting. Okay."

"Thanks a lot, Werner. Just bring him to my office once you're done. I really appreciate you staying and doing this after your night-shift."

The loud hammering noises engulfed them the moment the stairway door opened on the second floor.

"What's going on here?"

It still amazed Werner that the Italian spoke such good Norwegian and what surprised him even more was that he pronounced some words with a Vestnorsk accent; as if he were from Godshus.

"Oh, yes. Godshus General Hospital is getting an Intensive Care Unit. They're converting half of the maternity ward into it.

Hopefully, it'll be done soon. This construction project is just a huge mess."

They walked down the hallway where the hammering sounds were now mixing with the screams of a woman in labor. The workers were finally installing a door that would divide up the floor.

Werner wondered why they only did this now and had not done this right at the beginning of the entire construction project some nine months before.

As the tour of the hospital was almost over and he would soon drop the Italian at the chief physician's office, Werner decided on some small talk.

"So do you do any sports?"

"Well, as Italy didn't even qualify for the UEFA European Football Championship in Paris this year, I guess I'm giving up on soccer. How about you?"

"I ski. Mostly downhill, but also some cross-country."

"I'll have to try skiing as well. My wife, Charlotte, really likes to ski."

* * *

←⋯ 59 ○◎○ 66 ⋯→

June 15th, 1985
Dr. Werner Bjerknes
Godshus – Norway

Saturday

"I didn't know you were working today, Dr. Bjerknes," the emergency room triage nurse said as he walked by the desk.

"No. I'm not on. Just going up to the lab for some testing that needs to be completed."

It was just before noontime. All the morning labs would be done by now. There were no patients in the emergency room, so he would likely not be disturbed by his on-call colleague running any urgent labs. He entered the laboratory and out of precaution turned the key to lock the door. Of course, he could have completed all the tests with Dr. Gianetti yesterday. The reason he had given was just another of those small lies people like him occasionally had to tell because of the way society operated.

He sat down at the desk in the corner and took the light-blue band and wrapped it tightly around his left arm. He pumped his fist and a big blue vein appeared. Drawing his own blood was harder than he had imagined, but finally his blood started filling the tube with the red cap. There was no reason for him to do this. He felt healthy. Did not even have a cold last winter. But these days small nagging doubts always remained. As being together meant being apart for long periods of time, early on they had agreed with Akira that it was okay for both of them to be non-monogamous. Seek physical pleasure with others. Neither Godshus General Hospital nor the European legal department of the large Japanese bank in London, which Akira had been promoted to head a while ago, were places where one could be open about things. There had to be discretion and the occasional lies.

Therefore, in reality, most of the time their mutual openness meant that they shared this freedom jointly, either in the apartment in London or while traveling. Whenever the door closed behind the third man, with whom they just had shared their bed, there was even more clarity for Werner that it had not been just the physical attraction that brought them together. Of course, as soon as the reports of the mysterious cancers and cases of pneumonia had started arriving from the United States, they became careful. Since then, they always protected themselves. Neither of them ever felt sick. Their routine bloodwork was completely normal. He began following the literature. The test had false-positive results. The concerns about discrimination.

Of course, for the physician's mind in him, the sentence made sense:

It is inappropriate to use this test as a screen for AIDS or as a screen for members of groups at increased risk for AIDS in the general population.

—written in bold letters in the manual included with the test and the even more direct instruction in the letter which came in the package from the Norwegian Ministry of Health:

This test is **ONLY** to be used to test the blood supply.
NO TESTING OF ANY INDIVIDUALS,
even if they ask for it, is currently permitted
UNDER ANY CIRCUMSTANCES
with this test in Norway.

Why would you test someone just to tell them that there was no hope? A test just confirming the certainty of death. In this case, it is better not to know. Keeping hope alive. But the Werner in him wanted to know. Not only for himself, but also for Akira. The evening after the package had arrived from Oslo, they talked for a long time on the phone. They felt prepared if the sample would turn yellow. He made a plan. Given all the new equipment in the lab, he was not confident running the test on his own. He needed Alessandro's help with this. He read the test instructions several times. He went to the lab. Opened the fridge where the blood was stored. Counted. He realized that the seventeen samples would not all fit in the twelve slots of the centrifuge at once. That was the plan.

He took out the tube with his blood from the centrifuge and transferred his clear serum with the pipette to the other tube. He put it in the row with the other five tubes which belonged to the packed red blood cell units which they had not finished testing the day before. He unlocked the door.

Werner waited on the balcony of the conference room, trying to smoke his pipe in an unsuccessful attempt to calm his nerves. The timer he had put into the pocket of his lab coat started beeping. His feet walked him quicker than usual back to the laboratory. Except for the tubes with the positive controls which turned yellow as they were supposed to do, all other tubes remained clear. None of the blood tested in the laboratory of Godshus General Hospital on that grey Saturday morning contained antibodies to the virus, which was believed to cause AIDS.

It had started to rain by the time Werner was ready to drive back home.

* * *

←⋯ 70 ○◎○ 332 ⋯→

December 10th, 1990
Dr. Werner Bjerknes
Godshus – Norway

Monday

It was a tradition he tried to keep each year. Werner had taken his lunch with him to the office, turning on the TV and watching the live broadcast on NRK. Answering all the questions of the patient who needed his gallbladder removed took more of his time. He was late—the program had already started:

Immanuel Kant prophesied that mankind would one day be faced with a dilemma: either to be joined in a true union of nations or to perish in a war of annihilation, ending in the extinction of the human race.

He heard a knock at the door.

In this respect, the year 1990 represents a turning point. It marks the end of the unnatural division of Europe.

The door had opened and the face belonging to Hana peeked into the room. He had totally forgotten that he had asked her to stop by around lunch. It had been a pleasure to work with this young doctor who had joined them from Trondheim almost a year and a half ago. As her internship advisor, they needed to have a formal 'close out' talk before she would end her internship at Godshus General Hospital in less than a month.

But there are some very grave threats that have not been eliminated: the potential for conflict and the primitive instincts which allow it, aggressive intentions, and totalitarian traditions.

Breaking with his yearly tradition, he switched off the TV.

"Hana, sorry I forgot, please sit down."

"Are you sure? I can come back later."

"No worries. This will be very short. Well, it was wonderful working with you and this is exactly what your evaluation will say. You're a great person and an outstanding doctor. All the doctors and nurses are in full agreement on this. Any questions?"

"Thank you so much. I was also very happy here."

"So your last day will be on December 21st? But you will make it to the Julebord that evening? This is the first time ever that the entire team will be there as we will have a locum doctor covering. And we're doing it together with the nurses, too."

"Yes, I will be there. Tore is going to move everything to Oslo earlier that week and will drive ahead with Gunnar already and I'll take the bus on the twenty-second to join them."

"Oslo?" The last time they had talked Hana had told him she had been accepted for a cardiology training spot back in Trondheim.

"Yes. I know. Change in plans." There was a hint of sadness in Hana's eyes when she said that.

"Tore got a position at the Ministry of Justice. He really dreams of becoming a judge one day and this will help. He could work as a lawyer in Trondheim, but this is not what he wants. Always committed to public service for Norway! That's what you get when you marry into a freedom fighter family."

"Freedom fighter family?" Werner said, surprised a bit that Hana gave up a surely promising career as a cardiologist for her husband.

"Yes—his father was very active in the resistance during the war. I am sure you heard about the SF Hydro in school—it was actually Tore's dad who planted the bomb which sank the ferry."

The plaque with the three names written on it, which he had visited with his parents every year when he was young, appeared in front of Werner's eyes.

"Yes. Yes, of course. The SF Hydro," he said after a brief pause with a slight tremble in his voice.

JULEBORD (The Holiday Party)

They said goodbye and Hana left to finish her work for the day. Werner thought of his mother and turned the TV back on.

With my sincere wishes for peace and prosperity, Mikhail Gorbachev President of the USSR. This was the address by the winner of the Nobel Peace Prize for 1990, which I, as his personal representative, have had the honor of making on his behalf.

And a gentleman in a blue suit whose lack of hair made him look a bit similar to the actual laureate but without the characteristic mark on his head walked over to accept the golden medal.

* * *

←··· 336 ○◎○ 84 ···→

October 13th, 1994
Dr. Werner Bjerknes
Godshus – Norway

Thursday

Werner was sitting at his desk upstairs at home. He had put the things he would take with him the next day to his new office into a small cardboard box.

He felt that he was ready. When he heard the phone ring, he walked over to the bedroom.

"Dr. Bjerknes speaking."

"Good afternoon! My name is Anthon Berner and I work for *Aftenposten*," a male voice with an Oslo accent said.

"How did you get my number?"

"I'm a journalist."

Werner was surprised. Of course starting his new role as the Chief Physician of the Department of Medicine of Godshus General Hospital might be newsworthy, but hardly important enough to receive a phone call from Norway's largest newspaper.

"Dr. Bjerknes. Sorry for calling you at home, but I'm working on a story and wanted to see if you would be willing to talk to me about something?"

A phone interview with him? Werner was even more surprised. "Okay."

"Is it correct that you were one of the Norwegians on board of the Landshut?"

Werner's mouth opened. He felt his heart rate jump. This was something he had absolutely not expected to hear. The name of a small Bavarian town just east of Munich.

The Scandinavian Airlines planes he would fly on to London to visit Akira would be named after Vikings. Sigun Viking. Lage Viking. Using the names of the ancient mythological chiefs and kings, explorers and conquerors to refer to the ships of the air, which the modern Scandinavian Vikings used to easily spread across the globe. He had never understood why Lufthansa named planes after towns. German towns only. As if there was anything mythical, attractive, or nice about Frankfurt am Main or Buxtehude.

It suddenly seemed a good idea to sit down on the edge of the bed.

"Hello? Are you still there?"

"Yes. Yes, I was on board of the Landshut," he said, realizing that it was October 13th today. He had not thought about it in the morning. He had actually not thought about it in a very long time. Yes, he had been sitting in the Landshut, exactly seventeen years ago. A Thursday like today. But why would some journalist from *Aftenposten* write a story about this? Now. Half a generation later. Perhaps some German newspaper. But in Norway? This made no sense.

"It must surprise you that I'm calling you about this."

"Yes, it does."

"So just for you to understand. I'm contacting you because the only terrorist who survived when the plane was stormed in Mogadishu and managed to escape justice, was arrested in Oslo today."

Werner realized it that sitting down had been a good idea. His brain did not remember much from those four-and-a-half days. As if most of the memories had been blocked out. But not all.

The stench he remembered.

The putrid stench of the mix of fearful sweat, urine, and shit that started coming from the plane's toilets after the first day.

The heat he remembered.

The unbearable heat when the air conditioning stopped working under the hot Arabian sun.

The sound he remembered.

The piercing sound of the gunshot which killed the pilot in front of them.

The taste he remembered.

The bitter taste of the perfume on his lips, which one of the hijackers had poured over his head, so the alcohol contained in it would light up and burn him, just in case the explosive attached to the cabin wall next to him would have not been enough to kill him.

But other than clearly seeing the hatred in the woman's brown eyes, all else looked blurry.

As if the sudden glaring flash of blinding light from the stun grenades, which heralded that everything was over, had forever put a thin veil of opaqueness over these visual memories. Perhaps it had helped that he had kept his eyes shut for most of the time.

"It appears that she has been just living a normal life in Norway with her family for the last three years," the male voice on the phone said.

Soon he hung up.

He then dialed the number, which was still the same as seventeen years ago. He had memorized the handwritten digits written on the back of the card. Constantly repeating them in his mind during the eternity of those four-and-a-half days. So he would not forget. Not forget the number if the card were to be lost.

It was the number he asked them to dial after they had brought all of them to the white hospital with the palm trees upfront. And then again from the hotel. The hotel where you could see three towers from. Two square ones next to each other with the two smaller squares on top and the one round cylindrical one up front with the rocket-like tip above the balcony. The hotel they rested in shortly before getting on the plane to bring them back. He remembered the short priest who spoke only Italian, whom he had never expected in this country.

Some of the Germans had prayed with him at the hotel.

The phone rang five times. The voicemail Werner was not yet used to answered.

"Hello. You have reached Akira Kaku. I'm sorry, but I'm not home right now. Please, just leave me a message."

* * *

←⋯ 194 ○◎○ 256 ⋯→

August 5th, 1995
Dr. Werner Bjerknes
Hiroshima – Japan

Saturday

They had left their Ryokan in Kyoto early in the morning. It was not the first time Werner had traveled to Japan with Akira. But this was different. The speed and the efficiency of the trains which connected the country had always fascinated him. Akira's parents had moved back from Twyford to the town where Akira was born a couple of years earlier when it became clear that, despite the best treatment possible, the thyroid cancer his father had been battling for years would ultimately kill him.

They had promised Akira's mom to be at the ceremony. Akira's sister had come from Tokyo with her family and would stay at the house, so they dropped their luggage at the modern high-rise hotel which was close to the train station. Werner felt the summer heat as they took the short stroll through the streets lined with ferroconcrete buildings.

The scarred greyish-white concrete appeared framed by two big green trees on his left. As they continued to walk, the now-empty steel frames of the lattice of the dome, shining black-brownish-orange because of the rust started to stick out from above the vivid green of the crowns of the trees. It was only after they had crossed the street and walked by the river that the trees stopped hiding the building. Its barren windows looking from the greyish-white walls out onto the island, which was busy with the preparations for the ceremony the next day.

Werner's mind wandered back to the yearly winter pilgrimage of his youth. He felt a chill from the inside, despite the summer heat around him, as if he had taken in a deep breath of the ice-cold February air standing on the shore of Lake Tinnsjå.

Werner felt like sitting down and they found a bench that was out of the way under the shade of a tree. It felt good to hold on to Akira's hand and to lean the head against his shoulder for some time.

They decided to visit the nearby art museum. It was neither hot nor cold under the building's intact dome. They looked at the French paintings in their golden frames. When it was time to go, they took a taxi for the short drive up the hill to the house. The welcome was warm and loving. Akira's niece and nephew were full of smiles. Honoring the country she spent most of her life in, Akira's mom prepared the tea the English way. The cucumber sandwiches tasted fresh. The home was filled with laughter. He felt like smoking his pipe. He sat down by himself on the granite bench amid the small Japanese garden with the view of the city, which was bustling with living below.

"Werner, thank you so much for coming. It means a lot for me and it would have meant a lot for Akira's dad as well."

The woman who had been a Professor for Media and Communications at the London School of Economics and Political Science told him with a gentle smile after she left her kids and grandkids to themselves in the house.

"How are you feeling?"

The expression on her face indicated that she clearly understood what he wanted to know as they sat next to each other looking at the city below, although he was not able to ask more directly.

"Of course, there are memories which I will never ever be able to forget. But I had a wonderful life despite it all. I have not let what happened rule over the rest of my life. I know I'm rationalizing, of course, but clearly, I could have done nothing to prevent what happened to me and all the others that day. I was at the wrong place at the wrong time. But if you look at the effect it had on our world as a whole, I'm actually, in a certain way, proud of being part of it. I had always believed that humanity's three main 'lessons learned' from the Second World War would be: First, never again a war—at least not in Asia or Europe. Second, never again a genocide. And third, never again the use of the atomic bomb. Well, with wars that didn't take too long—among all of them Korea, Vietnam, and now Yugoslavia. And the butchering in Rwanda[1] shows that the first two hopes were, unfortunately, obviously wrong. So, it's only my third belief which is still here at the end of my life. And I'm nevertheless confident in that—with humanity realizing that the power of the weapon used here and in Nagasaki negates the very basis of life itself—it will never be used again. Life itself will prevent this. This is the legacy of all the ones who died and the few lucky ones, like myself, who survived. That's what I feel right now."

She briefly paused.

"But how are you feeling?"

Werner was not clear about what she meant.

"I am sure you have your thoughts, as the terrorist is going to go on trial in Germany soon. This must have brought up the past for you again."

"It must be much worse for others."

"I don't know if this can help you. I'm not sure if you know that I had done some research on terrorism before. It was back in the beginning of the 1980s when a lot of the IRA bombings were taking place. Of course, the world is in a much better shape today than back then, and this is no longer relevant."

"No, I didn't know. What was your research about?"

"I analyzed modern terrorism from a media and communications perspective, and basically the hypothesis I came up with is that we should regard it as a form of indirect communication. Of course, a fundamentally wrong, failed, evil, and unacceptable form of communication taking advantage of one of the pillars of democracy: the free press."

"Okay."

---

1 The **Rwandan Genocide** occurred between April 7th, 1995 and July 15th, 1995. Approximately 600000 people of the Tutsi ethnic minority were systematically murdered.

"Instead of directly communicating with each other, terrorism shifts this communication to the media—hijacking it in a way. Therefore, of course, the more horrible the committed acts are the more exposure. You of course have been a victim, but in no way were you—as me fifty years ago tomorrow—the intended victim. Neither of us were chosen for this because who we are, both of us—as terrible as it sounds—just happened to be at a very wrong place at a very wrong time. You were caught, by no fault of yours, in the middle of a totally flawed communication event. And, sadly, the victims end up always being the least important piece in the entire story."

Of course, Werner would never be able to completely forget the events on that Lufthansa plane, but in the end, if it had not happened, he would not be sharing the view of the bustling city below with Akira's mom now, who moved a bit closer to him on the bench.

"The other two hypotheses I came up with in my research—and gosh was I criticized by my colleagues for this—is that first it's the most fundamental mistake of the attacked to respond at all; to enter into this horrific dialogue of sorts, as this will inevitably bring on more attacks, as this indirect form of communication is now established in a way. Responding will also ultimately lead to the degeneration of the attacked as, if one wants or not, if one changes the way one lives life, one does exactly what the terrorists want to achieve. The whole thing ends up being a vicious circle very quickly."

Werner took a deep breath in through his pipe.

"The other point is the role of the media. Of course, we have the entire issue of the free press in a democracy at stake here, but one must say that it's a very slippery slope for the media reporting on terrorism between 'free press' and 'becoming a perpetuator'. Imagine a hypothetical world in which the public would still be informed about terror attacks, but no pictures, no motives, no naming of the responsible party. Just a black screen honoring the victims. No imprinting of a lasting visual memory in everyone's mind. There would be no media to hijack anymore, no more indirect communication that the terrorist could use and—again gosh was I reprimanded for this by the other faculty—I dare to hypothesize that this form of self-restraint of the media would lead to an end of terrorism very quickly."

"Sort of 'Sometime they'll give a war and nobody will come'?" Werner asked.

"Yes. That is a good way of putting it: 'Sometime there will be a terror attack and nobody will report about it'. But the very least thing the media should do immediately is put things into proportion if a terror attack happens."

"What do you mean?"

"I'm sure you've heard about the crazy sarin gas terror attack in the Tokyo underground in March."

"Yes, I did."

"Absolutely horrible. Twelve people killed on their way to work in the underground my daughter takes every morning. And many more people injured and scarred."

"Yes. Completely senseless."

"Yes. Crazy. And the Japanese media was full with it for a long time. But, and here is what I mean, when I say 'put things into proportion'—you know what fugu is?"

"Is that the toxic fish?"

"Yes. Some people regard it as a delicacy. And you know what? On average, about six people die each year in Japan after eating badly prepared fugu. So every two years, the same amount of people die eating fugu as were killed that morning in the terror attack. And despite this, people still continue to eat that god damn fish!"

* * *

←⋯ 256 ○◎○ 345 ⋯→

September 18th, 2001
Dr. Werner Bjerknes
Godshus – Norway

Tuesday

"But why does she show up at 21:13 at night in the emergency room? She should go to her primary care doctor in the morning!" Werner was a bit annoyed when the emergency room nurse called him about the forty-one-year-old woman with pain in her right breast. It seemed like a clearly non-emergent issue that really could have been taken care of the next day.

"I'm very sorry for coming tonight, Doctor. It's just hurting a lot. And I think the last couple of days were just a lot."

Based on her Vestnorsk dialect, she was obviously local, but her last name was not Norwegian at all.

"So when did the pain start exactly?" he asked the woman whose eyes looked scared while she was taking off her blouse for the exam.

"You know I'm a flight attendant. I fly for SAS internationally. The first time I felt the pain was actually on the flight back from New York on Saturday—so three days ago."

N Y
✈ O
E R
W K

The pictures which had flooded the news for the last week immediately came to his mind. He did not dare to ask. She was standing in front of him now with her torso unclad. He washed his hands in warm water in a small washbasin to make sure they were clean and warm. Her breasts appeared symmetrical, the skin looked normal. He carefully started examining them with a circling movement of his finger. His fingers retracted for just a split second as if a needle had pricked them, when he felt the hard cherry-sized lump in her right breast.

"I want you to come back first thing tomorrow morning when the X-ray department is fully open and we'll do a mammogram," he advised the woman who had every reason to be concerned and wrote Eva Redding on the request form.

* * *

←·· 197 ○◎○ 274 ···→

July 23rd, 2011
Dr. Werner Bjerknes
Godshus – Norway

Saturday

At one point early in the morning, Werner had gotten into the car and driven home to sleep a bit. It did not make sense for all of them to stay at the hospital. It became quite clear that they would very likely not be needed. They divided themselves into two groups—the ones which would remain at the hospital for now and the ones who would head home and return after catching some sleep. All patients who could be discharged were home by now.

Beds were available just in case there would be a need.

By the time he parked the car the sky started turning into a gold glow announcing the sunrise of the early summer sun. He put his cell phone next to the landline phone, which was standing on the nightstand next to a small clock with red numbers.

He was too restless to sleep well, but still felt somewhat refreshed once he woke up a couple of hours later. He got ready to return to the hospital. He had just opened the door of his Land Rover Defender 90 to get in and start driving when his cell phone rang.

He looked at the screen. The caller ID showed: Max Kjekshus.

"Max. How are you, my friend? It has to be horrible in Oslo. How're you managing this at the Rigshospitalet?"

"Werner. She's dead. She was on Utøya yesterday. He shot my wife in the head."

* * *

←··· 94 ○◎○ 281 ···→

June 24th, 2016
Dr. Werner Bjerknes
London – United Kingdom

Friday

Werner unlocked the front door and turned on the light. The envelope with the two tickets for the 17:04 train from London Paddington to Truro with the day's date on it was still in the same place on the small entryway table. He dropped the apartment keys next to it. A slightly unpleasant odor was coming from the living room. The breakfast table appeared unchanged from the morning before, except for some flies that had begun feasting on the leftover fried eggs and toast that they had just started to eat, when it all began yesterday morning.

The first thing Werner had noticed was how the newspaper slipped out of Akira's hand. When he looked over to him he saw how he was suddenly bending over to the right, his sparkling, almost black eyes full of alarm instead of light. The corner of his right mouth dropped with only the left half of his face moving as if he tried to say something. Akira put his left hand on the table, tried to stand up but then his body flaccidly fell over to the floor. Werner helplessly kneeled next to him while waiting the long minutes until the paramedics arrived. They allowed him to ride with them in the yellow ambulance, whisking him quickly to the modern red, blue, and silver-colored complex of buildings of 'The Royal London Hospital'. The lady doing the registration paperwork in the emergency department—called 'A&E'—separated them when they speedily wheeled Akira to the CT-scanner.

"We would need a next of kin information for his chart," she said.

"He has a sister. She lives in Japan. In Tokyo."

He looked up the phone number and gave it to her.

"And who are you?"

Her question took him by surprise. What should he tell her? How much did she desire to know? What single word to pick that anyhow could not describe what Akira meant to him. Would it be partner? Lover? Companion? Spouse? Mate? Husband? Pal? Consort? Fuck-Buddy?

"An old and very close friend," was what he decided to label himself in the end.

"Do you by any chance know if he has an LPA for Health and Welfare?"

"What's an LPA?"

"A Lasting Power of Attorney. It's a document where Mr. Kaku would have designated someone to make decisions for him in a situation like this. As he's not able to tell us his wishes right now."

Of course, they had similar papers in Norway to do this. Named differently, but basically achieving the same. And of course—a lawyer and a doctor—should have such documents in place. Especially considering their situation. However, it had somehow never crossed their minds that this would be needed. They had completely neglected this.

"No. He has no LPA."

He dialed the only Japanese number, which was left in the contact list of his phone.

"Akira is having a large stroke. I'm in the hospital with him... no, he cannot talk. It has affected the part of his brain which controls his speech."

The neurologist with the heavy German accent who rushed to Akira's side in the emergency room was cautiously hopeful.

"Clinically he's having a disabling acute left-sided middle cerebral artery stroke. Luckily ze CT scan doesn't show any bleeding. As everyzing started only one-and-a-half hours ago, he's in ze time window for getting tPA. Of course, zere's always ze risk of bleeding."

He saw how Akira looked at him, as if he was asking for guidance. Unable to speak, but likely still able to understand.

Werner knew the drug. On rare occasions, they would even give it at Godshus General Hospital, before putting the patients on the helicopter and flying them to Bergen. Although in Godshus patients would rarely make it to them within the necessary four and a half hours after starting to have symptoms.

Given too late the brain cells which were not supplied with enough oxygen and nutrients would have died already—and getting rid of the blood clot causing the stroke by blocking a blood vessel would make no difference. Unfortunately, sometimes the tPA could actually make things worse. If the medication designed to break up the obstructing blood clot, which led to the stroke would cause bleeding; anywhere in the body, but most catastrophically in the brain. If that happened, most of the patients would die or surely be left even more disabled than without the tPA, as they would basically end up with two strokes. The initial one because of not enough blood flow due to the obstruction caused by the blood clot and the second one precipitated by bleeding into the brain tissue. Actually, most of the times if this happened patients would die.

But for Akira, it undoubtedly was worth the risk. If it worked, he would be able to talk again. Move his right side again. None of this would likely be the case without the medication. The benefit of possibly making the effects of the stroke completely undone—of not being significantly limited for the rest of his life by not being able to speak and not being able to move the right side—clearly outweighed the about seven percent risk there was that the tPA would cause bleeding.

Werner looked at Akira and nodded his head.

A nurse with a Spanish-sounding name in the ER quickly prepared the medication and started the one-hour infusion. They informed him that Akira would be taken upstairs to the neuro-ICU ward with the number 3E. They asked him to come once they got him settled.

He briefly got lost in the enormously large and busy building. In principle, it served the same function as the intimate structure of Godshus General Hospital. But both buildings appeared a galaxy apart. He waited shortly in an uncomfortable dark grey chair in front of a double door.

"Mr. Bjerknes?"

"Yes. That would be me."

"You can come in now and see Mr. Kaku. He's in bed A1313." a nurse with a Lithuanian-sounding name said.

Werner pulled up a chair. Akira was resting with his eyes closed, hooked up to the monitor above him. As soon as Werner held Akira's hand in his, he opened his eyes. His sparkling, almost black eyes now again more full of light. His face even trying to smile back at him. Werner lost track of time, just sitting there, the nurse with the Lithuanian sounding name was coming in frequently.

"Akira. I'll be right back. I just have to use the restroom quickly," Werner said. Akira tried to nod his head and closed his eyes. The nurse had stepped out briefly and Werner leaned down to Akira's face after he had gotten up and whispered, "I love you." into his ear.

With his eyes closed, Akira smiled.

The visitor toilet was in the hallway outside and while Werner pressed on the doorbell to be let back into the neuro-ICU, there was an overhead announcement: "CCO Team and A Team to Ward 3 E, bed A1313."

"Yes. How can I help you?" a voice from the speaker next to the doorbell asked.

"Could you please let me back in to see Mr. Kaku?" Werner said.

"Wait, please."

Werner sat down again in the uncomfortable dark grey chair. Three people—one nurse and two doctors, based on what they were wearing—came running down the hallway and quickly entered through the double door. They had urgent looks on their faces.

He continued to wait. About ten minutes must have passed and just as he was about to get up and ring the doorbell once more, his phone rang. The caller ID showed the name of Akira's sister.

"Werner. What's going on with Akira?"

"What do you mean?"

"They just called me that there has been a problem."

It took the next fifteen to twenty minutes, or about the same time which it took to whisk Akira—now with a breathing tube down his throat—to the CT scanner and back, to make clear what had happened:

Shortly after Werner had stepped out of the neuro-ICU, Akira had suddenly started seizing. The nurse with the Lithuanian-sounding name and the neurologist with the heavy German accent had rushed in immediately to give Akira medications to stop the seizing. The big concern was that the tPA had caused bleeding into Akira's brain and therefore the Critical Care Outreach (CCO) Team and the Anesthesia (A) Team had been called to help with his management. They decided to intubate Akira to make sure his breathing would not be compromised. The ward secretary, whose job it was to answer the doorbell and control the traffic into the neuro-ICU through its double door, had been unaware who she was talking to when Werner rang the doorbell, but was well aware what was going on in bed A1313 of ward 3 E. Thus—following hospital procedure—she instructed Werner to wait. And Werner himself was no different than any other person, whose loved one had been just admitted with a large stroke to a sprawling large hospital complex and—although his brain retained the spatial awareness of where to find Akira's room, it amid everything that had already happened that morning did not even register, much less remember the alphanumeric code that had been assigned to the room and bed Akira was lying in.

This granted Werner ten short minutes of blissful unawareness about what was going on behind the double doors, ending the moment Akira's sister called, whose phone number had been dialed minutes earlier by the neurologist with the heavy German accent as her number was the only one listed in the section of Akira's medical record to call when there was 'a problem'.

"Mr. Bjerknes?"

"Yes."

"I am so sorry. Ze results of ze CT scan are back. Zere has been a massive bleeding into Akira's brain."

Werner did not need to ask about what this meant for the future prognosis for Akira when the neurologist showed him the scan of Akira's brain. Although Akira's heart was still beating, his lungs still enriching his blood with oxygen, his liver still metabolizing the last nutrients from the half-eaten breakfast which was still being absorbed by his intestines and his kidneys still filtering his blood and producing urine, all the neurons which made up Akira's brain—affected first by the stroke and now by the massive bleeding—were either dead already or would die soon.

"Mr. Bjerknes, we have now completed ze brain-stem death tests zat we talked about earlier. Ze tests have confirmed what we all suspected. Do you have any questions?" the neurologist said several hours later after it had become dark outside.

He continued to explain that all of Akira's brain function had been irreversibly lost.

"I know, I'm an internal medicine physician myself," Werner answered, knowing that this meant, not that Akira might die, not that Akira was going to die, but that Akira was dead.

"I'm really sorry. I didn't know zat you're a colleague. Do you work in London?"

"No, I work in a small hospital in Norway."

"I will ask Mariella Kyriakidou to stop by. She's a specialist nurse who we work wiz on ze ward here and who helps support families and friends during such difficult times."

Werner looked at Akira's body. He lay there as if in a deep, peaceful sleep. Connected to all the cables and the ventilator. He was not sure if he should pull up the chair again to sit next to him or just stand. His vision blurred from the tears. He needed to sit down. He shut his eyes, bent over Akira's body, face resting against the palms of his hands. He felt the palms turn wet.

"Dr. Bjerknes?"

He looked up.

"I am so sorry for your loss. Oh, let me get you something."

A middle-aged woman with long hair and deep brown eyes said. After a brief moment, she returned with a box of tissues, pulled up a chair next to Werner, and sat down.

"Can I get you anything else?"

"No. Thank you."

"I know this has to be a most horrible time for you. My name is Mariella Kyriakidou. Do you have any questions, or is there anything you want to talk about? Anything really."

She carefully listened as he shared what happened, how they had planned to go to Cornwall together the next day for a one-week summer vacation. She asked him other things from Akira's life. They talked and talked, and then after Werner told her that he had known Akira for more than 38 years, she asked:

"How do you think Akira would feel about organ donation? I'm sure you know that organ donation has the ability to save and transform up to eight other people's lives. Do you think this is something Akira would have wanted?"

They had never, ever talked about this topic together, but Werner knew it was something Akira would have wanted.

It, however, then took more than an hour until the further process of donating Akira's organs could be set in motion. The delay was mostly caused by the need, as Mariella explained in detail, that the 'Human Tissue Act' which had been passed in England and Wales in 2004 required the consent of Akira's sister in Tokyo. The piece of legislation placed her—hierarchically—above a 'friend of long standing'. It took quite some time to convince Akira's sister and a lot of explanations as her initial reaction had been:

"But is he really, really dead? You know here in Japan there was a huge scandal years ago where they removed organs from a person who was not actually dead."

"There is a long list of questions I would need to go through with you to complete all the necessary forms. Is this okay with you, Werner?" Mariella said after they had finally settled things with Tokyo.

"Yes, of course."

She went through a lot of questions that basically would judge if there was a risk of Akira having a serious infection in his body like hepatitis, tuberculosis, or even mad cow disease, which his organs could transmit to the recipient.

When she asked: "Any travels outside of Europe Akira did that you know of?" All their trips together flashed briefly through his mind.

"Just to Japan and the USA."

"Did he drink any alcohol?"

"Socially. An occasional glass of wine and just a little sake here and there."

"Did he smoke?"

"No."

"Ever any injection drug use?"

"No."

"Was he in prison for more than three days during the last twelve months?"

"No."

"Did he ever have oral or anal sex with another man?"

She had asked about sexually transmitted diseases previously. What was the need for such a follow-up question? They would surely run an HIV RT-PCR test before if this was what they were afraid of. Was this intimate question about sexual orientation really necessary in 2016? These were no longer the 1980s!

"Is this relevant?" Werner asked.

"The British Transplant Society policies oblige us to inform potential recipients about a potentially increased risk for transmissible diseases. Of course, no details will be shared and I fully understand that you likely don't know the answer."

A heart is a heart.

A lung is a lung.

A liver is a liver.

A kidney is a kidney.

Or are there 'gay' organs and 'straight' organs?

A neutral question about high-risk sexual behavior would be relevant. But this was not what she had asked. She asked just about sex between men.

"Yes. Yes. Akira had sex with men. Both oral and anal," Werner said.

She glanced at him, but in a way, which was a little different than she had looked at him before.

"I'm sorry, but our policies require me to ask a follow-up question in this case: Did Akira have sex within twelve months with a man who has had sex with another man?"

Who came up with these questions? Twelve months. Twelve months? What about less than twenty-four hours ago? Less than twenty-four hours ago when life was still normal. And not only once that night. What would she ask next? Whose hand had touched which body part? Whose tongue had stimulated what? Whose penis had penetrated which body orifice?

"Yes."

Mariella looked at him again, but now completely different than before with a slightly open mouth and after a short while said.

"Oh, Werner. I am so very, very sorry for you. I didn't realize. I had no idea. And I'm so very sorry for asking all these stupid questions."

And Werner, who had begun crying again, gladly accepted the embrace she offered to him.

He picked up the newspaper with the date of the morning when life was still normal from the floor next to the table. The one that had slipped out of Akira's hands when everything started. It showed a satellite map at night with the shining bright lights of Europe's cities and towns. The headlines read:

Who do we want to be?

and

Last-ditch push to stay in Europe.

* * *

←⋯ 217 ○◎○ 177 ⋯→

November 9th, 2016
Dr. Werner Bjerknes
Godshus – Norway

Wednesday

"What time did you put down, Louise?" Werner asked, looking at the flat line on the monitor in the patient's room. The cables were still connected to the patient's chest.

"8:33."

He put the switch on the ventilator into the off position.

"Let me call the family then. They said to call the granddaughter, correct?"

"Yes."

After taking off the isolation paper gown and gloves, and then thoroughly washing his hands, he sat down at the small nursing counter and dialed the number which was on the chart.

"Maria? Good morning. This is Dr. Bjerknes. I'm sorry, but your grandma has just died."

After he finished talking to the granddaughter, he put down the phone and opened the patient's electronic health records. He clicked on the menu option, which in this patient's case was quite inaptly named 'Discharge', and then created the final note which would ever be contained in her record called 'Death Summary'. He started typing:

86-year-old woman with underlying heart failure (EF of 35%), diabetes mellitus, mild dementia, hypertension, and chronic kidney disease stage III, initially presented from a nursing home with a one-day history of severe diarrhea and vomiting. Evidence of acute on chronic kidney injury on admission with highly elevated creatinine. Stool studies tested positive for Norovirus infection. Admitted to the Intensive Care Unit because of hypotension, but unfortunately developed acute hypoxic respiratory failure, likely due to an aspiration pneumonia caused by the preceding vomiting as she had a right lower infiltrate on subsequent X-rays. She required intubation and mechanical ventilation, but her acute kidney injury did not improve and she became more septic. Development or signs of multi-system organ failure as well as ARDS. After discussions with family, given the patient's pre-existing medical conditions, and unlikely survival, it was opted not to further escalate care and she passed away.

After saving the note, he clicked on the link to the national death certificate website and entered:

Multisystem organ failure in an elderly patient with pre-existing chronic medical conditions triggered by acute severe gastroenteritis secondary to Norovirus infection.

He then continued his rounds with the patient lying in the next bed in the Intensive Care Unit. The septuagenarian smiled at him, taking his eyes off the TV, which he now was again able to watch. They had removed the breathing tube the previous afternoon. His pneumonia luckily had improved.

"You look much better today. How is the breathing?" He noticed how the man had stopped making eye contact with him and was looking at the TV, slowly opening his mouth. Werner turned around. The text written in the lower quarter of the TV screen in a red box with the title 'Breaking News' read:

Hillary Clinton concedes Election in the United States of America.

* * *

←·· 168 ○◎○ 219 ··→

December 29th, 2017
Dr. Werner Bjerknes
Godshus – Norway

Friday

Werner checked the drawers for the last time. He had not forgotten anything. The box was ready to be closed.

Forty-one years and six months.

He had not thought that he would hand over the department in such surprisingly good shape. They were fully staffed as of a couple of months ago, and for now, it seemed that both Dr. Noor and Dr. Andersen would be staying for some time. They would need to find somebody for the junior physician position to start in January 2019, but this was more than a year away. The internship lottery was stopped in 2014. So nowadays the young doctors were free to choose. All of them. Not like him.

What would his life look like if his lucky number had not been '374'? There were things he regretted—getting into his car and driving all the way to Godshus from Oslo through the darkness was not one of them. That night his parents had told him to leave the house after he had spoken to them about Akira.

They would have to continue to look for his replacement, as Hana had only reluctantly agreed to serve as an interim chief physician after he had convinced her together with the management team from Ålesund Regional Hospital to do so.

"I'm going to be a grandma early next year, and I really want this to be my focus now and not the hospital. And, of course, I can never do the great job as Werner has done," was what she had told everyone.

Although he was convinced that Alessandro also would have never accepted the job, Werner was still a bit surprised at the reaction of the management team when he brought up his name.

"An Italian as a chief physician?"

179

What would be next? Of course, for the next two months, it would be Oslo. It was so nice of Max to offer him a stay at his house. It was close to the hospital where he would have the radiation treatment for his prostate cancer every weekday for the next six weeks. Max had insisted on only one thing. That Werner would take him to 'The London Pub' one night. Werner was not sure if it would be Max or himself who would look more out of place there nowadays.

But what then? He had decided to first see how things in Oslo would go before making any further plans. Of course, it was nice that they allowed him to stay on part-time in Godshus General Hospital. Help out a bit if there was a need.

There was one last thing that needed to be packed.

He took the silver frame from the desk, which now was no longer his, and looked at the picture. He had found the photograph with the slight yellow tint on the bottom of a cardboard box with papers in the apartment in London when he had to sort through Akira's life.

The picture showed two young men laughing into the camera with the dark blue ocean in the background. It had '*Where I first kissed my big Viking*' written on its back.

They had returned to the spot once together. In 2012. To celebrate their anniversary. Before they boarded a cruise in Palma de Mallorca.

Werner remembered the name of the cruise ship: Island Escape—it was quite old.

Looking at Akira's sparkling, almost black eyes full of light, he decided that the picture's new place would now be on his nightstand at home, and he carefully put it on top of the rest of his things.

Then he closed the box, stood up, took the box under his arm, and walked out of the office, which was reserved for the chief physician of the Department of Medicine of Godshus General Hospital.

He switched off the light and closed the door behind him.

* * *

←··· 222 ○◎○ 285 ···→

January 2nd, 2019
Dr. Werner Bjerknes
Godshus – Norway

Wednesday

"It really shouldn't be me giving this speech." Werner glanced at Hana, who was sitting across from him on the short side of the table.

"You're much better at these things than I'll ever be," Hana said.

They had gathered around the table in the conference room. It was one of the traditions he had introduced early on when he had started as chief physician. Whenever a new doctor would join their team, all of them would have a welcome breakfast. Nothing really fancy, just meant as a little gesture to welcome the new colleague. They had kept the tradition. Over the years the three of them who had been the 'old-timers' brought always the same: Hana the bread, Werner the cheese—always brunost—but as he knew that only the true Norwegians in the room would actually enjoy the simultaneous sweet and sharp taste with the hint of caramel, he also always brought a second cheese choice with him, most of the time, as today, a big piece of Jarlsberg. Alessandro, of course, always topped everyone with his version of laks og eggerøre.[1] Faiza, who had worked the night shift, had brought two large bottles of orange juice. Pia—if she had been present—would likely have brought two packs of Pålægschokolade[2] to stress her Danish heritage, which was what she had brought when they organized the 'welcome back'

---

1 **laks og eggerøre** – *Norwegian*: Smoked salmon and scrambled eggs—a very common Norwegian breakfast dish.

2 **Pålægschokolade** – *Danish:* Thin slices of chocolate which are used as topping on bread—common in Denmark—instead of a chocolate spread.

breakfast for him after he was done with his radiation treatment in Oslo. Whatever would be left over from this breakfast would be stored in the common small refrigerator for the next days for everybody to use if they were to become hungry at work.

"Well, a very warm welcome to the two of you, Anders and Per, to Godshus General Hospital. Also, of course, Anders as you're now the new chief physician, I wanted to say a big thanks to Hana for filling this role for the last year. We usually do this little breakfast gathering to get to know each other a bit better right from the start. So we usually say a little bit about us and then would ask you two to quickly introduce yourselves. We're actually all here today except for Pia—she is on vacation right now, but she'll be back on Monday."

And as so many times before, they all shared a quick story of their lives, which Werner knew well by now, as everyone always tended to say the same things over and over again. Dr. Per Nystrom-Miller introduced himself first to them. And then it was the new boss's turn. Werner was surprised that Dr. Anders Boisen-Jensen had opted to put *brunost* on his piece of bread, and given that he had already eaten half of it, Werner was even more surprised that the new boss seemed to enjoy it.

"So, I'm originally from Jutland in Denmark, but then studied medicine at Lund University in Southern Sweden and also did part of my training there and have worked as a cardiologist in several hospitals in Copenhagen the last couple of years," the new chief physician said.

"And we have talked about this previously here. As soon as the funding is approved, a small cardiac catheterization suite will be added in operating room number two. That way we'll be able to do cardiac stents here in Godshus and patients will no longer need to be flown to Bergen," Werner said.

"Such a great addition for the local community," Hana said.

"Okay. Now that we've done the introduction, let's go over the patients you admitted last night, Faiza, so you can get home," Werner said.

"So, you're doing this meeting every day here?" Anders asked.

"Yes. Somehow this is how it has always been done here. We usually all quickly meet at 7:30 in here to get an overview from the on-call doctor about the patients who got admitted over night and if something significant happened to the patients in-house. If a more detailed sign-out is necessary for the patients in the Intensive Care Unit, we do that at the bedside afterwards. But there's no breakfast. That's just today." Werner smiled.

"7:30?" Anders said.

"Yes, 7:30."

"I think we should move the start time to 7:15."

"Okay. Well, that's, of course, your decision going forward, but we had always started at 7:30," Werner said a bit surprised.

"Back in Copenhagen our aim was to get all patients discharged before ten in the morning to have the beds available for the next patients and although I realize that all of us meeting in the morning is important, I think we need to run things a bit more efficiently," Anders said.

"But we're not in Copenhagen here," Hana said.

"Perhaps Faiza can present the patients now and we can talk a bit more about this later?" Werner suggested.

"I really don't think we need to discuss more. Starting tomorrow, let's meet at 7:15 here," Anders said with a suddenly very firm tone in his voice.

After Faiza presented the new patients and the events of the night, and before everyone got up, Anders had one more question for Werner:

"I really like that cheese you brought, what is it?"

"Oh, the brunost. You really like it?"

"Okay. That's Norwegian brunost. Of course, I've heard about it, but I actually never tasted it. Love it!"

"Are you sure you're not Norwegian?" Werner looked over at Dr. Per Nystrom-Miller. The young Swedish doctor also had made himself a piece of bread with his brunost, but it was still sitting on his plate after he had only taken a single bite of it.

"No. Definitively not."

"Well, I guess you are the first non-Norwegian I have ever met who likes it. So I guess going forward it'll be you and me eating brunost here, as nobody else eats it in this department."

* * *

←··· 380 ○◎○ 384 ···→

December 18th, 2019
Dr. Werner Bjerknes
Godshus – Norway

Wednesday

The Dead Speak!

Perhaps it was this very first line that made everything in the movie feel disappointing for Werner.

Of course, they don't. Never. And, of course, it was an immediate reminder that he would never again sit next to Akira in a cinema.

Seeing the princess again made him smile. But was it really a dignified 'last performance' for her? But that was about it. At times, it felt almost like a parody. Flying Storm Troopers. Rey juggling all those stones, much more than Luke ever had. A 42-year celebration while trying to find a Sith Wayfinder—nice try. Chewie dies; but actually does not. C-3PO running around with some sort of memory reboot-induced dementia? The towering waves looked a bit like those in winter in Godshus. The scenes set in the death star wreckage. Guys… hello… it exploded… into trillions and trillions of little pieces…!!!!! Thousands of Star Destroyers equipped with lasers—so basically an entire fleet of Death Stars! And then all the resurrections: Rey kills a miraculously revived emperor, who—by the way—is her grandfather, and then dies. Kylo Ren then climbs out of the hole he just fell into and somehow uses the Force to revive her. Then a kiss between them. And then Kylo Ren dies—dead. Fin-ito. Somehow everybody can be resurrected except him. Chewbacca gets a medal.

Perhaps the movie could have never been what he wanted it to be. The expectations were just too high. A universally satisfying ending? Not that they really had a chance with this movie. But it felt like they did not even try. That they had just given up on the impossible task they faced.

Should he just allow it to exist and accept the imperfection? Yes, they wanted to show that you can choose your own destiny and that some things are more powerful than blood. How close light and darkness actually are. How very interchangeable. The divide between good and evil in everybody was the only thing clever in the script. Clearly, having power can yield unintended consequences and it will corrupt everyone. Of course, there were the old recognizable beats and the old familiar sites. But overall, this movie was not a royal farewell.

It was a whimper.

There was no new darkness or new light—just the same old battle. Same old stuff recycled.

In contrast to all the other eight movies, Werner did not wait until the long reel was over, but stood up and left the cinema wondering why exactly he used to love this stuff so much. He was relieved that it was over—because it stopped being fun. The director had achieved something extraordinary: for the first time in forty-two years and nine months, Werner did not care about *Star Wars*.

The first time ever.

It was a bad movie peppered with the occasional moments that did not suck as much as the rest of the film. He decided that for now, he would just pretend that the movie had not happened. For him, the saga and everything it had stood for had fallen.

The day at the hospital had been quite stressful, and he had to drive straight to the small cinema in Godshus without going home first. The one elderly man who had been sent over from the nursing home in the early afternoon with the bad nausea and vomiting and then started having profuse watery diarrhea as soon as they admitted him into a room on the second floor. Werner was just concerned and hoped that this would not be another Norovirus outbreak. They would have the test results from his stool sample the following morning as the laboratory technician had left for the day, and none of them knew exactly how to run that test. But he was worried. They put the patient into the isolation room. He called the nursing home and told them to isolate all the residents and staff members that might have been in contact with the man.

He remembered the disaster they had gone through a couple of years ago when all of the sudden they had eight elderly women and men come in from the nursing home with Norovirus. They did not have enough isolation rooms to put all of them in and then on top of everything they ran out of PPE. By the time sufficient gowns and masks were finally delivered another five patients in the hospital had been infected and one-by-one all the nurses except Louise and all the doctors except him became sick.

It was ten days of a—not only literally—shitty mess.

The management team from Ålesund Regional Hospital had then finally sent over help to get their nosocomial outbreak under control.

While driving home through the darkness, he thought of the evil emperor again. Clearly, Dr. Boisen-Jensen was not an evil emperor, but from all that had happened since January, it had become more than clear that he had not been the right choice to be the chief physician for Godshus General Hospital.

Of course, the good and the bad were close together. It was great that they now could offer to treat patients with heart attacks right here in Godshus, but what was the price the other doctors on the team were paying for this service? He definitively was medically very competent; but did that balance out his lack of leadership skills? He thought about what they had discussed and agreed upon with Alessandro and Hana at their meeting the previous week. They would start doing something in the beginning of January. They all were out of patience.

He went to bed immediately after he got home. Before falling asleep, he wanted to quickly check the headline news online and clicked the link on his iPad, which took him to the *Aftenposten* website.

The main announcement that evening was that there was a bitter debate happening in one of the chambers of the United States

Parliament as Werner called it to determine if a trial should be started to remove the forty-fifth President of the United States from office. A decision was expected later that night.

The reporter remarked in his article that it was only the third time this had happened in the history of that country.

And no president had ever been tried more than once.

Werner put his iPad down, glanced at Akira's sparkling, almost black eyes full of light in the picture in the silver frame on the nightstand, and turned off the light.

* * *

←··· 314 ○◎○ 245 ···→

December 20th, 2019
Dr. Werner Bjerknes
Godshus – Norway

Friday – 18:33

Werner had finished knotting the dark blue bow tie with the small white dots. Akira had bought it for him at an expensive store during the first time he visited him in London. There were not many opportunities to wear it in Godshus, but he had worn it every single Julebord.

But this evening would be different. After how the morning meeting went, he was not really looking forward to celebrating. The explosion of temper. The yelling. But traditions are there to be kept. He felt a slight squeeze in his stomach. Was it just the disappointment about how the evening would go? Or did he eat something bad during the day?

He thought about what he had eaten. He had overslept a bit, so only had one slice of crispbread with butter in the morning at home. He had too much coffee during the awful morning meeting and he had started to feel the acidity in his stomach. After seeing the two patients in the emergency room, Werner had returned to the conference room. He was happy to find the piece of brunost in the fridge. It was not his. He assumed it belonged to Dr. Boisen-Jensen. For Werner, it was a comforting taste of childhood.

After what had happened that morning, he did not care if he was stealing the cheese belonging to that asshole. He sat down at the conference room table and ate it all on two slices of crispbread. Then for lunch, he had the nondescript piece of meat with the brown sauce which the hospital kitchen had prepared that day. He had some chocolate cookies once he came home. The short, squeezy feeling in his stomach was gone now.

189

Werner locked the outside door and got into his Land Rover. He drove the familiar way through the darkness. The restaurant was about halfway between his house and the hospital. About a ten-minute drive. He drove straight down the small hill until he came to the trough with the steep cliff on his right side. In summer, when there was light, he always turned his head briefly here to look out at the ocean. Then he continued uphill again, reaching the small peak, and then drove down the hill where the road curved in a total of seven serpentines. When he reached the bottom, he turned right into the parking lot of the restaurant. Hana's parked car appeared in the headlights. He got out and walked over a small metal bridge. A light rain had started. He could hear the stormy ocean in front of him. A bike was leaning against the railing opposite the entrance door. Werner opened the door and stepped into the emerald-greenish light which rose from the depth of the restaurant.

* * *

←··· 125 ○◎○ 248 ···→

Chapter 3

Dr. Faiza Abdi Noor

October 1st, 1989
Dr. Faiza Abdi Noor
Kismaayo – Somalia

Sunday

Mom was shouting. Faiza was running. But she was not quick enough. Faiza started to scream. She tried to run faster. And faster. She would not escape. She screamed louder.

Turning around, she saw the quickly approaching white spume of the ocean wave. The warm water engulfed the soles of her feet. She stopped running. Her cousins and the other kids around started laughing. Some of them had outrun the wave, whereas others—like her—had not. Faiza joined them in laughter.

"Faiza! Careful! The ocean. You don't know how to swim. We need to go home soon," Mom said.

Faiza had met so many new faces the last days. The wedding of the distant older cousin would be tomorrow. The new face she liked the most was the one who called himself Uncle. Mom said he had come from a town far away called New York. And of course, she also liked the older man with the caring face. He was standing on the beach next to Dad.

* * *

Watching the joy of his almost three-year-old granddaughter playing around with the other kids on the beach made him for a short while forget the troubled weeks since they had recalled him from Stockholm.

As soon as they returned to the house, he would have to talk to his son.

At least he, his wife, and his granddaughter should be prepared to leave the country in case it should become necessary.

* * *

←··· 75 ○◎○ 79 ···→

March 8th, 1993
Dr. Faiza Abdi Noor
Hagadera Refugee Camp – Kenia

Monday

Her bare feet walking on the red dusty earth after Faiza was told it was *'her time'*.

The shack like all the others made of wood sticks with a tin roof and blue tarps as walls.

Her clothes being taken away.

The powerful hands holding her down on the ground.

The chanting.

Her screaming.

Her unbearable pain.

Her blood running down her legs and dripping onto the red dusty earth from where the piece of flesh had been cut between her thighs.

* * *

←··· 344 ○◎○ 156 ···→

May 17th, 1997
Dr. Faiza Abdi Noor
Oslo – Norway

Saturday

"So that's the king?" Faiza asked.

"Yep. That's him."

Faiza waved the flag in her hand even more. She almost could not see the man dressed with a cylinder through the sea of red, white, and blue. He and the other people standing on the balcony and looking down appeared so small.

"So is there also a king in the country where you are from?"

"My dad told me that we used to have a president. But now I guess there are just people fighting and killing themselves," Faiza answered. She had to talk quite loudly because of all the marching band music coming from everywhere.

"Well. I'll really miss the Constitution Day parade in Oslo. I mean, I really liked going every year."

"What? Why?"

"We're moving away from Oslo this summer. Dad got a job in a place really far away from Oslo. At the end of a fjord. I was actually there when I was a baby, but I don't remember that."

"Oh, that's sad. I'll miss you," Faiza said. The boy with the short hair had been her first friend after she had switched to the new school. They were now walking downhill a bit, under trees with fresh green spring leaves.

"I'll miss you too. My parents said that it's a good time to move now. That way my little brother can start school at the new place and doesn't have to switch like me. Was it hard to switch schools?"

"In the beginning, a bit. But it was much easier this time. What was really hard was three years ago when we just came here."

"Gunnar!"

Faiza saw how a tall man who was standing at the corner of the street in the distance shouted and waved. He was holding a smaller boy by his hand.

"Ah, there's dad. Will have to go now."

"You're not going all the way towards the end of the parade?"

"No. We live really close. Dad's picking me up and we'll go to visit my mom at the hospital."

"Oh gosh. Is she sick?"

"No. No," he said, smiling. "She has to work at the hospital today. She's a doctor."

"Ah. Okay. My dad also works in a hospital, but not today."

"Oh. Is he a doctor, too?"

"No. He just cleans."

"So is your mom and dad picking you up at the end of the parade?"

"Just my dad. My mom is dead."

* * *

←⋯ 258 ○◎○ 347 ⋯→

September 15th, 2001
Dr. Faiza Abdi Noor
Newark, New Jersey – United States of America

Saturday

"Faiza, please go and get on that plane. You have to go back to school."

"But Dad, I can't just leave you here. And I'm afraid going by myself," Faiza said.

"Sorry, officers. I'm going to be the purser on this flight. So what's the exact problem?" a woman in a blue Scandinavian Airlines flight attendant uniform asked.

"The girl is okay to board. But there's no way we'll give security clearance to the gentleman to get on this flight," the officer in the black uniform with the bulletproof vest and the helmet explained.

"But he's Norwegian," the flight attendant said.

"He's a Somali with a Norwegian passport. Ma'am we do not need to discuss this anymore now here. This is our judgment—not yours. We'll run a full background check and once that's completed and okay, he can take another flight in the next couple of days. But not this plane."

"I'm sorry. But you'll have to make a decision. All the other passengers are in the plane already," the woman looked at Faiza and dad.

"Faiza. Get on the plane, please. You have the apartment key. And please go to school on Monday. I'll come as soon as they let me."

"But dad!"

"Faiza!"

Dad gave her a quick hug and pushed her towards the flight attendant.

"Can you show me your boarding pass?" the flight attendant asked. "Okay, you have seat 14G. That's a window seat and right at the galley. Do you think you'll find it? I have to tell the captain something real quickly."

Faiza only had sat down and had not had time to fasten her seatbelt yet, when the overhead announcement came.

"Boarding complete. Arm doors and cross-check."

Faiza looked at the empty seat next to her, which would have been dad's.

She did not really hear any of the announcements that followed while the airplane slowly began rolling towards the runway. She only remembered how just a week ago all had started so well. How happy she had been. Dad and she had taken the brief walk from the small apartment in Tøyen with their suitcase to Oslo Sentralstasjon[1] and boarded the Flytoget,[2] which whisked them to the new airport north of town. She was excited. She did not remember too much of the flights she had been on when she was half the age she was now, and which brought dad and her to Norway. Their dark red Norwegian passports had finally arrived a couple of months earlier, and she was proud to show hers to the officer in the booth before boarding the plane. At one point she fell asleep during the flight. It was so nice to see uncle at the airport. He had come to pick them up. Uncle had visited dad and her several times in Oslo, but this was the first time they were able to visit him. Of course, she had a bit of a guilty feeling about the trip as she would miss a week of school. She had never seen such wide roads in her life before. That early afternoon she only had a quick glimpse of all the high buildings in the distance when uncle said:

"Faiza look to your right, we are going over the George Washington Bridge now. That's the skyline of Manhattan."

On Sunday they just rested in uncle's house in a place called Hartsdale and on Monday morning they joined uncle on his way to work. They took a train and got off in a majestic station. Faiza had never seen so many people rushing around. They changed to a subway line with the number four.

---

1 **Oslo Sentralstasjon** – *Norwegian*: Oslo Central Station.

2 **Flytoget** – *Norwegian*: Airport express train.

Uncle had a lot of meetings that day, and they agreed that he would only show them his office the next day. He had given them a map and he showed them where they would meet on a wide plaza with a water fountain around a sphere in the middle. From there it was only dad and she who walked down to a park. Lady Liberty stood in the distance, and they patiently waited in line to take a boat to visit the sights.

They bought a hot dog for a late lunch once the boat had returned them, and then strolled around the streets which appeared like narrow valleys among all the tall buildings—visiting places she had heard and read about.

They had a little time left before it was time to meet uncle and they went to a department store named 'Century 21'. She found a pink tank top, with the letter 'I', the emblem of love, and then the letters 'N' and 'Y' on it. She really liked the red glitter of the heart symbol.

When she tried it on, dad did not look too happy at first, but she enjoyed how snugly it fit on her body, which over the last year had changed so much. She knew how to look at dad and what to say and happily pulled it out of the plastic bag the cashier had put it in to show it to uncle when they met him, before they took the same subway and train back to his home.

He told them that he had to be in the office early the next morning, as a last-minute meeting had been scheduled, and suggested that the next day they would go to town separately. Uncle would take an early train in the morning and then meet them at the same place on the wide plaza at ten when the meeting was over. He would have time to go to Chinatown with them to have an early lunch and then would show them the view from his office. Dad and uncle agreed that this was a good plan.

Faiza felt how the plane made the turn onto the runway. She looked out of the window. In the distance, she could see the skyline, where what was now missing was more significant than what was there. A thin white plume in the air was all that remained from the office uncle was in on the 99th floor of the South Tower.

Dad and she had cried a lot the other days, but now the tears started flowing again, more than ever before.

As she felt how the plane's acceleration began to push her body against her seat, a caring arm was placed around her neck, and a hand gently cleared off the tears from her wet right cheek. Through her tear-filled eyes, she recognized the woman in her blue SAS uniform who unexpectedly had sat down in the empty seat next to her.

Faiza started sobbing, and the woman held her a bit tighter so that she rested her face onto the right side of her torso.

As the front of the plane lifted to the sky, Faiza's head must have pushed harder against the woman, as all of the sudden Faiza noticed how she briefly retracted. When she looked at the flight attendant, she saw how she was briefly brushing her right breast with her left hand.

"Sorry. I had a little pain there. But now just cry. Just cry," the woman said and before Faiza buried her face on the right side of the woman's torso again, she noticed the name tag with Eva Redding written on it.

* * *

←⋯ 351 ○◎○ 165 ⋯→

January 10th, 2007
Dr. Faiza Abdi Noor
Oslo – Norway

Wednesday

Faiza hated how everything smelled from the formaldehyde.
Repulsive. Nose-pinching. Throat grabbing.
She couldn't stand it for one more second.
Everything, absolutely EVERYTHING smelled like formaldehyde.
Especially her hair.
She had washed her hands at least three times with soap, but still had the feeling they smelled. And she had worn gloves, of course. Perhaps it was just in her mind now. Her eyes were still tearing.
It was interesting to watch the other students in her study group during the gross anatomy dissection class. Some of them appeared to really enjoy it, whereas others—including her—not so much.
It was snowing outside.
She took out the small flask with Opium from Yves Saint Laurent and put a single spray onto the back of her hands and rubbed them together. Getting the smell out of her hair was an entirely different story. Just a quick shower and shampooing was out of question. It would be a half-a-day project for Saturday. Precondition her hair for two hours first, then the shampoo in the shower and afterwards put in lots of avocado oil. She would braid her hair this weekend—perhaps that would somehow help to keep the formaldehyde smell out the next week a little better.
It was time to go to the library now to study. At least until 21:00. She would have a coffee to keep her awake from one of the machines there.

Faiza put on her heavy winter coat and wrapped herself up for the walk from the domus medica[1] to the T-bane[2] station. She took out her iPod to put on music for the trip. The new cell phone Apple had announced the previous day—iPhone—would be interesting.

People would just have all their songs on a phone and would not need to carry two devices around anymore in the future, perhaps.

She put the earplugs in and selected a song with the round wheel before putting on her gloves. Amy Winehouse started singing about not going to *Rehab*.

* * *

←··· 274 ○◎○ 353 ···→

---

1 **Domus Medica** (Latin) – Medical House. Name of the building which serves as main teaching site for the first two years for medical, dental and nutrition students of the University of Oslo.

2 **T-bane** – *Norwegian*: Tunnelbane. Oslo Metro.

JULEBORD (The Holiday Party)

April 19th, 2008
Dr. Faiza Abdi Noor
Oslo – Norway

Saturday

"Whit's yer name?"[1] Faiza had trouble understanding his heavy
Scottish accent through the deafening pulsating music in the club.
He could have picked any girl that night. As soon as he handed the
DJing over to the guy from South Africa around two in the morning, he went down to the dance floor and danced next to her. He
must have observed her throughout the night, she thought—she
definitively had. She loved the loud music on the Friday nights. She
actually just had come to dance. Just herself tonight. Her biochem-
istry exam had been on Thursday. She did not expect him to be as
sober as he was.

"Awright this is ma jab. Cann't dram oan th'jab. At least nae
awfy much. A'm an' a' booked tae wirk back in Auld Reekie th'nicht.
Sae hae tae be canny wi'th' swally. Cannae shaw up wasted tae a
gig."[2] The groove of the rave had changed once the South African
took over—softer, sexier, more sultry. They danced closer together.
Their bodies touching from time to time. She noticed how his hand
started playing with her hair above her ear. It surprised her how
good it felt when their lips touched. She could feel how his very
hard erection pushed against her tights, while they kissed passion-

---

1 **Whit's yer name?** – *Scots:* What's your name?

2 **Awright this is ma jab. Cann't dram oan th'jab. At least nae awfy
much. A'm an' a' booked tae wirk back in Auld Reekie th'nicht. Sae
hae tae be canny wi'th' swally. Cannae shaw up wasted tae a gig.** – *Scots:*
Hey this is my job. Can't drink on the job. At least not too much. I am
also booked to work back in Edinburgh tonight. So have to be careful
with the booze. Cannot show up wasted to a gig.

203

ately against the wall next to the entrance of the club shortly after. The decision to accept the offer to go to his room in the hotel just felt naturally right to her. She had never done something like this. Faiza had been naked with other men before, of course. She had met them at school or at university, one of them at the library—but it had always been gradual—not a choice made in the here and now, like tonight. Perhaps like this, things would end differently tonight than with the others? Perhaps it was the planning, the anticipation, the building excitement which made it impossible for her to open up when a naked man was ready for her. She never told them before. A conversation she never dared to start. What could she tell him? What should she say? The shame she felt about what had been done to her as a child. The memory of the intense pain. The perceived ugliness of self. The belief that she would not be able to enjoy.

The naked men had always tried gently, but her reaction made all of them insecure. It was more the scars of the past which did not show on her body than the actual visible one that blocked her. The guilty feeling about her inability to satisfy them, to be a true woman, made her resort to using her hands and her mouth. To reward them out of the notion of obligation. To at least return something to them for their efforts. To not disappoint. Their pleasure being more important than hers. Only two of them had been naked with her a second time—again unsuccessfully. All the naked men so far had just quickly given up on her.

Not mature enough themselves to provide any guidance or help for her to start to heal. She never blamed any one of them for their choice.

Therefore—from a pure definition perspective—she was still a virgin when she heard the sound of a condom package ripping open in the dark hotel room. Immediately, she felt the disappointing tensing in her lower body, the fear and the memory of the pain coming back. She knew right then, that the experience with the naked Scot would be the same like with all the naked men before him. She continued the passionate kissing, but he must have sensed that something was different.

"Urr ye okay?"[1] he asked with his sexy accent, while he turned on the too-bright light on the bedside table.

She tried to quickly and clumsily hide her body under the blanket while she grabbed the shaft of his penis with her hand with the plan to satisfy him that way.

"Awright—whit urr ye daein'? Let's juist get pumpin'."[2] His face looked surprised and annoyed a bit while he tried to free his cock from her grip and pushed the blanket off her body. Faiza let go of his penis, keeping her hand close to his groin while he energetically parted her knees, fully exposing her in the light to his eyes for the first time. She noticed how he paused, his gaze wandering back and forth between her altered anatomy and her eyes. In the light, she now could clearly see the long scar which was running from just below his sternum down to his pelvis. She held her breath and looked at the ceiling, not wanting to see the insecurity which would surely appear in his face; as it had with all the other naked men before. She felt how his body began to retreat. Perhaps he was ready now—she thought—and decided to proceed to gently roll his balls like if they were oversized marbles in her hand next. To stimulate him. At least please him this way. She was surprised when it was only one single testicle which filled her palm. Somewhat anxiously, she peeked back at his face. With even a bigger surprise she saw a warm, genuine grin of a smile.

Their mutual releasing laugh started out of nowhere.

"Juist huv a go. Tis safe,"[3] he proposed while they were sitting naked on the edge of the bed, sharing the blanket to cover their backs. They had laughed, kissed, and talked for a long while—and she shared thoughts she had not shared with any other naked man before.

"Come on, you want me to take a date rape drug to help me?" She told him in disbelief after he had quickly disappeared in the bathroom coming back with a small dropping bottle.

---

1 **Urr ye okay?**– *Scots:* Are you okay?

2 **Awright – whit urr ye daein'? Let's juist get pumpin'.** – *Scots:* Hey—what are you doing? Let's just fuck.

3 **Juist huv a go. Tis safe.** – *Scots:* Just try. It's safe.

"Howfur dae ye think a seventeen year auld laddie, wha's ane baw hud juist bin cut o'fur cancer ever cam up brave enough tae girls 'n' git thaim tae kip wi' him?"[1] The Scot answered defensively. "Th' nicht—dae ye think ah wid hae juist waltzed up tae ye oan th' dance flair wi'oot it? We baith hae bin broken in some ways. We baith hae oor scars. Whit haes helped me fur th' lest twelve years wis mah reels 'n' strathspeys 'n' th' GHB. O' coorse it knocks ye oot if ye tak an awfy lot. Bit that's nae howfur ye tak' it. Ye hae tae fig-ure oot howfur muckle wirks fur ye. Fur me a' that it does is kerry oot th' anxiety that a'm different. That ah will nae be liked fur th' doctors cut aff yin o mah baws. O' coorse, it does nae mak' th' scars disappear. Bit it helps th' mynd deal wi' thaim."[2] His sermon ended.

---

1 Howfur dae ye think a seventeen year auld laddie, wha's ane baw hud juist bin cut o'fur cancer ever cam up brave enough tae blether tae girls 'n' git thaim tae kip wi' him? – *Scots:* How do you think a seventeen-year-old boy, whose one ball had just been cut off because of cancer ever got brave enough to talk to girls and get them to sleep with him?

2 Th' nicht – dae ye think ah wid hae juist waltzed up tae ye oan th' dance flair wi'oot it? We baith hae bin broken in some ways. We baith hae oor scars. Whit haes helped me fur th' lest twelve years wis mah reels 'n' strathspeys 'n' th' GHB. O' coorse it knocks ye oot if ye tak an awfy lot. Bit that's nae howfur ye tak' it. Ye hae tae figure oot howfur muckle wirks fur ye. Fur me a' that it does is kerry oot th' anxiety that a'm different. That ah will nae be liked fur th' doctors cut aff yin o mah baws. O' coorse it does nae mak' th' scars disappear. Bit it helps th' mynd deal wi' thaim. – *Scots:* Tonight—do you think I would have just walked up to you on the dance floor without it? We both have been broken in some ways. We both have our scars. What has helped me for the last twelve years was my music and the GHB. Of course, it knocks you out if you take too much. But that's not how you take it. You have to figure out how much works for you. For me, all that it does is take away the anxiety that I am different. That I'll not be liked because the doctors cut off one of my balls. Of course, it does not make the scars disappear. But it helps the mind deal with them.

He had removed the filled dropper from the bottle. Faiza realized she had really nothing to lose by just giving it a try. It had to be because of him having one testicle only and his candid manner that she trusted this naked man she just had met. She swallowed the two drops of the salty clear liquid from the dropper after he had done the same.

Nothing happened.

She continued to talk with him, while looking out at the white silhouette of the modern opera building which was rising from the fjord into the dawn of the late spring sky like a forever stuck iceberg in the fjord of Oslo.

When she glanced back at his green eyes, she felt the uninhibited urge to kiss the freckles on the cheek above his short ginger beard. She also felt the desire, but with none of the fear, to feel him inside her.

And so it occurred, that about twenty-five minutes later—through the combination of a pale-skinned, freckled, redhead Scottish DJ with only one testicle and the anxiolytic and disinhibiting effects of a substance which in much higher doses is used to date rape women and men—Faiza, by definition, could no longer be considered a virgin.

She took the train with him to Gardemon airport that afternoon. After one last kiss, he gave her the dropping bottle which contained the rest of the salty fluid. He also noted down a phone number on a small wrinkled piece of paper. The number belonging to a guy who lived in Oslo from whom he had bought the dropping bottle with the salty clear fluid earlier during the week.

She was convinced that she had found a way that could control her fear, her shame, her self-loathing.

* * *

←··· 279 ○◎○ 86 ···→

May 29th, 2010
Dr. Faiza Abdi Noor
Bærum – Norway

Saturday

"Douze points vers la Georgie."

The woman with the black hair did not appear to be too happy or ecstatic about being the winner with her 246 points. But of course, it had been clear much earlier that she won. Faiza could only see from the distance how she walked through the booths where her co-competitors were sittings toward the stage; even so, seeing her live was special.

"The Winner of the Eurovision Song Contest 2010 is Germany." Okay, now it was official.

Norway's previous year's winner was the first to congratulate her and well, he was much more ecstatic than the entire group of Germans together who now had to perform the song again. She felt that Alexander Rybak, an immigrant like herself, winning the song contest for Norway the year before with his pop-folk *Fairytale* and his fiddle felt so special that she decided to go and see the live show this year in Oslo. She, as most of the women in Norway, was a bit in love with Alexander. In a platonic way, of course.

"Congratulations! Can you describe this moment?" Alexander asked this year's winner.

"It's. Ehm. Hi. I think…I'm not strong enough to take this the whole time. Thank you. This is so absolutely awesome. And I feel like this is not real. I'm so thankful. So happy. So thankful. So ahh."

Then the woman quickly just covered her face in the German flag which she had dragged along and the moderators had mercy and proceeded to the final item of the contest. Her song once more. Only the second-ever win for Germany in the many years of the competition.

"The stage is yours," said one of the moderators, and the woman looked anxious for a second.

"Do I have to sing now?"

Then luckily the moderators took over.

"The Eurovision Song Contest 2010 has come to an end. What an outstanding competition it had come to be. We had an amazing time in Oslo. Next year the final will be in Germany. Bonne Nuit!"

Then the singer who had just won and who now appeared more herself again started with her pop song named *Satellite*.

Upon leaving the Telenor Arena, Faiza noticed she had received a message on her iPhone earlier in the night:

Ubaxyow! Waxaan u maleynayaa inaan dhiig ka imaanayo xiidmaha. Jacayl. Aabe.[1]

* * *

←··· 86 ○◎○ 90 ···→

---

1 **Ubaxyow! Waxaan u maleynayaa inaan dhiig ka imaanayo xiidmaha. Jacayl. Aabe** – *Somali:* My flower! I think I'm bleeding from my intestines. Love. Dad.

April 11th, 2011
Dr. Faiza Abdi Noor
Elverum – Norway

Monday

It was absolutely clear to Faiza that she would never, ever become a primary care physician. Sitting on a chair for the majority of the time of the day. Listening to mostly completely trivial complaints. And in the rare cases that they indeed meant something serious, one would actually not treat anything, but immediately send the patient to the hospital. Faiza however really liked the precepting doctor. She had hoped to see a faraway part of Norway when she had signed up for the month-long 'rural primary care medicine clerkship' and was a bit disappointed having ended up just two hours north from Oslo by train. But this way she could spend the weekends home with her dad. She had taken the first train in the morning. It was the last time she would do this trip—the one month was over on Friday.

The early spring weather felt nice, and she had decided to walk from the red-colored old station building to the doctor's office in town instead of taking the bus. She crossed the quiet river using the odd-looking suspension bridge. The center of the town was filled with nondescript buildings constructed after the war. Judging from the appearance of the train station and the single surviving original building left in town, Elverum had to be a much nicer little Norwegian country town in the past— prior to being reduced to ashes by the bombs. With her mind set at the end of the rotation, the day passed more quickly than the others. After she was done with the last patient, she would walk back through the center a bit north of town to the assortment of old red wooden buildings that made up the Elverum folkehøgskole.[1] A historic place with so few reminders. Being housed with the students there only a couple of years younger made her realize how the last five years of medical studies had shaped her. The overwhelming amount of information, attention to detail, the endless studies in the libraries, and the hard exams had formed her mind differently. In a certain way, she envied the creative souls, which were spending a year studying how to organize a music festival, photography, or outdoor living while traveling Norway, Europe, and the world. On the other hand, Faiza was happy that in contrast to her fellow lodgers she always knew exactly what would have to happen next in her life, to achieve her goal of becoming a physician.

She saw the final patient of the day, like the others, on her own first. A stocky man looking older than his early thirties due to the receding and thinning hairline. He had a cough the entire week, but over the weekend also some fever. The phlegm he brought up at times was a little yellow. Tea and paracetamol had helped. His lungs sounded clear, no wheezes. His vitals were normal. No other medical problems.

Faiza went next door to the precepting doctor and suggested to just continue the tea and paracetamol. Why give him antibiotics for his bronchitis, which the immune system of his body would be able to very well manage on its own?

"So Anders, you had this cough for a while now?" her preceptor asked him after they both went back into the room. After examining and talking to him, she fully agreed with Faiza that there was no need for antibiotics. He was instructed to return if he did not feel better later that week. Faiza had the feeling that he was somewhat disappointed by the news that his body could handle the infection alone—without an antibiotic which would surely kill any of the bacteria in the lining of his bronchi, but also a lot of the microbes which were required in his gut; and in addition, have several other potential side effects.

---

1 **Folkehøgskole** – *Norwegian*: Folk High School.

She needed to finish a quick note on the computer in his chart. The system had logged her out of his record already, and therefore she re-entered his last name to open it again. She typed: Breivik.

* * *

← 90 ○◎○ 94 →

March 25th, 2015
Dr. Faiza Abdi Noor
Klampenborg – Denmark

Wednesday

"Tredjegenerationsindvandrer?"[1] Faiza asked.

"Well, you pronounce it in a Norwegian kind of way. But yes, third generation immigrant, that's what the kindergarten teacher called Taban. I mean, she's a nice person and didn't say it in a bad way at all. It was just like—'Oh yes, we have two other tredjegenerationsindvandrere in his group.' It doesn't matter at all that he, me, and his dad are all born in Copenhagen, have Danish passports, have never been to Somalia and, given that we speak Danish at home, I somehow doubt Taban will ever speak Somali. But well, he's a tredjegenerationsindvandrer. It'll be interesting to see what word they'll come up with for my grandchildren." Taban's mom smiled at this wacky Danish socio-linguistic concept.

It had been a beautiful late March day, which felt almost like June already, but it was slowly getting time to return to the Klampenborg S-tog[2] station and get back to Ballerup.

Faiza had visited Copenhagen several times before, but she had never been to Dyrehave.[3] She had gladly accepted her invitation to come over for the visit.

Now that her dad had died.

Her dad and Taban's mom's parents had visited each other frequently over the years and although she was four years older than

---

1 **Tredjegenerationsindvandrer** – *Danish:* Third-generation immigrant.

2 **S-tog** – *Danish:* S-train. Name of the urban-suburban rail system serving Copenhagen.

3 **Dyrehave** – *Danish:* The Deer Park. Forest park north of Copenhagen, consisting of mostly huge, ancient oak trees.

her cousin—which was what they called themselves, given the lack of a word which would exactly express the way they were related— she had fond memories of playing with her throughout the years. When the weather forecast and the sky outside promised that it would be a nice day both of them had agreed that Faiza would pick up Taban at the Kindergarten and then they met at the advertising agency in downtown Copenhagen where her cousin was doing an internship at the moment.

It was not clear to Faiza how her cousin managed all of this: having a very active almost-three-year-old while doing her bachelors at the Copenhagen Business School and Taban's dad working full time. With Taban in the stroller they walked through the park where, due to the unusually early warm spring weather during the last weeks, the oak forest had already started to be covered with fresh green leaves. They went up to Eremitageslottet where they let Taban out of the stroller and kicked the ball they had brought with them around in the large lawn covered by fresh green grass. They took a different way back and passed by the summer scene in the section called Ulvedale. When Taban saw the stairs leading up to the empty seats of the summer scene, he insisted Faiza walk up and down with him a couple of times while he was playing with his small red toy car that he let drive up and down the handrail several times. It required two adults to wrestle the toddler back into the stroller, as he somehow had loved this newly discovered game of his very much before they headed back to the train station.

They passed a couple who were holding hands. She was clearly no longer in her twenties and appeared to be slightly in the lead of the young, very tall, and definitively athletic man with a sharp chin and short hair. He sent a still boyish type of smile towards Faiza as they passed and she briefly smiled back. Besides them, there were only very few people walking around, especially in this section of the park.

"You know, in the end, the Danes and the Somalis are not so different. If you look deep down at things," her cousin said.

"What do you mean?"

"Well, you know how the whole clan thing is so important in Somalia?"

"Of course I do."

"In essence—basically the Danes are nothing different than a clan. I mean, the entire country is like a big clan. Either you are part of it or not, and there is not really a way to become part of it."

They now arrived at an old white house with a yellowish reed roof. Faiza remembered it was here that they had entered into the park a couple of hours ago.

"What's this house?"

"Oh. That's Peter Lieps Hus. There is a really hyggelig[1] pub in there. We could stop by, but it would be a bit difficult with Taban."

"Hooyo.[2] Where's my car?" Taban asked.

They both started looking in their pockets, then in the pockets of the stroller, and around a more and more angry and cranky toddler, who was convinced that the currently most important and irreplaceable thing in his life was forever gone.

"I guess we must have dropped it at that summer scene when we were wrangling him back into the stroller. He was playing with it there. Should we go back?"

They turned around and after a short while, Taban became suspiciously quiet. He had fallen into an exhausted, end-of-the-world/lost-my-favorite-toy toddler type of sleep.

About half the way to the place where they hoped to somehow find Taban's little play car, sounds started coming out of the woods.

"Aah."

Then again.

"Aaah."

Then.

---

1 **hyggelig** – *Danish:* Pleasant, nice, cozy. Derived from 'Hygge'. The concept of 'Hygge' is a prominent Danish (and to a lesser degree Norwegian) cultural category focussed on the feeling of coziness, wellness, and contentment.

2 **Hooyo** – *Somali:* Mom.

"Mmmmh."

They both stopped and looked.

"Oh, my god. What is he doing? Is he raping her?" her cousin asked.

Given that from the angle where they were standing Faiza could see the side profile of both of them in about a twenty-meter distance, she doubted this. He was using the stump of a fallen oak tree as a seat with her straddling him. His short hair and naked side of an athletic torso clearly identified him as the man she had just exchanged smiles with a couple of minutes ago.

"I don't think so."

Her suspicion was confirmed by the crescendo of a female voice which followed:

"Oh, ohh, ohhh, ohhhh, ohhhhh, yeah."

Immediately followed by a deep releasing male:

"Aaaaahhhhhh."

It must have been the somewhat bewildered expression in Faiza's face which made her cousin say.

"Well, you know, someone a long time ago already said that 'something is rotten in the state of Denmark'. But, oh my god, what is she doing now? I mean, can't she give the guy a little break?"

By the time they realized that someone who had unexpectedly woken up was also watching, it was too late to move the stroller around.

"Hooyo. What are the two people doing there in the forest?"

* * *

←⋯ 281 ○◎○ 283 ⋯→

JULEBORD (The Holiday Party)

March 21st, 2016

Dr. Faiza Abdi Noor

Oslo – Norway

Monday

She had absolutely no idea how they got her e-mail address:

From: Inga Öberg
Subject: Work as a Medical Doctor on board of the Ocean Gala
Date/Time: March 21st, 2016 – 13:13
To: Dr. Faiza Abdi Noor

Dear Dr. Abdi Noor,

Sorry for contacting you directly this way. We are currently looking for doctors who would be interested in staffing a medical clinic on the cruise ship 'Ocean Gala', which we plan to use for refugee housing. Further information is included as an attachment.

If you should be interested, please just contact me.
Yours sincerely,

Inga Öberg

Senior Project Manager—Working Group for Alternative Refugee Accommodation

Migrationsverket / Swedish Migration Agency
Huvudkontor/Head Office
Planeringsavdelningen/Planning Department

Norrköping
Organisationsnummer: 202100-2163

Faiza looked up from her computer. Interesting. A ship doctor.

Of course not cruising around. Taking care of refugees. It would likely mean more of a primary care type of setting, which was not really what she would be looking for. But perhaps it was time to take a break from working at a large university hospital. A little change for her while trying to help to advance the world for the better—just a tiny bit. Why not? Of course, now that Sweden had closed its borders, there were fewer refugees, but there was still lots to do. But what would the ship look like?

She looked up Ocean Gala on the internet.

Oh, interesting—the ship had even its own Wikipedia page. Not such a huge ship actually. Wow, quite a history for a simple cruise ship. And all the names it had before: 'Scandinavia', 'Stardancer', 'Viking Serenade', 'Island Escape'.

She pushed reply and started typing.

* * *

←⋯ 283 ○◎○ 168 ⋯→

February 12th, 2017
Dr. Faiza Abdi Noor
Taghazout – Morocco

Sunday

Annoyed, Faiza answered: "Norway."

"Yes, and I am from the moon! Or Mars! C'mon—I mean—where're you from?"

"Norway. I'm from Norway." If it had been anyone else but him she would have likely slapped him by now, but his face was just too similar to hers.

"Honey, I mean you have 'I'm from Africa' written all over your face, so just admit it!"

"Well, I was born in Somalia."

"Ah, there. I knew it. A fellow African. But you know. No need to be ashamed of being from Africa. All humans are in the end. Or not? Wasn't there that old African—Homo Erectus? Isn't she or he supposed to be the great-great-great-great-or whatever grand-dudess or dude of all of us?"

This universal insight formulated by the tall slim man who united being a Berber, surf instructor, and now apparently also an evolutionary biologist in one single body made her laugh. She had never expected to have so much fun on this trip. But now she was really hungry and took another huge bite out of the Batbout[1] sandwich, while sitting next to him in a circle with the other five people from the same one-week Yoga-Surf-Retreat like herself.

The link to the website had popped up when she used Google to do a search on 'warm' 'yoga' 'sun' and 'holiday' one afternoon, when it became clear she needed a little one-week escape from winter in Norway. The dates fit perfectly with her already approved vacation

---

1 **Batbout** – Moroccan pita bread.

time, and First Airlines of Norway had an unbelievably cheap direct flight from Gardermoen to Agadir. She remembered how in the first e-mail she had specifically asked if she could just book the yoga retreat without the surfing part. The answer was 'No, but we're sure you'll love it!' Realizing that the worst-case scenario would be to sit a couple of hours on a wide sandy beach between the morning and afternoon yoga sessions, she just booked the trip. Faiza was glad that the day had started off with the yoga session, as getting into the black wetsuit was not easy at all. She, of course, ended up in the 'novice surfer' group and not with the experienced surfers who were driven away in another old van to a different beach.

The Berber/surf instructor/evolutionary biologist had briefly explained to them what to do on the beach, throwing words at her which she did not really understand, and off they went into the North Atlantic.

Wow, this was hard.

The waves did not look so big from the shore, and it always looked so easy when you watched what surfers were doing.

Suddenly he was standing next to her, holding her surfboard a bit, until he shouted:

"Paddle."

She did.

And all of the sudden the power of the ocean took over not only the surfboard she was lying on, but also her mind.

It must have been the sudden release of the perfectly balanced mixture of catecholamines and endorphins in her brain, which made it impossible to remember the amount of time she managed to actually stand on the surfboard before she fell off.

Her face emerged out of the ocean water with the biggest smile of her life.

She looked at him.

"Stoked? You are a surfer now!" he yelled, holding up his right hand with only the thumb and smallest finger extended, while he kept the other three fingers curled, repeatedly rotating his hand back and forth so that Faiza could see the hand's front and back in alternation.

"Do you have another sandwich for me?" Faiza asked.

"A hungry surfer. Here you go," he said and handed her the third Batbout sandwich.

"Thanks."

"You know, you're lucky, you can surf back home if you want."

"In Somalia?"

"You just said you're from Norway."

"It's way too cold to surf in Norway."

"You'll need a thick wetsuit. But you know liquid water can never be colder than zero degrees Celsius," the Berber/surf instructor/evolutionary biologist and now apparently also physicist replied and continued: "There is even a Norwegian pro surfer now on the World Surf League Men's Championship Tour. Erik Rønneberg. Cool dude. Really, really good surfer. Think he'll win some of the big competitions in the next couple of years. He stops by in Thagazout at least once a year. Just surfed with him in January for a few days. He said that there are quite some nice waves around a place called Godshus, or something like that."

Later that day in the evening when Faiza was lying in bed, her body and mind miraculously content despite the fact that every single one of her muscles seemed to ache, she decided to check on the internet in the morning if there was any hospital located in Godshus.

Perhaps she could find a position there, after the entire fiasco with the Ocean Gala. Perhaps it would be a place where she could work and learn to surf at the same time.

Back home. In Norway.

* * *

←··· 177 ○◎○ 222 ···→

December 6th, 2017
Dr. Faiza Abdi Noor
Godshus – Norway

Wednesday

It was always inspiring for Faiza to see Rima Iraki[1] and Yama Wolasmal[2] announce the news on NRK Dagsrevyen. Palestinian-Lebanese. Afghani. Little symbols that integration might work. But, of course, today it would also be interesting how NRK handled who would report the news. Not that she really cared if the embassy of the United States would be located in Tel Aviv or Jerusalem, but surely a lot of people would.

Okay, interesting it looked like a Norwegian colleague would take the controversial news block for Rima—a diplomatic solution.

The phone rang.

"Yes?"

"Dr. Noor, sorry for calling but the patient in bed number three is starting to desaturate on the BIPAP. Could you come over, please?"

"Of course. On my way, Louise."

She had the feeling that the BIPAP would not be enough for the patient and that he would end up intubated. The man looked like he would be easy to intubate, but perhaps it still would be better to call the anesthesiologist for help. Of course, situations like this had been much easier to deal with back in Aker Sykehus in Oslo

---

1 **Rima Iraki** – Norwegian journalist and news anchor for NRK's evening news program Dagsrevyen. She came to Norway when she was five years old. Her parents are Palestinian and Lebanese.

2 **Yama Wolasmal** – Norwegian journalist and news anchor for NRK's evening news program Dagsrevyen. He came to Norway when he was four years old. He was born in Kabul, Afghanistan.

where there was always somebody in the building to help. Here at Godshus General Hospital, it was just herself at the moment. It was not too late in the evening, so at least she did not need to wake them up. Perhaps she could adjust the BIPAP settings a bit so that at least her anesthesiology colleague could finish watching Dagsrevyen.

She opened the door of the call room and walked over to the intensive care unit.

* * *

←··· 219 ○◎○ 179 ···→

May 9th, 2018
Dr. Faiza Abdi Noor
Godshus – Norway

Wednesday

Faiza parked her car in front of the building, which housed the bowling alley and the Vinmonopolet[1] store. Across the street was the one structure in town which managed to be even uglier than Godshus General Hospital. It contained the Folkebibliotek.[2] She walked down the street, past the flower shop. She never quite understood why it had to be the flower shop that size-wise was the biggest store in the short street, which had been simply named 'Gate 1'[3] and was what one would consider the bustling downtown center of Godshus. After that, she passed the first of two hairdresser salons, in fierce competition with the other about fifty meters down the street.

Of course, neither of them knew how to deal with her hair and therefore she did not frequent either. She entered the lobby of the Sparebanken Vest[4] where she had opened an account after she realized how high the fees were when she used the ATMs to pick up money in Godshus from the account she had with DNB[5] in Oslo. She picked up some cash from the ATM and then crossed the street to a small store, which was a mix of drugstore and beauty shop. After trying out several of the perfumes, she bought one in a small black square-shaped flacon: The One Desire from Dolce&Gabbana.

---

1 **Vinmonopolet** – *Norwegian*: 'The Wine Monopoly' is an alcoholic beverage retail chain owned by the Norwegian government.

2 **Folkebibliotek** – *Norwegian*: Public library.

3 **Gate** – *Norwegian*: Street.

4 **Sparebanken Vest** – *Norwegian*: 'Savings Bank West'.

5 **DNB** – *Norwegian*: Den Norske Bank. 'The Norwegian Bank'.

She then returned to her car.

Faiza did not meet anybody on the street—neither on her way from her car to the drugstore/beauty shop nor on her way back. It was just herself walking around in the bustling downtown center of Godshus that early Wednesday afternoon.

She turned on the radio in the car on her drive back home. It was announced in the news that the day prior the president of the United States had decided to withdraw from the Iranian nuclear agreement.

* * *

←··· 285 ○◎○ 380 ···→

July 13th, 2019
Dr. Faiza Abdi Noor
Godshus – Norway

Saturday

The phone in Faiza's hand began to tremble when she read what had popped up in her Facebook feed:

Inna lillahi wa inna ilayhi raji'un.[1] It is with great sorrow and regret that we confirm the unexpected and tragic loss of ...

The woman had been such an inspiration to her. Posts on Instagram showing the country she was born in not in the normal way. Not war, but palm trees. Not people fleeing, but children playing on a beach. Because of her, she had briefly even thought about how to help. She had found out that a nursing program was now being taught in the port city of Kismaayo.[2] She had considered perhaps one day going over to help. Maybe teach?

But now the woman who had been such an inspiration to her was dead.

Killed when the hotel she was staying in was attacked by terrorists.

* * *

←··· 390 ○◎○ 103 ···→

---

1 **Inna lillahi wa inna ilayhi raji'un** – *Arabic:* We belong to Allah, and we will return to Him.

2 **Kismaayo** – Somalian city located in southern Lower Juba with a population of about 150000 people.

July 16th, 2019
Dr. Faiza Abdi Noor
Godshus – Norway

Tuesday

Faiza pushed down the key labelled CNTR and the key with the S on it simultaneously. The window on the screen opened. She updated the file name to 'CV—Dr. Faiza Abdi Noor—2019' and saved it that way.

She would need it for all the e-mails she would be sending out. Working at Godshus had been fun. Yes, she got to surf a bit—but the waves here were just too big for her most of the time of the year. Unfortunately, she had been just too old when she became a surfer to be charging here. She would have completed all the requirements to be allowed to do her Internal Medicine specialty exam by the end of the year. But what was next? Should she specialize further? She always liked cardiology. Perhaps she should give that a try? But there were just so few training spots. She would have to apply all over Norway. Maybe even to some places in Sweden.

Faiza then opened the internet browser. She decided to check out the website of *Verdens Gang*. Amid all the gossip on the daily tabloid it was interesting to read that earlier that day Ursula von der Leyen was elected President of the European Commission, the first woman to hold that office.

* * *

←⋯ 103 ○◎○ 294 ⋯→

October 8th, 2019
Dr. Faiza Abdi Noor
Godshus – Norway

Tuesday

"Hey, Faiza. Pia just called me from the hospital. She just got a fifty-something-year-old guy, who has an anterior ST-elevation myocardial infarction. I'm going to drive in to put a stent in. If you want, meet me there in twenty-five minutes and we can do it together."

She was just about to scrub the pot in which she had prepared her pasta breakfast-dinner, after she woke up about an hour earlier. She had been on call the night before. The clock in her car showed 21:27 when she started driving to the hospital. It still surprised her how helpful he had been since she had handed in her resignation. He had been nice enough to contact the professor of the cardiology department in Lund, where she would start January. It would only be a six-month job for now, but she wanted to really try the cardiology thing. He also went on allowing her even more than before to assist him, when he was doing his cardiac catheterizations and for the non-emergent ones allowed her to do the procedure on her own while he was standing next to her; his hands carefully guiding her motions if this was necessary. He had asked for her private cell phone number. They had agreed that he would always call her if he was called in during the night to do an emergent stent for somebody having a heart attack. But she had the feeling that there was something more than him just being a friendly mentor. It was as if the way he smiled at her had changed the day she had dropped off her resignation letter in his office.

But it might just have been an impression.

"But Faiza, you're moving to Malmö in December. How do you think that should work with us then? Let's just be honest to each other. We had fun together. Let's stay friends." The math and physics teacher, who had started teaching at the Godshus Upper School the school year prior, had told her this back in September when they decided to mutually end their relationship, which had lasted a little over a year. He had always been gentle with her but she could understand that his patience had run out. Of course, she only found out later from one of the nurses who worked in the operating room that all along he had been cheating on her with the history and sociology teacher. In a way it was good—she would leave Godshus behind with no sort of attachment.

She hurriedly put on her scrubs, but did not have time to put her contacts back in and she drove to the hospital wearing her glasses with the heavy black frame.

"With the STEMIs it is basically the same like the routine stents. But, of course, one tries to do things as quickly as possible." Both had gotten sterile and the patient, who was a fisherman, was lying on the cath lab table in operating room 2.

"Also, one can see much more arrhythmias—Ventricular tachycardia and Ventricular fibrillation—during the procedure. That's why I always put the defibrillation pads on the patient. It's an extra cost, of course, and a single-use product. But it can be quite a hassle to defibrillate under the C-arm with everyone being sterile."

He used his right hand to steer hers, holding the probing needle when she missed the artery the first time. The pulsating splash of blood appeared in the syringe and she quickly put the guide-wire into the patient's femoral artery. She was able to perform the subsequent steps quite efficiently on her own.

As always, Dr. Boisen-Jensen had put on some classical music in the background, which was coming from a Bang & Olufsen speaker, which he had insisted to be kept for this purpose on one of the shelves in operating room number '2'. Classical music was definitely a habit of his.

After they injected the dye, it was clear that the patient's LAD was completely obstructed about half-way and that its occlusion was causing his heart attack. The fisherman's other coronary arteries looked okay. Faiza got the stent that Dr. Boisen-Jensen had selected into the right spot and they inflated the balloon, carefully watching what the patient's ECG rhythm was doing on the monitor. No serious arrhythmias, just a couple of PVCs.

"How are you feeling, sir?" Faiza asked.

"Much better," the fisherman said.

Faiza felt proud.

The images they did after the stent was in place showed that blood was again flowing normally through the patient's coronary artery.

"Great job, Faiza! Your first stent in a STEMI patient. Should we look at the images once more on the computer in my office and write the note?" Dr. Boisen-Jensen asked.

They walked over to the chief physician's office. He pulled up a chair next to his and loaded the films showing the fisherman's coronary anatomy on his computer screen. He explained to her what made him decide on the size of the stent they used and pointed out some minor narrowings in the other arteries, which however were not really relevant for tonight. Faiza then logged into her EMR profile from his computer and quickly typed up a note summarizing what they had done. She logged out of the system and as she was about to get up from the chair Dr. Boisen-Jensen took out a box with AirPods from his pocket.

"Should we have a small dance to celebrate your first successful stent in a STEMI patient?"

This was absolutely not what she had expected.

"Dance? Here?"

Faiza noticed a confident, knowing smile in his face, a smile that appeared warm and genuine.

"Well, there aren't too many places to go for a dance in Godshus, are there? So why not use our conference room?"

Faiza looked into his eyes and saw that they were full of power and desire. He stretched out his palm, which was filled with one AirPod. She looked back at him. His still warm and genuine smile made her take the one AirPod and put it into her ear.

"Anders, are you trying to seduce me here?"

He was silent for just a moment.

"You're a very smart and very beautiful woman, Faiza."

As Tango music started playing in her right ear, he stood up from his chair and held out his hand. She hesitated. Clearly, she had mistaken her mentor's patience with her in cardiology things, with something else.

But what was wrong with a dance? Purely objectively, he was not completely unattractive. Of course, at least fifteen years older than her—much older than the other men she had ever dated. But the starting grayness of his sideburns and his slim, almost ascetic body had something attractive about it. In its own way. Plus, she would be out of here soon. Her last shift at Godshus General Hospital would be at the end of December. She would be celebrating this year's New Year's eve in Southern Sweden. Why not have a small celebratory dance in the conference room of a rural hospital in the middle of nowhere in Norway? And it was tango. She would not have expected him to be a tango dancer. And how could he possibly know that she liked dancing tango? In the end, it was the genuine and not at all desperate look on his face, which made her reach for his hand and get up from the chair. He led her out of the office into the conference room, which was only dimly illuminated by the light shining through the glass partition wall from his office. Gently he pulled her towards himself and they started dancing, their bodies separated at arm's length, embracing just with their arms and their hands.

They fell quickly into the music as they danced around the conference room table. He was a very good dancer.

Tango dancing in the hospital's conference room. It was fun. Relaxing in a special kind of way. Perhaps even a bit romantic.

After a while, the music stopped.

"Faiza. Thanks for dancing with me. Okay, one last tango before we call it a night," Anders said. "Hey Siri. Play *Por una Cabeza*."

"Okay, let's hear *Por una Cabeza* by Carlos Gardel with lyrics by Alfredo Le Pera," the virtual voice said, acknowledging his request.

She felt how his palm slid from its prior position on top of her right shoulder blade and now lingered on her lower back. The force with which the fingers of his left hand were threaded through hers increased. And just like that, their embrace was suddenly no longer at arm's length.

They started dancing again.

Her breasts pressing into his chest.

The lobe of her ear feeling his breath.

When the music stopped both of them were standing at the edge of the table which was closest to the fire escape exit. Farthest away from the Chief Physician's office, next to the chair Dr. Andersen would sit on during the morning meetings. Faiza's back was facing the conference room table, only able to make out a silhouette of Anders in the room, which was almost completely dark. She felt how he let go of her and how their bodies separated. For a very short while, there was nothing but silence and darkness, until she saw how the shadows of two hands lifted from below. In a powerful but gentle way, his palms cupped her cheeks from both sides. She retreated a step backward, bumping into the conference room table. Before she could think anything more, his shadow leaned down towards her.

"Can I kiss you?" Anders whispered. "You can say 'no'." The shadow of his body moved closer to her.

Should she shove him back now? Knee him in the groin? Faiza wanted to look him in his eyes, but could not see anything because of the darkness. Would he respect a 'no.'? Would he let her go? Step away from her?

She recalled his confident and knowing smile, the power, and desire in his eyes. Therefore, she decided not to resist. His hands moved away from her cheeks onto her biceps. She felt how their foreheads touched, then their noses. She could feel his breath on her lips when they became impossibly close. Then, when he barely brushed his lips over hers, she first pulled back just a bit, but then shifted forward, sealing both of them together. The way his tongue slipped into her mouth sent shivers through her body. Hesitantly and softly, at first, her tongue started kissing him back. She felt how his hands appreciated her, touching her shoulders, brushing against her breasts. She was surprised how good his hands felt on her body. She did not know what made it happen, but she desired Anders' hands to touch her bare skin. Her left hand searched for his right, and when she found it, guided it under her scrub top. She sensed how his fingers explored her. Moving up from the left side of her abdomen, circling her left breast through her bra. Then two fingers carefully entering under her bra from above, seeking her nipple, caressing it briefly before moving away towards her breastbone. His hand wandering downwards now, halting just above her navel.

It was only now that their lips parted.

"Belly-button piercing. Very sexy," spoken softly, before his lips started kissing her in a path leading from the corner of her mouth towards her left ear while his hand continued moving downwards on her abdomen. The prickling feeling on her cheek made Faiza tilt her head backwards, exposing her neck. He immediately altered the route of his kisses, burying his face in her neck, while his fingers slipped underneath the worn elastic of her scrub pants that were strung across the points of her hips. By now neither his lips nor fingers felt frightening. He knew very well what he was doing. And there was no way she could deny that her body liked, what his skillful hands, tongue, lips, and teeth were doing to her.

And so what happened next was as if Faiza's body had pushed ▶ whereas her mind desperately tried to find ⏸.

Her glasses were suddenly on the midst of the conference room table.

Her scrub top dropped on the middle chair where Dr. Gianetti always sat.

Her bra on the floor close to the fire escape door, where it had landed after it initially had been thrown against the glass partition wall next to it as it had been removed so energetically.

Her naked buttocks sitting on the conference room table approximately in the same place where Dr. Andersen would push her elbows against, when she listened to the stories of the new patients

233

who had been admitted over night, after his hands under her knees had lifted her there.

By the time she heard Anders ripping open a condom package, her mind had given up on finding 🔳. At that point in time—due to the lack of any GHB in her system—it of course would have been Faiza's body who would have pushed 🔳 as she became aware of the tensing in her lower region caused by the memory of the pain coming back.

But actually no 🔳 or 🔳 was necessary at all.

Because, so it occurred, that in the very moment, when Faiza felt how the condom wrapped glans of Dr. Boisen-Jensen's penis started pressing against her outer sex a brief cracking sound in the hospital loudspeaker system was followed by an overhead announcement:

"Medical Code ICU bed 4. Medical Code ICU bed 4. Medical Code ICU bed 4."

⏏

* * *

←⋯ 363 ○◎○ 303 ⋯→

November 22nd, 2019
Dr. Faiza Abdi Noor
Godshus – Norway

Friday

Faiza felt the slight vibration of her phone. It was a new Messenger message from her relative—Taban's mom—in Copenhagen.

How are things? All packed? When shall I pick you up?

She typed back:

Working tonight. But all good. Not packed yet. Have my flight booked for the 29th of December How're you doing cousin?

Was super busy. But the project is finished. Wanna see it?

The ad for SAS?

Yep. It's done now. Just completed the editing.

It was more out of wanting to be polite and respectful towards the creative mind of her cousin, than out of any actual interest in what a video advertisement for an airline would look like that she wrote back:

Of course. Would love to see it!

Okay. Here you go. Let me know what you think. Don't share it with anyone, please!!! It'll only come out in February 2020. They'll fire me if it gets sent around before that.

Given the slow network connection in Godhus, it took some time until the small picture with the play button in the middle had completely loaded in the Messenger app. She started the video and a voice of a female narrator said the following:

What is really Scandinavian? Abso-fucking-lutely nothing.
Nada. **Niente.** *Nope, there's*
NO. SUCH. THING.

All is copied. EVERYTHING.
Our democracy?
Credit goes to **Greece**.
Parental leave?
Dankeschön—Merci beaucoup—Grazie mille—Engraziel fetg.
Switzerland.
*The iconic Scandinavian windmills were actually invented in **Iran**
and we made the **German** bicycle a staple of our cities.*
Rugbrød?
It's **Turkish**.
Smørrebrød?
The Netherlands.
Love licorice?
It's **Chinese**.
And what about the midsummer maypole?
German.
*But it gets much, much worse: Rumor has it even Swedish meatballs
might not be as Swedish as you think, but from **Türkiye!***
HUH!
Even the Danish isn't Danish.
It's from Vienna.[1]

*And the very pride of Norway—the paperclip[2]—was actually in-
vented by an **American**. (But anyhow, thanks to everyone in Norway
who was wearing them in the 1940s …)*

---

1 In Denmark the 'Danish' is called *wienerbrød ('Bread from Vienna')*.
2 Following the Nazi occupation of Norway in spring 1940, students at Oslo University started wearing paperclips on their lapels
as a non-violent symbol of resistance. As the wearing of Norwegian
insignia had already been outlawed the symbolism of the paperclip
holding things together was chosen to project national unity, further
strengthened by the widespread, but false, belief that the Norwegian
Johan Vaaler was the original inventor of the paperclip.

JULEBORD (The Holiday Party)

*While we're at it **America**, thank you for taking the first baby steps in empowering the women's rights movement and—in general—taking it upon you to try to use your power to stand up for freedom, liberty and universal human rights in this world.*

*OK, **America** sometimes you screw up big time in doing so—but overall?*
To err when you try is human—true failure is only twofold:
you either don't try at all or you don't learn from the errors of prior tries.

(Because sometimes wearing a paperclip is not enough. If really needed you must untwine it and stab eyeballs to blind aggressors ...)

We in Scandinavia are no better than our ancestors with their Viking longships. We just take everything we like with us when we travel abroad, adjust it a tiny bit and
voilà.
It's something uniquely Scandinavian.
Travelling the world inspires us to think
BIG
even though we are quite
small
because every time we go beyond our border, we add
progress, innovations, colors,
adding the best of everywhere ... to right *HERE.*
In a way, Scandinavia was brought here.
Little piece by little piece.

By everyday humans, who found the very best of our home away from home.
So, we can't wait to see what amazing things you bring home next.
WE ALL ARE TRAVELERS. SAS.

237

With a wide-open mouth, she put down her phone on the table. After some time, a new message arrived:

Still there?

WOW. I LOVE IT!

Thank you!

So if we ever go to Somalia to visit, we should definitively fly SAS.

I don't think they ✈ there …

Well, if they ever will, I'll ✈ with them!

But what would you do in 🏴??? 🎥

You know the 🌊 🏄 *must actually be really good in some places there! And the weather* 🌑 *is definitively better than in Scandinavia in the middle of winter!*

A surf trip to 🏴 *?!* 🙉

Why not? Some day?

LOL. Okay. What airline are you flying from Godshus to Copenhagen?

SAS—that's the only airline we have here.

* * *

←⋯ 111 ○◎○ 113 ⋯→

December 14th, 2019
Dr. Faiza Abdi Noor
Leonkulen Glacier – Norway

Saturday

"I'll be right back," Faiza said.

"Okay. I'll put on some music."

Anders had taken off the bathrobe already, and the state his penis was in was a clear indication of what would happen next. The unusually large vein, which continued to fascinate Faiza, was throbbing expectantly.

He had surprised her with the short trip.

"You'll be off to Malmö soon. We might not see each other that often anymore."

She liked the hotel. There were very few other guests. The receptionist had greeted Anders in a very friendly manner, and Faiza got the feeling that she knew him. They ate an early light dinner and then went to the spa. There were only two other couples. She had put her head into his lap while they were in the sauna—he preferred to sit while she opted to lie down. While he was stroking her sweaty forehead, she felt his growing erection through the towel. It quickly vanished, after he plunged into the ice-cold pool.

Laws of nature also applied to Anders; at least temporarily.

She went to the bathroom. Her cosmetic bag was on the granite sink countertop. She opened it and took out the dropping bottle with the GHB. She had two of them. She always kept one in her cosmetic bag and one in her handbag. Anders had insisted that they always meet at the house he was living in for the last two months since they had started sleeping with each other. Meeting there afforded both of them discretion, which was not assured in her apartment complex where several of the nurses working at Godshus General Hospital also lived. Anders had even given her a key, so she could sleep at his house after being on call, before he would come back in the afternoon and wake her up with a 'dinner-breakfast' in bed. A fanfare of horn music began playing from the room. She lifted the bottle with the salty clear liquid and was startled. It was completely empty. The last two months she had only used the GHB, which she had in the bottle in her handbag before they had sex. She had forgotten to check the bottle in her cosmetic bag before leaving. And where was her handbag?

At home, of course.

"But you have your key and your phone. Do you need anything else? We'll be back tomorrow afternoon." was what Anders had told her when she had realized that she had forgotten her handbag after she sat down next to him in the passenger seat of his car. When she looked at the mix of snow and rain falling from the sky outside, she had decided not to return to the apartment but stay in the warmth of the car.

What should she do now?

Never had she slept with a man without first taking her little dose of GHB. It was her necessary ritual. To relax her. To enable her to take control of the memory of the pain.

Of course, she had not told any of them about the salty, clear liquid. Not to the ICU nurse, she had been dating for almost four years while she was still in Oslo, but who ended up being less of the support she expected during the time when her dad became sick. It also became more and more clear over time that his ego could not handle the inherent: he—nurse, she—doctor divide between them going forward. Clearly, she did not confess to any of the few Tinder dates she had hooked up with, in the times after she had broken up with him, and neither to the Berber/surf instructor/evolutionary biologist/physicist in Morocco, whose advances she just could not resist in the end. And likewise not the math and physics teacher at the Godshus Upper School. And clearly, Anders knew nothing about the bottles with the salty, clear liquid in them. Flutes and violins now joined the horns in the fanfares, which were coming from the bedroom.

JULEBORD (The Holiday Party)

She recalled how Anders had been the first night when they actually did have sex at his house. When she, after that unexpected advancement in the hospital's conference room in the middle of the night, had reluctantly agreed to meet once more, after he had apologized the next morning in the catheterization lab; after he had shown her how to change a pacemaker generator. His convincing "I can't stop thinking of you". His invitation to take her out to the fancy underwater restaurant. His stories during the dinner about how he learned to dance Tango in Argentina. All his words that made her feel special. Her attitude being that in any case things would not last long as she would be in Malmö soon, so why not try to perhaps have some fun. The glass of wine in his living room. Him talking about the classical music that he put on.

And then—once they got naked in the bedroom—how it had been him, who totally unexpectedly hit ⏸️ that night. Immediately after he fully realized what had been done to her as a child. Not like the other men, who Faiza always suspected pretended they did not notice and just kept going. And if they would ever ask her anything about it, would only do so after they had satisfied themselves. Of course, with the exception of a pale-skinned, freckled, redhead Scottish DJ. But in contrast to him, Anders did have two intact testicles and not just one. Anders starting the conversation: "I know it will not be easy for you to talk about this."

How Anders then, after he had not only asked her about what happened, but wanted to know every detail of how it affected her, what worked for her and what not, what he needed to be aware of. His non-judgmental way about all of it. Then, after they were done talking, he just began giving her a back massage. How the conversation and the following massage took so long that she actually needed to quickly disappear into the restroom for a second time that night and for the first time ever in her life needed to take a second small dose of her GHB, as the first dose had long been out of her system by the time they were ready to hit the ▶️ button together. And how the ▶️ that followed, not only that night but all the others as well, was definitively the best ▶️ she had experienced.

241

It was time to return to the bedroom.

The fanfares of horns, violins, and flutes paused briefly, and then it was mostly the violins taking over.

"What's playing?" she asked.

"Tchaikovsky. Guess it's almost Christmas, so I thought *The Nutcracker* would be appropriate."

He was holding a small flask-shaped bottle labelled with a number '1' in his hand. It was opened.

"What are you drinking?"

"Just having a little nightcap of flavoured akvavit."

"Flavoured akvavit?"

"Yes. I found it in the Duty-Free in Copenhagen Airport when I was flying back from Paris in the summer. A tiny distillery on Bornholm makes it. They have eight different flavours. Number '1' is flavoured with chili peppers—that's my second most favorite. The one I like most is number '7'—flavoured with licorice."

"Akvavit with licorice or chili peppers?"

"Wanna try?"

"Nah. No, thank you."

Anders took another small sip from the bottle, closed it, and put it down on the bedside table.

"Look at me," he whispered into Faiza's ear. "You're so sexy."

He gradually took off her bathrobe. He tasted a bit like hot chili peppers. She felt how his hands were touching her in all the places. Caressing her patiently. His lips moving around her. His eyes observing her for her reactions. His fingers tangling her hair.

Then slowly and unrushed, the light pressure of his warm hand clasping her, fingers slipping inside her, his lips against her lips now again. Him now tasting less like hot chili peppers. Her body was shortly surprised when his lips were suddenly gone; but she knew from before that they would swiftly return after the ripping sound coming from the condom's foil wrapper stopped.

Anders and condoms. Never, ever having sex without one. Well, at least she did not have to restart taking the pill. She never liked how it affected her mood.

He was gentle. Not frightening. Knowing what he was doing. He parted her legs with ease. She felt his crown pressing against her opening. There was no anxiety with him. No tensing. The only thing she felt was how wet she was—how very fucking wet. He was no longer tasting like hot chili. She felt how he pressed into her. She gasped as he slowly entered her without her mind being manipulated by the small molecule she thought she would always need. A sense of liberation made her exhale loudly.

"Shhh," he murmured—falsely interpreted the heavy breath as a sign of discomfort and not of relief. "Shhh, it's all right, don't worry, just relax, listen to your body."

His hands touched her soothingly. Then he started to rhythmically pulse his hips back and forth, slow and gentle, but determined. It was his firm, patient approach, which made her flesh melt around him. No more pain. The way he filled her with sweetness overwhelmed her. He pushed everything away. The memories of the pain, the scars, the unsure naked men, the salty taste of the clear liquid. She lost all sense of time, as he skillfully fucked her from her past into her future. Her entire body shook and shook and shook.

When just before the music ended with an intense drum finale, his thrusting stopped, she wanted to continue to feel him inside herself.

Faiza stroked his right cheek with her hands and their eyes briefly met.

"Please stay. Stay. Just stay within me. Don't go."

He looked surprised, perhaps even tired a bit, in the yellowish light of the lamp standing on the nightstand which they had kept on. She felt how he gave in to her desire to hold on to him. His body spread out on top of her. She felt how he was gradually getting flaccid inside her. He appeared more relaxed to her than the other nights. He rested his heavy head on her left shoulder. She felt how his breathing was getting quiet and regular. She glanced over to look at his eyes and saw that he had fallen asleep. She lay there for a while with him. Just still. Enjoying the moment. Then she decided to carefully roll him over to her left side. His body only shivered briefly once, but he did not wake up.

She could no longer feel him inside her.

And so it occurred that when his no longer erect penis, with the nevertheless still prominent vein, brushed first against her left inner and then outer thighs she could sense an unusual wetness on her skin. She took the index and middle finger of her right hand and brushed them over the moist feeling places and sensed a slightly viscous fluid on her fingertips. She carefully sat up in bed looking at his penis, which still had the now wrinkled condom attached. After she had carefully removed it so that he would not wake up, she could see that it was empty. It had a small rip at its tip. She got up, went to the bathroom, and put the contraceptive in the garbage after wrapping it in a piece of toilet paper.

She decided not to wake him up because of this and fell into a deep sleep next to him.

* * *

←⋯ 367 ○◎○ 407 ⋯→

December 19th, 2019
Dr. Faiza Abdi Noor
Godshus – Norway

Thursday

Faiza allowed her torso to collapse onto his chest. The fine sweat from their bodies started mixing, and she felt how the repeating contractions of his chest wall muscles gently stimulated her nipples differently than his hands had before. In between the radiating waves of pleasure, his pulsations in her slowed and weakened. She had never felt closer to Anders than now, not even during the past weekend. Simultaneously shared bliss. The other times he had always been the gentlemen. Finishing only after her. She had needed tonight.

Like last Saturday—and then again Sunday after he brought her breakfast to bed, she had not taken the couple of drops of the salty clear liquid. But tonight was the first night she had done so by choice. Leaving the about a third filled bottle with the GHB in her handbag. Was all of this with him just sex? Or has it become something different? Was making love a better word? At this moment, she just had the urge to kiss him. She moved her head up towards him. Pressed her lips on his and made her tongue enter. All she wanted was to taste him. He slowly slipped out of her. Faiza stopped kissing him and lay down her head left ear first onto his chest, hearing his irregular and slowing heartbeat and the metallic sound from the artificial valve in his heart. She closed her eyes. It was only now that she noticed. The room was silent. No classical music playing for the first time. Just the noises coming from their bodies the entire evening. Anders' hand caressed her hair.

Eventually, he got up and went to the bathroom. She heard how he peed. When he came back, he just stood at the end of the bed, naked. She glanced at him. His face appeared strange. Insecure.

245

Pensive. A moment later it turned hard, which contrasted with the current state of his penis with the ever-present prominent vein. Anders seemed to be searching for what words to say. But before he could say anything, Faiza smiled at him.

"Anders. Come to Malmö with me."

"What are you talking about?"

She sat up in the bed against the headboard. The insecurity in his face was gone.

"I want you to come to Malmö with me."

"No. Never. Faiza. What do you think this was about the last two months? This wasn't about fucking love. Or fucking commitment. This was just about fucking, nothing else. And don't tell me I ever promised you something else."

"Anders!" For a short while she felt like crying.

"Faiza! What do you want? My soul? I'm not built that way!"

"But we do have a relationship?"

"Faiza. What relationship? Never. We didn't have a relationship. Never. I don't do relationships. I have sex with women. That's it."

For the last time, she looked at him in a questioning way.

"Faiza. We had a lot of good boom, boom—but now is clearly the time to say ciao! Just go now. And please leave the keys on the kitchen table."

She was trembling. But she knew one thing. This was not the time to show weakness. She got out of the bed and stood next to him. She wouldn't let him hurt her. She was stronger than this. What a loser. It was she who would have the last word.

"You have said enough, Anders. I understand you now. I just have to be ashamed of what I thought my feelings were about you. I'm sorry for taking up so much of your time. Live long, and prosper!"

Faiza quickly collected her clothes, closed the bedroom door behind her, and walked down the stairs to the living room. She got dressed in a hurry. It was the moment she took out Anders' keys from the handbag that the anger in her came up and the loathing for revenge. She noticed the dipper bottle with the GHB at the bottom of her purse. With shaking hands, she took out the bottle and the keys and went to the kitchen. She opened the refrigerator. She saw the two small flask-shaped bottles of the flavored aquavit. Number '1'—chili peppers, number '7'—licorice. She decided to take out the bottle with the number '7' on it. It was about half empty. She hastily unscrewed the bottle. Her hands were shaking a lot more now, and she had to take two deep breaths, but then was able to remove the dropper from her GHB bottle and poured whatever GHB was left into the aquavit bottle. Her hands stopped shaking; and she screwed the lid back on, put the licorice-flavored Aquavit/GHB mix into the refrigerator, dropped the keys to his house on the kitchen counter, and walked out.

The moment she got into her car, her phone announced a new message. It was from him: three four-letter words separated by two hyphens. The first two identical words written in small caps only and the last word written in ALL CAPS. Angrily, she first deleted the message, and then his contact info from her phone.

* * *

←··· 185 ∘◎∘ 125 ···→

December 20th, 2019
Dr. Faiza Abdi Noor
Godshus – Norway

Friday – 18:27

boom – boom – CIAO

Anders' message still hurt. But just a bit. Much less so than last night.

Faiza stopped the car in front of the small modern apartment building. She was about five minutes early. She had agreed with Per to pick him up. She would never drink more than one glass of wine during a Julebord, and that way at least her colleague could celebrate a bit.

She had only worked from 12:30 until 17:45, when the doctor from Bergen whom they hired to work as a locum for the night took over. A couple of more hours working on Sunday and that would be it here. Done with Godshus General Hospital. Done with Godshus. And as things were solely about boom-boom, she would leave with no strings attached. In a way, it was good that way. She had considered showing up to the morning meeting just to say a formal goodbye to her colleagues. But she woke up still a bit too upset, and as she would see all of them in the evening, it was not really necessary.

On her way to the hospital, she longed to reward herself a little and therefore decided to quickly stop by at the small perfume store in town. Her mood liked a Chanel perfume the most—aptly named 'Chance' when she considered her situation.

Perhaps all of this was a chance for her future? Of course, she still felt hurt—upset about Anders. He had clearly just used her, but had she been abused? She did not say no to dancing tango with him back in October. And honestly, she had enjoyed things. Just because

Anders had rejected her did not mean she should also reject herself. It would not mean that no one would ever love her anymore. She understood why things had to happen this way. He was too old for her. But mere understanding does not chase away pain. On the other hand, letting someone go sometimes could be the best thing you could do for yourself.

Just before paying, she remembered she was out of tampons. Her period would start in a couple of days, perhaps on Sunday already, and she, therefore, walked back to the appropriate aisle and grabbed a box of Mini Tampons made by Ginger Organic.

After a very quiet several hours at Godshus General Hospital, that had been mostly spent chatting to the nurses about everything that had happened in the morning, Faiza quickly gave her signout to the locum from Bergen and then changed into something festive in the call room. She refreshed her makeup, put on her deep red lipstick, and used the newly bought perfume. Then she left the hospital and drove off to pick up Per.

Teetotalist waiting outside—take your time.

The very moment she had sent the text to Per, the lights on the outside walkway turned on. She tracked how Per walked down the outside stairs and towards her car. He opened the door on the passenger side and got in. His face looked surprisingly fresh for having worked the previous night, and then also considering what had happened in the morning.

"Ciao!"

Although something in her almost made her ask 'BOOM-BOOM?' after a momentary pause she ended up saying:

"Goddagens![1] So you're Italian now?"

Per laughed. "No. It was actually Dr. Gianetti who told me to greet you this way tonight."

"Dr. Gianetti?"

---

1 **Goddagens** – *Swedish*: Formal way of saying 'hello' in Sweden, that is a little more happy or friendly than the very formal 'goddag'. Overall, most often the informal 'hej' is used.

"Yes. He asked me after today's morning meeting how I would get to the Julebord tonight and if I would need a lift with Dr. Rønneberg and himself. But then I told him that we had already agreed that you would drive tonight. So he just said: 'Well make sure you greet her with a 'Ciao', that's really nice of her, driving you, so you can party."

Faiza started the car and drove out of the parking lot.

"The nurses told me it was quite a show this morning at the meeting."

"Ah, whatever. He was somehow pissed and in a really bad mood. Honestly, it's his problem." Faiza was a bit fascinated how easily Per brushed things aside.

"How was your partial call?" he asked.

"Quiet. Friday before Christmas. Did you get some sleep?"

"Got a short surf session in right when I came back from work and then slept. It was still quite blown out and choppy. But tomorrow morning should be really nice waves. Erik will be back here for the holidays. Hopefully, we'll get out just before my call tomorrow. You want to join us?"

"Per. You know that even in summer G-point is always too big for me. The only thing I can surf is gentle summer waves at H-bay."

The fact that Per had invited her to surf together, however, made her feel special in a way.

"Mind if we put on some music?" Per asked.

"No, of course not … go ahead? What are you gonna play?"

"R.E.M."

While she was driving, Per somehow managed to convince her car's entertainment system to play a song from his phone. After a short drum roll, the lyrics started playing:

That's great.

Finally. No more flutes, horns, or violins. They sat silently for the rest of the drive. It started to drizzle outside, but the cloud cover was thin and the sea appeared stormy on the driver's side under the faint light of the half-moon.

250

JULEBORD (The Holiday Party)

It's the end of the world as we know it ... was how the song ended just as she turned left into the restaurant's parking lot.

She parked the car next to a Land Rover.

They got out and walked over a small metal bridge. A bike leaned against the railing opposite the entrance door. Per held the door for her and Faiza stepped into the emerald-greenish light which rose from the depth of the restaurant.

* * *

←··· 189 ○◎○ 317 ···→

Chapter 4
Dr. Pia Andersen

March 17th, 1985
Dr. Pia Andersen
Frederiksberg – Denmark

Sunday

"There was a pool on the ship?" Pia just could not understand.

"You know, they built it more like a cruise ship."

"A cruise ship? But where do they put all the cars, then?"

"Well, it's a very special ship. The lower part was built like a ferry, so all the cars can go in there. And the upper part is more like a cruise ship. They had it sail in America first."

"In America?"

"Yes. Between New York and the Bahamas. But that didn't work out as they had planned. So now it's sailing between Copenhagen and Oslo. But not for much longer."

"Why?"

"Well, they just sold it. So it's going to be a cruise ship again."

"So people will swim in the pool again."

"Yes. I guess so. If it's going to go somewhere warmer. My boss also told me they are going to rename it."

"They can just change the name of a ship?"

"Yes. If the new owner wants, they can do that."

"So is that why you and Mom did the trip? So that you can see the ship while it's still here?"

"You are so smart, Pia. Yes, that was one reason. Also, mom and I just wanted to have a little mini vacation. And you had a good time with Grandpa? Or not?"

"Of course, we always have a good time with Grandpa! So what will the new name of the ship be?"

"Stardancer."

"I think I liked the name Scandinavia better."

JULEBORD (The Holiday Party)

Pia was happy that her parents were both home. It was so nice that Dad was at home much more now and not away on a ship for such long stretches as before. As before mom got sick and needed to sit in her wheelchair.

* * *

←·· 66 ○◎○ 70 ··→

April 15th, 1995
Dr. Pia Andersen
Copenhagen – Denmark

Saturday

The smile in grandpa's face made Pia sad. It was still difficult to see him no longer living in his apartment, but in the home with all the other old people. But of course, it was not safe for him to stay alone anymore. After the fire. After he forgot to turn off the stove and the food he had left there started burning.

It was a nice day, so she took grandpa outside to sit in the small garden.

"So grandpa. We're learning about the Second World War in history at school right now and the teacher has given us the assignment to talk to people who are still alive from that time and write an essay about it."

"So my little girl wants to interview her grandfather?"

"Yes. Sort of, I guess."

"Those were bad times."

"Mama always says that you were working for the Danish Foreign Ministry at that time."

"Well. You know Denmark was occupied by the Germans, so I'm not sure it was a real 'Foreign Ministry' as we had to check everything with Berlin. But yes, I was working there."

"She also told me that you went to one of the camps?"

"Yes. Unfortunately, that was part of my job."

"Which camp was it?"

"It was Theresienstadt in Bohemia. A bit north of Prague. It was where they had sent a lot of the Danish Jews who didn't make it over to Sweden in time. The king felt like something needed to be done, so after lots of back and forth we agreed to a visit with the International Red Cross."

"That had to be horrible!"

"Pia. It was during the war. People struggled everywhere."

"So how was it there?"

"It was more like a closed city for Jews. You know, what I saw actually didn't look so bad. They could play football and the kids even gave a performance for us."

"But I thought the Nazis killed all the Jews?"

"Of course, they did. But in that camp, which I visited, they treated them well. That's also what I and the two others I was with, wrote in our reports."

"And that was the only camp you visited?"

"Yes. They didn't allow us to visit any others. But my little girl. Why are you so concerned about all of this? In the end, these people were just Jews."

* * *

←·· 156 ○◎○ 160 ··→

July 27th, 1996
Dr. Pia Andersen
Copenhagen – Denmark ▷ Frederiksberg – Denmark

Saturday

"How old are you?"

"I'm eighteen," Pia said.

"So we have an 18-year-old female, who collapsed on the dance floor at the Rust nightclub. No obvious trauma. Smells a little drunk. Likely alcohol intoxication. Please advise where we should take her?" She overheard the paramedic say on the radio.

No, she was not drunk.

Well, perhaps a little. But something else had to be wrong. She had not felt well for a couple of weeks now. So tired and thirsty all the time. It must have been the summer heat. She also had to urinate a lot. Well, not only a lot but basically all the time. Two nights ago she even ended up wetting herself in her bed. Of course, it was nice that she lost some weight—despite being constantly hungry and eating such large portions and drinking all that orange juice.

Pia really had to push herself to go out dancing tonight. But she wanted to go with all the friends from school. Yes, she had sipped on the margarita before the song started. Although she felt too tired to dance the entire evening, she had to when they started playing *Macarena*. Then the third jump. Her legs gave out. She woke up on the stretcher in the ambulance.

"Okay. We'll take her to Frederiksberg Hospital."

The nurses in the emergency room were not too friendly. There were lots of patients there.

"Doc. You want any labs?" one of them asked.

"Neh. Think we just let her sleep a bit and give her some fluids. The only thing, check a blood sugar for me please," the ER doctor said.

"It's going to be a little prick here in your finger, sweetheart."

She felt a short sting on her right index finger. After about a minute, she heard the nurse call over to one of the other nurses in the emergency room.

"Hey. Can you give me the other meter? I think this one is broken. We need to recalibrate it. It's giving me an 'Extreme High Glucose' reading."

It took about one more minute until she felt how now her right-hand middle finger had been pricked. Shortly after, she overhead the nurse calling the doctor.

"Sorry, doc. I think we have to send some labs on her. I got two 'Extreme High Glucose' readings when I checked her blood sugar."

A couple of hours later that day, she felt much better than in a long time. She was connected to a drip, which was infusing into one of her veins on her arm. Dad was sitting on her hospital bed. There was a knock on the door and a middle-aged woman in a white lab coat entered. She said the following with a soft but concerned voice:

"Pia. I hope you are feeling a bit better. I'm an endocrinologist. We now know why you have not felt well for a while. You have type I diabetes mellitus. You'll have to inject insulin for the rest of your life."

* * *

←⋯ 345 ○◎○ 195 ⋯→

DAVID ØYBO

October 1st, 1998
Dr. Pia Andersen
Copenhagen – Denmark

Thursday

Pia's new Nokia 5110 bleeped:

When we are together, we stay up all night.
When you're not with me, I can't get to sleep.
Praise the Almighty for these two insomnias!
And their difference.
RUMI

She started smiling. Asif. Typical. Never sure if he should become a neurosurgeon or a poet. But perhaps he could be both at the same time? He recited her a section out of the poem *Alfabet* by Inger Christensen when they first met at the FADL[1] party given for the first semester students like her. He was in his fifth semester.

She looked up from the functional anatomy book. Shoulder muscles. The big exam was on Monday. There were another three-hundred-fifty pages left. The library would close in thirty minutes. She realized how her buttocks had become numb from sitting there the entire afternoon. It was time for learning anatomy hands-on; and some poetry. She took the phone and repeatedly typed the number keys to write the following SMS:

Shoulder muscles. Live object needed tonight.

They would always use her dorm room at the Rigshospitalets Kollegium. The verses he whispered in her ear would alternate with

1 **FADL (Foreningen af Danske Lægestuderende)** – *Danish:* Danish Medical Student Association.

his thrusts. He would scream out a haiku, almost panting when his deep brown eyes turned glassy as he was about to cum—which occasionally was too soon. The sonnet he would recite when his arms held her tight, his little belly pushing against her back when they lay next to each other and were about to fall asleep.

The phone bleeped.

Only shoulder muscles?

She composed her reply with the keypad:

And the function of musculus cremaster ...[1]

She was about to leave the library when the phone bleeped once more:

Your Frontal Cortex
Sexiest Part Of The You I Love
Goggling At Your Breasts

* * *

←··· 347 ○◎○ 262 ···→

---

1 **musculus cremaster** (Latin) – Cremaster Muscle. Muscle covering the testes and spermatic cord.

June 30th, 2000
Dr. Pia Andersen
Roskilde – Denmark

Friday

"Who the fuck do you think I am!"

"Pia. You fell in love with a guy whose family is from Pakistan. Did you really expect I could get out of this?"

"I'm not your girlfriend anymore. It's over. I'm done."

"Pia—I'm only going to marry her because of the paperwork. Nothing ever is going to happen between her and me. And everything stays the same between us."

"You're the worst thing that has ever happened to me."

"But Pia! Let's talk. I love you, but we can't escape the fact that our backgrounds are different."

"Get out of my life. Get away. You're just a fucking asshole! Don't touch me! Don't fucking touch me! I hate you. I hate you!"

And the moment Asif tried to grab her hand, she slapped him in his face and began darting towards the exit.

"Wait! Pia! Please wait! Come back!" he yelled.

She did not turn around. She walked away faster. After a while, he stopped following her.

She could hear the crowd of cold and damp fans cheering in the distance. And then Pearl Jam started playing *Corduroy*.

* * *

←⋯ 260 ○◎○ 349 ⋯→

July 7th, 2000
Dr. Pia Andersen
Malmö – Sweden

Friday

Pia knitted her fingers into his thick hair, quivering slightly as she felt her third climax coming closer.

This was not how she thought the night would go.

She had crossed the new bridge to Malmö early that evening. She needed some distraction after getting dumped for the NDF-P[1] bride. Among the loud music in the bar, it was clear to her from everything about him that this was just for one night.

It was refreshing that he did not pretend otherwise.

"I'm Pernille," she said.

She did not care about his name. His body was way too lean for her taste. Tonight it did not matter. He seemed about her age, perhaps a bit older.

All she had hoped for was a mediocre orgasm generated by the product of friction and time.

---

1 **NDF-P** – *Neologism*: Substitute for any vulgar or demeaning word Dr. Pia Andersen would use for a human being who does not share the same national, racial, or ethnic background as herself. Whereas the author could have used a number of expressions, he strongly believes that certain words carry so much negative power in them, that they should no longer be spoken, written, or read and he does not want to utilize these words in his writing. Honoring the tradition of the home country of Dr. Pia Andersen, which—despite its small size—in 2018 accounted for about 9% of the global pork exports (and likely is the nation with the highest pork exports per capita) the acronym **NDF-P** stands for **N**ot **D**ansk (Danish) **F**ødt (born) – **P**ig. The suggested corresponding acronym that would be used for humans sharing the beliefs of Dr. Pia Andersen is **DF-P**, standing for **D**ansk (Danish) **F**ødt (born) – **P**ig.

They wasted little time in the bar after he ordered the cocktail for her. Pia had never sipped a Cosmopolitan before, but after trying could not understand why everyone was so excited about it—she really did not like the taste.

His talk and kisses were seductive. He was clearly well trained at giving women the illusion of feeling good.

The walk through the beachside park to his apartment was short. The summer sun had just started to disappear in the waters of the Øresund to their right.

The room stayed lit by the lamp standing on the floor on the left side of the bed.

He knew very well how to unhook her bra.

The 'South America on a shoestring' Lonely Planet book on the nightstand reminded Pia of the trip Asif and she had planned to go on in about a week from now.

She had canceled everything.

The repeating spasm rolling through her body made her groan in pleasure. The force of this orgasm caused her to gasp and her eyes fluttered shut. She jerked and quivered beneath him as she came.

Being fucked by him had nothing of Asif's poetic energy, but the masterful perfection of how he executed the physical act blew her body and mind.

"As much and as long as you want it," was his answer to the questioning look in her eyes once she realized that he had no intention of stopping with the perfectly timed rhythm of his deep thrusts.

The feeling in her cunt started changing from a pleasurable ache to a pain.

She decided to lift her hips a bit, resting her knees on his torso, which was glittering slightly from sweat.

He looked surprised—perhaps even slightly annoyed—and she felt his initial resistance through the increasing force of his thrusts.

Determined, she pushed him out and rolled him over onto his back.

"My turn now," she whispered, sitting on his flat belly, his erection pushing against her ass.

264

The hint of annoyance quickly left his face when she pinched his nipples and then glided her fingernails over his rib cage, shoulders, and arms.

He held his breath momentarily when she started following the long scar running down the middle of his chest with her kisses.

His skin had a salty taste.

She gently bit the point where the end of the scar met his stomach and then quickly turned around—now facing his legs and her wetness mixing with the sweat of his scar and chest.

Her hand grabbed the colorless condom and slid it off.

She lowered her lips to the tip of his circumcised cock, which had an unusually large vein running down its shaft, disappearing in his trimmed pubic hair.

Pia did not expect his tongue to start to lick her after she had moved her butt towards his face.

She rested her forearms on his thighs.

His tongue slipped into her.

Carefully she formed a seal with her lips around the thick shaft of his dick, the large vein throbbing against her lower lip.

He slowly resumed the rhythmical movements with his hips as she pulled him further into her mouth.

His body started trembling.

She sucked him harder.

He responded with deeper thrusts and Pia felt him at the back of her throat.

His licking became more intense but less directed.

She enjoyed the feeling that it was finally she who was going to make him lose control.

But Pia was wrong. Very wrong.

Unexpectedly, his hands grabbed the hair just above her ears, holding her head firmly in place. His tongue entered her deeper than ever before.

Pia saw the rhythmic contractions of his balls.

An unexpected pleasureful warmth started spreading in firing waves from the depth of her pelvis, this time even more intense than the three times before.

He made a loud primal noise.

She completely lost control of her body and mind as the abrupt rush of his warm semen began spilling into her mouth.

And then,
the

♀♀♀S
♀♀♀E
♀♀♀X
♀♀♀I
▽
◀▶=♂=♂=♂= ▶ ooo[1]
△
D♀♀♀
E♀♀♀
N♀♀♀
T♀♀♀

happened.

His pelvis arched up into her face with a forcible final thrust, and he filled her oral cavity even more. The orgasm caused a sudden unexpected jerk of his upper torso, his contracting muscular strength pushing her body towards his legs just a bit. At the same time, he let go of her head as his hands started clenching to form fists out of pleasure. Her released head moved in the direction of his feet forcing her bare lower teeth against the unusually large still throbbing vein on the back of his penis.

Pia immediately noticed how the mild bitterness of semen mixed with the metallic taste of his blood in her mouth.

"Oh gosh. Sorry," she said as soon as she was able to.

---

1 **Sexident** – *Portmanteau word*: Combination of the English words 'sex/sexy' and 'accident' that creates a slang word that mostly refers to an accident that occurred during sexual intercourse.

A trickle of blood was coming from a small gash that her teeth had cut into the vein in the lower third on the shaft of his still engorged penis.

It was bleeding quite a lot.

Now kneeling in the bed next to him, Pia just saw the blissful expression in his face—his eyes looking at the ceiling. His brain was obviously still busy processing his orgasm and had not yet registered the pain.

"Hey, you're bleeding!"

"What?" His confused eyes glanced at her briefly before he lifted his head slightly and saw all the blood.

"Is this coming from you or me?"

"I'm so sorry! Does it hurt?" He had sat up on the edge of the bed in the meantime, applying pressure to the gash on his gradually shrinking penis with his thumb.

"It's OK. That part of my pik[1] isn't so sensitive. But can you get a pack of gauze from the bathroom? Look in the medicine cabinet. I'll just have to apply pressure for some time. I'm taking a blood thinner and I don't want the floor to get full of blood."

Pia opened the medicine cabinet. Packages with condoms took up more than half of the space inside.

It surprised her to see all the medications for such a young guy:
Warfarin – Diltiazem – Potassium – Lasix

She returned with the gauze.

He applied pressure for some time until the bleeding stopped.

Then, their naked bodies rapidly fell asleep uncovered next to each other in their post-coital bliss on sheets smelling of sweat, semen, and blood.

The sky was finally dark outside.

* * *

←⋯ 349 ○◎○ 268 ⋯→

---

1 **Pik** – *Danish*: Vulgar word for penis.

July 8th, 2000
Dr. Pia Andersen
Malmö – Sweden ▷ Skodsborg – Denmark

Saturday

A wet feeling on the skin of her left side started to wake Pia up. Gradually she blinked her eyes open. The brief summer night was ending outside and a faint light of the early morning dawn came in through the window. She heard him breathe next to her and out of instinct shifted herself away to the right. She moved her left hand towards her hip. The liquid felt slimy a bit, and when the back of her hand carelessly prodded against the mattress, it was like it had immersed itself into a body of liquid. Now fully awake, Pia held up her hand against her face and saw that it was completely covered in blood. Her mouth opened but she did not scream and she recoiled even more to the right in the bed. In the dim light, she could see that the man at her side was lying in a large puddle of dark red blood, which extended from his knees halfway up his back. The parts of his body which lay against the mattress were covered in blood, as was her left hip, thigh and part of her abdomen. His skin was almost the color of the white sheets he was lying on. The parts of his naked body not covered in blood were coated with a film of tiny little pearls of sweat. His breathing was rapid and shallow.

"Hey, wake up!"

He did not react. She started shaking his chest. He felt cold.

"Urgh." He opened his eyes and looked at her.

"Who, who're you? What's going on with me?" he said in a barely understandable way, rolling his eyes upwards in a weird way, clearly not being fully present.

She remembered the trauma course from university last summer. She tried feeling a pulse on his cold right wrist. It was rapid, very rapid—at least in the 130 beats per minute range—and very faint. He was obviously in shock and needed help.

"I'm going to help you. I'm going to help you!"

She jumped out of the bed and scrambled to remember where her phone had ended up during the lustful frolic when they had undressed each other a couple of hours earlier. She found it and with shaking hands dialed 112. A male voice answered:

"SOS Alarm."

"I'm here with a man in hemorrhagic shock and need an ambulance. Quickly!" Pia said.

"What happened?"

"He's lying in a bed full of blood."

"Did he get stabbed?"

"No, no. No. No. I didn't do anything to him."

"Where's he bleeding from?"

"I think he is bleeding from his dick."

"From his penis? Is he able to talk?"

"No. I told you he's in shock!"

"How do you know?"

"I'm a medical student!"

"Is he dead?"

"No. He has a weak pulse, I think around 130, and he's clammy and barely responsive. Please send an ambulance, quickly!"

"How old is he?"

"I don't know, I guess in his late twenties."

"What's his name?"

"I have no idea. We met in a bar last night and then had sex."

"Okay." The male voice on the phone paused for just about a second. "So where are you calling from?"

"Malmö!"

"Okay. But what's the street address?"

"I don't know!"

"I can't see your caller ID. Are you calling from a Swedish phone?"

"No. I'm calling from a Danish cell phone. I live in Denmark."

DAVID ØYBO

"Unfortunately, I can't locate your phone as it's not a Swedish phone. Any idea what the address could be?"

"It's an apartment building. I think I'm on the third floor. We took the elevator up. We walked from the center. Past Malmöhus and then through the park which looks out onto the Øresund."

"Okay, so you're likely in Ribersborg somewhere. Is there anybody there who can give you the exact address?"

"No. It's just the two of us in the apartment. He needs help!"

"Okay. Just try to be calm. You said you're in an apartment building. Can you knock on one of the neighbors' doors?"

With the phone in her hand, she ran into the hallway, opened the entrance door—carefully putting a chair against the door, so the door would stay open—and stepped into the small landing of the staircase. There were three doors.

"Okay, I'm in the stairwell here," she said to the emergency dispatcher.

She picked the door which was closest and started knocking.

"Help! Please open the door!" she shouted while she intensified the knocking that rapidly turned into a banging. Finally, she heard some noise coming from the inside.

"Help. Please help!"

The door opened just a bit.

"Aaaahhhhhh. Farhad there's a naked woman covered in blood in front of our door!" the voice belonging to a sleepy-looking woman, who had opened the door screamed.

"Help! Please! The guy's bleeding to death. This is the emergency dispatcher. He needs the street address!" she shouted at the woman while trying to make her take her phone and at the same moment realizing that under the stress of the situation she had completely forgotten to cover herself when she ran out onto the stairwell landing. The bewildered woman in the door took the phone from her, which allowed Pia to instantly retreat into the decency of the man's apartment. It surprised her how speedily she could put her clothes on. By the time the woman with her husband entered the apartment still holding her phone, she heard the sirens of the ambulance already.

270

Then everything went very quickly. The paramedics immediately recognized the seriousness of the situation and started two I.V.'s. The face of the older one of them remained completely professional without any hint of an expression when she confessed the little sex accident which had occurred.

"Do you know if he takes any medications?" he asked her.

"His medicine cabinet is full of prescription medications."

"Could you please get them for us? And can you come with us to the emergency room?"

It was a quick ride in the ambulance. He still was very pale lying on the stretcher, but after receiving two bags of normal saline, he seemed a little more coherent. They asked her to wait in a small ground floor room, which was the waiting area of the emergency department. She was alone. The leaves of the small shrub outside of the window appeared to get greener as the light increased. She still had all his medications in her handbag. After some time a doctor showed up.

"So, I was told that you were with Anders last night?"

Anders. Guess that was his name, which she forgot immediately after he had introduced himself in the bar.

"Yes."

She braced herself for another embarrassing retelling of the details of what had exactly happened, but it appeared that the doctor already knew.

"Such a bizarre case. But as his INR was greater than 12 on his laboratory work, the small laceration of that vein on his penis just didn't stop bleeding. Now what I'm totally unclear about is why his INR went up so high. I pulled up Dr. Boisen-Jensen's medical record and he's on Warfarin."

"Dr. Boisen-Jensen?"

"Yes. He is one of our new interns, actually. So the paramedics told me that you took his medications with you?"

"Yes. They're here." She removed them from her handbag and one-by-one handed them to the doctor.

"Oh. Okay. This is likely what happened. See here. These are 4 mg Warfarin tablets. The record states that he is taking 2 mg. It's really bad if the pharmacies do that. If they don't have the 2 mg tablets in stock, they dispense the 4 mg tablets to patients and tell them to take half a tablet. Most likely he continued to take the full tablet and was taking too much. He has to be quite sensitive to Warfarin when just doubling the dose almost made him bleed to death."

Pia recalled the pharmacology lectures she had back in the spring. She had read that Warfarin indeed was a very tricky medication, and this was now a real firsthand experience.

"How's he doing?" she asked.

"He was lucky. But he should be fine. He's getting blood at the moment, and plasma. We just put a small stitch into that vein." The doctor now grinned a little and added: "The organ itself shouldn't have any lasting damage."

Pia felt that her face was flushing.

"You can see him a bit later if you want. Oh, I forgot to ask. What's your name?"

Pia decided to keep her cover and said: "Pernille."

"Okay. Pernille. There's one more thing. It seems like you scared the neighbors out so much this morning that they called the police. The officers will be here shortly. They'll just need to quickly talk to you."

The doctor left.

She had done nothing wrong. It was an accident. She decided she would not talk to the police. She was the only one in the waiting area and the door was closed. She saw the green shrub on the outside of the window. Quickly she put all of Anders' medication on the chair, opened the window, and slipped out.

It was a short walk from the hospital to the train station and she was happy when she sat down in the seat of the train which still smelled new. She took out her insulin pen and her glucometer and pricked her finger. The reading was 10.4 mmol/L. She injected three units of short-acting insulin using her insulin pen. She would need to check once more when she had breakfast at home.

She got off at Skodsborg Station and walked the short distance to the small apartment building on Skodsborg Strandvej, where she had bought her one-bedroom home with the money she had inherited from grandpa.

She turned on the radio in her kitchen.

Oops! ... I Did it Again sung by Britney Spears was playing.

A feeling of filth overcame her, and she went to the bathroom and stripped off the clothes, and put all of them directly into the washing machine. She could see in the mirror that her left side was still covered with dried blood. Pia felt she needed more than just a shower. She put on her grey bathrobe.

The lyrics coming from the radio implied something about lacking innocence when she stepped outside the apartment. She walked to the end of the small pier which belonged to the building. She was alone. Pia stripped off the bathrobe and jumped headfirst naked into the refreshing summer cold salty water of the Øresund to purge her body from Anders' blood.

* * *

←··· 263 ○◎○ 351 ···→

December 26th, 2004
Dr. Pia Andersen
Ko Phi Phi Le Island, Thailand

Sunday

It was the first time ever Pia tried sex on The Beach.[1] She still had the peachy-orangy-cranberishy taste on her tongue when Joakim, or Jack as everyone called him, had gently woken her up.

"Let's go for a walk under the stars," he whispered into her ear and then tenderly bit her earlobe.

In the light of the enormous tropical full moon, she saw that the other twenty or so tourists who had booked the overnight tour with them were deeply asleep on the simple bamboo mats covered with the thin sleeping bags. The limestone karst surrounding the bay appeared in a lighter gray than during the daytime under the glittering sky full of stars, which made the ocean appear more light-greenish than the day's turquoise blue. Once they had walked a bit, they could no longer hear the snoring guy from Birmingham, and the only sound was the gentle rhythmical splashing of the waves on the soft white sand of the beach. She noticed the small backpack Jack was carrying on his naked shoulders, with the rest of his torso covered by the tank top with the logo with two elephants and Chang beer written on it. The thought that the walk under the stars was not as spontaneous as it seemed crossed her mind. The entire trip had been quite a surprise. Of course, she did not say no.

"I have to use all those airline miles, so let's just book the tickets. Let's go."

She had been able to get the week before Christmas off and then also Christmas as an exchange for working New Year's Eve.

---

1 **The Beach** – Adventure drama film released on February 11th, 2000 with Leonardo DiCaprio.

She would have to be back at work in the hospital the next day after their return to Copenhagen on December 29th. Jack had to be in San Francisco on January 3rd for a project management meeting for the inhaled insulin he was supposed to market for Novo Nordisk at one point in the future. So timing-wise things worked out.

They always had endless discussions about insulin. Of course, the idea of not having to inject her insulin appeared great when she first heard about it, but once she thought it through a bit more, it just did not really make sense. She still had to take it, and instead of a thin pen, she needed to carry around a big block of an inhaler device. She preferred the insulin pump in any case, but for her first trip to the tropics, she switched back to the pens.

The climate was pleasant in Thailand. The poverty and the intrusiveness of the people, much less so.

Perhaps the only error Denmark had ever made in history was that they sold the Virgin Islands to the U.S. It would have been nice to have a true Danish tropical paradise.

She missed the way she used to celebrate Christmas when she saw the small plastic tree which had been put up in their hotel bungalow on Phi Phi Island. The overnight 'Sleep on The Beach' tour was a surprise. The Beach was wonderful. It looked even more stunning than in the movie. It was a fun group of people from Europe and the U.S. The main guide was a hunk of an Australian and there were only a few NDF-Ps.

After reaching the end of the large sandy beach, they carefully waded through the shallow water under the overhanging cliffs. From the daytime, she remembered the small sliver of beach which the cliffs separated from the main beach. This must be where Jack was leading her. She was glad she had put her flip-flops on to walk over the in-places sharp coral.

They reached the short deserted much smaller strip of sand which was surrounded by high cliffs on three sides, opening up towards the large beach where they had slept before, in the distance; separated just by the incredibly clear water, in which they had frolicked with the group during the early night, playing with the phosphorescence of the light-up plankton.

Jack put the backpack next to him while they sat down. He started kissing her less clumsily than usual. They undressed themselves mutually.

Unfortunately, Jack had managed to get some of the fine white sand to stick on his penis, which was not a pleasant experience for her. But they continued after a quick interruption, washing themselves off thoroughly in the salty water of the bay. The sex was nice.

They fell asleep uncovered, lying naked on a blanket from Jack's backpack.

A slight trembling feeling which appeared to come from the earth gently woke them up in the morning. The sun had risen already and she could see in the distance that some people in their group were slowly getting up on the large beach. She was confident the distance was far enough so nobody could tell that they were naked and made Jack skinny dip with her and wash off all the sand on their bodies from the night. When they noticed how the first boat with the tourists started appearing, they retreated into the small assortment of shrubs towards the back of the beach at the bottom of the steep cliffs. After making good mutual use of Jack's morning wood using the support of the limestone cliffs, she put her bikini back on and Jack his boardshorts and tank top. They lingered for quite some time on the blanket and observed the arrival of more boats with the tourists, who would just visit the bay on a day-trip. Soon they would have to return to the big beach to unite with their group and travel back to Phi Phi Island in the longtail boat. Pia also knew that slowly she would need to give herself her morning shot of insulin. She had left her insulin pens together with all her other possessions on the main beach.

They were about to get up and start walking when they noticed that the tide had suddenly become unusually low, fully exposing large stretches of sand and coral, which otherwise would lie at the bottom of the bay. Jack grabbed his backpack and followed her after she said:

"Hey. This is interesting. Let's check out that coral in front."

After walking around a bit on what had just a short while ago been the bottom of the bay and seeing some nice colorful fish stranded in several shallow pools of water, it had definitively become time to head back.

They turned around and walked back to quickly grab the blanket. As Pia bent down to pick it up, she noticed that Jack had fallen behind a little.

With the blanket in hand, she turned around and saw that he was down on his knees on the white sand of the beach about a meter away from her.

Pia's heart started beating faster after she realized that he had removed a small black box from the backpack and was now looking at her with an unsure smile and bigger eyes than usual, holding the small box in front of him in both hands as if it were heavy.

"I have something very important to ask you, Pia. I've known you for a little while now. You're the most amazing woman I've ever met, and I believe there's a wonderful future for us. Pia, will you …"

While Jack was saying the lines he had surely carefully rehearsed numerous times, she noticed something strange appearing in the corner of her eye.

She focused her eyes away from Jack's face to the opening of the bay towards the deep blue of the Andaman Sea.

Pia saw it before she heard it. A very high white-tipped more wall than wave was rapidly crashing into the bay. It was neither deep blue, nor turquoise or green, but its deep grey color blended with the grey limestone of the cliffs surrounding the bay.

"Jack!" But he had turned his head already towards the sea, alerted by the deep enormously loud growling noise which now echoed from the cliffs in the bay.

"Oh, shit!"

They hurried back to the shrubs at the back of the beach and started climbing up the cliffs in the spot which they were familiar with from earlier that morning.

Pia went first, closely followed by Jack. When she was about three meters up, her left foot misstepped on the slippery sandstone. The trunk of a tree that was growing out from the cliff and which she held on to with her cramping arms was all that prevented a fall into what was no longer a beach or shrubs, but a rapidly rising grey body of angry water beneath her.

It had already reached her knees.

Jack was next to her.

"Never let go," he said.

"I promise. I'll never let go, Jack. I'll never let go."

And then Pia watched how Jack swiftly continued his climb to safety while she felt how the water now reached her breasts.

* * *

←··· 165 ○◎○ 201 ···→

July 8th, 2007
Dr. Pia Andersen
Klagenfurt – Austria

Sunday

She could no longer feel her legs. Pia heard all the people cheering around her. A man ran past her. This was the last turn now. She could see the finish line. She would not be able to speed up anymore.

It looked like another five hundred meters.

Would it be enough this time? Enough for the spot? The finish line was coming closer. She was able to see the sign with IRONMAN written on it.

About four hundred meters.

She saw the group from the triathlon club waving small Dannebrogs[1] and shouting at her. She was unable to acknowledge them. One more man passed her—but no woman.

Three hundred meters.

Now she could recognize the red numbers above the finishing booth.

Two hundred meters.

Another group from the triathlon club. More cheering and more Dannebrogs.

One hundred meters.

Nine hours, nineteen minutes. The seconds were ticking. This would be her best time ever. All the endless training had paid off.

Nine hours and twenty minutes.

Fifty meters left now.

---

1 **Dannebrog** – *Danish:* Flag of Denmark. Red with a white Scandinavian cross that extends to the edges of the flag—the vertical part of the cross is shifted to the hoist side.

Nine hours and twenty minutes and twenty seconds.
Ten meters or so to go.
Nine hours and twenty minutes and twenty-two seconds.
Three more strides.
Nine hours and twenty minutes and twenty-four seconds.
That should be enough for a spot in Hawai'i.
Do not stop running now.
Walk. Walk. Legs walk.
Oh, no. Don't fall now.
Shit.
Autch.

* * *

←⋯ 353 ○◎○ 203 ⋯→

May 12th, 2014
Dr. Pia Andersen
Hellerup – Denmark

Monday

Pia had never seen Helsingørmotorvejen[1] backed up all the way to the Tuborgvej[2] exit. She would be late to work. And now, of course, the radio had to play the song that had won last night: *Rise Like a Phoenix*.

So much was so wrong with this song. First and foremost the performer. What was she? Or he. Pia in general had no problem with gay people, but, well, this was simply too much. A clear sign where all this liberalism in Europe was heading. She had always liked the Eurovision song contest, but all it was now was a clear sign of the degeneration spreading throughout Europe.

Now it was nothing but leftish propaganda. And what a name: Conchita Wurst—Conchita Sausage? And the lyrics. Threatening. A warning about vengeance in the future.

From which ashes? When in human history did people like him or her ever make the rules about who was normal?

What vengeance—if anyone would have the right to retaliate it would be the normal people like Pia.

Normal people who made society work by standing in a traffic jam, heading to work. Not people who were self-centered on life pleasures only and not even sure what gender they were.

If someone or something had to rise like a phoenix, it was the good old values. Family, nation and traditions.

---

1 **Helsingørmotorvejen** – *Danish:* Highway in Denmark connecting Copenhagen downtown to Helsingør.

2 **Tuborgvej** – *Danish:* Tuborg Road. Derived from Thuesborg ("Thue's castle").

Making sure that Denmark became strong, proud, independent, and sovereign again. Of course, there was envy in the world.
Envy for the rich history, Danish design, the monarchy.

If a phoenix needed to rise it was this phoenix who all the traitor politicians had burned. And it was this phoenix, who would
eventually rise, full of vengeance and retribution!

She pushed the button to turn off the radio in the car.

Finally, the cars in front of her had started moving.

* * *

←⋯ 167 ○◎○ 213 ⋯→

September 24th, 2015
Dr. Pia Andersen
Copenhagen – Denmark

Thursday

"Næste station Københavns lufthavn. Next station Copenhagen airport."

They were everywhere. Thousands and thousands of them just pouring in. Pia was horrified as even more of them boarded at København H[1]. She should have taken a taxi to the airport.

And their smell! Can't they take a shower?

And what is this now? Stay away from my Evoc bike bag. Nothing to steal there. Okay. Finally, almost at the airport.

Oh my god. The constant aggressive undertone in the unintelligible language they were speaking. So many of them. She would not be able to get off the train. She needs to get through. All these NDF-Ps walking on the highways, clogging traffic, and now because of them, she would miss her flight. Enough already. Finally, off the train. What is this now! What kind of sign?

REFUGEES WELCOME

What mental morons in yellow vests put up such a sign. They are not refugees—this is an invasion of migrants.

If they were refugees, they all should just stay in the first safe country in Europe they arrived in.

But they were invaders—marching all the way through Italy, France, Austria, Germany, and all the other countries.

Pia could only shake her head. If the West is to have any chance, one would need to, first of all, get rid of such people—such traitors.

---

1 **København H** – *Danish:* Abbreviation of Københavns Hovedbanegård. Copenhagen Central Station, the main railway station in Copenhagen.

How could the country stay a strong, proud, independent, and sovereign nation with people around, who put up 'REFUGEES WELCOME' signs?

"Where are you flying to?"

"To Kona, Hawai'i."

"Ironman?"

"Yes."

Well, at least for a short time she would be away from all this. But once she got back, she would have to do something. She did not want to wake up in the morning with the feeling of the immediate danger of getting mugged, carjacked, or worse. Living in constant fear. Needing to lock her windows and bolt the doors.

Clearly—already now—she could no longer go to most parts of Copenhagen. And this invasion would only make things worse. Much worse. Perhaps it was time to seek refuge elsewhere for herself. Someplace safe.

Somewhere pure.

Without all those NDF-Ps.

Perhaps in Norway.

In some small hospital at the end of a fjord.

"Good luck with your race. You'll have to drop your bike at the oversize counter."

* * *

←⋯ 213 ○◎○ 217 ⋯→

May 4th, 2018
Dr. Pia Andersen
Godshus – Norway

Friday

In order to get the stupid permit, Pia needed to pretend that she wanted to hunt moose. It was such a complicated process. But now finally she was almost done. She needed this. She had to protect herself. She opened the door to the Godshus police station. Several police officers were sitting at their desks in the big room.

But what was this? Another NDF-P! Not that the one at work was not enough. Did Norway nowadays also import policemen from Africa? Not only doctors?

"Hello, can I help you?" a young female police officer with grey-blue eyes asked her.

"Yes. I'm here to get the final approval for my Våpenkort."[1]

"One moment, please. Let me get Chief Investigator Redding. He handles this here."

In disbelief, Pia watched how the young police officer walked over to the desk of her colleague, who then got up and walked over to her.

"Dr. Andersen?" the chief investigator asked.

"Yes." Pia made the muscles of her face gently lift both corners of her mouth.

"You work at Godshus General Hospital?"

"Yes. Started there last fall."

"Welcome to the community. We're glad to have you here. They're always having problems getting doctors to stay there. Okay.

---

1 **Våpenkort** – *Norwegian*: Firearm license.

Let me stamp and sign this. Here you go. Have fun with your gun and please only shoot moose."

* * *

←··· 179 ○◎○ 224 ···→

January 7th, 2019
Dr. Pia Andersen
Godshus – Norway

Monday

Pia could not believe who just got into the elevator with her.

"So, I was told that you are the other Dane here?" Dr. Boisen-Jensen said.

It was clearly him. Older. Less hair. Still too lean for her taste. But it was him.

What had the doctor in the Malmö hospital emergency room told her: Anders—Dr. Boisen-Jensen? She should have noticed before.

The world was so small. The large vein on his penis. His blood on her body.

Nothing in his expression indicated that he recognized her.

But she, of course, remembered.

"Yes, good to meet you. Sorry, I was on vacation last week."

"You didn't miss too much. So, you also came from Copenhagen?"

"Yes, Bispebjerg Hospital."

The elevator doors opened on the second floor.

"That's about the only hospital I never worked in in the capital. No wonder we never met before. Okay. See you at the morning meeting then. You know that we moved the start time a bit earlier to 7:15, instead of 7:30?"

"Ah. Okay."

She would have to hurry up to leave her things in the office.

* * *

←⋯ 356 ○◎○ 386 ⋯→

April 15th, 2019
Dr. Pia Andersen
Chessy (Seine-et-Marne) – France ▷ Paris – France

Monday

In front of Pia was a water feature of sorts. A boat full of kid figurines sitting on top of a stylized half globe with a map of Europe in violet below it. All the children had to squeeze together in one single boat. All children having to sit in the same boat irrespective of their skin color. That could not be comfortable. They should all have a boat of their own. On top of this, four flags which Pia realized must indicate the name of the ride:

it's __ a __ small __ world!

She could see that there was no line this late in the day. Her Garmin Forerunner 945 watch showed 18:40. She felt a little tired. She would just take in this last attraction and then get back on the train to the hotel, which she was spending so much money on. At least the view from the small hotel room terrace was nice. She was the only one who got into the front row of the orange boat. The ride started to move, and the boat advanced into a dark chamber filled with dancing dolls, scenes in psychedelic colors, and a hard to forget simple song:

Something about laughing …

Oh, actually the ride did not start off badly. Of course, the color scheme was totally un-Scandinavian, but the first castle had some resemblance with Kronborg.[1] A ride starting with the resemblance of the Hamlet castle in Denmark. What a sympathetic gesture. And then there were also some reindeer, so a bit of Norway and Sweden as well.

---

1 **Kronborg** – Castle in the Danish town of Helsingør, north of Copenhagen. Also called 'Elsinore'. Shakespeare chose it as the location for *Hamlet*.

... something about crying ...

Okay, after passing something which gave the impression of being the London bridge, things took a turn for the worse. Eiffel tower. Paris. The city which had disappointed her so much during her trip. So dirty. So many NDF-Ps.

... something about hope ...

Oh, the Leaning Tower of Pisa and now Venice. At least Italy today had a government that would finally start putting an end to all the NDF-Ps coming over in the boats.

... something about fear ...

Looks like this is the Kremlin now. The Russians. Always—always—need to be careful with them. And if they offer you black tea, never, ever drink it.

... something about sharing ...

Japan. What in the universe did she share with Japan? People with crooked eyes and false smiles. She had seen enough of them in the Louvre the day before—or were they Chinese? Who cares. Would not make any difference. Same. Same.

... something about being aware ...

Taj Mahal. Aware of what? That all NDF-Ps from that part of the world are assholes like Asif had been?

It's a small world ...

It's a small world ...

It's a small world ...

It's a small world ...

It's a tiny, tiny world.

Something about a single moon ...

Perhaps she should just go to the moon next. A moon colony for pure people like her only. Perhaps NDF-Ps would not be able to get there through the vacuum of space. They would need a doctor on the moon, or not?

... something about the sun ...

Denmark's only mistake ever made in history—selling the Virgin Islands. Now whenever one needed some sunshine in the middle of the Scandinavian winter, one would have no choice then go to a country full of NDF-Ps.

... something about smiles and being friends ...

What stupidity. Clearly not from the always smiling Japanese. Or the Chinese.

... something about partitioning peaks ...

Well, considering that she had to deal with the NDF-P at work every day in a hospital in the sticks in Norway obviously showed that NO, they were not high enough.

... something about the broad seven seas ...

Given all the NDF-P who didn't drown, the Mediterranean was clearly not wide enough. Oh, how lucky the Americans are. At least they will be able to keep things at bay by just building a wall.

It's a small world ...
It's a small world ...
It's a small world ...
It's a small world ...
It's a tiny, tiny world.

By the time the orange boat passed by two giraffes, a zebra, and a rhinoceros, Pia was so enraged about this pathetic indoctrinative ride of propaganda aimed at small children, that she did not even bother listening to the third verse of the song:

It's a world of miracles, a world of goodness.
And in the future, there will be peace on our planet.
We will stop being blind, and we'll all realize
It's a tiny, tiny world.

She took an enormous sigh of relief the moment she got out of the boat. This ride should be demolished.

A chirp on her phone announced a new message.

Pia! Are you okay?

She was not sure why her friend in Copenhagen where she had just stopped by on her way to Paris would write her such an SMS. She typed back:

Yes. Well, except that Paris is a real disappointment!

OMG. So sad. Notre Dame!

Actually, the cathedral had been the only part she had enjoyed. She quickly wrote:

No. Notre Dame I actually liked.

Pia! Notre Dame is on 🔥 🔥 🔥 *! Where are you? Look at the news!!!!!*

She looked up from her phone; her data plan was only valid in Norway, Denmark, and Sweden.

The French couple with the toddler in front of her who had sat behind her in the boat were both looking at the man's cell phone, their eyes and mouths wide open.

Quickly the sounds of laughter that had filled the place were replaced by an eerie silence, only pierced by an occasional,

"Oh, mon Dieu! Notre Dame!"

THEY must have done it.

And SHE was in an American amusement park.

What if it was one of those coordinated attacks? Clearly this would be their next target.

She had to get out of here. Taking the train back to Paris. No way. Too dangerous. What if they would blow up the trains? Taxi. Taxi. Where? The hotel at the entrance. Legs run. Sprint. Not a marathon. Get out. Safety.

Why the fuck had she gone to Paris!

She got out of the taxi after paying the driver a hundred and eighty Euros at her expensive hotel. He looked like an NDF-P, so she did not give him a tip. He was the only taxi that was available. Otherwise, she would have of course taken another one. He only spoke French, as did the radio which he had turned on. The only thing she could understand was 'Notre Dame' spoken quite frequently.

The security guard directed her to the reception, "Out of precaution, Madame. For your safety."

She waited impatiently until the Japanese or Chinese woman behind the reception finished talking in Japanese or Chinese to the Japanese or Chinese couple in front of her. She got a new magnetic card and took the elevator up to the sixth floor and opened up the door with the number 69 on it.

She saw the Eiffel tower surging to her right and could see the smoke rising in the far distance. There and then she knew that she had to get out of here as soon as possible. Out of this Paris shit-hole. She did not bother to check any of the news once her phone had connected to the hotel's Wi-Fi, but standing on her room's terrace just quickly looked up the website.

Pia found the number which she needed to dial from France.

"You have reached the customer service line of First Airlines of Norway—the low-cost way to fly. Your estimated current wait time is 69 minutes."

As it became dark the Eiffel tower lit up in a bright golden light and the blue searchlight atop started turning as if nothing had happened, whereas in the distance she could only make out a very distant reddish glow.

"Hello, my name is Madhuri. How can I help you today?" A female voice said, after what seemed like eternity. She spoke a very clear Norwegian, with just a hint of an accent. Despite Pia trying to speak Danish to the female voice as clearly as possibly—much clearer than when she spoke to her patients in Godshus General Hospital—she ended up switching to English.

But only after finding out that Madhuri's office was not located in Bærum a suburb of Oslo, but in a town called Bangalore, in India.

"I need you to change my trip from Paris back to Ålesund to the next available flight. Please. It's really urgent."

"Of course. The next available flight leaves at 11:45 tomorrow. It's via Oslo and you'll be in Ålesund at 16:05."

"That's great. Thank you so much."

"Of course. You're welcome, Mrs. Andersen. Could I please have your credit card number to process the re-booking? Your charge will be NOK 1500."

"I only paid NOK 499 for the ticket back and forth."

"Sorry. But we have to charge a change fee and the difference in the price of the ticket."

"It's very irresponsible how you are taking advantage of people who are trying to get away from an act of terrorism. You should waive your charges. I will never ever fly your airline again."

"But Mrs. Andersen, the French President just announced that the fire in Notre Dame was an accident."

* * *

←⋯ 100 ○◎○ 390 ⋯→

August 28th, 2019
Dr. Pia Andersen
Godshus – Norway

Wednesday

Apart from his penis, his body was pure perfection. Pia had never expected to find a specimen like him in Godshus. She had his number stored as 'Mr. Sweden 2018' in her phone. Getting him to sleep with her had been easy. She simply combined the two strategies that she had perfected over the years back in Copenhagen to get men in their twenties to fuck her.

She had one for athletes and one for the young guys she would meet at work. 'Mr. Sweden 2018' happened to be eligible for both of them.

After accepting that there was just no 'Mr. Right' for her, her life became so much easier. Of course, she signed up with the famous app which starts with a 'T' when it launched in Copenhagen. But as a woman rapidly approaching her forties, it meant that the men who swiped her picture to her right were almost always her age group or older. Either single weirdoes or married trying to cheat on their wives. The app gave her practically no chance with those who she was actually interested in. When they saw the number which was written on the right side next to 'Pia', they would do a quick immediate swipe to the left. She could have easily lied about her age. Her carefully cared for athletic body looked at least ten years younger; but why would she try to compete with women in their twenties when her strategies worked so well for her:

For the athletes, she would usually make use of the swim training of the triathlon club. The men at work—in contrast to the X-ray/CT-technician 'Mr. Sweden 2018'—were mostly the young paramedics.

Of course, her reputation and positions were more than helpful: All the competitions she had won, co-founder and board member of the North Copenhagen Triathlon Club, finisher of the Ironman in Hawai'i twice over the years, specialist physician in gastroenterology, lecturer at the paramedic training course and vice chairwoman of the medical emergency room of Bispebjerg hospital.

The first conversation would always be short:

"I watched you swim. The little twist you're adding to your arm stroke is really unique. Would definitely like to get some more details how you're doing that. Send me a text. Perhaps we can also go over our training plans together." Said to the law student at the edge of the Kildeskovshallen pool, who was determined to become an Ironman and who felt clearly flattered that she commented on the way he swam—although it was in no way different from the way all the others were swimming.

Or a quick:

"You really managed the patient very well out there! Such an interesting case! Send me a text. Perhaps we can meet to sit down and talk about what was going on with the patient in more detail some day." Spoken towards the young paramedic, after he finished his report in her emergency room. He had taken the job just for a year, hoping to make it to medical school the next semester.

Most of the time she would get a text message within the following three days. If the guy was single and tolerable during the beer she would take him to in the cozy pub, in the old white house with the yellowish reed roof close to Dyrehavsbakken, she would start to follow her script:

The opening act was to surprise him totally out of the blue with a precisely timed: "Wanna fuck?" spoken softly, while he was swallowing the last sip of his beer. Over the years only two of the men had said no. Of course, all the guys would be nervous. Therefore, the sex, either—if the weather was nice in spring or summer—performed after a brief walk against a tree somewhere in Dyrehave or, after the short drive, in her apartment in Skodsborg, was always too quick and seldom satisfying for her. This was a calculated loss and just an intermission of sorts before moving on with her script.

The second act would start immediately after he pulled out of her. The blowjob took some time, but men so young would never go completely limp on her and their energy returned quickly.

The closing act would take place while she was driving him home, her assurance of continued future benefits with no obligations for him at all, just a quick text message away.

JUST   like   THAT:

🍻 — 🦴 — 🍌 — 🌮 — 💦 — 🍭 — — 💦 — 🤪 — 😈 — 📱

Three or four active numbers was all she really needed at a time. Regularly, men would fall off her list. Mostly after meeting a woman around their age, who would only trade benefits for seriousness. But with her strategies in place, she had no problems to move on—quickly entering a new number in her phone.

What had surprised her was the discreetness with which she was able to operate:

Women would share stories. *Men* never did.

Apparently, no man in his twenties would ever brag around about sleeping with a woman in her position, almost twice his age. She had no problem with that. It suited her well.

Of course, after moving to Godshus, she needed to build a new list from scratch: By the time 'Mr. Sweden 2018' showed up, fresh out of radiology technician training, more than a year before—purely for the quick money promised to him as a summer replacement—she already had two names stored in her phone. Both paramedics: very skinny 'Mr. Kinky'—the bondage thing, if not done excessively, felt stimulating and novel to her at times, and the quite chubby, shortish but really very well endowed 'Mr. Big'.

Both were serving their purpose well.

It was the toned muscular body of a young athlete that she longed for. 'Mr. Sweden 2018' did not stand a chance against her combined strategies. Sleeping with him had the additional convenience that the physical act could be performed during work, if her overnight call started to feel too long and lonely. The pay they offered in Norway had to be so much better for him than in Sweden, as he continued on after the summer.

She never had any illusion that he stayed because of her.

During winter, to remain undisturbed, they would use the small patients' changing room next to the CT scanner after she told the nurses that she would work on her X-ray reports in the radiology department. If the weather was nice during the never really dark summer nights, as tonight, they would carefully walk up the fire escape stairwell—unnoticed—to the second-floor conference room.

As always, he had moved one of the chairs onto the balcony. Pia was sitting naked on his lap. Her white lab coat, blue scrubs, bra, and panties were lying on the conference room table inside, next to his white scrub top. He had dropped his pants and black sport boxer briefs to his ankles. He would always keep on his white clogs.

The palm of her right hand was tightly holding the dense muscle of the back of his neck and pushing her own lean body against the V-shape of his muscular torso. With his almost two meters, her forehead was just touching his cheekbones, which appeared like they were chiseled out of marble. The skin between her eyebrows gently rubbed against the mild roughness of his well-kept short black beard. He still carried the slight scent of chlorine. She concluded that he must have gone to work directly from his training session at the pool that afternoon.

The physique of 'Mr. Sweden 2018' was not just the one of an endurance athlete. She had got to know multiple examples of these wiry bodies intimately over the years. He was not afraid to sacrifice a couple of seconds of time in a race for aesthetics. She knew that he spent long hours with weights in the gym as well, apart of all the regular swimming and running.

She felt the stimulation of the nipples of her firm breasts, which were pressing from below against the pure strength of his hard

297

chest. The somewhat larger size of her boobs, the only evidence left on her body that she had only started with endurance sports later in her life. The ÖTILÖ[1] race, a 75-kilometer course across 26 islands in the Stockholm archipelago, would take place the following week. He was leaving to go there on Friday. All the training over the last months had melted away the remnants of any subcutaneous fat covering the muscles of the eight-pack, which formed 'Mr. Sweden 2018"s abdomen. She felt the rhythmic contractions of these thick strands of muscles which he used in isolation to action his pelvis to thrust into her. His powerful hands on her buttocks, holding her firmly in place.

He was not using a condom. After her ovaries had shut down early on her some years before, she always gave the men the option not to use any. 'Mr. Sweden 2018' was like most of the others and had gladly accepted her offer.

At least she did not need a plan for how to discard a used condom so nobody would notice what was being done at night in Godshus General Hospital.

Sadly, the only part of his body which failed to stimulate Pia was his cock. In every position they had ever tried, she could barely feel him inside her.

It was a size issue.

His dick was not just small—it was too small. And just too thin.

What a waste of such an impressive body.

She had started smoking again because of his penis. She needed the nicotine from just that one cigarette after sleeping with him to help her cope with this recurring disappointment.

It was not clearly obvious.

He was a shower.

---

1 **ÖTILÖ** – Name of the original swim-run race, which was the result of a late-night challenge in a bar in 2002 and which is a 75-kilometer course across 26 islands in the Stockholm archipelago. The literal translation from Swedish is 'island to island'.

Therefore naked in the shower at the pool or gym his just about less than ten centimeter length might have not appeared so irrefutably catastrophic to him, if he, in secret, compared himself to the other guys.

The problem was that he was only—and only—a shower.

Not a grower at all.

Stimulation would just make his cock stand up. Solely a variation in position, but no change in length or girth at all. Absolutely none. You would get exactly what you saw before, and not a millimeter more.

She was sure that no woman who had slept with him ever said something. The rest of his body was just too perfect. No woman—including herself—who, after feeling the triumph of having seduced him to have sex with her, would ever openly talk about this.

Not really because of him, but first and foremost because of herself.

Occasionally, however, she suspected that deep down he knew.

His careful attention to all the muscles, his beard, just because of the part of him which would always stay too small no matter how many weights he would lift.

Genes can be so very, very cruel at times.

She felt bad for the one woman he would meet later in life. What kind of man would he become once he grew old; a young, beautiful body no longer a compensation for his totally inadequate size.

Could gene therapy help?

What would happen to the world if the dick dimension of every guy was adequate?

Would all the competing and compensating just conclude?

Pia noticed the quickening pace of the contractions of his abdomen. When she felt how the muscles surrounding the base of his cock were tensing up against the back of her left hand, she decided to stop stimulating herself with her index and middle finger.

His climax—in contrast to hers—was coming closer. She then moved her left hand onto that spot on his chest, where she could start to play around with the fingerlike strands of muscles that attached to his ribs from his back.

Soon, she would smoke her cigarette on the balcony after he returned downstairs. She tried to force as much of the skin of her body against all his perfectly sculptured fibers of lean meat. She also tried to imagine the feeling of having the penis of chubby and short 'Mr. Big' inside her. Although Pia was quite sure 'Mr. Sweden 2018' did not care at all, it would be time for some Kegel exercises in the very near future.

She decided that for the soundtrack she would just stick to her regular tonight:

"Mmmmh ..." followed by:

"Oh, ohh, ohhh, ohhhh, ohhhhh, yeah."

Shortly after, an "Aah." from Mr. Sweden 2018 signaled that it was time for:

Lights—Camera—ACTION

and Pia responded with just a slightly bored:

"Mmmmh."

And her performance that followed was definitely not worthy of a Bodil Award.

* * *

←··· 227 ○◎○ 106 ···→

September 15th, 2019
Dr. Pia Andersen
Godshus – Norway

Sunday

A red circle with a number one in it appeared on the right upper corner of the blue app symbol with the small 'f' in it. Pia opened the app. A new friend request. She did not recognize the name at all, but the picture looked vaguely familiar. She opened his profile. Yes. She recognized him now. The hunky Australian who had saved her; after Jack had left her to die. Yes—it was definitively him. Older, but still looking hunky. Appeared to still be living in Thailand and running a boat business. She scrolled through his profile.

Alternating female faces next to him.

Likely in no serious relationship.

Still single.

No pictures with children.

Funny that he had contacted her now. It had been he who saved all of them in the bay that day. By some miracle, nobody had died on Ko Phi Phi Le Island. She had been bruised and had scratches everywhere, but nothing really serious when he rescued her from the tree trunk. The hunky Australian somehow got them back to Phi Phi island in the slightly damaged longtail boat later that afternoon. It was then that they realized the overnight trip to the bay had likely saved their lives, as there was absolutely nothing left from either the bungalow or the rest of the hotel they had stayed in.

But it was then when things started getting serious. Of course, all her insulin was gone. All the insulin which she had taken to 'The Beach', and all the insulin which she had left in the bungalow in the hotel. And because of the complete disorganization of all the NDF-Ps in their NDF-P country, she was now going to die going into diabetic ketoacidosis. Why was this NDF-P country not prepared for something like this?

And then it was he who saved her.

After he found out what she needed, he put her together with some other people on his longtail boat and through the night got them over to Phuket. The hospital there was terrible, but at least she managed to get some insulin.

She decided to accept his friend request.

Shortly after, she got a new message on her messenger app. It was from him:

G'day, Pia! How's it hangin? Been a long time, hey! Looking well. Do you remember me? It'd be bonzer to see you, you great galah! Wondered if you fancied popping over to Thailand in December? We're planning a bit of a memorial service here with people from the gang to mark the 15 years since the tsunami. Having a bit of tucker and grog in the arvo, too. Whadday think? Cheers.

Pia really did not care at all about any type of memorial service. But the hunky man who had once saved her life looked interesting.

Of course, he was neither Danish nor Scandinavian. But considering that the future Queen of Denmark was from the country he was from, Pia decided to write back.

* * *

←··· 393 ○◎○ 363 ···→

October 9th, 2019
Dr. Pia Andersen
Godshus – Norway

Wednesday

Pia was extremely careful not to touch the table at all. Of course, she had wiped it before the meeting started. Twice. But she did everything she could to stay away from it. Instead of leaning her elbows onto it as she would usually do during the morning meeting, she had just kept her hands in her lap. She was still sitting on the chair in the conference room. On her regular spot at the table like every morning, closest to the fire escape stairway door with her back facing the balcony window. On a chair designed by Arne Jacobsen—a Model 3107 chair. The chair which she and 'Mr. Sweden 2018' would use at night in summer on the balcony. It was her chair. Of course, she would never use someone else's chair. She was respectful of other people's space. Not like the NDF-P.

She was tired from the night call and ready to go home and straight to bed. The morning department meeting was finished and everyone but her had left the conference room. Ordinarily, she would already be driving home by now, but today was unexpectedly different. She needed to stay for another fifteen minutes until 8:00 when the tall old Norwegian guy with the long white beard would arrive. The 'device' doctor of Godshus General Hospital, whose office was located in the small separate building on the opposite end of the hospital's parking lot next to the morgue. She would have to walk over there with the broken pager which she held in the hands in her lap. The pager which she would usually put on the worn ash wood of the conference room table in front of her. But, of course, not now. After the call the previous night, she would never, ever sit at this table the same way. A table Poul Kjærholm had called PK55™ when he designed it back in 1957. She realized that the

303

furniture in the conference room was likely still the same as when the hospital had been built in the 1970s. Originals. Scandinavian, but especially Danish, design aged really well. Perhaps she could somehow request that the hospital buy a new table now?

Her call night had started with the excitement of the 54-year-old chain-smoking fisherman. Around 21:15 his concerned wife had driven him in. Crushing chest pain for the last two hours or so, beginning shortly after he started smoking his after-dinner cigarette. As all the local fishermen he was very stoic, but his ECG showed clear anterior ST-elevations in leads V2-V4, which lead to an immediate phone call to Dr. Boisen-Jensen and the activation of the catheterization lab team. The morphine and nitroglycerin she had given him had made the patient comfortable by the time Dr. Boisen-Jensen arrived. And soon after him, all of the sudden the NDF-P had appeared like out of nowhere. She guessed they had an arrangement going for her to get some training with regard to her future career ambitions as an interventional cardiologist. Although now Pia very much doubted that the arrangement between the two was limited to cardiology things. They rapidly took the fisherman to the catheterization laboratory, and the ICU knew he would be coming up to them after he had his stent placed. She agreed with Dr. Boisen-Jensen that he would write all the necessary orders for the ICU. After quickly seeing one more patient in the ER who only needed some prednisone and an inhaler for his asthma, the ER was completely empty around 22:30. As 'Mr. Kinky' was in the process of getting deleted from the memory of her phone because of a 20-something-year-old woman who was serious about him, Pia was very happy when she got a message from 'Mr. Sweden 2018':

22:45—CT-scan?

She let the nurses in the ICU know that she would be in the radiology department working on some of her overdue X-ray reading reports and took the elevator downstairs. She had just locked the door to the patients' changing room, while 'Mr. Sweden 2018' had already taken off his scrub top, revealing the chiselled torso she was longing for, when his pager beeped. The stent in the fisherman's LAD had been successfully deployed, but they had trouble transferring the digital film record of the catheterization from the radiology computer to the general electronic medical record and 'Mr. Sweden 2018' was also asked to help transport the patient to the ICU. He put the scrub top back on and she waited for his return about ten minutes later, using the time to undress completely. It had to be around 23:40 when she—filled with the usual ambivalent (non)-satisfaction after having sex with 'Mr. Sweden 2018'—started walking up the fire escape stairway for the necessary ritual of the quick nicotine fix from the one cigarette on the balcony of the conference room.

To make sure the nurses would never find out, she was used to walking up the stairs in total darkness. There were nine steps in each flight; with a total of four flights to get to the door leading to the conference room. Initially, when she and 'Mr. Sweden 2018' had decided to explore the balcony she would use the flashlight function of her iPhone, but nowadays she could walk the staircase in complete darkness, just counting the steps and holding on to the balustrade. Turning on the timed light in the stairwell could have given 'Mr. Sweden 2018' and herself away as the nurses sitting in the first-floor nursing station would surely at some point in time have noticed the light coming from below the door. From the time of her internship in the small Bornholm hospital, she knew that nurses (especially the night nurses) somehow always knew where the doctor was in the house. As if they had attached some sort of tracking system to her. But she was smarter than them.

When she reached the first-floor landing, she noticed things differing slightly from the usual. A very dim light shining through the conference room window illuminated the last two flights of stairs. Somebody must have left a light on in the conference room somewhere. Suddenly it made sense to her why the architect of the hospital had put in the glass partition wall next to the door leading from the conference room to the fire escape stairwell. At least part of the stairs would be illuminated if the light was on in the conference room. She walked up the remaining two flights of stairs and had almost pushed down the door handle when the sounds coming from the conference room caused her to freeze. Muffled sounds of heavy breathing, followed by a male voice, which sounded like Anders, saying "Belly-button piercing. Very sexy." At that point, she decided to carefully lean forward over the railing and peek through the glass partition wall into the dimly lit conference room.

Pia was very sure that Poul Kjærholm would have never envisioned what the table he had designed was being used for.

The light was very dim, the conference room only lit by the light coming out of the chief physician's office. So mainly she could only make out the shadows of the two persons who were in there. But it was clear who they were. The shorter person leaning against the table right at what was usually her place and the taller person leaning down towards her head. Next through the continuing sounds of heavy breathing, she heard a brief clacking sound, as if something had been hastily placed on the table. Then it appeared like the smaller person lifted her arms and shortly afterward she saw a fleeting shadow, like as if a piece of wardrobe had been thrown through the air. Pia almost screamed the moment when out of nowhere a soft something hit the glass partition wall just in front of her face, before it fell to the ground next to the fire escape door. It now appeared that the silhouettes were moving closer together at her place of the table.

Her hypothesis, which she had briskly formulated, of what was unfolding in the dimly lit conference room was unequivocally confirmed the moment she heard the characteristic melody of a condom package being ripped open.

Any further analysis of the entire revealing situation, however, was harshly interrupted when a brief cracking sound in the hospital loudspeaker system was followed by an overhead announcement:

"Medical Code ICU bed 4. Medical Code ICU bed 4. Medical Code ICU bed 4."

It had to be the fisherman, as bed 4 had been empty when she had taken over her shift and had briefly rounded in the ICU. In a split second full of panic, Pia realized that the piercing loud beep which would start coming from her pager after a couple of seconds would surely reveal the presence of her hidden observatory to the two people in the conference room. She therefore quickly grabbed the pager and tossed it over the railing—the beginning of any beep aborted and muffled by its crashing sound on the stairwell landing one floor below.

In contrast to the fisherman, who was likely having a light breakfast in ICU bed 4 at this very moment—of course, with a sore chest from a couple of broken ribs from the chest compressions and the electrical shock that successfully stopped his ventricular fibrillation—Pia was not sure that even the tall old Norwegian guy with the long white beard could resurrect her pager back to life from its fall. She looked at her Garmin Forerunner 945 watch: 7:54. It was time to bring her pager to its special little hospital. As so often before, she slightly bumped her knee against the heavy metal legs of the worn PK 55 table. Perhaps, after all, Poul Kjærholm did have some intentions making them as sturdy as they were?

When she passed the red garbage bin, which was standing next to the small table with the coffee machine, her tired eyes by chance spotted the clear evidence that the play of shadows she had observed the night before had not been a dream. A hastily and carelessly deposited condom with not even the slightest attempt made to hide its presence. How amateurish. She was about to open the door to the conference room when she realized that she really did not know about anyone else besides her, 'Mr. Sweden 2018', Dr. Boisen-Jensen, and the NDF-P having sex in the hospital. As someone could make the same discovery as she did and as any rumors, potentially involving her, needed to be avoided at all cost, she returned to the garbage bin. Pia grabbed the clear plastic bag containing the incriminating evidence and took it out with her to one of the garbage cans located on the hospital parking lot.

After the tall old Norwegian guy with the long white beard confirmed that her pager was deader than dead, she quickly drove home. It had started to become light outside.

She had found the white wooden house with the balconies on both sides shortly after she had accepted the job in Godshus. Compared to Copenhagen, real estate was dirt cheap in this part of Norway. It was a short, about three-kilometer drive from the hospital on a small quiet one-way road. A bit out of town, but still close. Her closest neighbors lived about 250 meters away. The privacy was useful when her visitors came. And she could start biking right away in front of the house for her training when the weather was good.

Pia entered the home which would always be too big for her. Thirsty, she grabbed a glass of water from the kitchen. She had re-done the kitchen—it had been such a pain to get the black granite countertops installed. All that the local contractors had offered her was a black composite material.

She thought about what she had witnessed at night. ,

Treason.

Dr. Boisen-Jensen betraying his origin, his race, his nation with the NDF-P. There was no chance the country could stay a strong, proud, independent, and sovereign nation with people like him around.

He deserved punishment.

She would have to do something.

Pia craved something stronger than water to calm her nerves. She rinsed a celery stalk, grabbing the Worcestershire and Tabasco sauce, the lemon juice, and salt and pepper before she took the ice cubes and bottle of Danzka vodka out of the freezer.

Mr. Big's message arrived while she was returning the tomato juice into the fridge. He let her know he was free after 17:00 in the afternoon. It was Wednesday—the pool would only close at 21:00, so she could do her training from 19:00.

She texted back:

JULEBORD (The Holiday Party)

I'll leave the door unlocked and sleep. Wake me up! I'll be naked. Will be Zzz about your 🖐.

She made sure the entrance door was unlocked before walking up to the bedroom on the first floor with the view of the blue water of the fjord. The cocktail combined with the warm water of the shower made her sleepy in a good way.

As she had promised, she went to bed nude. She covered herself with the blanket she had shared with the bodies of so many men.

All by herself in her bed.

As always.

As none of them would ever stay and fall asleep next to her.

Later that evening when she was driving back home from her swim training, the news on the radio announced that earlier in the day a synagogue had been attacked in Halle, Germany.

* * *

←··· 228 ○◎○ 397 ···→

December 10th, 2019
Dr. Pia Andersen
Godshus – Norway

Tuesday

"Anders, that was what the pharmacist from Legemiddelverk[1] wrote in her e-mail. If you want, I can forward it to you." Pia was getting frustrated a bit. She was not Anders' doctor and just because she was the senior physician responsible for overseeing the medications the hospital stocked did not mean she was the right person to deal with his personal problem.

"So because of Brexit, the English manufacturer has stopped selling diltiazem in capsules in Norway altogether? They haven't even left yet, or have they?"

"No, they didn't leave yet. And yes, that's what happened. What she wrote is that Norway is such a small market it just doesn't make sense for the company to get all the approval paperwork done for the future, once the automatic reciprocal approval expires after Brexit. So they decided to stop selling this medication in Norway altogether."

"I cannot believe how fucked-up all of this is."

Seeing how his facial muscles had tensed up, Pia almost started feeling sorry for him. All of this had just come up, when during the routine quarterly medication review report she was required to do, she mentioned the e-mail she had received from the hospital pharmacy department at Ålesund Regional Medical Center, which was also responsible for overseeing Godshus General Hospital.

The subject line of that e-mail had been:

---

1 **Legemiddelverk** – *Norwegian*: Norwegian Medicines Agency. National authority responsible for supervising the production, trials, approval, and marketing of medications in Norway.

Discontinuation of all CAPSULE-based diltiazem extended-release formulations in Norway (ADIZEM—PAN Pharma Ltd., United Kingdom) and transition to sustained-release TABLETS only.

It had surprised her when he started asking all the questions after she mentioned this to him the previous day. But then she remembered a condom-filled medicine cabinet in Malmö on a summer night many, many years ago.

He told her, "But I have been taking ADIZEM for years for my heart!"

From an overall perspective, this was actually a tiny change and Anders was upset out of proportion. First of all, diltiazem was a relatively old drug. Still a useful one, but nowadays mostly newer drugs—for which there was better data showing that they lowered mortality—would be used. Only if they did not work, one would go back to good old diltiazem. And although there were some very small differences between the capsules and the sustained-release tablets, in practical terms they were really interchangeable. Anders must know that, so she was not sure why he was so unnerved about all of it.

"So going forward, once we use up all the ADIZEM capsules, we will switch over to sustained-release tablets. CARDIZEM Retard for the 90 mg, 240 mg, and 300 mg dosages. That's what they'll actually do in all the hospitals in Norway." she said.

His face got even more tense.

"So there will also be no more capsules available in the outpatient pharmacies as well?"

"I guess so. Seems like it will be just the sustained-release tablets in the entire country."

"Can you forward me that e-mail from Legemiddelverk, please?"

"Of course, Anders. You really seem very upset about this, and I understand that it's hard to switch from one medication to another. But sorry for asking about this—why can't you just take the tablets?"

"I'm allergic to vanilla."

"Okay, but it's diltiazem."

"Some asshole at a pharma company unfortunately at some point must have decided that their pills should taste better and added vanilla extract to the coating of the pill."

Pia had never considered such details when she prescribed medications. What a series of coincidences! Well, the devil is always in the details, isn't it? But as Anders was talking now, perhaps it was a good opportunity to find out why he was taking all those medications. Given the scar on his chest, which she remembered from that night, it looked like he had open heart surgery at one point. But why he had been on the diltiazem for years did not fully make sense. She needed a bit more information. And it would also appear that she was caring about him. With a dose of false empathy, she said:

"Oh, Anders. That's clearly a no-go then. I'm really sorry about this. But I mean, why are you taking the diltiazem in the first place?"

"I had a valve replacement as a teenager. Atrial fibrillation. Rate control. To make sure my heart rate doesn't go too quick."

Now also the Warfarin which led to the bloodbath that morning made sense.

"I'm not a cardiologist. Only a gastroenterologist. But couldn't you just switch to a beta-blocker?"

"I don't like the side effects of beta-blockers."

"Okay."

"Pia, I mean this is a huge favor I want to ask you. And please keep it personal—just between us two."

Interesting—the empathic and caring aspect had worked as well. She was now all interested in what he would request.

"First of all, thanks for writing that email to Legemiddelverk. After you told me about all of this yesterday, I checked how many ADIZEM capsules I have left. I'll run out on December 16th. I'll try to get them somehow, but just as a backup."

"As a backup?"

"Yes, could you please check how many ADIZEM capsules we still have in the hospital pharmacy? And perhaps stock the CARDIZEM Retard 90 mg tablets now already and start giving those to patients? Just in case I won't be able to get these in some way or form by December 16th? I would use the hospital stock then. Of course, I would buy some CARDIZEM Retard 90 mg tablets and exchange them with the hospital stock."

Pia very briefly paused. An idea came to her mind and with a smile she said:

"Of course, Anders. No problem. I'll do that."

* * *

←··· 364 ○◎○ 403 ···→

December 17th, 2019
Dr. Pia Andersen
Godshus – Norway

Tuesday

"Pia. Thank you so much for the diltiazem."

Satisfied, she smiled back at Anders.

"No problem. Let me know on Sunday before you fly to Copenhagen if you need more. I'll be in the hospital."

"Yes, I'll stop by if needed."

She had met him in front of the door leading to operating room '2'. He just finished the one cardiac catheterization which was scheduled for the day. And she would now do the screening colonscopies on four patients.

She watched how he walked towards the door leading to the ER with the envelope she had given him full of the seven ADIZEM capsules inside. She knew exactly what he would do next. Walk up to the conference room. Enter into his office. Take the black pill organizer and put in the seven ADIZEM capsules in their places, and then take one of the ADIZEM capsules together with his other pills. Of course, he would never know or suspect that the capsules would not only contain diltiazem.

Because Anders would never ever suspect what she had done:

Later the Tuesday afternoon the previous week, after he had asked her to give him the ADIZEM capsules from the hospital supply, just before going home, she had stopped by the ICU.

"Louise, I have a terrible headache. I'll just get two Panodil tablets," she said before stepping into the small room in the ICU where all the medications were stored. She took her time taking the two 325 mg tablets out of their blister pack and watched how Louise and the other nurse had stepped into the patients' rooms, away from the nursing counter. She then quickly took the seven

ADIZEM capsules as he had instructed her to take, but—in addition—also took seven light blue 2 mg Warfarin tablets still in their blisterpacks with her, putting all of the tablets into the pocket of her lab coat. As soon as she was home, she placed all the tablets into a drawer in her kitchen.

The next two days she did nothing.

On Friday evening, once alone and done smoking her cigarette—after 'Mr. Sweden 2018' had left—she came back to the kitchen and took out the capsules and the pills. She took one of the capsules and compared it to the Warfarin tablet. The large white yellow ADIZEM capsule was about one and a half centimeters long, much bigger than the little blue round five-millimeter Warfarin tablet. This would work. Using her black granite mortar and pestle, which she would use to make guacamole from time to time, she ground up one of the Warfarin tablets. The last step was to carefully open one ADIZEM capsule, remove a little bit—but not all the diltiazem powder—and fill in the Warfarin containing powder from the mortar. Then she closed the ADIZEM capsule. The capsule with the added Warfarin looked exactly like the other ADIZEM capsules. This would definitively work. That was all she did on Friday.

On Saturday just before noon, after she got back from her swim training, she gradually added powder containing 2 mg of Warfarin each to the remaining six ADIZEM capsules. She found a white envelope and put the seven capsules in there.

Today, she handed him the envelope with a very friendly smile.

She knew nothing would happen immediately. Over the next two to three days Dr. Boisen-Jensen's liver would start producing even less of the clotting factors than it had for years as her action had doubled the dose of the Warfarin he would take; a total of 4 mg of Warfarin instead of his regular 2 mg. Perhaps as early as Friday this week Dr. Boisen-Jensen's blood would clot very little, like during that summer night many years ago in Malmö. Then it was just a matter of time until he would bleed. It was unpredictable what would happen. A bleed into his brain if he bumped his head somehow? Bleeding somewhere in his gut; with blood gushing out of either his mouth or anus?

Pia did not know. She knew she potentially might need to give him more of the specially prepared ADIZEM capsules before something would happen. And she would prepare more of them on Saturday to give to him on Sunday before she would leave for Thailand.

Eventually something would happen to Dr. Boisen-Jensen, which would either significantly harm or kill him, but most importantly punish this traitor. She imagined his bloodless body lying in a bed with white sheets soaked with his blood, hands stretched out, as if his body would form a cross.

Like a Dannebrog.

ii

Like the flag of her nation he was betraying with the NDF-P. She stepped into operating room '2' to start her first colonoscopy.

Satisfied.

Her action had assured that, while Dr. Boisen-Jensen would assume that he would be taking his regular 2 mg dose of Warfarin, he—in reality—would be taking double the dose.

* * *

←··· 121 ○◎○ 185 ···→

December 20th, 2019
Dr. Pia Andersen
Godshus – Norway

Friday – 17:40

Pia opened the door for him.

"Okay, see you once you're back from Thailand."

"Yes. I will text you as soon as I land. Have a quiet shift."

She closed the door behind 'Mr. Big' in his paramedic uniform. He was getting even more chubby. It was her turn to shower now. She let 'Mr. Big' shower and change first. He had stopped by before his overnight shift, which started at 18:00. She finished running her 5 km training run on the treadmill while he was taking off his clothes.

They did it in the kitchen. She always liked the stimulating contrast of the cold radiating from the black granite countertop, her still warm buttock muscles from her run, and the heat generated by him inside her.

Her smoking was getting out of control. Her body craved the nicotine, and she smoked a cigarette against the open window after she put on her bathrobe. It was already dark outside and there was a light drizzle. Except for the out-of-control morning meeting, it had been a regular Friday. After Dr. Boisen-Jensen was done with his one cardiac catheterization, she did her four colonoscopies of the day and the one EGD. She had removed three polyps. One lady had a really poor prep. The EGD likely showed some gastritis only, and she took two biopsies. She then helped on the first floor a bit and left the hospital in time. Once she got home, she went right to the treadmill for her run.

Before stepping into the shower, she checked her phone again. Like at least twenty times before that day. Still no message from him. It would be forty-eight hours soon.

In the shower, Pia had to scrub a bit to get the sticky whitish transparent patches off her inner thighs, which Mr. Big's semen had turned into after dripping out of her while she had been smoking. While washing her hair, she thought about what she should wear for the Julebord. Not that she was really eager to go. She selected the black skirt with the origami birds pattern in different shades of red and the shoulder free top with the deep cleavage. If it was cold in the restaurant, she could always use her black pashmina scarf to cover up her shoulders.

She needed to put back on her insulin pump. She had taken it off before she went for her run on the treadmill. After she had dried herself off, she checked the pump. She would only need to refill the insulin reservoir the next morning. Pia took out a new pack that contained the tubing and the cannula and opened it. She attached the tubing to the pump and primed it. She felt the short sting of the cannula as she drove it into her skin on her lower abdomen. She attached the sticky gauze which would hold everything in place and then pricked her finger to check her blood sugar. It was okay—she would not need to give herself a correction bolus right now. She decided against wearing her continuous glucose monitoring device tonight and went to the bedroom to get dressed.

Before she went back to the bathroom to put on some mascara and light make-up, she checked her phone again—still no message.

Once she was done, she went downstairs. She would do all her packing for Thailand the next day. The clock in the kitchen showed 18:42. She would need to get going. It was a fifteen-minute drive to the restaurant.

Pia opened her handbag to put her phone inside. She glanced at her Glock P80 pistol, which she always kept there. She would never leave her house without it. She wanted to feel safe. These were dangerous times in the world.

She got into the car and began to drive. After she turned left into the restaurant's parking lot, she parked the car next to the car she recognized as belonging to the NDF-P, whom she had to work with. Luckily, Faiza would soon be gone.

JULEBORD (The Holiday Party)

Pia got out of her car and walked over a small metal bridge. A thin, cold rain had started. A bike leaned against the railing opposite the entrance door. She opened the door and stepped into the emerald-greenish light which rose from the depth of the restaurant.

* * *

←⋯ 248 ○◎○ 374 ⋯→

Chapter 5

Dr. Hana Rønneberg

August 21st, 1968
Dr. Hana Rønneberg
Prague – Czechoslovakia

Wednesday

"Haničko[1]—wake up." Grandma's soft hand was gently stroking her forehead. But her face was not the same when Hana blinked her eyes open. "All is okay. All is okay. Haničko. But I need you to get up now."

A humming sound filled her bedroom from the sky beyond the window. It was earlier than the other summer holiday mornings. Yesterday they went to the zoo, after they had returned to the city from the summer house in the countryside. She always liked the elephants the most. She wanted to see them again. School would restart soon. Mom and Dad were back to work. The door to her room had been left half open and she could hear the radio from the living room:

'Všemu lidu Československé socialistické republiky. Včera dne dvacatého srpna devatenácetšedsátosm kolem třiadvacáte hodiny večer ...'[2]

The humming sound from the sky returned.

---

1 **Haničko** – *Czech*: 'Haničko' is the diminutive version of Hana in Czech—meaning 'little Hana'.

2 **Všemu lidu Československé socialistické republiky. Včera dne dvacatého srpna devatenácetšedsátosm kolem třiadvacáte hodiny večer ...** – *Czech*: To all the people of the Czechoslovak Socialist Republic. Yesterday, August 20th, 1968 around 23:00 ...

'... *stalo se tak bez vědomí* ...'[1]

Through the door, she now felt Mom and Dad walking around.

'... *aby zachovali klid a nekladli* ...'[2]

Mom appeared in the door.

'... *odpor.*'[3]

She quickly brushed her teeth. Mom, Dad, and Grandma were whispering in the living room. Dad walked up to her and bent down so their faces were close.

"Haničo—listen," he said after he lowered a nervous fist from his mouth. "Today we'll all go to Mom's and Dad's hospital together. All the four of us. You, Mom, Grandma, and me."

Shouting noises started coming from the street. Grandma had stuffed two bags with food. The plushy krteček[4] who shared the bed with her, her pillow, and several children's books were quickly arranged into a small suitcase. A terrifying rattling noise started rising from the street and met with the humming sound from the sky just as they walked down the stairs from their third-floor apartment.

* * *

---

1 ... **stalo se tak bez vědomí** ... – *Czech*: ... this happened without the knowledge ...

2 ... **aby zachovali klid a nekladli** ... – *Czech*: ... to remain calm and ...

3 ... **odpor**. – *Czech*: ... not resist.

4 **Krteček** – Little Mole. An animated character created by Czech animator Zdeněk Miler.

Dr. Ruth Singerová—Hana's mom—could see the black tanks rattling near the Czechoslovak Radio Broadcasting Center to her left and the Antonov transporter planes humming above in the cloudless blue sky as soon as they stepped outside the front door of their building with the number 16 on Vinohradská Street.

* * *

←⋯ 128 ○◎○ 325 ⋯→

September 10th, 1968
Dr. Hana Rønneberg
Malmö – Sweden

Tuesday

"Mom, mom! The houses were so small and it was so fun flying through those white clouds." The excitement of her first flight was definitively the best thing that had happened to Hana during the last two weeks.

She was missing Grandma.

"Yes, the houses were much smaller this time than I remember from before," her mother answered. "Guess the planes are flying higher today."

"You've flown before?" Hana was surprised. "Did you also fly from Vienna?"

"It was a really long time ago, before you were born. It's how I got back to Prague from …" Her mom paused briefly. "Well, I guess they didn't quite call it Israel back then. But the plane was much smaller than ours—and it had propellers and not those modern engines."

"Where's Israel?"

A tall woman with a gentle smile prevented mom's explanation. She had appeared in front of them and gestured to Hana and her parents to follow her to a small office, which was just down the hallway from the waiting room they were sitting in with the others at Malmö Bultofta Airport. An older gentleman was there to translate.

"Welcome to Sweden," he said. "We only need to quickly fill out a family immigration form with some basic information before a bus will take you to the welcome center. We know you are exhausted. Everything else will be taken care of in the next couple of days."

* * *

Dr. Ruth Singerová briefly hesitated twice after she wrote down 'Anesthesiologist' in the form below the 'Obstetrician' which was her husband's medical specialty:

First she decided not to include 'German' on the line asking about language skills.

Then under 'religion' she felt safe not to copy the four print letters: NONE which were on the line belonging to her husband, but instead wrote down: JEWISH.

She did the same on the line belonging to her daughter.

* * *

"How many suitcases do you have?" Hana noticed that the tall woman looked surprised after her mom pointed to Hana's small suitcase, which still contained just what had been hastily packed nineteen days before.

Hana's mom explained: "Most of the fighting happened in the street we lived in. People got shot there and died. The house our home was in burnt out completely the first day."

* * *

←··· 322 ○◎○ 129 ···→

October 6th, 1973
Dr. Hana Rønneberg
Trondheim – Norway

Saturday

Hana recognized his curly hair from school. He sat just across the aisle.

עַל חֵטְא שֶׁחָטָאנוּ לְפָנֶיךָ בְּגִלּוּי עֲרָיוֹת
For the sin which we have committed before You with immorality.

She had dressed all in white for the day. She was tired, but the break when they could go home would come soon now. She had only left the place next to her parents for a very short time once that morning to abide the custom. He looked over to her now and smiled. Hana smiled back. He was either one or two years above her. She liked his smile. She had been too shy to talk to him yet, but she would ask him on Monday. Mostly she liked the new school.

עַל חֵטְא שֶׁחָטָאנוּ לְפָנֶיךָ בְּדַעַתוּבְמִרְמָה
For the sin which we have committed before You with knowledge and with deceit.

The synagogue in Stockholm had been much bigger than the one here. But they lived very close here. He was sitting next to a man who must be his dad, as they both had the same curly hair.

עַל חֵטְא שֶׁחָטָאנוּ לְפָנֶיךָ בִּהוֹנָאת רֵע
For the sin which we have committed before You by deceiving a fellowman.

He and his presumed father got up now and started walking back up the aisle. One more man who was older joined them. He smiled at her once more as he got out of the bench.

327

So he was one of them. They would soon return without shoes and stand up front and recite the blessing:

May G_d bless you and keep you. May G_d make His face shine upon you and give you grace. May G_d lift up His face to you and give you peace.

Their white scarves covering their heads, they would hold their arms up. First facing the ark before turning around. Then they would stretch out both arms at shoulder height. Initially, their palms would face downwards, but then they would raise them, revealing that the little and ring finger of each hand were held together and separated from the middle and index finger, these again touching and separated from the thumb with both thumbs touching each other.

Of course, she was not supposed to know this as she should not have gazed at them directly, but full of curiosity she had peeked out under the white scarf last year in Stockholm.

עַל חֵטְא שֶׁחָטָאנוּ לְפָנֶיךָ בְּזָדוֹן וּבִשְׁגָגָה

And for the sin which we have committed before You intentionally or unintentionally.

The chazzan now started to recite:

"For You are the Pardoner of Israel and the Forgiver of the tribes of Yeshurun in every generation, and ..."

His voice began to change and slow.

"... aside from ..."

Hana now looked up. She saw that Mom had also glanced up, as had most of the other members of the congregation. Perhaps that was how they did things here in Trondheim?

"... You ..."

People now started turning around, looking towards the exit. But neither the boy from school nor his dad nor the other man had come back through the door yet.

"... we ..."

Some people started to murmur.

"... *have* ..."

The face of the rabbi looked just a little bit annoyed.

"... *no* ..."

More murmurs and more heads turning towards the entrance door.

"... *King* ..."

The entrance door now opened.

"... *who* ..."

The older man as well as the boy from Hana's school and his dad stepped inside. Their faces had a scared, disbelieving look on them.

"... *forgives and* ..."

Only the older man walked down the aisle. Not gracefully, but with quick steps. He had not taken off his shoes. The building was filled with murmurs now. The boy from school and his dad stayed behind at the door.

"... *pardons.*"

The older man had now walked up to the rabbi and uttered something, which made the rabbi's face turn worried. The rabbi asked the man, and the man only nodded his head. Some silence followed before the rabbi said:

"News has just reached us that Israel has been attacked."

* * *

←⋯ 129 ○◎○ 133 ⋯→

January 14th, 1977
Dr. Hana Rønneberg
Trondheim – Norway

Friday

"But what about your mother? Wouldn't it cause problems for her if we sign?" Hana's mom was a bit concerned about her dad's plan.

"I think she would support the idea. Perhaps she'll even sign herself." Dad seemed determined to put his name under the document. "It is not like we'll ever be able to go back anyhow."

Mom had made dinner and had lit the two candles, saying the blessing as she did every Friday. Of course, it would always be too late in winter, as it got dark so early in Trondheim.

"Should we try to call the neighbors to see if we can talk to her about it?"

"Ruth, you know that they are listening in on phone calls. I don't think it would be fair to involve the neighbors and cause them trouble. Let's just send them a letter or a postcard to give to her. That might be safer."

"So what would you write?"

"We'll have to be a bit cryptic, I guess. You know, the secret police people are usually not the brightest. Any suggestions?"

"What about: Dear Grandma! As you are turning 77 this year, we wanted to make sure you know that we all signed your birthday invitation cards here in Norway."

"That should work. They'll never check that she's actually turning 84. She'll understand this."

* * *

←⋯ 137 ○◎○ 141 ⋯→

November 20th, 1979
Dr. Hana Rønneberg
Trondheim – Norway

Tuesday

She had not seen Dad cry before. The telegram arrived in the afternoon. Grandma had died on Sunday already.

Hana decided to go to her room. She put on the radio. The song which played after the news announcer had long talked about the Grand Mosque in Mecca being seized by armed men that morning was Gloria Gaynor with *I Will Survive*.

* * *

←··· 144 ○◎○ 146 ···→

March 1st, 1986
Dr. Hana Rønneberg
Bergen – Norway

Saturday

Her future father-in-law reminded Hana just a tiny little bit of Indiana Jones. Not only because he looked similar to what she imagined an older Harrison Ford would look like.

Hana's mom wasn't really like Marion—except for her smile and hair that had a close resemblance to Karen Allen's in the movie. Nor was she like Willie, barring that mom shared the character's dislike for elephants and—as mom at least formally tried to keep kosher as much as this was possible in Norway—foods with not clearly defined contents.

It was still fun watching them bantering at the table. Observing their debate, she also got the feeling that if Tore's dad and her mom had somehow, somewhere met at the right place and time in the past—when they were young and free—and not just tonight in the restaurant in Bergen, neither Tore's mom nor Hana's dad, and of course as a result neither her future husband nor her would sit here tonight.

What had happened in Stockholm the night before had made the meeting start in a somber atmosphere, but not only Hana's nervousness about it quickly dissipated.

"So there wasn't much of a resistance against the Nazis in Czechoslovakia during the war?" Tore's dad asked.

"Of course there was resistance. Lots of it. But different from here. You know, there're just no deep fjords and also no high mountain peaks or endless forests where one could have really hidden from the Germans," Hana's mom answered.

"Yes, of course, Norway is a much bigger country."

"I mean, they were just everywhere. It was a cage. And there was also no Sweden next door where one could run away to if needed. Of course, Sweden and its 'neutrality' in the war. But it still was a place one could go. Escape to if needed, or not?"

"Interesting. I have never really thought about the Swedes in this way."

"Well and for myself, as you already know, they locked me up in a concentration camp. So, there's only so much you can do if you have SS guards around you all the time."

"Theresienstadt."

"It's called Terezín in Czech."

All six of them had a pear chocolate ganache tart with a small scoop of pear sorbet for dessert.

"So, what would you say was the most memorable thing you did for the resistance?" Despite knowing Tore's dad for almost three years now, Hana had actually never really asked directly about that time. It was more through what Tore had told her that she knew, but all mom's talking had encouraged her to ask. The smile on the face of her future father-in-law disappeared, and any resemblance to Indiana Jones suddenly vanished.

"I don't think there is such a thing as a memorable thing I did. These were things that needed to be done. But I know what is and continues until today to be the hardest thing I did during that time."

"So, what was the hardest thing?" Hana asked.

"Arming the bombs."

"Which bombs?"

"The ones I placed in a circle in the Hydro's keel."

"The SF Hydro? The ferry with the heavy water, which the Nazis needed for their atomic bomb?"

"Yes. And full of families who just wanted to take a ferry on a Sunday morning."

A bit later, when Hana was about to get out of her parents' car in front of Tore's family home, mom said:

"Well, you know they seem to be really very nice people. If only they were Jewish, it would be perfect. But what am I talking about, I didn't marry a Jew either."

* * *

←·· 150 ○◎○ 73 ···→

June 6th, 1989
Dr. Hana Rønneberg
Godshus – Norway

Tuesday

Four tanks with red stars and a man in a white shirt.

Hana had seen the footage on NRK Dagsrevyen the previous day. But now seeing it again on the front page of *Bergens Tidende* felt equally disturbing. Tore had brought the newspaper home from court. The judge he worked for as a saksbehandler[1] had given it to him.

Gunnar had finally fallen asleep. He still had to get used to daycare. Her not being around him all the time. Work today and yesterday was fun. Everyone was so nice and helpful.

"When is your first night-shift?" Tore asked.

"They first want me to get used to everything. So likely not until August. They want to make sure I'm comfortable. I'm going to be the only doctor in the hospital over night. So they don't want to rush. Being in a small hospital like Godshus General Hospital does have its advantages. If I had stayed in Trondheim, I am sure they would have made me work nights the second week already."

"So you are okay that you didn't stay in Trondheim? You could have selected to go anywhere in the country."

"Well, but it was the court in Godshus, which had the only opening in the country for a saksbehandler. So that one day in the future, hopefully, I'll be married to a sexy judge. No, I think the hospital will be an exciting change for me for some time. By the way, before I forget. Could you buy some diapers for Gunnar tomorrow? We're running low."

* * *

←⋯ 73 ○◎○ 75 ⋯→

---

1 **Saksbehandler** – *Norwegian*: Court clerk.

May 7th, 1990
Dr. Hana Rønneberg
Berlin – East Germany

Monday

Hana felt how the train stopped. She heard the martial sounding announcement coming in from outside. She could only understand parts of it:

"Berlin Lichtenberg. Am Gleis Drei gerade eingefahren Nachtzug Number Drei Eins Neun aus Malmö, via Trelleborg, Saßnitz und Stralsund. Zur Weiterfahrt nach Wien, über Dresden und Prag um Acht Uhr und Dreizehn Minuten."

(Berlin Lichtenberg. The overnight train number three one nine from Malmö, with stops in Trelleborg, Saßnitz and Stralsund has arrived on track number three. The train will continue to Vienna with stops in Dresden and Prague at eight thirteen.)

"What time is it?" Hana turned around in her bunk bed and looked at her mom. She had thought that mom was still asleep.

"7:16."

"We have roughly an hour."

They had never talked about it, but she knew her mother understood German very well and likely would still be able to speak it fluently without an accent. Her dad had told her once. It was actually German mom had spoken at home with her parents in Prague. When she was growing up. Before the war. Mom clearly had a talent for languages. Obviously Czech besides the German. But still, before the war she had been taught English very well and a little Hebrew. Then when she studied medicine the bits of Latin. And Russian, the only language, which she was told to study without actually wanting or needing to do so. It must have been the German and the English which allowed her to pick up Swedish much quicker than dad. In order to make things easier for Hana to integrate after arriving in Stockholm, mom only spoke Swedish with her once she had grasped the basics herself. In Trondheim, the Norwegian came easy. "Granted, it's different. But not so different. A bit like Czech and Russian type of different." Mom never actually mentioned if she considered the Norwegian to be more the Czech and the Swedish more the Russian or vice versa. With Hana, she surprisingly continued to mostly speak Swedish, and Hana switched over to respond in Norwegian over time. Only rarely—and really only if mom wanted to tease her—mom would say something in Czech to her.

Like yesterday during the long train ride from Oslo to Malmö:

"Haničko! We will be in Prague for the first time in over twenty-one years and the thing you want to see the most are the elephants in the zoo?!"

"But I like elephants. I always liked them. And it was you and dad who dragged me to a country where there is no zoo with elephants."

Had dad been with them, they would likely not have had this conversation at all. The three had planned to drive. All together. Tore's mom had come to Godshus to help with Gunnar while they were gone for the week. But in the last minute, one of the senior obstetricians got sick in Trondheim. So dad had to stay and work. He would go the next time. Therefore, they decided to take the long train ride instead. It was somewhere shortly before Göteborg when Hana asked:

"But why did you and dad actually pick Sweden? Back then in Vienna. Why not Switzerland? Israel? Canada?"

Mom did not answer right away.

"Hearing all the German in Vienna suddenly made all the memories come back."

"Which memories?"

"The ones from Terezín. I could not sleep at night. I had nightmares. I knew I couldn't stay in a country where everyone spoke German."

"But why Sweden? Why not Israel?"

"You know. It's funny. Your dad was actually all excited about Israel."

"Really?"

"Yes. 'Ruth—it is warm there. Ruth—the ocean. Ruth—you said there's a beach in Tel Aviv.' And so on."

"Well. You know when dad's right, he's right."

"I wanted for you to grow up in peace." Hana's mom paused a bit. "And also there was really no one there whom we would have known anymore. Perhaps if famous uncle Asherman wouldn't have died earlier that year, we would have ended up there."

"Mom. But it was you who made uncle Asherman famous!"

"Hana. I only translated his paper into English for him. It was uncle Asherman who researched everything and wrote it."

"So he wrote the article in German?"

"Those were different times, Hana. There was no reason to learn English in school when he was growing up in Prague. All the medical books were in German at that time. And I think once he moved to Israel he just refused to learn English as a protest against the British."

"But he published the article in the *British Journal of Obstetrics and Gynecology.*"

"Hana! Science and politics only rarely work well together."

"You know. You actually never told me why you went back to Prague from Israel in 1947?"

"Well, I guess I should have just stayed with dad right away and not gone to Israel at all in the first place."

"Why?"

"When I finally got out of Terezín, the only people I had left in the world were uncle Asherman and your dad and his parents. They immediately took me in when I knocked at their door in Prague, but I was just not ready to stay. After contacting uncle Asherman in Tel Aviv, he told me to come. And you know that entire adventure. How complicated it was back then."

"The boat and then the camp?"

"Yes. Basically, I exchanged a camp run by the Nazis for one run by the British. But no. Of course Atlit[1] was much better than Terezín. And then they liberated us and uncle Asherman took me in. He only knew me from pictures and letters."

"And?"

"I was actually determined to stay. And I guess if I hadn't taken that bus I would have."

"Which bus?"

"Funny. What a difference buses have made in my life ..."

"What?"

"I just realized something. Well, but back to the bus in Israel. So on November 30th, 1947 I got on a bus to go to Jerusalem. I wanted to go and check what I needed to do to study medicine at the university."

"Okay."

"Well, the bus got ambushed and I almost got shot."

"You never told me about this!"

"Well, I am now. I guess they consider the event the start of the Milkhemet Ha'Atzma'ut[2] now."

"Okay."

"And then the next couple of days there was more and more violence—it was a war. And then the telegram came from dad."

"A telegram?"

"Yes. A man one day stood in front of their door and asked for me."

"In Prague?"

"Yes, in Prague. They told him I had gone to Tel Aviv to be with

---

1 **Atlit**: Coastal town south of Haifa that had been the location of a detention camp established by the authorities of the British Mandate for Palestine.

2 **Milkhemet Ha'Atzma'ut**: 1947-1949 Palestine war. It is called 'War of Independence' in Hebrew and 'The Nakba' ('The Catastrophe') in Arabic.

uncle Asherman. And then he left them an envelope with a lot of money. Like twenty-thousand Czechoslovak crowns, which was really a lot of money at that time. And they sent me a telegram to ask what they should do with the money."

"Who was that man?"

"I still don't know to this day. We never found out. Your grandma always said that she thought he was Italian."

"Okay."

"And after what had happened, I just sent them a telegram: 'Buy me a plane ticket back to Prague'. And they did. And my adventure in Israel was over. And a couple of months later the communists came to power in Prague and the borders closed."

"So were there other buses in your life?"

"Well, you wanted to know why I picked Sweden, didn't you? Yes, there were other buses."

"So what buses?"

"So these were actually things that happened in Terezín. The first thing was at some time in early summer of 1944. Suddenly there was quite a rush to make the camp more 'beautiful'. It was also then when they sent your grandma and grandpa away to the extermination camp. One day they had all the jews who were from Denmark come together. It was when the International Committee of the Red Cross made their visit to Terezín. I got a peek how the three men they had sent there walked down the main street of the camp and I guess they believed the show the Nazis had staged for them. The jews who were not from Denmark were strictly forbidden to talk to them. But, all right, at that time the war was already coming to an end. The invasion of Normandy was ongoing, and Paris was liberated less than two months later. Of course, we didn't know any of this."

"But what about the buses?"

"That happened when the war was then really almost over—in mid-April 1945. Suddenly one day about twenty white buses showed up in Terezín. They again gathered all the jews from Denmark, loaded them, and drove off with them to safety in

Sweden. And that's how we ended up in Sweden, Hana. I remembered those buses in Vienna. I said to myself that if a country can send buses through a continent filled with only fighting and chaos at the end of a terrible war and get people who needed it most to safety, it would be a good country for my Hanička to grow up in."

"And then we ended up in Norway."

"Well, that was just because of the better salary they offered us. And Hana, they were one country until 1905."

Mom stood up in the train coupe. She looked out of the window.

"Berlin. Never thought I would come here voluntarily. Should we go for a walk?"

They got out of the train. The sky looked like it would be a nice day. They walked around. Mom stopped at a small kiosk in the entrance hall of the train station, which was colored in the hue of neglectful grey. She seemed to study the headlines on the front page of a newspaper with the name *Neues Deutschland*. When she finished reading she just mumbled:

"They will allow the monsters to unify again. Do they really believe that mentioning the Shoah in an article on the same page will help?"

* * *

←⋯ 79 ○◎○ 153 ⋯→

January 18th, 1991
Dr. Hana Rønneberg
Oslo – Norway

Friday

Hana made sure that she closed her winter coat well. It was cold outside, although not as bitter cold as it would have been in Trondheim or Godshus at this time of year.

She stepped outside the modernist hospital building. Compared to Godshus General Hospital, it appeared worn. It was good that the parliament had decided to build a completely new hospital—the Nytt Rikshospital—out in Gaustad. It would not make any sense to modernize this building. Although, without a doubt, the current location of the hospital was ideal for her.

Tore and she had been very lucky with the apartment in the center. But it would still take a long time until the new hospital would be finished. She quickly walked down Pilestredet and turned left onto St. Olavs Gate. She had to walk against the cold wind which was blowing up from the fjord when she turned down Frederiks gate. The streets were crowded despite the cold. When she reached Karl Johans gate, she decided to take the detour walking up to the Royal Palace and not directly down to Henrik Ibsens gate.

Slottplassen was filled with people. The light from the sea of candles arranged in the piles of snow gently illuminated the yellow façade of the palace. Folkekongen[1] had died the night before.

She wanted to dwell longer but did not have the time to do so.

When—back on Henrik Ibsen gate—she passed by the triangular building designed by Eero Saarinen and home of the US embassy, she was surprised that there were only two police cars

---

1 **Folkekongen** – *Norwegian*: The People's King. Nickname given to Olav V (1903–1991) of Norway.

guarding the building. She had expected more security measures now that the war had started.

She briefly stopped by the pharmacy in the Handelsbygningen building and bought what a woman must buy if her period has been late for two weeks. She crossed the street and opened the light blue wooden door of the apartment building on Inkognitogata 86.

The somber atmosphere from in front of the royal palace was reflected by the announcers in the TV studio on NRK Dagsrevyen that night. Black dress. Black tie. After seeing the footage of the Scud missile attacks on Israel from the day before, she needed to pee and left for the bathroom. Luckily, it had been only conventional explosives and no gas.

She collected her urine in the small cup and inserted the test. Not unexpectedly, a blue stripe appeared.

Before she could start thinking about what this meant, she heard mom call from the living room:

"Hana. There's a new attack!"

When she got back in front of the TV, NRK had switched to a live feed from the CNN newsroom in Jerusalem, showing all the journalists present wearing gas masks.

* * *

←⋯ 84 ○◎○ 344 ⋯→

August 29th, 1991
Dr. Hana Rønneberg
Oslo – Norway

Thursday

"The last love of my life can finally go home from the hospital. I can't believe it, Hana. And it has to be on the same day they are banning the communist party in Russia!"

Seeing mom's joy how she carefully cradled her baby boy made Hana smile.

The last two-and-a-half months had been very long and difficult. Her baby boy had arrived much too early. Much, much too early. June 12th instead of during the second week of September.

Only 873 g. Twenty-seven weeks.

His chances to live had been fifty-fifty.

But now the day had finally come to take him home to his brother and her husband.

* * *

←··· 342 ○◎○ 194 ···→

JULEBORD (The Holiday Party)

November 6th, 1995
Dr. Hana Rønneberg
Oslo – Norway

Monday

"A jew killing another jew. This is the beginning of the end." Hana's mom appeared only a grey resemblance of herself at breakfast. It was not clear what shocked her more—that Jitzchak Rabin had been murdered less than thirty-six hours ago, or the fact that he died by the hand of another jew.

The family rushed through the normal routine. Hana went directly to the hospital and Tore dropped off the boys at pre-school and school, respectively, on his way to the Ministry of Justice. Other than mom's grey face that morning, the day seemed no different than any other busy Monday morning for the Rønneberg family.

Luckily it was a relatively light day at work for Hana and she looked forward to a relaxed evening at home after she picked up the boys.

"Hana. I don't feel well. Please call an ambulance," was the first thing her mom had said to her after she had unlocked the door and found her sitting on the recliner in the living room, with her face even more grey than when she had left in the morning.

"What's wrong, mom?"

"My chest hurts. It has been hurting all day!"

Then everything went very quickly. The paramedics arrived a few minutes after she had called. They hooked her up to oxygen. Started an I.V. The portable ECG showed clearly that she was having a major heart attack. The boys started crying. She called Tore's number at work. He would come home immediately. Mom looked a bit better after the paramedics had started the oxygen. They told her they would take her to the Rikshospital. She would go there as soon as Tore was home to take over the boys. She gave her mother a hug before they took her away on the stretcher. As soon as Tore arrived, she did not walk her regular way to work, but mostly ran. The moment she saw her colleagues' faces in the familiar emergency department, she knew something had to be awfully wrong.

"Hana. I'm so sorry. She arrested one minute after the paramedics brought her in. Ventricular fibrillation. We did CPR for thirty minutes, shocked her ten times, but we couldn't get her back."

Mom was dead.

* * *

←··· 160 ○◎○ 258 ···→

December 11th, 1997
Dr. Hana Rønneberg
Godshus – Norway

Thursday

"So, Hana! How does it feel being back for your first call night at Godshus General Hospital?"

"Good. Feels like not too much has changed."

"What are you talking about! I don't think we had the TVs in each of the patients' rooms when you were here before.

"Well, yes. Those are new." It was fun for her to see how proud Dr. Bjerknes was about all the changes.

"And next month, thanks to you, the dialysis machine!"

"I think the hospital getting the CT scanner is much more important."

"Well, but a CT scan never actually treated a patient differently. Now we soon can provide the community with dialysis on-site without having to transfer all the patients to Ålesund or Bergen. That's really a huge change. Perhaps as huge as when we got the intensive care unit started."

"Werner. Don't exaggerate!"

"Once more, good to have you back, Hana. Call me if you need anything."

"I'll be fine. See you in the morning."

It was nice that Dr. Bjerknes stayed so late and checked on her before going home. There was no patient in the emergency room right now and only one patient in the intensive care unit. The early December Christmas time lull. People busy preparing for the holidays and not having time to be sick in the hospital.

Perhaps she could get some sleep tonight. She would have to start preparing for the holidays as well. The boys would enjoy double this year. Chanukah and Christmas at the same time. They would light the first Chanukah candle on Lille Julaften this year. It felt good to be finally back at work. The last four months had been all about getting settled in the new house and making sure the boys got used to the school. It was a bit rough for Gunnar in the beginning in his new class, but otherwise, everything else went smoothly.

She looked at the clock. 19:28. Perfect, she could check Dagsrevyen. She turned on the TV. A lot was talked about a protocol that had been adopted by the United Nations. The goal of it was to minimize global warming by reducing greenhouse gas emissions into the atmosphere. The final negotiations had taken place in Kyoto.

* * *

←··· 195 ○◎○ 260 ···→

July 1st, 2000
Dr. Hana Rønneberg
Long Beach, California – United States

Saturday

"Mom, can we go to the pool? Please? Please!"

It was rare that Hana's sons would ever be in full agreement on anything.

"You know, I don't know if it's open already. We haven't left the port yet. But what if you go and check it out and then come back and let dad and me know?"

The boys stormed out of their cabin on the MS Viking Serenade, which would be their home for the next seven days. The second week of their family dream summer vacation.

They had started out in Seattle after the long flight via Copenhagen. While walking around the city, they had coffee at a place called Starbucks. She had never heard the name before. The latte was really good, despite it being served in a paper cup.

Then Las Vegas. They gave in to the boys and went for a ride on a roller coaster on top of an observation tower named Stratosphere Tower. Tore was not good with heights and had vomited afterwards.

The Grand Canyon reminded her of Norway a bit. A reddish-yellowish Norway.

The drive to Los Angeles.

Now the one-week cruise down the Mexican Riviera—to break up all the road-tripping.

Once back in L.A. they still had to visit Disneyland before driving up Highway 1 to San Francisco.

It was funny that a family from Norway ended up on a cruise ship in L.A. that had 'Viking' in its name.

Hana looked out of the window of the cabin. In the distance, she could see a billboard announcing that a Democratic National Convention would take place in Los Angeles the following month. It had the picture of the vice president of the United States on it.

* * *

←⋯ 262 ○◎○ 263 ⋯→

September 28th, 2000
Dr. Hana Rønneberg
31º 46' 36.12" N 35º 14' 4.2" E

Thursday

Hana, Tore, and her sons getting out of the taxi.

Yellowish-white limestone.

> *– NEXT YEAR IN YERUSHALAYIM –* ירושלים

Chatting briefly about the reception that would follow with the nice family from Los Angeles they had met on the cruise ship, whose son Daniel's thirteenth birthday two days ago was on the same day as Gunnar's.

Yellowish-white limestone.

> *– NEXT YEAR IN YERUSHALAYIM –* ירושלים

Making sure she had enough soft jelly candies.

Yellowish-white limestone.

> *– NEXT YEAR IN YERUSHALAYIM –* ירושלים

Gunnar clumsily strapping on his tefillin[1] for the first time, which were bought the day before, helped by the father of his friend Daniel.

Yellowish-white limestone.

       – NEXT YEAR IN YERUSHALAYIM – ‎ירושלים

Hana separated from her sons and Tore, just behind the partition wall—annoyed a bit—but following the laws of religion that needed to be followed.

Yellowish-white limestone.

       – NEXT YEAR IN YERUSHALAYIM – ‎ירושלים

Angry noises intensifying just above them.

Yellowish-white stones starting to fly randomly.

       – AT THIS VERY MOMENT IN AL-QUDS – ‎القُدس

* * *

←··· 268 ○◎○ 197 ···→

---

1 **Tefillin** – Set of small black leather boxes containing scrolls of parchments with verses from the Torah written on them.

June 26th, 2007
· Dr. Hana Rønneberg
Godshus – Norway

Tuesday

"SAS flight number 1313 to Copenhagen is now boarding through gate number 1."

Hana thought that it did not really make sense that they said 'through gate number 1' as the airport only had one gate.

The newly introduced once a day early morning flight from Godshus Regional Airport to Copenhagen was helpful, as otherwise they would have had to drive all the way to Ålesund airport for the trip. Like when he went for the interview in December. It was time to say goodbye now. Gunnar got up from the grey seat in the small waiting area. He looked funny with his blue russelue[1] on his head, but he had insisted on wearing it for the flight. At least he had agreed to cut off the tassel with the russeknuter,[2] but perhaps if he had not done that they would send him right back?

"You have your boarding passes?" Hana asked.

"Yes, mom. Here, Godshus to Copenhagen and then Copenhagen to Tel Aviv."

She was not sure at all if he fully realized that his decision was a serious one. She had endless exhausting discussions with him about it, but he insisted.

---

1 **Russelue** – *Norwegian*: Russ Cap. The 'russefeiring' (English: 'russ celebration') is a traditional month-long celebration for high school students in Norway just prior to graduation. It is customary for the graduates to wear colored overalls and russelue.

2 **Russeknuter** – *Norwegian*: Russ knots. These knots are attached on a tassel which is part of the russ cap and signal that the student has fulfilled a certain accomplishment during the russ period.

"If you must join an army, just do it here in Norway!" she had tried to convince him.

"And do what? Sit around in the arctic and watch birds?"

On her side of the family, all men always tried to run away from armies—the Austrian one, the Czechoslovak one. It must have been Tore's freedom fighter genes, which made Gunnar want to run around the desert with a gun in his hand. Of course, he was also now twenty, so there was no way of stopping him. Well, there was still the chance that he would have so much difficulty with learning Hebrew that they might just send him back. Who knew? But, as he had taken at least one hour a day even during russefeiring[1] to study from the 'Hebrew Self-Study Guide for Mahal[2] Soldiers' which The Jewish Agency had sent him, she doubted that. Well, at least for now, he would just be sitting in an army base somewhere close to the Sea of Galilee trying to learn Hebrew.

"Son—your grandfather would be proud of you!" Tore said while he hugged him. She was not sure at all about what her mother would have felt in the current situation. After the brothers had said goodbye to each other, it was her turn.

"Love you. And please be careful."

"Yes, I will. Love you, mom."

She watched him walk away.

"Eva! Eva!" a man dressed in a black Norwegian police officer uniform shouted, who had come through the terminal door. A lady in a SAS flight attendant uniform who was in line behind Gunnar turned around and walked back a bit. She and the man met just in front of Hana.

"Honey! You forgot your purse in the car!" the police officer said.

---

1 **Russefeiring** – *Norwegian*: Russ celebration.

2 **Mahal**: Acronym of 'Mitnadvei Hutz LaAretz' – 'Volunteers from Abroad'. A volunteer program associated with the Israel Defense Forces (IDF), that allows overseas residents to serve in the IDF.

"Thank you!" the flight attendant replied.

"Safe travels. Don't work too hard and say hello to The City!" the police officer said, before kissing her.

* * *

←⋯ 201 ○◎○ 279 ⋯→

January 6th, 2019
Dr. Hana Rønneberg
Jerusalem – Israel

Sunday

Hana only started to vaguely recognize the place while walking across the crosswalk from the stop where they had gotten off the tram. The tram looked like it had been dropped right from a science fiction movie and they had boarded it after emerging out of a deep cavernous railway station, which resembled an underground space-ship. The entrance pavilion was the first thing that did not appear completely different from how things had looked like ten years ago.

She had initially hoped they all would go together. Not only Tore and her. Her son as well. But Erik was busy.

"They want you to go where?" Hana had asked.

"Unstad. It's up in the Lofoten," Erik replied.

"But it's January. It will just be dark and freezing cold."

"Well, of course, it's cold. With the darkness—I actually didn't know. Apparently, the sun starts coming up again after January 6th up there. I guess forty-five minutes of daylight, or so."

"So you'll just be sitting around for the rest of the day? And that for a month?"

"The photographer ideally wants to get a shot with me surfing under the northern lights. They say the light is really special. But again, that happens really rarely. And then, of course, the waves have to cooperate as well. That's why they booked me for the entire month. Of course, we might be lucky and the conditions are ideal the first day. If they are happy with the shot, all is done and I am free to leave. But again, that's not very likely."

"Well, I had really hoped you would come."

"Mom, I know."

"And who is this for?"

"Noreg Liv. Life Insurance company. They will do a national campaign next year with this. TV. Internet. Billboards."

"They make a TV spot to sell life insurance to surfers in Norway?"

"No. Of course, they want to sell life insurance to everyone. They really want young people to sign up. New parents especially. Actually, think they have a really good marketing idea for it."

"Yes?"

"Besides me, they also hired two other Norwegian athletes with kids. A cyclist and a cross-country skier."

"Hmm."

"The first part of the shot is showing us doing our sport—like me surfing, the other athletes on their cross-country ski or bike. Of course, all filmed in Norway."

"But why would anyone buy life insurance because of this? I guess I'm too old to understand this."

"Well, the second part of the shot we say: 'For jeg vil ikke be-kymre meg mer for: …'[1]"

"Erik. I'm sorry I still don't get it."

"Well, so for me I then say: Sharks. The cross-country skier says bears, and I think the cyclist says wolves."

"Okay, I think I'm getting it."

"For the second part of the shot, they also show us with our kids."

"So you are taking my grandson Gunnar-Kai[2] to the dark, freezing-cold Lofoten for a month with you? And what about your wife? She's going to freeze off her, I guess what do they call it 'okole',[3] where she's from."

---

1 **For jeg vil ikke bekymre meg mer for: …** – *Norwegian*: Because I don't want to worry anymore about: …

2 **Kai** – *ʻŌlelo Hawaiʻi*: (🏄🏂🏔👍🌺🌊) Ocean.

3 **Okole** – *ʻŌlelo Hawaiʻi*: (🏄🏂🏔👍🌺🌊) backside, butt, gluteus maximus region.

Hana had been afraid that he would fall in love with one of the local woman from Godshus, none of whom had ever cared about him while he was still in school, but the moment he was the first not only Norwegian, but Scandinavian to be selected to be on the World Pro Surf team four years ago suddenly were all so very interested. But when, after he came home in the middle of winter after his first full year on the tour, bringing with him the woman from Kaua'i, who had been, quite understandably, just cold all the time in Godshus, she knew that all would be good. A happy end. Erik had not only found the love of his life, but had found all of this by following his passion and had excelled at it. Never had she thought this would happen, when Tore and she had just very reluctantly agreed that it was okay for Erik to 'pause' school after his VG-2 year that summer, only five months after the last time they went to Israel ten years ago. That evening over dinner the three of them had first just screamed at each other for almost an hour, before then ending up crying and hugging.

It was only later that she understood the reason he needed to go away, so he would no longer be forced to see the ever-present devastation in his parents' eyes. When they bought him the ticket to Australia, she thought it would be a gap year of sorts for Erik. Like the kids signing up to 'study' at the Elverum Folkehøgskole for one year—exiting as lost as they entered. Then Erik came back earlier than planned from Australia. With a new sparkle in his eyes, now convincing them that he needed to spend some time in Portugal, after supposedly surfing was all he wanted to do now. An afternoon spent at Bondi Beach resetting his life. The ticket to Portugal was the last time he asked them for help with anything. Since then he managed it all on his own.

From Portugal, his next stop was a dusty town north of Agadir the name of which she could not recall. Working some odd job for two brothers/surfers/surf hostel owners from England. But Erik was so full of happiness and life when Tore and she went to visit him that winter. So she decided to put whatever reservations she had about all of this aside.

Initially, she thought it would just be for some time.

But then came new friends. Travel to exotic places. Bali. Fuerteventura. Ireland. Tahiti. Iceland. Sheboygan. Pictures of Erik surfing in some magazines. Him winning some contests. Asking if he could park the old VW bus he had bought at the house when he was traveling. A TV crew showing up at their doorstep the day he qualified for the World Pro Surf team, wanting to interview the proud parents. The evening he called over Facetime and told Tore and her that the wedding would be on Kaua'i. The ceremony to be held on a beach—leaving out the ketubah,[1] chuppah,[2] and even the broken glass. People dancing hula[3] instead of the horah.[4] But Erik would be happy, and that was all that mattered. Chatting to his best man, Per, on the beach who as a surprise to her was not only a surfer but a physician and whom she then hired last year when he applied for the open position at Godshus General Hospital. The name of her grandson, which not only honored the ocean but also the memory of his older brother. Gunnar.

Hana paused briefly before she climbed up the six steps leading to the entrance pavilion. Searchingly extending her hand towards Tore. Without words their hands met, and they passed through the opening between the white metal rods, directly under the signage reading:

World Zionist Organization – MT. HERZL

Hand in hand they stepped under the flat open roof of the building and back under a light blue sky with high white thin

---

1 **Ketubah**: Marriage contract.

2 **Chuppah**: Covering. Term used for a canopy under which a Jewish couple stands during their wedding ceremony.

3 **Hula** – ʻŌlelo Hawaiʻi: (🌴 🏄 ⛰️ 🗿 🌺 🐚) Hula dancing is a complex art form that was originally developed in the Hawaiʻian islands.

4 **Horah**: Circle Dance that originated in the Balkans, but was adopted by the Jewish diaspora.

clouds, turned right, and walked on the asphalt path flanked by the irregular cypress trees.

Up to the asphalt path, they had travelled differently this time. On Thursday after work they had driven to Ålesund. Booking the tickets from there had been so much cheaper than from God-shus Regional Airport. They stayed in a hotel close to the airport overnight, then catching the earliest morning flight. She had a window seat from Oslo, and for the longest time, she just watched the magnificence of the changing colors of the winter sky as the sun was just rising on the flight to Frankfurt. She was sure her mother lying in her grave hated her for this, but it was Lufthansa that had the best-priced deal and connection. They landed in Ben Gurion some time after sunset. Even in Israel, Shabbat would start too early in winter. They had opted to stay at a large hotel at the beach in Tel Aviv. The day of his death was a Saturday this year—so the strictly followed laws of religion forbade them to visit that day.

The day was several months after their sons had convinced her and Tore to give up their landline and only use cell phones. She would Skype with Gunnar. Technological advancement. It had been such an exhausting time at work. After Tore had left for court in the morning, she went to the bedroom to try to rest. Sleep. She was supposed to work that night. The hospital had been full. She wanted to be sure nobody woke her up until Erik returned from school. She had turned off her cell phone. They only had her cell phone number, not Tore's.

The doorbell woke her up. She remembered opening the door. Seeing the police officer in his black uniform. She vaguely recognized him as a relative of a patient of theirs.

"Dr. Rønneberg?"

"Yes. That's me. What happened?"

"Dr. Rønneberg. I'm so sorry."

And then he said the same words she had had to say to so many relatives before in her life.

After that, she really did not remember clearly what went on until the three soldiers in their green uniforms picked up Tore, Erik, and herself at Ben Gurion.

"We're so sorry."

She had never expected that they would say:

"Your son has been killed by friendly fire. He was taking cover in an abandoned building in Jabalya north of Gaza with his unit from the Golani Brigade as part of the ongoing Operation Cast Lead. One of our tanks accidentally fired at the building. Your son was heavily wounded at the scene but was still airlifted to Rabin Medical Center in Petah Tikva. But they could not save him. We lost three more men in the incident."

The sound coming from their steps changed once the asphalt path switched over to a walkway formed out of irregularly shaped white sandstone. The same stone which all the low walls were made of, that contained the always same elevated small rectangular patch of green rosemary with a big rectangular stone at one end. With a writing on it using an alphabet which only she could read but not Tore. It only was now that the resemblance struck her—a dormitory of identical eternal beds, with army-green blankets and white pillowcases.

She opened her handbag and took out the small splinter of the dark grey Norwegian granite which she had found in the soil from digging a hole to plant a tree in their garden last spring. It was close to the place where a metal swing had once stood.

Gunnar had always loved to swing—even in the middle of winter in Norway.

She placed the small splinter of the dark gray Norwegian granite on the white sandstone next to his name written in gold in the alphabet, he had struggled so much to learn.

"Dr. Rønneberg? Mr. Rønneberg?"

She turned around. She had not noticed the man with the still-young face behind the double stroller before. She looked at him. Vaguely, he resembled someone she knew at a different time.

"Daniel?"

"How are you? We must have missed each other all the other years."

Daniel was no longer living in Los Angeles, but in Tel Hashomer[1] now with his wife and the twins. He would come here and visit his friend once a year. He had taken the twins with him this year. They shared stories. Things she did not know, which happened when Gunnar had spent a year in Los Angeles as a high school exchange student living with Daniel's family. Of course, everyone only called him 'The Viking' at that time.

Some of the stories made her smile.

After they had exchanged the numbers of their cell phones and the promise that they would meet for dinner on Monday, so Daniel's wife would get to know them it was the first time ever that Hana felt like she could one day possibly move a little away from all the pain that was inside her. For so many years, she thought that if she let go of the past, it would mean that Gunnar would be forgotten. Forgotten how beautiful he was. How full of life.

Tore and she then walked over to the newly built memorial for the soldiers who had died in Israel's wars.

Built by the defense force that had killed her son.

* * *

←··· 384 ○◎○ 287 ···→

---

1 **Tel Hashomer**: 'Hill of the Guardsman'. Neighborhood in the city of Ramat Gan East of Tel Aviv.

September 27th, 2019
Dr. Hana Rønneberg
Godshus – Norway

Friday

"But it's okay, Hana. I really don't mind."

"Are you sure? You basically will have two night shifts back to back that way," Hana asked Faiza once more.

"It's totally okay."

"So, let's make sure we get this correct: Pia, you are going to work on the 8th of October instead of me and not on the 9th as on the original schedule. And Faiza then works the night on the 9th of October as an extra shift."

Hana was happy that in the end it all worked out somehow. How could she have forgotten Yom Kippur! It was only when the schedule was out already that she realized that Anders had put her on the schedule to work. Of course, she would have worked if her colleagues would not have switched. But if there was an option not to work, that was preferable.

"Yes. Looks like we are all set then," Pia said.

Later that evening when Hana had time to sit down at the computer and browse through the news of the day she read that around half a million people had gathered on the streets of Montreal to highlight the risks of climate change as part of the 'Global Week for Future'.

* * *

← 301 ○◎○ 228 →

December 5th, 2019
Dr. Hana Rønneberg
Godshus – Norway

Thursday

"Okay, I think this is a good plan," Hana concluded. She was happy how the meeting with Alessandro and Werner had gone.

Although initially, she had been much more radical, demanding the 'it's either him or us' type of thing. But Werner had patiently convinced her that this was not the right way to proceed. That the right way for the hospital and community it served was for the three of them to drive over to Ålesund at the beginning of January. Werner would reach out to the management team over there and arrange for it. Via a long phone call and not a long email with all the potential of various misunderstandings. They would hopefully, after a lengthy discussion, convince the management team to recognize the shortcomings of Dr. Boisen-Jensen and would have to start helping to settle the conflicts, which they were no longer able to solve themselves. The three of them discussed that likely a type of mediator would be sent out to Godshus General Hospital. There would be coaching sessions and meetings. And hopefully, all would end well.

Hana realized just how silent Alessandro had been most of the time. Werner and herself had done most of the talking.

Perhaps it was because of the place they had selected for the meeting?

This had been a mistake and they should go somewhere else if they ever needed to meet again. Of course, the place had a new name—it was called 'Pub på Hjørnet' now. Less of a restaurant these days and more a bar, if ever something like a real bar would exist in Godshus. But the interior had changed very little from that night now roughly 29 years ago. The place their table was standing on had been the dancefloor that night. Alessandro and she had never talked about that night. She had left for Oslo the morning after and once she returned to Godshus almost seven years later, all of it had been distant history.

She had made the decisions she had made.

The past was the past.

The past should not bring pain to the future.

Hana looked around. There were other reasons this had been the wrong place to meet.

The waitress who had brought them their beverages. Two, or three years ago, she had admitted her with seizures. They were never able to find out exactly what caused them.

The man sitting at the left end of the bar, of course, had started drinking again. He had spent five nights in the intensive care unit about two months ago, because the delirium that began once he decided to stop was so severe that they had to put him on a Precedex drip and get out the heavy leather restraints for his arms and legs; after he had punched Louise in the face. Hana had the feeling that she would likely see him in the hospital anew before this year's New Year's Eve.

The couple holding hands who just walked through the door:

· He—single—had puzzled all of them for almost three weeks when he came back to the emergency room repeatedly in April one year because of fevers, headaches, a poor appetite as well as a reddish-pink, non-itchy rash on his trunk and extremities—including his palms and soles. Hana did not remember who had the genius idea to test him, but she remembered very well the incredible mess it caused when his syphilis test turned out positive. He had been in Thailand for his winter vacation… In the end, he was actually the one who might have been affected the least by the entire imbroglio. But once all the contact tracing, which had luckily been done by the health department in Bergen, had been completed, Tore had been busy with working on the judgements of the resulting three divorces, that the incident had triggered in Godshus for the next two years.

She—while still married—showing up severely beaten up one night by her then-husband, whom Tore subsequently had sent to jail.

"Okay, my dear colleagues. I think it's time for me to go home now."

* * *

←⋯ 118 ○◎○ 310 ⋯→

December 12th, 2019
Dr. Hana Rønneberg
Godshus – Norway

Thursday

Hana had noticed the bleeding from her gums when she brushed her teeth before coming to work the night shift. It took even longer to stop than the other times it had happened in the two weeks before. She had also been feeling so tired lately. Very tired. Perhaps she just should check her labs.

After she had seen three patients in the emergency room and everything seemed quiet on the floor, she decided to stop by in the intensive care unit.

"Louise. Can I ask you a favor?"

"Of course. What can I help you with, Dr. Rønneberg?"

"Could you just do a blood draw on me—I've been feeling really exhausted recently and just want to check my labs."

"Have a seat."

A short while later Hana entered the lab with a red and violet tube containing her blood. She switched the programming of the analysis machine to 'manual output only' which would prevent an automatic upload of the values into her electronic medical record and then followed the steps necessary for the laboratory analysis. The first results of the values of her blood chemistry looked okay. Nothing special. About a minute later, the printer connected to the analyzer started working again. Once it stopped, she took out the paper and looked at it:

COMPLETE BLOOD COUNT

TEST *RESULTS* UNITS NORMAL RANGE **COMMENT**

HAEMOGLOBIN [Hb] *9.7* GM% 11.5 TO 14.7 **LOW**
RED BLOOD CELLS [RBC] *3.85* M/CMM 4.2 TO 5.4 **LOW**
PACKED CELL VOLUME [PCV] *31.5* % 37 TO 47 **LOW**
MEAN CORP. VOLUME [MCV] *78.77* CU MIC. 78 TO 100 **normal**
MEAN CORP. HB [MCH] *27.57* PG. 27 TO 31 **normal**
MEAN CORP. HB CONC. [MCHC] *36.25* % 32 TO 36 **HIGH**
RDW *17.15* % 11.5 TO 14 **HIGH**
PLATELETS *0.37* /CMM 1.5 TO 3.4 **CRITICAL ***
TOTAL W.B.C COUNT *24700* /CMM 4000 TO 10500 **HIGH**

DIFFERENTIAL COUNT:
NEUTROPHILS *82* % 40 TO 75 **HIGH**
LYMPHOCYTES *15* % 20 TO 45 **LOW**
EOSINOPHILS *03* % 01 TO 06 **normal**
MONOCYTES *00* % 01 TO 10 **LOW**
BASOPHILS *00* % 00 TO 01 **normal**
BANDCELLS *00* % 00 TO 03 **normal**
OTHER ABNORMAL W.B.C.BLAST CELLS DETECTED **CRITICAL ****

RBC MORPHOLOGY: NORMOCHROMIC NORMOCYTIC
* CRITICAL LOW PLATELET COUNT—HIGH BLEEDING RISK
** BLAST CELLS DETECTED—OBTAIN MANUAL DIFFERENTIAL—POSSIBLE ACUTE LEUKEMIA

368

Hana looked at the paper again. Then she sat down on the chair in the lab. She looked at the printout a third time.

CRITICAL LOW PLATELET COUNT. BLAST CELLS DETECTED. POSSIBLE ACUTE LEUKEMIA.

She put down the printout on the desk and used her hands to feel for the lymph nodes in her neck first. Then under her armpits and then in her groin. Nothing. None of her lymph nodes were enlarged.

Hana looked at the paper once more.

CRITICAL LOW PLATELET COUNT. BLAST CELLS DETECTED. POSSIBLE ACUTE LEUKEMIA.

Next, she did two things. There was enough of her blood in the tube left to run the sample again in the analyzer. She also took a glass slide from the drawer which was under the table which the old microscope was standing on. Nowadays they used the microscope so rarely that it took her some time to remember where the on/off switch was. She took a pipette and put a single drop of her blood on the glass slide. A bit clumsily, as she had not done this in a very long time, she took another glass slide and dispersed the drop of her blood over the slide's length. She let the slide dry and then quickly dipped it in methanol before using the fluid from a bottle with a label that read 'Wright-Geimsa' to stain it. In the meantime, the printer started printing again. She looked at the second printout. There were minimal differences in the numbers listed, but the same words still appeared on the bottom:

CRITICAL LOW PLATELET COUNT. BLAST CELLS DETECTED. POSSIBLE ACUTE LEUKEMIA.

She put the slide she had just prepared under the microscope. She looked through the eyepiece and adjusted the focus:

They were everywhere. A large number of purple-colored circles against the background of smaller light pink circles. Purple-colored circles which were never supposed to be there. Never. All the blast cells in her blood against the background of her red blood cells.

There was no doubt. A single cell in her bone marrow had gone crazy and had started

multiplying and multiplying and multiplying and multiplying
and
multiplying and multiplying and multiplying and multiplying.

Egoistically
pushing
everything
else to the side.

That was the reason that her red cells were low. The reason that the platelets, which were there to stop bleeding, were low. The reason why her gums bled. The reason why she felt so tired.

Although a bone marrow biopsy and some additional testing would need to be done to confirm everything, this was the laboratory and clinical picture of an acute leukemia. And it was not one of those better ones. The ones patients could live with for a number of years. This was one of those leukemias that kill quite rapidly; weeks—perhaps months. Not years. For which patients are given the really, really harsh chemotherapies. The chemotherapies which make patients nauseated. Which make you lose your hair. The chemotherapies which were only done at the university hospitals. The leukemias for which younger patients would sometimes get bone marrow transplants. And, in the end, after all this, more or less only a quarter of all patients would be alive after five years. Of course, that included all the younger patients—not the patients who were older.

Like herself.

Herself?

Yes. Herself Hana.

This was not a patient here who had leukemia.

This was her—Dr. Hana Rønneberg—who had acute leukemia.

This was her—Dr. Hana Rønneberg—who would very likely die from her acute leukemia sooner rather than later.

Shit. She really did not have time for this shitty leukemia right now. Erik had promised to be in Godshus at the latest next Friday evening with his family. With her second grandchild, who would just turn two months that day. Her second grandchild, whom she had not met yet. Of course, that meant that Erik and his family had to get on the plane in Honolulu, the latest on the 19th at 8:00 in the morning local time there. He had absolutely promised her that they would get on that plane even if it meant giving up winning the Pipe Masters, which in theory, as he had explained to her, could run until December 20th. But if he stayed that long, that would mean that he and the two kids would not be in Godshus in time to light the first Hanukkah candle on December 22nd. It just took time to get from one end-of-the-world to the other end-of-the-world. She was secretly hoping that the waves would be good the next week so that the event would be finished in time—so that Erik would not have to choose between 'career' and 'family'. He had made it to the Round of 16 scenario already. She never understood how it worked and what it meant, but he was quite excited when he had called her about this earlier in the day. She would feel bad if he needed to leave early and give up potentially winning. But, well, he had already won the Vans Pro in Sunset and the Hawaiian Pro in Haleiwa in November. Perhaps it was time to let some other surfer win this time. She was sure Erik would be okay with that.

Okay, Erik would be here for the holidays. When would she tell them? Spoil Hanukah and Christmas for everyone? Likely her last Hanukah and Christmas. Bad idea. December 30th? She liked that date. Of course, they would have to cancel the trip to Israel now. Because of her. Well, not really because of her, but because of the blast cells. But they were her cells. So yes, in the end, it was because of her. But what would she tell them?

Hello, everyone … by the way, mom has leukemia …

Well, she would need to tell them that. But perhaps much more importantly, she would need to tell them what she would want. And what was that? Did she want treatment? To be away from home? Either in Bergen or most likely all the way in Oslo? Get all

371

the chemo? The blood transfusions. The platelets. The sores in her mouth. Loosing her hair. And all this with only a very slim chance that it would work. What about Erik and his family? He was part of the World Pro Surf team. The season for him would start in Australia at the end of March—the Corona Open Gold Coast—Snapper Rocks', Coolangatta, Queensland, Eastern Australia. If she would go for treatment, he would surely insist on staying in Norway. And that would be the end of his career. Why would she want to destroy the life of her son? And Tore. He would retire in two years. Even if she would achieve some form of remission, it would mean none of the trips they had talked about. Just staying in Norway. Close to a hospital for the tests, blood transfusions. Her immune system too weakened to travel anywhere. And what would all this be for? For potentially a bit more quantity of life. But what would the quality of such a life be? Her life, which at the moment at least felt as good as it would ever get considering all what had happened in the past. Two beautiful grandchildren, which of course she would love to see grow up. One son who most definitively found his way in life and the other one who had lost his way too early, but who, as she knew now, would never be forgotten. A husband with whom there had been their share of ups and downs throughout the years, but with whom she, in the end, had lived—everything considered—a happy life. Perhaps it was just the time to leave the party a bit earlier? Not linger around. In a bit a similar way like mom, who was all of the sudden gone. Just continue to be herself. Perhaps even go to work until likely one morning she would either start bleeding from somewhere or get a fever because of some infection, which she definitively would end up getting. Then, if she would still be able—just call and say that she was sick with the flu. Take a Panodil and go to bed. Perhaps this was the better way. For her. And for the people she loved. She would really need to think about all of this.

Oh. She realized that there was just one thing she now absolutely needed to do urgently. One person in the world who needed to know about this. And not only this. And in contrast to everyone else, she would have to tell him earlier than December 30th. She would have to tell him as soon as possible. Not only about the cells she found in her blood. It would just not be fair otherwise. But how and when? Hana thought for a brief moment and then took out her phone and started typing a message.

Ciao Alessandro! How will you get to the Julebord next Friday? I can pick you up and drive. That way you can drink a couple more glasses of wine than me. Let me know. Hana.

She pushed the send button. Concerning the rest, she still had time to think about everything. How to tell her family. If she should get treatment or not. But it was definitively the time to talk to Alessandro about everything. She felt relieved that she had sent the message. Just as she made the only other definitive decision which she would make tonight—that she, no matter what, would be cremated—her pager beeped. It was the triage nurse from the emergency room. She called back.

"Dr. Rønneberg. Sorry for this. Everyone's old friend is back. He says that he quit drinking three days ago. He's shaking like crazy and his heart rate is up to 130."

"I'm on my way. Can you please get out the leather restraints?"

* * *

←··· 403 ○◎○ 239 ···→

December 20th, 2019
Dr. Hana Rønneberg
Godshus – Norway

Friday – 07:58

The very moment Hana closed the door of the laboratory behind her, she got even more angry. How should Per have known this? He was just a junior physician. She as a specialist had only seen two such cases during the entire time she had worked in Oslo.

And then the explosion because of the other patient. The putz had no right to put Per down the way he did. To embarrass him in front of the rest of the team.

The patient, of course, would be fine. The university hospital in Bergen had accepted him already after her quick conversation with her nephrology colleague. Alessandro was getting the paperwork ready. Now she would have to process all the day's labs as the laboratory technician had called in sick. She had briefly returned to the conference room after making the phone call. After all this excitement, she needed a coffee and poured whatever was left in the coffee machine into her mug. Per must have made it in the morning.

She wanted to add some milk and not drink it black, but there was nothing in the fridge except for a piece of brunost and some crispbread. She would have to remember to buy milk and bring it on Monday.

Before Hana turned on the light, it was only the different colored control lights of all the laboratory machines which she could see. She put down her mug next to the holder into which the nurses had collected all the patients' blood samples from the morning. After putting on gloves, she quickly started processing the samples as usual. Once the samples were running in the machines, she took a sip of the coffee. It was only lukewarm and tasted bitter.

Then she took the holder with the remaining blood samples and opened the laboratory refrigerator to put them inside, just in case they would need to run additional tests on the blood later on. The moment she saw the container with the light brown fluid in the fridge, she had an idea. The container had the name of the man, who had been admitted on Wednesday from the nursing home, on it. The stool sample from his profuse watery diarrhea had—as they all expected—tested positive for the Norovirus yesterday. It must have been the light brown hue of the liquid which made her think of the piece of brunost she had just seen in the conference room fridge. The piece of brunost belonging to Dr. Boisen-Jensen, which he would eat in the chief physician's office as soon as he would be finished with the one cardiac catheterization he was doing this morning.

She took a clear plastic specimen bag and put the container into it. The container filled with light brown diarrhea and the Norovirus particles which were causing it. She then put the specimen bag into the pocket of her lab coat. She removed her gloves and put another fresh pair into the same pocket. Hana checked the machines—the samples would be processing another five minutes. Time enough to quickly walk over to the conference room and back.

Once she entered the conference room, she locked the door behind herself and put on the gloves. She kneeled next to the refrigerator, unscrewed the orange lid from the specimen container, and quickly took the piece of Dr. Boisen-Jensen's brunost out of the fridge and dunked it into the sample of light brown diarrhea, which had the exact same hue of light brown as the cheese. She then put the brunost back into the fridge, screwed the orange lid back on the specimen container, and put the container back into the specimen bag and back into the pocket of her lab coat. Then she took off her gloves.

Hana did not remember the exact incubation period of the Norovirus, but with such a high dose of the contagion, Dr. Boisen-Jensen perhaps would start vomiting and having diarrhea already before the beginning of the Julebord. There was hope he would not show up in the evening and the team could have fun without him. Satisfied, she returned to the lab and continued with her responsibilities for the day.

Around noon, a text message arrived.

Safe in Copenhagen. Love! Erik+3.

Just before leaving work, Erik's next text arrived:

Back home in Norway.

The house was empty when she walked in. Tore had left already. She checked the rooms. All was ready. Erik, his wife, and the baby would sleep in the guestroom and Gunnar-Kai would sleep in Erik's old room. What was now the guestroom had been Gunnar's bedroom.

She opted to take a relaxing bubble bath. Her gums bled a bit again when she brushed her teeth afterwards. She realized how pale she was when she looked in the mirror to put on her make-up.

Hana found some rouge at the bottom of the drawer and put it on. Better. Less dead looking. More alive. After putting on the pantyhose with the fine fishnet pattern with different solid black stars woven into them, she picked the black chiffon dress with the scoop neckline and long sleeves. The dress ended just below her knees. She liked the stars on her ankles and they contrasted nicely with the bright red satin Manolo Blahnik Butina pumps she had long planned to wear for this year's Julebord. She would not have too many occasions left to show off these shoes with their semi d'Orsay design with their singular crossover strap and stiletto high heels.

Just after she got into the car to drive to Alessandro, Tore's message arrived.

They landed. Hope we will catch the 19:00 ferry.

It was Charlotte who opened the door after she rang the doorbell.

"Hana. So good to see you. Please come in. I guess Alessandro will be ready in a moment."

"Thank you so much. How are things at school?"

"All good. Christmas Break now. Wow! I saw the interview with Erik on the news yesterday. You must be so proud. The best surfer in the world!"

"Thank you. Well, no, only the second-best. But I'm so happy that they're coming over. They just landed in Ålesund. Tore is picking them up right now."

Of course, Hana would have wanted to pick them up at the airport, but now, with the two kids, they would have just not fit. She would have breakfast with all of them in the morning.

"It has to be such a long trip for them," Charlotte said.

"Yes. More or less twenty-six hours. Honolulu to San Francisco. Then Copenhagen, Oslo, and finally Ålesund. It takes time to get from one end of the world to the other."

"Well, at least when they open the new bridge next year, there'll be no more need anymore to take a ferry. That should save us a lot of time when we have to go to Ålesund."

"Yes, I guess it'll take us only an hour and a half to get to Ålesund then. Imagine half the time it takes right now. It'll be interesting if they'll keep the Godshus airport open or shut it down because of this. Guess most people will just drive to Ålesund and fly from there."

"Ciao!" Alessandro said as he walked down the stairs. Hana noticed he was wearing cuff links. The same cuff links like every year. The same cuff links like twenty-nine years ago.

"Well, have a nice Julebord you two!" was what Charlotte wished them as they walked back to her car.

Hana started talking as soon as she turned out of the driveway. Alessandro's first words after she told him about the blast cells in her blood were, "No, that cannot be true! Did you double-check?" He said them with a tremble in his voice. She countered with what she knew was a lie:

"All is okay. All is okay."

He was too shocked, and the drive to the Dypthav restaurant was too short to tell him about the more important thing in the car. She parked the car. A light rain had started. He carefully held the umbrella over her. In a protective way. They walked side by side in silence down the small concrete pathway which then lead to the small metal bridge. Hanna took one step ahead and grabbed the handle of the entrance door to the underwater restaurant. She regretted it had taken her this much time to share the truth. But now was the time to come clear.

She pushed down the handle of the door and pulled the door towards herself. Stepping aside one step so that Alessandro could pass after he had clumsily collapsed the umbrella, she noticed a bike that was leaned against the railing opposite the entrance door.

"Alessandro, there is one more thing you need to know," she said, holding the door for him so he could step in first.

"Erik is your son," Hana said the moment after he had stepped inside the emerald-greenish light of the restaurant and then she swiftly joined him.

* * *

←⋯ 317 ○◎○ 412 ⋯→

Chapter 6

Dr. Anders Boisen-Jensen

December 30th, 2018
Dr. Anders Boisen-Jensen
Oslo – Norway

Sunday

Usually, Anders would only rarely resort to pay for sex. He however had noticed that there appeared to be a positive correlation between the occurrence of this happening and the length of time since he started to use glasses to read about two years before.

But today, because of timing, things would not have worked out differently. She barely understood any Norwegian; or any other Scandinavian language he had tried to speak to her. Her English was basic, bad, and came with a heavy either Ukrainian or Russian accent. He had pre-booked her to the hotel the night before leaving Copenhagen.

In reality, she looked much better than the leggy woman with big breasts on the internet picture.

The trip from Copenhagen through the short day had taken longer than expected. And this was just halfway to Godshus. In the future, he would fly, but he had to drive up his car this first time. A Škoda Octavia with a 1.2 TSI engine.

He had never been one of those men who considered that an automobile was part of their sex appeal.

For the next day—New Year's Eve—he had made a reservation at a fancy-looking hotel with a big bar and a spa at the Leonkulen Glacier ski resort. Google Maps had told him that it would only be about another two-and-a-half-hour drive from there to Godshus. His start date at Godshus General Hospital was Wednesday. He was confident he would find a woman tomorrow night at the ski resort without the need to exchange money.

But tonight was different. Anders had read that hotel staff in Norway would get you in trouble if you were not discreet with a woman whom you paid for sex. Therefore, he instructed her to meet him in the parking lot outside the nondescript modern hotel somewhere in an uninspiring area of Oslo. They filled out the registration as a couple.

They were both naked now. She lay wide open. He was entering her while standing next to the bed, hooking each of her legs with his arms. She was clearly trying to forge her orgasm. This was almost always the case with hookers. At least during their first time with him. He hated that. He felt ashamed for the other men who had taught them to do this.

"Oh, you dick so big, ooh, so hard, oh yes, ooh you like bull. Oh, ooh, I come. Come I will soon." Her fake dirty talk began annoying him.

Something was clearly not working for her.

Sex for him with any woman—even if he would pay her before or later—was always more than the actual silly act of penetration. He never allowed it to be reduced to the simplistic, testosterone-driven, instinctively controlled performance of desperation of shoving his pik into someone.

Anders never just fucked for fuck's sake.

He wanted to satisfy women. Any woman. Women of all ages, all shapes, and all sizes. He craved to lick them, tickle them, play with them. Only satisfied himself when he knew in the frontal lobes of his brain that she had to subject to him.

The only downside of fucking he dreaded was the risk of creating a human being with half his set of genes.

Because of his past, the thought of this utterly disgusted him.

Anders, therefore, had his prime directives. Initially, just two:

Never commitment.

Always condom.

Because of a peculiar event many years back in Malmö, he later had added a third:

No blowjob from a woman with teeth.

This directive had a single exception: Madame Professor.

He stopped, pulled out of her, walked over to his small duffel bag, and reached for the white box containing his AirPods.

"Put this one in your ear and turn around. I want you on your stomach. And psst, no more talking, okay?" Anders noticed her slightly perplexed face, while he placed the other AirPod into his ear. They were set on mono anyhow, as he would always only wear one at work. He double-tapped the white device in his ear with his index finger. The clock on the nightstand showed 21:33. He had agreed for an hour with the woman. More or less twenty-five minutes left. He would need to hurry up.

"Hey, Siri. Play *Boléro*."

"Okay, let's hear *Boléro* by Maurice Ravel," the virtual voice acknowledged his request.

The music started. He really did not like the piece too much. Too mechanical sounding—industrial almost—but given its only about fifteen-minute length it was the right choice for the current situation.

He entered her vagina from behind, syncing his moves to the accelerating rhythm of the music, massaging her neck and back and on occasionally lowering his mouth to gently bite her in the back of her neck. For some time she was just lying there—quiet—but eventually could not suppress her moaning. Shortly after, her entire body tensed and he felt how she tightened around him. He continued to speed up his movements with the quickening tempo of the music and although he would have preferred to keep going to enhance the intensity of his own orgasm, tonight he decided that, after she had moaned, tensed, and tightened for a second time, it was the moment to let go already. It was a long drive tomorrow. Soon after, he sensed the pleasurable feeling resulting from the release of his semen.

He stayed in her for a while longer, resting on top of her back. His pik was gradually getting flaccid still inside her. She continued to breathe heavily. Her body slightly sweating. Then he slowly pulled out, rolled onto his back next to her, and removed the condom. Anders glanced at her. The look on her face indicated that this might have been the first time she had a paid-for-orgasm.

He gave her NOK 1000 more than the price they had agreed upon.

After letting her out of the room, Anders took out his black pill organizer from the duffle bag and all his medications and put them on the nightstand. It was Monday tomorrow and he would have to refill his pill organizer for the next two weeks before continuing his drive to Godshus. Usually, Anders would do this at work, but tomorrow was different. Then he lay down in bed. Naked. The faint smell of her cheap perfume lingered in the room.

The no longer crisp hotel sheets smelling of recent sex reminded him of Madame Professor.

* * *

←··· 224 ○◎○ 181 ···→

January 5th, 2019
Dr. Anders Boisen-Jensen
Godshus – Norway

Saturday

The last thing Anders needed to do was to connect the high-end speakers. Basically, he was done unpacking. He had not brought many things with him from Copenhagen. He was keeping his apartment there for now, but he had taken the amplifier and the speakers with him.

The team he was now tasked to lead was definitely interesting. A mix of 'old-timers' who had been at Godshus General Hospital almost all their lives—with a deep sense of entitled ownership—and then the ones who just had arrived recently. He yet would have to meet the doctor, who was also from Denmark. Anders was curious if he might know her from somewhere—in the end, Denmark was a tiny country.

He still had no plan on how to solve the first task the Godshus General Hospital Management team had asked him to do: Implement the goals of the National Colon Cancer screening program at the hospital. At least his plans for New Year's Eve earlier in the week had worked out perfectly. Of course, by now he had forgotten her name. She—mid to late twenties—had grey-blue eyes and really, really very nice breasts. They both had good fun. It was a thoughtful touch of the hotel to have the Bang & Olufsen BeoPlay Bluetooth speaker in the room. He was able to connect his phone and play music. He first banged her to Charles Marie Widor's *Piano Quartet in A minor, Op. 66* and then put on Tchaikovsky's *Swan Lake* for the rest of the night.

The ski resort would be a good place for the future. Especially after the receptionist had told him that they expected a lot of ski tourists from England, now that a seasonal direct flight from

London to Godshus had been started. Likely none of them would be great at skiing and would not have considered that it was getting dark so early this time of the year in Norway. He had booked two nights for the next weekend at the ski resort already and was almost certain he would be successful at the bar with a spinster working at a London investment bank.

Anders turned on the stereo. It was pitch dark outside the rented house and it was likely still snowing heavily as it had around noon three hours ago, when he had last peeked throughout the living room window.

He contemplated which the inaugural piece should be for Godhus and decided to play the *Concerto for Orchestra BB 123* by Bartók; it seemed like the best match for the atmosphere outside.

After updating himself on the news of the day where the only headline that caught his interest was that Bartholomew I of Constantinople decreed the independence of the Orthodox Church of the Ukraine from the Russian Orthodox Church, he remembered that he still had to find a storage spot for the other essential items he had brought with him from Copenhagen.

Anders took the box filled with Pasante King condoms in their yellow packaging and went to the bathroom to check if they all would fit in the medicine cabinet.

* * *

←⋯ 181 ○◎○ 356 ⋯→

March 15th, 2019
Dr. Anders Boisen-Jensen
Godshus – Norway

Friday

Anders got on his bike. It was a fresh sunny morning. The air was cold still, but it finally felt like some sort of spring had arrived in Godshus. The rented house was the last one at the end of a dead-end one-lane country road. Behind it, the coastal cliffs soared towards the sky. A week ago he had started to bike to work again. Like he had always done in all the places he had worked before; be it in Malmö, Lund, or Copenhagen. The hilly terrain of Godshus was something he had to get used to, but he was glad he finally could get some exercise. He instructed Siri to play his biking song, and the lyrics began playing from the AirPods in his ears.

Anders started biking down the small hill past the three other houses that were scattered at the end of the road. All of them old wooden farmhouses. Two of them red like his and one white. There was a Land Rover parked in front of the white house. The hill continued downwards until a small trough. Here the view on his right went out to the North Sea ahead of him and the blue calm water of the fjord cutting into the grey towering cliffs as he turned his head back over his shoulder. The clear sky allowed even for a glimpse of the glittering white of the glacier peaks in the far distance. It was uphill from now, but straight. He had to peddle a bit harder until he reached the small peak. Now came the serpentines down the hill with their seven turns. He liked the roller coaster feeling of this section. The rest of the ride would be more flat. Shortly after, he passed a concrete monolith building that submerged itself like a giant periscope into the ocean on his right. The restaurant which it contained had been opened with great fanfare just at the beginning of the month. He had gone there for dinner in the first week.

He made sure he gave the maître d' a very generous tip in the end, which led to the assurance that he could call anytime he would want to dine there again and 'they would always find a space for him, no matter how long the official reservation list was.'

It was now about half of the way to the hospital. Anders passed the first of the two intersections—just another single-lane road that continued up the north side of the peninsula on the south side of which the hospital was located. He sped up on the flat section of the road here until he reached the bigger second intersection and turned to his right. He quickly biked through the town of Godshus, passing the harbor with the large fish factory on his left, and then he already could see the aging building of Godshus General Hospital. A slight wind was blowing from the North Sea and the air felt saltier. Anders got off his bike and left it in the empty bike rack that recently had been installed next to the heliport. He walked to the entrance and the sliding doors opened.

"Good morning, Dr. Boisen-Jensen," the triage nurse said.

"Good morning. Quiet night?"

"So, so. Could have been better. Could have been much worse."

"Get some rest!"

He stepped into the elevator and pushed the button for the second floor. He walked down the hallway. It was quiet. He opened the door to the intensive care unit with his ID card.

"Good morning, Dr. Boisen-Jensen. How was your bike ride this morning?"

"Good morning, Louise. Good, thank you. Refreshing. Quiet night?"

"Regular I would say."

He continued down the hallway until the second door on his right. He knocked. Nobody answered, so he entered. The state the bedding was in on the bed indicated that it had been used last night, but the room was empty. Anders closed the door behind him. He opened the cabinet where he kept the stash of scrubs, underwear, and socks as well as his white clogs into which he would change for the day and took the ensemble outfit with him into the ensuite bathroom.

He stripped out of his biking clothes and stepped into the shower. Feeling the need for a quick relief, Anders started stroking himself. Once he was done, he briefly wondered why mother nature had designed semen in a way that it always created a mess, and he made sure that none of the strands of the coagulating liquid remained stuck in the mesh of the rusty shower drain.

Nobody was in the conference room yet. He entered his office and opened the computer workstation with his password. The numbers in the right lower corner of the screen showed 7:04. He checked his work e-mail and saw that he had received a new message late in the evening the night before:

From: Godshus General Hospital Management Team
Subject: Additional Gastroenterologist Physician Position for Godshus General Hospital
Date/Time: March 14th, 2019 – 21:13
To: Dr. Anders Boisen-Jensen

Dear Anders,

We are sorry that we have to inform you that after lengthy discussions we must at this point in time deny your request to open up an additional Gastroenterologist Physician position. Although we have full understanding that it will be extremely difficult to achieve the national colon cancer screening colonoscopy target this year at the current staffing level, we must ask you to somehow make this work by utilizing the 'work smarter not harder' principle and make sure that both Dr. Andersen and Dr. Gianetti adhere to it.
Thanks for your understanding!
Best greetings,

Godshus General Hospital Management Team

Anders felt bad for both Dr. Andersen and Dr. Gianetti.

He only had a quick moment to open the website of CNN before the morning meeting would start.

The latest news update was the following:

12:04 a.m. ET, March 15, 2019

New Zealand police: Don't share video of the shooting

Police has asked social media users to stop sharing graphic footage circulating online relating to the incident in Christchurch.

"We would strongly urge that the link not be shared. We are working to have any footage removed," the New Zealand police said.

Police earlier told CNN they were "aware" of a specific video, but were unable to confirm or deny its veracity.

The disturbing video which has not been verified by CNN, purportedly shows a gunman walking into the mosque and opening fire.

CNN is choosing not to publish additional information regarding the video until more details are available.

* * *

←⋯ 287 ○◎○ 100 ⋯→

May 10th, 2019
Dr. Anders Boisen-Jensen
Godshus – Norway

Friday

His iPhone rang. He recognized the voice immediately.

"Anders! How are you doing in your little fjord up there, my friend."

"Well, it ain't Copenhagen or Malmö."

"Listen, did you book your tickets already? I just booked mine. Will fly Air France via Paris again like last year."

"You'll stay the entire time?"

"I'm actually going to fly over a bit before the festival starts. Reserved the flight for the third of August and will stay a couple of days afterwards. Flying back on August 24th."

"So you are staying a total of three weeks. You lucky bastard!"

"Well, summer vacation time!"

"I'm not sure I'll be able to get away from this place for a total of three weeks."

"But you are the Chief Physician! Aren't you? Just make them work harder!"

"Well, it's not that simple here. The other issue is, I'm going to Paris at the end of August for a little over a week—European Society of Cardiology meeting."

"But man! You are coming, aren't you?"

"Of course, I am. Eager to dance again. Not really too much of an opportunity here. You know, send me your flight info. What I might do is fly there with you on the third of August, but then leave a bit earlier."

"Okay, I'll email you."

Asif and Anders had become instant friends and travel companions the moment they—as the only two Danes—met in the hostel in Cusco. Their encounter happened at the beginning of what they both had thought of as 'solo-South-America-backpacking trips' now almost twenty years ago. Asif always joked that it was his honeymoon; although the arranged marriage with the woman from Pakistan which his parents had planned for him later that year was much less on his mind than the still-fresh breakup with his long-term girlfriend.

Initially, Anders had quite some trouble with the altitude in the Andes, due to all the blood he had lost just a week earlier as a direct result of a summer Friday night sexual encounter. That this was the reason for Anders struggling so much when they hiked the Inca trail together was basically the only thing he had never shared with Asif.

The experimental night Asif and Anders spent together in the tent with the view of Machu Picchu made it clear to both of them—beyond any doubt—that they were only heterosexual. But they discovered their shared passion for dancing tango the week they devoted going from one milonga to the other in Buenos Aires, before it was time to return to Copenhagen.

To the great surprise of everyone, Asif's arranged marriage had actually produced a very functional family with two wonderful, now relatively well-behaved teenagers and a wife who occasionally would share her knowledge of the Kama Sutra with various Danish men in Copenhagen.

Asif, instead of joining other Scandinavian men for an annual winter pilgrimage to Thailand, would leave Copenhagen every summer—when the temperature there threatened to rise above 22° Celsius—for the cooler days of the Buenos Aires winter and hotter nights of tango dancing during the 'Tango Festival y Mundial'.

Although throughout the years it had actually been Asif, who had taken more of the minas—the "chicks"—with whom he had danced the last tanda of the night with, back to the hotel, Anders had the feeling that this year might be different.

Casual encounters were hard to find in Godshus—and the seasonal flight to London had stopped at the end of March.

When he put down his iPhone, he saw the brief notification which popped up from the *Politiken e-avisen* app. The trade war between the USA and China had further escalated with the imposition of a 10% tariff hike. The notification that followed was that bookmakers were still betting on a song called 'Arcade' performed by an unknown singer from the Netherlands to become the winning Eurovision song the following weekend in Tel Aviv. There were few things in the world which could interest Anders even less than the odds of a tragic heartbreak pop song winning a song contest taking place in Asia. Another article in the entertainment section mentioned that Volodymyr Oleksandrovych Zelenskyy—a Jewish vaudeville stand-up comedian—would soon be inaugurated as the President of Ukraine; a role he had previously played in a political satire comedy television series called *Servant of the People*.

Anders stopped reading when Asif's e-mail with the flight information arrived.

As with all his e-mails, Asif had included a poem at the end:

FRIENDSHIP

Што ёсць сяброўства? Лёгкі запал пахмелля,
What's friendship? The hangover's faction,

Крыўды вольная размова,
Resentment-free conversation,

Абмен пыхлівасці, гультайства
The exchange of vanity, inaction,

Ці заступніцтва ганьба.
Or bitter shame of patronage.
Пушкін —Pushkin

* * *

←⋯ 288 ○◎○ 226 ⋯→

392

September 12th, 2019
Dr. Anders Boisen-Jensen
Godshus – Norway

Thursday

"Dr. Boisen-Jensen, do you by chance know anybody working in the cardiology department at Lund University Hospital?"

Dr. Abdi Noor was sitting in his office. The subject line on the letter she just had handed to him stated: RESIGNATION

She had decided that she wanted to give cardiology a try, and after receiving several rejections from hospitals all over Scandinavia, she had received an acceptance for a six-month temporary training position close to his former home. Her last day at Godshus General Hospital would be at the end of December.

Of course, Anders knew somebody.

The department Faiza was going to work in was headed by a woman who had been flown to Sweden from Vietnam as an orphan in the late 1960s. She was a full professor of cardiology and one of those women who aged very well. Perhaps with a little help from an expensive plastic surgeon and some Botox. Things of no relevance, as—if it had been done—had been performed artistically and professionally.

Madame Professor looked absolutely stunning the early Friday evening not even two weeks before when she had opened the hotel room door in Paris. As a petite woman she knew very well how to wear high heels, and that evening she had opted for greeting Anders with nothing touching her body, but a pair of freshly purchased black Christian Louboutin stilettos on her feet and the golden band she always would display on her left ring finger. Her Paris outfit was capturing the essence of her so much more than the Bavarian Dirndl in which she had greeted him the year before in Munich.

Madame Professor, and not all the advancement of the science of cardiology, was the only reason he had attended all the European Society of Cardiology Congresses since 2016: Rome, Barcelona, Munich, Paris. And he was already looking forward to the Amsterdam meeting in 2020. Anders was sure that the man she had married many years ago and who was the father of her three kids knew about their regular once-a-year meetings. In that regard, one could even say Madame Professor and Anders had a 'committed relationship' of sorts. Her husband was clearly one of those wise old men who comprehended that this type of freedom would only make their marriage stronger. In Paris, they first made use of the luxurious bed in the expensive room. The pharmaceutical company, for which she was giving her talk, had reserved it for her in the very pricey hotel.

Anders doubted that the suggestive room number '69' was purely coincidental. For himself, he had booked a room in a simple three-star hotel just down the road, in a white painted old building. They drank a quick glass of champagne as a break. He recovered. It was a beautiful warm summer night in Paris and it had got dark outside. He enjoyed every minute of the sex with the woman who had the maturity and wisdom to know what she liked. Being satisfied by him on the terrace belonging to her hotel room with a view of the illuminated Eiffel tower was one of them. He hardened thinking back.

Apart from enjoying an incredible panorama, things with Madame Professor from Lund were somewhat special in other ways as well. Over the course of the four or five nights they would spend together once a year, they would actually have breakfast together in the morning. Room-service, of course—but still breakfast. This year served on the terrace with a view of the Eiffel tower. Back in Barcelona, they observed the harbor full of cruise ships from the balcony.

With the women whom he would only meet for one night, he had established the rule to try to leave as soon as they fell asleep. That most of the time they would end up in the woman's bed and not his own made this so much simpler for him. Being at her place made it easy for him to disappear into the night. Perhaps at times, she would wake up in the morning unsure if she only had been dreaming. The rare occasion when things could get problematic was when he took the woman home to his place. He had tried to avoid this. Prior unpleasant experiences. It rarely ended well. The woman who wanted to hold on to him by getting up and preparing breakfast. The one who had waited for him at his entrance door. At a certain point in time, he, therefore, started introducing himself as 'Klaus' at the start of the night.

With Madame Professor, there had never even been the need to discuss such matters.

His current situation was very different now in Godshus than back in Malmö or Copenhagen. He was running out of options here. The last six months in this place had not really worked too well for him. Not having the anonymity of Malmö or Copenhagen was causing him problems. His aimless wandering in the night—a glass of wine here, a glance and a smile there—this did not work at all in Godshus. Out here, he could not just take sex for granted. At least he had his little break in Buenos Aires and then in Paris.

But now? The ski resort would only open in about three months, and reportedly it was unlikely that the seasonal flight to London would return.

Anders was never looking for a relationship and he realized that the young woman, sitting in front of him with the beautiful brown eyes, would likely not yet have the wisdom of Madam Professor from Lund. But this was an opportunity. She would leave this place in a bit more than three months. He should be able to do breakfast in the morning for that period of time.

Of course, starting something with Faiza could cause gigantic problems. Although she had just resigned, he was still her boss.

Well, at least she was not a nurse.

But knowing the professor from Lund could give him an advantage. It would take some effort for him to make her sleep with him. But there was a chance it could work out. He realized that he was in an extraordinary situation and that this justified extraordinary

395

means. He knew he needed to smile a little differently. This was something that would need to last around twelve weeks and not just a night.

As he was neither willing nor ready to retreat from satisfying women into a world of masturbatory loneliness in the call room shower, he knew that his current condition required him to break the rule of his first prime directive.

In this situation he had to commit, at least for a short while. He had to do things differently with Faiza. Her frame was graceful with long limbs and slender, playful fingers. Toned legs. Her laugh was delicate. He imagined how he would run up one of his fingers from her calf up her thigh and then to her hipbone, ending at her by then slightly quivering stomach.

He mustered a confident, knowing smile—a bit different than the ones he would usually use. Still flirtatious, but pretending to be more genuine.

After a brief moment of looking into Faiza's deep brown, contact lens-covered eyes, he said:

"Yes. I know someone in Lund. Let me write her an e-mail."

And then he noticed the gold in her deep brown eyes.

The news that night reported that water had been discovered on K2-18b—an exoplanet orbiting a red dwarf in the star's habitable zone located about 124 light-years from earth.

* * *

←⋯ 106 ○◎○ 301 ⋯→

October 12th, 2019
Dr. Anders Boisen-Jensen
Godshus – Norway

Saturday

His palms carefully touched her cheeks. Faiza's skin appeared beautiful this close, smooth and radiant. Anders still could not fully comprehend what had been done to her.

Already that night at the hospital when his fingers had explored her, things had felt different, but—of course—he was not able to see anything in the darkness. But then tonight, he clearly recognized what had been done to Faiza, when he spread her thighs to enter her. He had never seen something like this before.

He had stopped immediately. She just lay there, silent. Not looking at him. And thus he just said: "I know it will not be easy for you to talk about this."

They must have talked for an hour, and then he decided to give her a back massage. Luckily he had selected Wagner's *Tristan and Isolde* as the musical theme for the night—so there was no need to get up and put on new music.

Anders felt a bit unsure if she had really enjoyed the sex that followed after the massage. Faiza appeared strangely absent after she had returned from the bathroom. This had definitely been a first for him, and the insecurity in Anders' mind in a way reminded him of the first time he had sex.

Or perhaps more appropriately, his 'two' first times.

Before he had the heart valve replaced, he was the always sick, nerdy kid; so nothing had ever happened until he finally healed from his surgery.

But was that bloody mess really his first time?

The moment his way too short frenulum[1] ripped after he had entered Gry with a first unsecure thrust. Of course, it was painful, but it was the bloody mess that made her scream; and then everything was 'over' before—well, it was really—'over'.

The bleeding from his frenulum, which would not stop because of the warfarin. The trip to the hospital in Hjørring that evening. The circumcision which they did the next day so it would not happen again.

Therefore, perhaps his real 'first time' was later that year, while working the summertime job at the Klitmøller Badehotel—helping out in the kitchen, preparing breakfast, cleaning the rooms a bit—and having the afternoons free to stroll on the beach.

Malin had been older than him—a medical student from Stockholm. In Klitmøller to surf with her American boyfriend. They called him 'Wipeout Miller'.

The bonfire on the beach which lead to some kind of bonfire of vanities between Malin and 'Wipeout Miller', from which in the end he benefited. In hindsight, Anders had no illusion that Malin selecting him to walk her home to the campground was nothing but an arbitrary act to instill jealousy in 'Wipeout Miller'.

It was never really clear to Anders how Malin and he ended up in one of the old concrete bunkers the Nazis had built as part of the Atlantic Wall for the rest of a sleepless night.

But from there on, he was hooked to these random acts. The only thing which differed from this first time to all the ones that followed was that he now would always wear a condom.

The chlamydia infection Anders had got from Malin was unpleasant enough, especially because of the erection he got in front of the young nurse, who did the urethral swab.

---

1 **frenulum** (Latin) – Although the literary Latin translation is 'little bridge', in anatomy in general it refers to a small fold of tissue securing the mobile portion of an organ to the body. The word is most often used to refer to the frenulum preputii penis (frenulum of the prepuce of the penis) that in un-circumcised men connects the foreskin to the penile shaft and holds the foreskin in place over the glans.

But in a way, the young nurse's smirky smile felt encouraging.

And then, of course, what happened later that year made him always wear a condom, so he would not end up in a similar situation one day.

His prime directives.

Gry and Malin were also the few women he remembered by first name from thereon.

Anders looked down at Faiza's closed eyes and peaceful face. Was she sleeping already?

He watched her for another moment. The gentle swell of her breasts, the flat plane of her stomach, the points of her hipbones.

Yes, she was sleeping.

He never particularly enjoyed waking up next to a woman. In a certain way, it would make him feel claustrophobic. Never liked the expectations it carried. The potential disappointments the morning could bring with it. But surprisingly to him, the thought of waking up next to Faiza had a different appeal.

Perhaps having breakfast in the morning with her for the next little more than two months would be easier than he had thought. Carefully, he placed his hand on her shoulder and fell asleep next to her.

* * *

←⋯ 303 ○◎○ 400 ⋯→

October 24th, 2019
Dr. Anders Boisen-Jensen
Godshus – Norway

Thursday

"Anders."

"Madame Professor."

"Oh gosh. Stop it, will you? I always feel really ancient when you call me that!"

He knew very well that in this moment the best thing he could do was just to continue holding the phone against his ear and not say anything.

"So, I did ask around for you as promised. Right now there seems to be no openings that would be a match for you in any of the hospitals in Copenhagen. I really asked everyone. The one hospital I know which will be looking for a chief of cardiology right now is in Esbjerg—the Sydvestjysk Sygehus."[1]

Jutland.

Well, that would feel like going back to his roots.

"Thanks so much for asking."

"Of course, just for you to know. If you decide to apply for the job in Jutland: It hasn't been posted yet. They told me, that the day they would interview all the applicants would be December 23rd. I mean what a stupid date, just before Christmas. So be aware of that, if you would need to travel."

"That's great. Thanks for letting me know."

"Do you think I should wear klompen[2] next year?"

After a playful discussion focussed on the pros and cons of klompen versus Christian Louboutin stilettos in relationship to Madame Professor's feet, he hung up the phone.

---

1 **Sydvestjysk Sygehus** – *Danish*: Hospital of South-West Jutland.

2 **Klompen** – *Dutch*: Traditional all-wooden clogs from The Netherlands.

Jutland.

The place he left on the day of his eighteenth birthday and never returned. Back to his roots? But being at the end of Denmark would still be better than here—at the end of Norway.

A three-hour drive to Copenhagen, or Hamburg.

Not ideal, of course.

Clearly, nobody at Godshus General Hospital should know about these plans. If he were to be invited for the interview on December 23rd, he would just tell everyone he had an important meeting in Copenhagen that day.

Sitting at this desk in the chief physician's office, Anders decided to check out the website of the Sydvestjysk Sygehus hospital. A notification popped up indicating that he had received a new e-mail.

From: Godshus General Hospital Management Team
Subject: Selection of 'Advancement in Healthcare' consulting agency
Date/Time: October 24th, 2019 – 13:13
To: Dr. Anders Boisen-Jensen

Dear Anders,

We just wanted to inform you that the 'Advancement in Healthcare' consulting agency has been selected to perform the work, which we had talked about at our last face-to-face meeting. We expect they will complete their report shortly before Christmas.

Yours sincerely,

Godshus General Hospital Management Team

After Anders completed a draft cover letter and made sure his resume was updated to have everything ready when the position in Jutland got posted, he opened www.nature.com. It was interesting to read that Google claimed that they had achieved 'quantum supremacy' with a 53-qubit 'Sycamore' processor.

* * *

←⋯ 397 ○◎○ 111 ⋯→

December 11th, 2019
Dr. Anders Boisen-Jensen
Godshus – Norway

Wednesday

Anders still had difficulty getting the content of the e-mail from Legemiddelverk, which Pia had forwarded, out of his head.

Why of all people did he have to be affected by this? Why did it have to be a British pharma company that produced his ADIZEM-capsules?

And therefore it was he who had to be affected by a decision directly resulting from democracy's two fatal flaws:

First, assigning the same value to Stephen Hawking's vote as to a person, for whom warnings like *'DO NOT PUT PETS IN THE MICROWAVE TO DRY THEM'* are deemed necessary.

And **second**—even more important and detrimental—making a ballot cast by a human of an age at which Liverpool Victoria under no circumstances would offer to underwrite a life insurance policy count the same way like from someone who only just was legally allowed to order their first pint of beer in a pub.

Well, in the end, it was because of his problem with vanilla. Or the vanilla ice cream to be precise.

Vanilla ice cream—the taste he associated with dad. It was at the time when mom still allowed dad to see him. It was 'their' food. Either at dad's home or the café in the zoo. Or in Legoland when dad took him there. At home—dad always had vanilla ice cream for Anders in the freezer. ALWAYS. No matter if it was summer or winter, spring or fall. Visits with dad had the flavor of vanilla ice cream. And grandma knew about this. And she held on to that rule. To always have a package of vanilla ice cream in the freezer. Just in case. Just in case Anders would show up at the door one day. So when he finally did, on that Sunday in December 1990, grandma in

her deep mix between grief and happiness offered him just that—
vanilla ice cream; although it was in the middle of winter. First, he
thought that the funny feeling in his throat was only a reflection of
all what had happened that day. But the moment he started itch-
ing all over, sweating, his heart racing, and his breathing becoming
harder, he knew that something else was wrong. The paramedics
treated him right away, and he felt better already before they even
brought him to the Rigshospitalet emergency room. They were not
sure what had caused it but just kept him over night to observe
him. He did not sleep well in the hospital, but that was not because
of the allergic reaction. And then the next morning they almost
killed him. Like now for the whole of Norway—the Rigshospitalet
had switched to diltiazem tablets and did not have the capsules he
was on at home. Stupid tablets. Idiotic pharma industry. It's okay
if your pills taste bitter. It's not okay if they almost kill you because
you added vanilla flavoring to the coating to make them taste better. And while the vanilla ice cream the evening before was just a
near miss, swallowing the diltiazem tablet instead of the capsules
that morning was the direct hit. Yes. Confirmed. Repeated exposure to the substance you are allergic to does tend to make allergies
worse—and Anders' immune system was no different in that regard.
The last thing he remembered was that he could not breathe. And
then, the next thing was the small Christmas tree the nurses had
put up on the nursing counter in the Intensive Care Unit, where he
spent two nights. The chief allergologist had been the detective to
piece everything together. So it was capsules since then. Carefully
reading the entire ingredient list of any pill he would take, and—of
course—never, ever eating any of the food associated with memories of dad.

And no, just because one island nation gave in to the delusion
that they were better off alone out at sea than in the company of
twenty-seven others, did not mean that he would stop taking his
diltiazem.

Of course, as capsules. Ultimately, he would find a solution.
And no—Anders would not switch to the alternative.

No beta-blockers for him. Beta-blockers might be the better choice for his heart, but most definitely not for his dick. That one single time was traumatizing enough for him when he had tried them after his cardiologist had insisted. He took them for exactly five days. Until that completely embarrassing night. It was so perturbing that he did not even remember if the woman had blue, green, grey, brown, or black eyes. Or perhaps she indeed had different colored eyes? After that night he was back on diltiazem and never, ever touched a beta-blocker again. And the problem that occurred that night never, ever happened again.

He looked at the clock on the kitchen wall. It was ten minutes to 19:00. Just enough time to book his train ticket for his interview before watching Dagsrevyen. He opened the DSB[1] app on his iPhone and booked the last train from Copenhagen Airport to Esbjerg on Sunday, December 22nd—he already had his flight tickets, but made sure he had ample time in case there was a delay, although SAS was usually on-time. He had not expected to hear back from the Sydvestjysk Sygehus so quickly. Of course, having the interview scheduled for December 23rd was a huge inconvenience. Not so much for him, but for the entire team. Anders felt bad about the last-minute change he had to make to the call schedule. But was it his fault that SAS gave the vast majority of their employees off for Christmas and did not operate most of their flights?

But hopefully, he would get the job in Jutland and this would never be a concern anymore. He had not decided what he would do in Copenhagen waiting around the three days until he could get back on December 27th. He would make plans for this tomorrow.

Once he finished booking his train tickets, he walked over to the living room and turned on the TV. After he watched the announcement that the court of the World Trade Organization was no longer able to adjudicate on trade disputes as the current US president had refused to approve the appointment or reappointment of any judges on this appellate body, he decided he had enough of learning about

---

1 **DSB (Danske Statsbaner)** – *Danish*: Danish State Railways.

the day's news and switched over to his Netflix profile. Faiza was on call in the hospital, so it was time for a little Netflix binge.

Anders selected the series which recently really hooked him. Asif had recommended it to him in Buenos Aires in summer. He had already started watching season two. Anders chose the motif with people dressed in red overalls with Salvador Dalí face masks and episode nineteen started:

La casa de papel—Boom, Boom, Ciao

* * *

←⋯ 310 ○◎○ 367 ⋯→

December 15th, 2019
Dr. Anders Boisen-Jensen
Leonkulen Glacier – Norway

Sunday

"I'll be right back." the server said and asked: "Do you want some coffee or tea to take with you as well?"

As Anders did not really remember, he requested both.

The waitress disappeared towards the kitchen entrance of the hotel's restaurant to get him the tray and beverages he had asked for, so he could surprise Faiza with breakfast in bed.

The only thing in the world Anders was sure about this morning was that Faiza would definitely not want to eat brunost for breakfast as he started putting together a plate for her from the breakfast buffet.

What had happened last night?

What was going on with him?

Limbic System

against

Frontal Cortex

Intuition

against

Reason

Emotions

against

Rationality

Animalistic Instinct

against

Human Behavior

He had fallen asleep in her arms; only to wake up next to her half an hour ago. What the heck was going on with him?

What was this?

Was he falling for her? What had happened to his first prime directive? What was the thing about no commitments?

This had to stop.

Not for his sake.

But mostly for Faiza's sake.

It was his 47th birthday today. How old was she? He had never asked. In her early 30s, perhaps. Something like a fifteen-year age gap. Half a generation apart. He was too old for this. He would have to change too much to make it work, and even then it just would not work. The young Swedish doctor—a much better match for her. Approximately the same age.

All this with Faiza should not have happened in the first place.

It was this fucking place that made it all happen. Godshus. This fucking place which had turned him into the desperate guy who had to masturbate in the call room shower in the morning!

Having sex with women was easy. It was a skill he had mastered over all those years.

Friendship between men—like with Asif—was easy.

But sex and friendship between a woman and a man both together at the same time?

A relationship?

What a fucking nightmare!

A made-up human concept that was always doomed to fail in the long run.

Like the one of his parents.

Why did shit always have to happen on his birthday?

Shit like seeing his dad, and then finding out he would never see him again a year later?

Seeing dad through the glass window. Not sure how his father had found out that Anders was in the hospital. They had replaced his heart valve on Tuesday already. Anders was recovering well, but still had the chest tube. They had moved him to the stepdown unit. His mom had been there with him. She had stepped out just for a couple of minutes. He heard a knock at the glass window, which went out to the small hallway in front of his room. He saw his dad smile and wave at him. He looked older, but it was dad.

Although mom had thoroughly trained him to do otherwise, he smiled back—just for a very brief moment.

But the moment mom's angry face appeared in the window, Anders turned away.

He could not understand their heated screams outside of his room. He remembered that he cried; just a couple of tears so that mom would not notice.

Just a couple of tears, like in the courthouse's toilet when he was twelve. After he told the judge and the social worker exactly what mom had told him to tell them.

That he never wanted to see or even talk to dad again.

And that was exactly what happened until the face behind the glass window showed up for that very brief moment almost five years later.

A knock, a smile, and a wave.

Then mom.

Anders pretended he was sleeping when mom came back into the room after a while. He could hear that she was still breathing heavily.

Much later that evening, after mom had left for the day and after the night nurses had come in after shift change, the same nurse who had taken care of him the night before entered. She spoke Norwegian. Explained to him the other night that she was in Odense just for a couple of months. Wanting to become an ICU nurse in her small hospital at the end of a fjord somewhere in Norway. Some extra training which she needed to get in Odense. Some sort of rotation.

"So how was your birthday? So sorry you have to be in the hospital for it."

"It was okay."

"So I have a little card for you. From your dad. He also wanted me to tell you that no matter what, he will always love you. And you know, he really means it."

He had long forgotten the name of the Norwegian nurse, but Anders would always remember what she had done for him. Every year on Christmas Eve he would remember another thing she told him later that night. It was how she would spend the Christmas Eve in Odense that year as she was scheduled to work that day.

That, after she was done with her shift, she would go home, lie down under the Christmas tree and just pretend she was a gift.

And then exactly one year later, when after a huge fight with his mother, he just took the train to Copenhagen on his eighteenth birthday. Because now he could. He was eighteen now. She had no way any more to stop him. How he got off the train at København H and then walked expectantly. He had looked up the address before. The address which was written on the card he had gotten a year earlier: Nyvej 16, Frederiksberg. How the anticipation had made him so happy. The anticipation that he would see dad again. Be able to talk to him.

And then grandma's face when she opened the door. Her disbelief first. Then her "Anders. It is you! My Anders! You came!"

Her hug. Her tears of joy.

And then her words, after he asked. "Where's dad?"

"Your mother didn't tell you? You don't know? Oh, my poor boy!"

The last thing he had ever expected and wanted to hear on his eighteenth birthday.

It had happened a couple of months earlier. One of those incredibly stupid, tragic, and sad things which happen on boring, and slightly rainy Tuesday mornings. Completely mundane Tuesday mornings which will not be remembered for anything special in the history of the world, because of something that will never, ever make sense and that nobody will ever be prepared for.

But things that still happen.

A father on a bike and the blind spot of a car's side mirror.

And later that afternoon grandma served him vanilla ice cream.

"So here's your tray and the tea and coffee. Anything else I can help you with?"

"No. Thanks."

Anders knew that he would have to stop things with Faiza.

410

But what to say? He really had never done 'breakups'.

When?

The coming Thursday? They both would not be on call at the hospital that night, and she would likely be over at his house.

He would definitely need to come up with a plan of what to do, what to say—but clearly, he had to do it in the most brutal possible way. He had to burn all the bridges right there and immediately.

Hurt her.

Make absolutely sure that there was no ⏪.

Okay. It was time to stop analyzing all of this.

Now it was time to go back to the room for some breakfast in bed and then some quality time with Faiza before the tea and coffee would get cold.

* * *

←⋯ 239 ○◎○ 121 ⋯→

December 20th, 2019
Dr. Anders Boisen-Jensen
Godshus – Norway

Friday – 05:45

The emptiness of the bed stung Anders when he woke up. For a brief moment, he closed his eyes again. The pillow still had the slight scent of Faiza's perfume. Even now he could not believe how easy she had made things for him yesterday: 'Come to Malmö with me'. Just before she had said that, he had not been sure if he could do the 'breakup' thing at all. But this way all he needed to do was react. Defend his boundaries. It went differently than he expected it would. He was not a guy for breakups. Actually, it was a really unpleasant first experience. And here he was, feeling only the absence of Faiza in the bed.

Her tears, her screaming, affected him more than he thought they would. But Faiza deserved someone better than him. She deserved someone who would love her and take care of her, something he could never do. He had done the only right thing.

After getting up, he dressed in his cycling clothes as usual, with the exception that he put on the Ole Mathiesen Classic 1962 watch. It was from dad. Its black leather band would fit nicely with the suit he would wear for the Julebord. He had already dropped off his formal outfit at the Dypthav restaurant on Wednesday afternoon with the car, after having slept a couple of hours following his overnight call. He would change at the restaurant tonight. Cycling back from the Julebord allowed him to have a little bit more to drink than if he were to drive.

He remembered the dinner he had with Faiza there back in October—he had some fancy non-alcoholic concoction, which the restaurant had named 'juice', created from white currant, pickled turnips, and black currant leaves. He did not like it very much.

As it was Friday, he also took the small duffel bag with him—he would need to take his pill organizer home from work for the weekend and for the trip to Copenhagen and Jutland. Passing the refrigerator, he also took whatever he had left over of the aquavit from the small distillery in Bornholm with him and put the two bottles—one with the number '1' on it and the other with the number '7'—into the bag. They were both already more than half empty, but that way he had something with him he liked in case the liquor selection at the restaurant would not be satisfying.

The bike ride to the hospital was uneventful, and he took his usual shower but had no urge at all to masturbate.

When he entered the conference room, everyone was sitting at their places already, except for Faiza, whose chair was empty. In a way, it relieved him that she clearly had decided to skip the morning meeting.

"So how was the night?" Anders asked, looking at Per, who appeared surprisingly fresh after his night shift.

"Super quiet. Only two patients showed up in the emergency room. One, I admitted, the other one I sent home. I'm not really sure what's wrong with the one I admitted though."

"Okay, let's start with the patient you admitted then."

"A 57-year-old man. His wife brought him in. He has been feeling weak overall for a couple of days, nauseated on and off. But the reason she drove him in was that he got a headache in the late afternoon and then became more and more confused. Only past medical history is high cholesterol. Never had any surgeries."

"Vital signs?"

"His blood pressure was a bit on the higher side, but apart from that nothing really abnormal."

"Anything on physical exam?"

"Well, he's a bit obese and was a bit confused. He thought it was 2015, and that Stoltenberg is the prime minister. But otherwise nothing, really. Well, he had this rash."

"What kind of rash?"

"Small red and purple discolored spots basically everywhere."

413

"Sounds like a petechial rash. So what tests did you order?"

"So, of course, I did a head CT because of the confusion. But that was unremarkable. I thought about doing a lumbar puncture, but you know then his labs came back. And that's the confusing part."

"Okay?"

"Well, his white blood cell count was a bit up, but he is also quite anemic and his hemoglobin was 8.4 and then his platelet count was only 24000. And his creatinine was mildly up. I really have no clue why his labs are so abnormal."

"Well, the patient likely has TTP," Anders said.

"TTP?" Per asked, looking unsure.

"Yes. Thrombotic Thrombocytopenic Purpura, caused by an acquired severe deficiency of ADAMTS13, which is the protease that cleaves large von Willebrand factor multimers in the vasculature and if it's deficient platelet microthrombi form. And the microthrombi get stuck in the kidneys and in the brain—that's why his creatinine is up and the reason he's confused."

At this point in time, all doctors present in the room started looking at Anders in silence with their mouths slowly opening.

"Does he have schistocytes?" Anders asked.

"Let me look at his lab printout. Oh, yes—here it is. All the way at the bottom of the paper. Yes, it says schistocytes detected."

"So how did you treat the patient?" Anders asked.

"Well, as I had no clue what was going on with him, I just admitted him to the first floor and gave him an infusion of saline. The nurses did call me during the night to say that he seemed to be getting more and more confused."

"So I mean. It's clear to you that the patient needs to be urgently transferred. He must have a plasma exchange today. Of course, it's Friday before Christmas, so I'm sure the University Hospital in Bergen will be extremely happy to have to deal with him this afternoon." It was unmistakable from the tone in Anders' voice that he was getting just a little bit angry.

"But the patient is not crashing at all. I mean, he looks okay. I stopped by his room bef—"

"Per," Anders said, cutting him off. "Do you understand that he has a 90% chance of dying if he doesn't get a plasma exchange as quickly as possible? And once he starts crashing, it will be too late. So as soon as this meeting is over, let's get him transferred to Bergen. Hana, please take care of that."

"Yes. Yes, of course," Hana answered after she had stopped looking at the patient's laboratory printout which she had taken from Per.

"Okay, and the other patient?" Anders said.

"A young twenty-three-year-old student. High fevers and a dry cough for the last four days. He also said that he is short of breath at times. He studies sinology and just got back to Norway two days ago after being in China for almost a year. In some place called Wuhan."

"Seems to me like he brought 'la grippe' with him from the Red Middle Empire," Anders said.

"What is 'la grippe'?"

Anders now only rolled his eyes at Per's question and then after a while said:

"Well, continue."

"His influenza A and B tests were negative. Interestingly, he also complained that he could not smell or taste anything."

"Okay. Still, sounds like he brought some kind of virus with him. So what did you do with this guy?"

"He really insisted on getting a prescription for an antibiotic. He said he would fly to Milan later today to be with his girlfriend in Italy for the holidays and then go skiing in Austria and wanted to have some 'just in case'. So I wrote him a script for azithromycin and sent him on his way."

"Per. I surely do hope you know the difference between bacteria and viruses. Do you? I mean, I get it, TTP is a bit advanced, but bacteria and viruses are more basic, so even you should know this. I'm not sure at all an antibiotic will help this young man." Dr. Boisen-Jensen now was shouting.

Anders then continued: "Perhaps the next time you can just give him an anti-malaria medication. What about hydrochloroquine? And did you at least tell him not to travel and stay home if he's sick? And that he should be wearing a face mask, so that he doesn't spread his virus to others?"

While getting up from his chair, signaling to everyone that this meeting was over, Dr. Boisen-Jensen concluded: "Per, you are a fucking moron—you should go back to medical school!"

There was nothing but silence in the conference room as Anders walked out to go downstairs and perform the one cardiac catheterization which was scheduled for the day.

After he was done with the patient, whose coronary arteries were unremarkable for his age, Anders went back upstairs to his office to take his medications and eat two slices of crispbread with brunost. He was a bit annoyed when there was no brunost at all left in the fridge. He was very sure he still had a leftover piece there from yesterday. Why did some people just feel that they could eat whatever they found in the shared fridge? In the future, he would put his brunost into a Tupperware box labelled with his name.

He opened his pill organizer and swallowed his daily medications, while he ate two dry pieces of crispbread. Somehow it felt like his heart was racing all this week, beating more rapidly. It likely had to do with Faiza, but if this continued he would have to increase his diltiazem dose the next week. Perhaps he needed a bit more. He decided to put his pill organizer into his duffle bag, so he would not forget to do this later on.

After rounding on the patients on the first floor and then in the intensive care unit, Anders had the nondescript piece of meat with the brown sauce which the hospital kitchen had prepared for lunch that day. Knowing that Faiza would work from 12:30 he retreated to his office for the afternoon so that he would avoid running into her somewhere in the building. He spent most of the time completing charts and doing other administrative work on his computer until a pling announced a new e-mail:

From: Godhus General Hospital Management Team
Subject: STRICTLY CONFIDENTIAL: Economic Viability Analysis and Management Team Decision
Date/Time: December 20th, 2019 – 16:43
To: Dr. Anders Boisen-Jensen

Dear Anders,

We hope this message finds you well and we are sorry for sharing the following information with you just prior to Christmas.

Please find the full report of the 'Economic Viability Analysis' regarding Godshus General Hospital included as an attachment to this e-mail.

The report has been completed by the internationally very respected 'Advancement in Healthcare' consulting agency, which we had hired back in October.

We kindly ask you to keep the following information STRICTLY CONFIDENTIAL at this time.

The decision the Management Team has taken, based on the above report, is that going forward the continuing operation of Godshus General Hospital is no longer economically feasible, nor clinically justified.

Our decision very strongly considers the expected completion of two road infrastructure projects in the summer of 2020.

These are definitively the most significant projects affecting Nordre Bergenhus since the completion of the Grasdalstunnelen project, now over 40 years ago.

Once completed, the Hjørungavåg fjord suspension bridge will reduce the driving time between Godshus and Ålesund roughly by half to about one and a half hours, and no more ferry rides will be necessary. In addition, in several years, once the Hareidlandet road tunnel projects will be built, this will lead to a further reduction of driving time to about one hour. Additionally, the Nordfjordeid-Volda street tunnel, which is also expected to be completed by summer 2020, will again roughly half the driving time between Godshus and Volda to about one hour.

It is expected that these projects will further speed up the demographic shift and modeling data suggests an accelerated decline in the population of Godshus.

The physical plant of Godshus General Hospital, which is close to fifty years old would require significant capital investments over the next five years, which—given that the newly updated Ålesund Regional Hospital, as well as the much newer Volda General Hospital, now will be a much shorter drive away—are not justified.

Therefore, the Management Team has decided to terminate all inpatient, obstetric and surgical operations at Godshus General Hospital on September 30th, 2020.

Starting October 1st, 2020 only the emergency room and the radiology department will remain operational, and patients from Godshus requiring inpatient or obstetric care will be transferred to either Volda General Hospital or Ålesund Regional Hospital. An emergency physician team will staff the emergency department. A new, purpose-built freestanding emergency room only will be constructed over the next three-year-period in Godshus and once this is completed the physical plant of Godshus General Hospital will be decommissioned and torn down—very likely at the latest by October 2023.

The Management Team is currently working on a 'Closure and Transition Plan' and will work on this during the Christmas Holiday period. We will share the details with you as soon as the plan is finalized. All employees will be offered transfers to either Volda General Hospital or Ålesund Regional Hospital and severance packages if they do not choose to transfer.

The public and all Godshus General Hospital employees will be informed about the above on Monday, January 6th, 2020 at 08:00.

Please do not hesitate to contact us if you have any questions regarding our decision.

Yours sincerely,

Godshus General Hospital Management Team

Just like that. Fuckers. There had never, ever been any indication that this was the Management Team's goal when they informed him about the consulting agency. The only thing they had told him was that they wanted a 'set of external eyes' to do a '360-degree' evaluation of the care provided at Godshus General Hospital so that areas of improvement could be defined for the future. But a closure? They had never, ever mentioned that this was an option they considered.

And why?

Not that Norway didn't have enough money to run a small rural hospital.

All this was about was a false set of priorities. Because isn't that what budgets are about? For Norway it was clearly not the question if there was money, but how to allocate it. So from next fall, if a grandma in Godshus got sick, was the expectation that the family would spend at least two hours in a car a day just to visit her?

Anders was so upset that he hit the 'reply-to' button and already started typing 'Fuckers', but then ended up controlling himself and deleted the unfinished draft.

He would need to do something about this, but first needed to calm down and think. Realizing that not too much time was left until the locum physician would show up in his office before the start of his shift he quickly went to the call room and changed into his biking clothes as he did not really want to see Faiza, who would surely change there before going to the Julebord.

The chat with the locum doctor was quick, and Anders gave Faiza until 18:15 to leave the hospital.

Trying to distract himself from the content of the e-mail, he read the news online—in a couple of hours the President of the United States of America was scheduled to create a new independent branch of the US military called 'Space Force' by signing into force the United States Space Force Act in Hangar 6 of Joint Base Andrews near Washington, DC.

He left the building using the fire escape staircase and cycled through the darkness to the restaurant.

Anders got off his bike and leaned it against the railing opposite the entrance door.

He opened the door and stepped into the emerald-greenish light which rose from the depth of the restaurant.

"Good evening, Dr. Boisen-Jensen," the maître d' greeted him.

He was quickly handed the suit cover bag with his formal clothes for the night and went to the restroom to change. He took out the two bottles of aquavit from his small duffle bag and put them into the pockets of his dress pants.

The moment he stepped outside the restroom, he saw Alessandro enter. He had never seen such surprise in Alessandro's face before it turned back to the entrance door towards Hana who just entered.

He quickly greeted them, but had the feeling they were preoccupied with thoughts of their own. Shortly after, Werner walked in, and the maître d' helped all to get out of their winter jackets in the narrow hushed oak wood-clad foyer. The moment the maître d' started leading them down the oak stairway to the dining room filled with the emerald-greenish light, Anders spotted the creature through the massive window. An utterly inelegant—but with its at least three meters—enormous animal, lumpish, slowly passing in front of the window on the other side of the array of tables.

"What's that?" Anders asked.

"Oh, we call it Quint. It has been hanging around for the last couple of days. It's a Greenland shark."

"A Greenland shark?"

"Yes. Greenland sharks are among the world's largest predatory sharks, although they are mostly scavengers. But you know what's interesting—they're thought to have the longest lifespan of all vertebrate species. They can live up to 500 years."

"So are you going to serve us one of its family members tonight?"

"No. You would need to go to Iceland for that. You can't eat the meat of Greenland sharks raw. It needs to be cured and fermented for months, and then it becomes the famous kæstur hákari."[1]

They were quickly seated, and informal conversations began. Anders saw how Faiza arrived with Per. She made eye contact with him and greeted him defiantly, before taking a seat at the other end of the table. As soon as Pia appeared, the food and drink started to be served. The atmosphere however never felt festive; the talking was kept in a low voice, and Anders' suggestion to sing a holiday song was only met with silence.

---

1 **kæstur hákari** – *Icelandic*: Fermented shark which is considered the national dish of Iceland.

Anders looked around the table. What would all of them do once the hospital got closed down? From a practical perspective, it would be easiest for Werner, who was retired already. But likely it would be Werner who would feel the worst about it. Anders always had the feeling that Werner considered Godshus General Hospital as a child of sorts. Alessandro and Hana would have no other choice but to transfer to either Volda or Ålesund until they could retire. Perhaps both of them would carpool? All the driving in winter through the darkness would not be easy—especially with all the moose around. Pia would likely do the same as he and return to Denmark. Well, and Per and Faiza were still young—they still had all the possibilities open to them.

After the riskrem had been served and eaten, and as Anders felt bad about being so harsh to Per in the morning, he decided to ask Per if he was up for a round of aquavit at the bar. The young Swedish doctor—who definitely still needed to catch up reading Harrison's[1] and Tolstoy—agreed, and they quickly found themselves sitting next to each other at the small bar in the dining room. Anders was not sure what he should talk about, so after both of them had a shot of aquavit from the restaurant's selection, Anders just asked a somewhat boring question:

"So where in Sweden are you originally from Per?"

"I was born and grew up in Stockholm."

"And being from Stockholm, why of all places did you decide to come to Godshus?"

"Well, you know I surf, and Godhus has some quite good waves—some of the best waves you can find in Scandinavia, actually."

"So did you learn to surf in Stockholm?"

"No way. You know the Baltic isn't really a sea in which you can surf too much. My dad's a surfer, and he taught me."

"So your dad made you a surfer?"

---

1 **Harrison's Principles of Internal Medicine** is a two-volume American text-book of internal medicine.

"Yeah. My mom and my dad separated when I was really small. My mom is actually a cardiologist who works in Stockholm, and I stayed with my mom. My dad is American—you know—that's where the 'Miller' in my name is from. He first stayed in Stockholm, but eventually ended up moving to Biarritz in France, and he lives there now. When I started school because of the distance, my parents agreed that I would spend most of the vacations with my dad. So I spent a lot of time in France, of course, but actually, we spent most summers in Denmark. Biarritz is just totally overrun that time of the year. Not sure if you know the place—Klitmøller at the northeast tip of Jutland. They call it 'Cold Hawai'i'. And that's where I learned to surf."

"Really! Klitmøller?"

"Yeah. You know the place?"

"Yes, I do. I had a summer job there when I was still in school one year. Summer of 1990."

"Wow. A year before I was born."

"So, are the Nazi bunkers still around? Or did they get swallowed by the sand? I haven't been back there since then."

"Yeah. The Nazi bunkers. They're still there. Pretty sure Hitler never imagined what they are used for now, after bonfires on the beach at night these days."

The smirky smile of the man, who was of an age that he could be his son, showed Anders that it was time to change the subject and start talking about manly things.

"So Per, are you more a breast, or a leg type of man?" He saw the hint of surprise in Per's face, but quickly an even smirkier smile than before appeared.

"Actually, I'm more an eyes type of man."

Eyes … that was quite a surprising answer. And while Anders thought about deep brown eyes with a touch of gold, Per added:

"Also, you know, what's really important in a woman is that the sum of everything is more than the individual parts. You know what I mean?"

Okay—it was time to stop talking and start sharing some good aquavit with the young one next to him, not the stuff the restaurant had served.

"Chilli peppers, or licorice?"

"Licorice, of course. I'm Swedish."

"Okay."

Anders had to stand up briefly from the barstool to take out the two aquavit bottles from his dress pants. This brought the table back into his field of vision, and he saw that Pia had risen. She had clearly noticed him, sending him a quick wave with a smiling face. Then she pointed up to the stairs with her index finger before she moved her flat hand to the side of her head and tilted her head against it. Anders just nodded towards her. He then placed the two small flask-shaped bottles onto the bar.

"Danish Akvavit time. This is from Bornholm, but we'll drink it the Norwegian way," Anders suggested.

"Okay. Akvavit at room temperature then," Per said, smiling.

By that time, Werner had walked up to the bar:

"Sorry, Anders. I somehow don't feel well. I'll go home early. Have a good rest of the night."

Anders first opened the small flask-shaped bottle with the number '7' on it and poured it in one of the glasses so that the glass was about a third full. He then closed the bottle and put it back into the left pocket of his dress pants as there was still some 'licorice' flavored akvavit left over, but not really enough for him to have a glass. He passed the glass in front of Per and then emptied all what was left of chili pepper-flavored akvavit into his glass.

"Licorice for you and chili peppers for me," Anders said.

"Skal!"

The taste of chili peppers in his throat made him immediately think about the last weekend at the ski resort. He glanced over to the table to look for Faiza, but she had gotten up and was heading towards the stairway with a rapid pace. Her face appeared tense in a way.

Anders chatted a couple of more minutes with Per and then decided it would be time to get back to the table where now only

Hana and Alessandro were left. He briefly looked at Per and noticed that his eyes suddenly had a glassy appearance.

Per was silent and walked wobbly over to his chair at the table and then to the surprise of everyone when trying to sit down pushed the chair aside in an uncoordinated drunken way, and landed on the floor. Faiza who had just gotten back to the table let out a short scream.

The brief commotion and Per's drawled speech clearly indicated that Per had had too much to drink for the evening.

It was decided that Faiza should get him home as quickly as possible; and as she—with the help of the maître d'—got Per up the stairs, she briefly glanced back at Anders. Her deep brown eyes with a hint of gold in them appeared defiant.

Although Anders tried really hard to come up with a conversation, after a couple of minutes it was quickly clear that, with only Hana and Alessandro now remaining, the Julebord had ended far earlier than he had thought it would.

Getting up from his chair, he noticed that the Greenland shark had reappeared. Anders glanced into its small eyes and somehow got the feeling that the animal looked hungry.

Hana, Alessandro, and Anders exchanged the formulated remarks of a farewell and, while Anders paid the bill for the night with the maître d' in the narrow foyer, he watched Hana stepping out of the restaurant with Alessandro holding the door for her. The maître d' handed him his credit card receipt with a time of 21:23 printed on it and, although Anders very briefly considered changing into his biking clothes, he just decided to bike back home in his formal clothes and quickly stuffed the bike clothes into the small duffel bag on top of the pill organizer.

Anders then opened the door of the restaurant and stepped into the darkness of the night.

* * *

←⋯ 374

425

Chapter 7

December 20th, 2019 – FRIDAY – 20:57 ▷ 21:38

Godshus – Norway

20:57

As soon as he was outside, Werner needed to hold onto the railing next to a bike. The door closed behind the emerald-greenish light. Taking deep breaths of the cold air made the nausea subside a bit. He felt the slightly salty taste of the air on his tongue.

He had to make it home somehow.

After several more deep breaths, he slowly walked over to his Land Rover Defender. He got in. A grumble came from the depth of his stomach. Werner started the car. The moment he turned out of the restaurant's parking lot, pearls of cold sweat appeared on his forehead.

He never had driven up the seven serpentines so slowly in his entire life. As soon as he reached the top, he knew he could no longer suppress his body's imminent urge to vomit. He got out of the car just in time. He lost track of the number of times his body expelled any remnants of food and drink in a wavelike fashion through his mouth. It felt like he was forever standing next to his car on the top of the small coastal hill, just after the turn of the seventh and last serpentine.

Finally, a feeling of slight relief settled in, but it came paired with the sensation of shivering cold. He sat back behind the steering wheel and started the engine. With shaking hands he turned up the heating to maximum and quietly rested there, appreciating how the more and more warm air from the vents was brushing over his face. The drive home would only be another five minutes now.

The car's clock showed 21:23.

Werner forced himself to start driving down the straight small hill. Almost immediately spasms of pain started coming from his abdomen. A powerful wave of nausea made him stop the Land Rover again. He already felt the taste of vomit in his mouth when he hastily opened the door. Tumbling out of the car and over the shoulder of the single-lane road, he in the last second held back his body.

The sounds of the waves crashing against the bottom of the cliff were silencing the purgatory noises his body was making him do. He shivered at the thought that he would have fallen off the cliff if he had taken one more step.

Then an intense crampy spasm coming from his lower abdomen announced the beginning of the next chapter of Werner's misery.

Feeling that the passenger side of his car was a safer locale, he barely managed to walk over, drop his pants and squat down while supporting himself by gripping onto the car's thick front rubber tire. And just that very moment there was no more holding back of the profuse watery diarrhea.

When he finally felt empty, he pulled himself up with shaking hands. The realization that he had no means at all of cleaning himself caused a sentiment of deep embarrassment, which peaked the second he—after a long interlude of hesitation—did the necessary and pulled up his pants over the coldness of his butt.

He slowly walked over to the driver's side of his Land Rover to get back in.

Preoccupied with his feeling of self-reproach, it was too late to do anything when he lifted his head and saw the light.

Werner just froze.

21:01

Stepping out of the emerald-greenish light of the restaurant, it surprised Pia to see how the Land Rover belonging to Dr. Bjerknes slowly disappeared into the night, making a left turn when it exited the parking lot. Of course, she had spent a lot of time in the ladies' room to refresh herself for the rest of the evening on her way out, but there was no indication that, when she said her goodbyes, Dr. Bjerknes also wanted to leave early.

His name was Jonas.

She had noticed him in the pool on Wednesday. He was new in town. She knew exactly what to do after he asked:

"Sorry, but didn't you compete in the Norseman triathlon this year?"

Jonas had just finished his Ph.D. in marine biology in Oslo. Something about some sort of shark. A Greenland shark, if she remembered the name correctly. His job with the local branch laboratory of the Havforskningsinstituttet[1] was his first one. He had competed in triathlons for the last eight years and was really hoping to qualify for Hawai'i in 2020. Finally, the text arrived the moment when she took the first sip of the 'Nordic Mule' cocktail the server had talked her into trying:

Dear Pia, so great to meet you at the pool. Thanks so much for the offer to go over my winter training plan with me. I know it's just before Christmas and you will be off to Thailand soon. Would you have time this weekend? Best greetings, Jonas

He was a bit older than her usual, towards the end of his twenties, perhaps. Of course, his physique could not beat the one of 'Mr. Sweden 2018' but the bulge of his swimsuit looked promising. Very promising.

---

1 **Havforskningsinstituttet** – *Norwegian*: Norwegian Institute of Marine Research.

She typed quickly:

Hey Jonas!!! Great to run into you! Of course, let's meet. I know it's last minute, but I'm actually free tonight—21:20 for a beer at the 'Pub på Hjørnet'? Otherwise tomorrow??? Regards, Pia 👜 🚴 🎿

His response did not take long:

Wow, fantastic! See you soon. 21:20—Pub på Hjørnet

Promptly after Dr. Boisen-Jensen had stood up with Per to make him taste some aquavit at the bar, she seized the opportunity:

"Sorry! You know it has been quite a week! Also, have to get myself to the pool early tomorrow. Behind with my training plan! And I still have to pack for Thailand," was what she said before she rushed to disappear into the restroom on her way out. She left her not-even-half-consumed cocktail behind; surprisingly Pia did not enjoy its Nordic twist and would have preferred just a plain Moscow Mule.

Seeing Faiza come in surprised her.

Not that she cared at all about the woman, who would never have the right to belong to her world. She noticed the NDF-P woman's shaking hands while she was washing them in the wash-basin next to her. Faiza's breathing appeared somewhat deep and heavy. While finishing up with perfecting her mascara, she asked out of false pretending courtesy:

"Everything okay?"

"This is just an awful night for me. I should have stayed home. Anders dumped me yesterday!" was the NDF-P woman's reply after a brief pause.

"Ahh, find someone else." Pia added the 'but one of your own kind' only in her mind—while putting her mascara back into her handbag next to the Glock P80 pistol. Then Faiza's stunningly open answer spoken with a slightly melancholic tone took Pia completely by surprise:

"I would have never ever thought that he would be so good in bed. Well, but he's an asshole. And you know—I'm sure that in the long run, I'll be very happy that it ended."

Memories of a summer night many years ago back in Malmö appeared. Then Pia decided to seize this opportunity—after inspecting her hands for a while and noticing a small chip in the nail-polish of her barren left ring finger—and added insult to injury. The nail-polish had the hue of fresh arterial blood.

The moment the NDF-P took out a small pink atomizer perfume bottle after having put on more dark red lipstick, Pia just said:

"Yes. I know," and then quickly stepped out of the restroom.

Sitting in her car, while Pia tried to visualize what was hidden under Jonas' swimsuit—as so often before—an image of a penis with an unusually large vein flashed before her eyes.

21:13

Slowly the door swung closed behind them, making the glow of the emerald-green light disappear.

"Per, listen! Listen to me! You have to get all that nasty stuff out of your stomach. Here, lean over here."

Faiza had known all along that it likely would not be a pleasant evening. But she never thought it would end up in such a mess. At first, she had felt so strong, as she managed to defiantly greet Anders as if nothing ever had happened. Of course, the strain between him and the rest of the doctors clearly overshadowed the festiveness of the night, but she did chat a bit with her colleagues. The food was nice. It was a relief when Anders got up with Per to get a drink at the bar. The moment he left, it was as if a lot of the tension had gotten up from the table with him. But then it seemed like it was just a signal to declare that the Julebord was over. Dr. Andersen quickly excusing herself and then to her big surprise shortly afterwards Dr. Bjerknes said:

"I'm so sorry, my dear colleagues, but I feel somewhat unwell. I think it's better I head home. Have a nice rest of the evening."

Faiza recalled that Dr. Bjerknes' face indeed had a greenish-pale tint to it, which was visible even in the emerald-green light of the restaurant. And then, when she finally wanted to chat with Dr. Rønneberg and Dr. Gianetti and ask if it was more appropriate to say 'Ciao,' 'Goddagens,'[1] or 'God kveld'[2] when picking up somebody to go to a Julebord, the completely unexpected happened.

Glancing over to the bar, she noticed that Anders had taken out two small flask-shaped bottles for what it seemed like was a second round of shots. One with the number '1' and one with the number '7' on it. Her hands started shaking uncontrollably the moment she

---

1 **Goddagens** – *Swedish*: Formal way of saying 'hello' in Sweden.

2 **God kveld** – *Norwegian*: Good evening.

realized that the content of the bottle with the number '7' on it had been poured into the shot glass belonging to Per. In the quickest possible way, she tried to excuse herself under the pretense of a needed visit to the bathroom.

But by the time she started walking towards the bar, it was already too late. The contents of the shot glass containing the liquid from the small flask bottle with the number '7' had already made its way down Per's throat. Quickly she diverted her steps in the direction of the oak stairway and walked up to the foyer and entered the ladies' restroom.

To Faiza's big surprise, Dr. Andersen was there and given her very concerned:

"Everything okay?" Her distress must have been clearly evident.

Of course, there was no way she would share that she had just witnessed the poisoning of her young Swedish colleague with a quite significant dose of GHB, for which she ultimately was responsible.

Therefore, after a split second of thinking, Faiza decided it was easiest to simply blame Anders for everything and then refresh her makeup and perfume to justify her presence in the restroom.

Given the absence of any splashing sounds next to her for some time, she realized that Per likely had completely emptied the contents of his stomach directly into the ocean below him, while leaning over the railing opposite the entrance door next to a bike. Although it was unusual that Dr. Andersen would refresh her mascara just for the drive back home and a surprising remark her colleague made on her way out of the restroom, Faiza had more pressing issues to think about at the moment.

Looking at Per, it was clear that part of the contents of his stomach had ended up on his light gray winter coat. Together they stumbled across the parking lot to her car, and after some struggle got in.

"Per, stay awake now! I need to get you into your bed."

After a drive which seemed to take so much longer than the drive earlier that evening, she somehow pulled him out of the car and dragged him up the outside stairs in darkness. While almost stumbling several times, Faiza realized how much darker the night had become. The cloud cover was heavier now and completely obscured the faint light from the half-moon.

"Where are your keys?"

By now Per was just leaning against the wall next to the door of his apartment—eyes closed.

She went through the pockets of his winter coat. There was something hard in the inside chest pocket. Faiza opened the zipper and while she retrieved the key was surprised how muscular Per's chest felt. The loose scrubs he was always wearing at work never gave her that impression. She somehow unlocked the door and got him into the apartment. His body was now leaning heavier against her and she needed both of her hands to hold him up. She dropped his key-chain on the floor.

"Per! Stay awake here. You're almost in your bed."

She shook him, and he lifted his head. Quickly she used the time to take off his light grey winter coat, hang it up, and then support him to the bedroom. She sat him down at the end of the bed.

"Good Per. Almost ready to sleep."

She felt his muscular shoulders and arms while peeling his jacket off his limp torso. For the time, she just folded the jacket and put it on the floor next to a dresser. While she was taking off his second shoe, his body suddenly went completely limp and his torso collapsed backwards into the bed. For a very brief second, Faiza was relieved that this had only happened now and not earlier. She left the shoes at the foot of the bed, one of them facing upwards. Pushing a pillow onto the floor, she kneeled down in the bed and slid both of her hands into Per's armpits from below and with a single rapid jerking movement moved him towards the headboard.

She murmured, "Mission accomplished," and stood up.

Per lay there, in front of her. Completely out. His body filling the right half of the double bed. The GHB was doing what it was supposed to do at such a high dose. In the end, it was a date rape drug. She looked at him, still surprised at how muscular his torso felt compared to the lean and skinny body of Anders.

435

A typical surfer—like from the ads.

While for a very brief moment she imagined him lying there without clothes, she immediately realized how inappropriate it would be to see her work colleague naked.

And then, Per all of the sudden stopped breathing.

"Oh, no! Per! No, no, no, no, no. Per breathe, breathe, breathe please!" But even the vigorous shaking of his shoulders did not help.

Per did not breathe—his face was turning bluish.

"Okay, Faiza! Okay! A–B–C. Airway, breathing, circulation."

She had all the training. She had gone through this numerous times before with crashing patients in the hospital.

But here in Per's bedroom—just by herself—was different. Nobody to call for help. No nurses. No gloves. No Ambu bag. No crash cart. Just herself and Per, who was not breathing. She quickly checked the inside of his mouth. He had not vomited. She tilted his head back a little. He still would not breathe. Of course, this was how people died from a GHB overdose. They stopped breathing. Having no other choice, she pinched his nose with the fingers of one hand, took a deep breath in, and lowered her head to form a seal between his lips and hers and did a mouth-to-mouth breath. Previously, she only ever had done this on a plastic mannequin. It was surprisingly easy to do on an actual human.

After she gave Per another breath, she knew she needed to check for a pulse. Faiza had trouble getting to his neck because of the collar of his dress shirt. Quickly, she lowered her ear to his chest. Yes, she could hear his heart beat.

In the split second of relief from this, her face accidentally touched his dress shirt, leaving a faint stain of her red lipstick next to his breast pocket. She moved back to Per's head now; another mouth-to-mouth breath, and another one, and yet one more. She tried to glimpse at his chest to see if it was rising. But she had trouble appreciating this with him still having his dress shirt on. In between the mouth-to-mouth breaths she had been able to nervously open a couple of buttons of the shirt, so she now could check Per's pulse by feeling for his carotid artery. It was strong and

436

rhythmical. The bending down towards his face while standing next to the bed became uncomfortable. She decided it would be better to kneel down on Per's left side in bed and after giving him a larger mouth-to-mouth breath than the others, she did so.

The position immediately felt better for her, but from this angle, it now was even harder to check if Per's chest was rising properly. She always thought that it was somewhat excessive when the paramedics used scissors in the ambulance to quickly cut through T-shirts, shirts, jackets, or bras to expose a patient's chest—but now she understood.

In a rapid movement between her mouth-to-mouth breath, she grabbed Per's dress shirt and ripped it open. The fabric did not rip, but she noticed some buttons flying through the air. However, she was now able to easily check that each of her mouth-to-mouth breaths made Per's chest rise and fall.

And so she continued.

After what seemed like an eternity, Per appeared to gradually begin to breathe on his own again. Just shallow breaths at first, which made her continue her mouth-to-mouth breathing intermittently. Over the next twenty minutes, his breathing became more regular, and she needed to do this less and less. His body started to metabolize the GHB and the peak effect was slowly over. She sat on the side of the bed, looking at Per.

The red pigment from her lipstick was all over his face.

What should she do? Should she call an ambulance? But what would they do differently now? He was breathing on his own. Unless she told the truth about what she had done, everyone would just think that he was incredibly drunk. She was leaving Godshus, but he was planning to stay.

If she called an ambulance, it would tarnish Per's reputation in the small community: 'The drunk Swedish doctor' people would call him. Of course, unless she confessed the truth—for which she could easily end up in jail; even in Norway. Faiza glanced at his face. At work, she had never noticed how sharply defined it was. She saw all the red pigment from her lipstick.

It looked like the result of an incredibly wild make-out session.

Her colleagues knew they had left together—assuming that she would drive him home. Because of the GHB, Per would have no recollection of what happened after they left the restaurant. She would likely only see him once more in her life—in a little bit more than 24 hours when she would take over the call from him just after midnight on Sunday. She would mention nothing. She would be off to Southern Sweden in less than a week. What would be his conclusion waking up in the morning with lipstick all over his face? Julebord? Julebord and its one rule:

What happens at the Julebord stays at the Julebord.

Why not take advantage of this?

The only thing she needed to do was to take off his clothes. First, she pulled off his dress pants and put them onto the jacket on the floor next to the drawer. Per was wearing boxer shorts. Not low-rise briefs like Anders. She always thought that boxer shorts looked sexier on men. Carefully she opened the remaining buttons of his white shirt, exposing his flat abdomen with the slight hint of a sixpack, and after that, she squeezed his torso out of the shirt. She now could fully see the tattoo covering his pectoral muscle—blue lines forming multiple interlocking waves. If it would have been a different situation, she would not have minded tracing along these lines with a finger to feel his bare skin. Per must be shaving—his torso was hairless. In contrast to the moderate amount of hair on Anders' chest.

With one swift movement, Faiza pulled down his boxer shorts. Indeed—he was shaving:

Everything. Everywhere. Even there.

No hair at all.

Per still would need to grow up a bit. Still a bit of a boy, not fully a man yet.

Penis: Size normal. Foreskin intact. Interesting large vein.

After she pulled off the boxer shorts from his legs, she dropped them next to the pile containing his dress jacket, pants, and shirt.

He was lying on the bed, naked, in his deep GHB-induced sleep. She took her eyes off him and walked into the hallway. Faiza had her hand on the handle of the front door already. Then she remembered. She turned around and went back into the bedroom. As she could not imagine anything which lowered the sex appeal of a nude male body more than wearing nothing but two black socks, she peeled them off and dropped them on the floor next to the boxer shorts. Better. Much better. Faiza grabbed the blanket and covered Per as good as she could—so he would not get cold during the night.

Then she left the apartment, got into her car, drove home, and went to bed.

The one decision Faiza made that night before she fell asleep as the result of everything that had happened over the last 24 hours was that, whoever the next man in her life would be, with whom she would want to have sex with, he would first hear about what had happened to her as a child.

There was absolutely nothing wrong about telling him.

And if she would not like his answer, she would simply say *Ciao* then and there. Because if he could not explore her head first, he would not be worthy of exploring her body.

21:22

It did feel nice for Hana that Alessandro held the door for her as she walked out of the emerald-greenish light.

They began to talk as soon as they got into the car. There was nowhere to go in Godshus to talk and so in the end after driving around aimlessly for some time Hana simply pulled over at the side of the road. Although at times reluctantly, Alessandro agreed to stick to her plan.

Then, when she started driving again to drop him off at his home, he admitted to her that once, only once, he had been suspicious.

It was just after she came back to Godshus from Oslo. When he had learned that she had had another son. When one night he had sat down and tried to calculate what the due date would have been. But how he then disregarded that possibility completely once he found out that Erik was going to Barneskole[1] already. Meaning that he had to be born latest in June that year and not in September, which was the date when a child from him would have been due. How he completely disregarded the possibility of Erik arriving too early. How Alessandro concluded that she simply had already been two months pregnant from Tore. How he even for a short while thought that Hana was really irresponsible for getting so drunk while being pregnant already.

Alessandro had insisted on just one thing.

"Please give these cufflinks to Erik. I really want him to have them," he said, taking them off the moment Hana stopped the car in Charlotte's and his driveway. Somewhat reluctantly, she put them into her purse. She would give them to Erik as an unexpected gift.

"Thank you for tonight," Alessandro said, as he got out of the car. She saw how he remained just standing there while she steered back onto the road.

---

1 **Barneskole** – *Norwegian*: Elementary school.

When Hana got home, she tried to be as quiet as possible not to wake anyone.

She startled a bit when she realized that Erik was sitting at the dinner table in the dimly lit kitchen, checking his phone.

"Why are you awake?"

"The baby cried and I guess now the jetlag is catching up with me."

"Do you want to eat something?"

"Somehow—not sure why—but some ice cream would be nice. Do we have any?"

"You know—you're back home in Norway. It's cold here. Ice cream in the middle of winter?"

"Yep. I know."

"I think we have some chocolate ice cream in the freezer."

Hana took the box with the chocolate ice cream out of the freezer. She prepared two servings. One for Erik and one for herself. She would not have time to wait until summer to eat ice cream.

So why not do it now?

Tonight.

With her jetlagged son.

In the kitchen.

In the middle of winter.

"Here you are."

"Thanks, mom."

She put the lid back on the box with the chocolate ice cream and opened the refrigerator door.

"Mom! Is everything okay with you? You just put the ice cream into the fridge and not into the freezer."

And at that very moment, Hana knew that absolutely nothing was left anymore from all what she had so carefully planned.

21:23

At least this time he was able to do the right thing, Alessandro thought as he stepped out of the emerald-greenish light of the restaurant after holding the door for Hana. They walked over to the car quickly.

"So when can I see my son?" Alessandro asked even before Hana had started the car.

"Alessandro, we cannot do that!" Hana said.

He tried to argue with her, convince her, while they were still driving aimlessly through the night. But then when Hana stopped the car at the side of the road, he gave in to her arguments. Alessandro understood them. All she wanted was to protect Tore. Why would Tore, who would be a widower soon, also now have to lose another son? Alessandro agreed that this would be too cruel. And Hana's plan made sense. The letter she had written for Erik where she had described everything and which she gave Alessandro to read. He agreed he would do the same and that they would leave both letters with the notary in town. With the instruction to be handed to Erik only after both Hana and Tore would be dead.

So there was hope for Alessandro—he would just have to live long enough.

Then after they had agreed on everything, when Hana started driving again, Alessandro for a short while considered sharing the conversation he had with Charlotte many years ago with her. When he first admitted to Charlotte that an indiscretion had happened at the Julebord the year before 'with a woman from the hospital', upon which Charlotte shared that she as well had a secret Alessandro did not know about until then. That she had elected to have an abortion many years prior to meeting him. Charlotte and he both agreed that it was really irrelevant for either of them to know who the father of the child would have been and who the woman at the

Julebord was—but also—that these would be the only secrets they would have between them going forward.

Alessandro would really have to think what to do with tonight's information in face of that promise.

Instead, Alessandro started telling Hana:

"Just so that you know, there was one time I was a little suspicious ..."

Charlotte was asleep already when he walked into their bedroom. He undressed—uncarefully—not in a way that would have prevented her from waking up.

"How was the party?" she asked.

"Special," Alessandro answered.

And then they made love.

21:25

The door closed behind Anders. The emerald-greenish light no longer surrounded him. After securing his small duffel bag on the luggage carrier in the back, he put his AirPods into his ears and asked Siri to play his biking songs.

Well, more correctly the one song with its two versions which he would play on a continuous loop only while biking. The only non-classical music he would ever listen to voluntarily.

The original version of the song started playing:

Alla mattina appena alzata ...

In the morning as I got up

He swung onto his bike. What a weird bunch. They could have had fun at what possibly was their last Julebord ever, but they chose not to. Unless, of course, they would win the fight against the Management Team's decision. Perhaps it had been wrong not to inform everybody about the e-mail tonight. But now it was too late. He would tell them Monday. No way he would play along with the Management Team's little dirty 'Closure and Transition Plan' and the surprise they were planning for people just after the Christmas break. What would they do—fire him? Be my guest—I mean, he did not want to stay anyhow. It would definitely be an uphill battle, and realistically there would likely be no Godshus General Hospital left in December next year. But it was worth fighting for.

After he had made a left turn out of the restaurant's parking lot, it was time to pedal harder. The serpentines started.

Of course, all of them would be surprised when he would show up at Monday's morning meeting. He would cancel the interview in Esbjerg. In the end, what would he want 'back home' in Jutland? Other positions would open up somewhere for sure—this was not the time to jump ship. Well, he had a plan of what to do on Monday. And at least he would not have to rush back from the ski resort on Sunday to catch his flight to Copenhagen.

Shortly after passing the second serpentine turn, the newer, more known, version of the song started playing. The biking uphill made his heart beat faster, and he began to sweat slightly. Just at the fifth turn, the original lyrics of the song started playing again. He started sweating even more. He felt the alcohol in his blood. The slight taste of chili peppers from the akvavit he had with Per still lingered in his mouth. He decided that as soon as he would get home he would drink whatever of the licorice-flavored one was left over in the small bottle in the left pocket of his pants.

In the end, the only good thing about this evening was Faiza's defiance. His plan had worked. The way he had broken up with her burnt all the bridges. No emotional skeletons left in the closet. Poor Faiza. How she had to drag drunken Per back home. But Per was a good guy—what did he say? "An eyes type of man." Sounded promising. Age-wise Faiza and he would definitely be a suitable match. Anders only hoped that Per would appreciate the gold in Faiza's deep brown eyes—and that he would treat her well.

Just as he made it up the peak after the seventh and last turn, the newer version of the song started playing again:

Una mattina mi son svegliato,

O bella ciao, bella ciao, bella ciao ciao ciao! Una mattina mi son svegliato,

E ho trovato l'invasor.

One morning I awakened,

Oh bella ciao, bella ciao, bella ciao, ciao, ciao! (Goodbye beautiful) One morning I awakened,

And I found the invader.

He thought about the night before. Faiza's passionate kiss. Their last kiss.

O partigiano portami via,

O bella ciao, bella ciao, bella ciao ciao ciao! O partigiano portami via,

Che mi sento di morir.

Oh partisan carry me away,

Oh bella ciao, bella ciao, bella ciao, ciao, ciao! Oh partisan carry me away,
Because I feel death approaching.

Thinking of Faiza made Anders' penis react. He was able to stop pedalling. It was straight downhill from now until the small trough with the nice view of the ocean; well if there was any daylight.

E se io muoio da partigiano,
O bella ciao, bella ciao, bella ciao ciao ciao! E se io muoio da partigiano,
Tu mi devi seppellir.
And if I die as a partisan,
Oh bella ciao, bella ciao, bella ciao, ciao, ciao! And if I die as a partisan,
Then you must bury me.

He really wanted to fuck now.
In Copenhagen, he would have made it over to Istedgade and would have just paid to have sex.
But here at the end of a fjord in Norway?
As soon as he would be able to in January, he would need to take a couple of days off. Visit a big city.
Berlin perhaps? Just to have a fucking good time.
At least he would go to the ski resort hotel tomorrow again. Hopefully, he would find some distraction there to help him forget Faiza.

Seppellire lassù in montagna,
O bella ciao, bella ciao, bella ciao ciao ciao! Seppellire lassù in montagna,
Sotto l'ombra di un bel fior.
Bury me up in the mountain,
Oh bella ciao, bella ciao, bella ciao, ciao, ciao! Bury me up in the mountain,
Under the shade of a beautiful flower.

At the ski resort hotel hopefully, there would be some lonely willing woman who was on a quick pre-Christmas ski weekend.

Perhaps a woman like the one he had been with the first night there.

Last New Year's Eve; if he remembered correctly. Anders remembered little about her, but he definitively remembered her boobs. Close to perfect.

So close to perfect he had a hard time remembering the color of the woman's eyes—and he was usually an eye-man, not a breast-man.

But he did remember—her eyes were grey-blue.

E le genti che passeranno,
O bella ciao, bella ciao, bella ciao ciao ciao! E le genti che passeranno,
Mi diranno "che bel fior".
And all those who shall pass,
Oh bella ciao, bella ciao, bella ciao, ciao, ciao! And all those who shall pass,
Will tell me "what a beautiful flower."

The state his penis was now in, due to his imagination running wild, made sitting on the bike saddle become increasingly uncomfortable.

As Anders was not pedalling and as he also did not want to brake—because he wanted to gain as much speed as possible so he would be carried up the last small hill to his house—he decided to stand up on the bike's pedals.

Standing up felt liberating.

He felt the salty, freezing air blowing past his face.

The unlit car standing on the right side of the one-lane road emerged only late in the illuminated cone of his bike light.

It would be tight, but he could pass it on the left.

But then a shadow appeared and blocked the road completely.

Out of reflex, he jerked the bike handle to the left.

He shot out over the cliff.

ANDERS

F
E
L
L

A
N
D

T
H
E
N

H
E

SAW THE FACE OF HIS FATHER.

Ma verrà un giorno che tutte quante,
  O bella ciao bella ciao bella ciao ciao ciao! Ma verrà un giorno che
tutte quante,
  Lavoreremo in libertà.
But the day will come when us all,
  Oh bella ciao, bella ciao, bella ciao, ciao, ciao! But the day will
come when us all,
  Will work in freedom.

At least Anders died with most of his mind preoccupied with
the only thing that really gave him joy in life.

And YES—just in case you are wondering—he still had a
hard-on.

December 23rd, 2019 – MONDAY

Godshus – Norway

11:55

The chime coming from chief investigator Redding's computer indicated that he had received a new e-mail. It was from the Godshus General Hospital Management Team.

He opened it.

After he was done reading, he got up and walked over to the auto-drip coffee machine. There was very little of the black liquid left in the cold glass carafe and its smell lacked any freshness, and James, therefore, performed the necessary steps to brew fresh coffee.

Back at his desk, he moved the cursor over to the other e-mail which he had received and read it once more. It was from the forensic pathology department in Ålesund and contained Dr. Boisen-Jensen's preliminary autopsy results. As James had expected, the conclusion was that Dr. Boisen-Jensen had died from massive blunt head trauma possibly caused by a fall from at least ten meters. The almost normal weight of his lungs and very little, if any, *emphysema aquosum*[1] meant that there was no conclusive evidence that he had drowned. A larger than predicted amount of bleeding was reported, consistent with the fact that Dr. Boisen-Jensen was taking Warfarin as they had learned from the review of his medical record in the National Health Database. Blood toxicology results would not be available until after the New Year. The traumatic amputation of Dr. Boisen-Jensen's left leg above the knee and the large wound on his left pelvis were likely caused by a shark. The exact species of shark would still need to be determined by further analysis of the bite pattern, but it likely was a Greenland shark. Jonas Strøm, a national expert on Greenland sharks from the Havforskningsinstituttet, would be consulted.

---

1 **emphysema aquosum** – Latin term used by forensic pathologists to describe hyper-expanded and waterlogged lungs found during an autopsy. This is one of the signs that a person died of drowning.

It surprised James that Jonas was working at the local branch of the laboratory—right here in Godshus.

At times the world is such a small place.

Overall, the preliminary conclusion of the forensic pathologist was 'no evidence of somebody else causing his death'—preliminarily classifying the death as either 'suicide' or 'accidental'.

All in all, this fully supported James' first impression on the beach back on Saturday morning.

He would have not given Dr. Boisen-Jensen's death another thought had there not been the initial reaction by the doctors present in the conference room. The fleeting expressions James had seen on all their faces, now a bit over 48 hours ago. During his busy years of murder investigations in New York City back in the 1980s—before he moved to Norway to be with his Eva—he had never experienced something similar. For him it was always the hardest part of his job to inform the people who knew the victims; be it family, friends, or co-workers. But the situation in the hospital's conference room was different. The reaction of every single one of the doctors had made his instinct set off an alarm.

He could not pinpoint why. It was nothing but a sense. He had tried to rationalize. Perhaps it is just that doctors react differently when they are told about the death of a person—something they are so familiar with. It is part of their job to deliver such news routinely—isn't it? Was it because this was Norway and not New York City? It still left a strange feeling in him. Not about any single one of them, but about the entire group. Back in New York City people would be shocked, surprised, or something in-between when they received an announcement of this sort. But this group was different. The seconds after he had said the words:

"I am sorry that I have to inform you that Dr. Boisen-Jensen was found dead."

The silence.

The gazes towards the floor, out of the window, at the wall.

The avoidance of any eye contact with him.

The brief, transient hardening of the muscles in their faces.

451

The hand made into a fist which was raised towards the mouth.

The dropped shoulders.

Were they expressions of guilt?

In every single one of them?

Of course, all that tension and the expressions changed the instant the young doctor from Sweden with his bleeding wound on his face had stepped into the room.

Arriving in the conference room on Saturday, James had not at all been prepared to interrogate any of the doctors. All he had planned was to deliver the news of the death of the chief physician of the hospital his Eva had died in, to his doctors' colleagues in a decent and respectful way. Not having them find out through rumors or hearsay, as, of course, his passing would impact the community.

There had been no reason to suspect any one of them. But he had not been prepared at all for that same very brief and fleeting expression in all of their faces.

It had thrown him off.

And thus, after the commotion, which had been caused by the appearance of Dr. Nystrom-Miller, had subsided in the room, he—slightly bewildered—asked:

"It is my understanding that you all were at a Julebord yesterday evening together with Dr. Boisen-Jensen. I would therefore need to ask you when every one of you last saw him."

Based on the doctors' answers, it was quickly clear that Dr. Boisen-Jensen had been the last one to leave the restaurant. All of them had left before him. At a time that seemed way too early for when a normal Julebord was supposed to end. From the way they answered, it appeared like it had not been a fun night full of celebration for any of them.

James ended the brief discussion with "Okay. Thank you for all your time, doctors. I'll let you know if I have any further questions."

After this, all doctors gradually left the conference room until only Dr. Bjerknes remained.

"Can I help you with anything else?" the former chief physician asked.

"No. Not at this time. Thank you. Well, actually yes. Could we look if we can find any next of kin info for Dr. Boisen-Jensen?"

Unfortunately, the information Dr. Bjerknes found in the Godhus General Hospital electronic human resource database was neither promising nor helpful:

It listed a Zusanne Jensen. Relationship: Mother. There was no phone number, only an address: Ældrecentret Lundgårdends— Demensby.[1]

James took down the information so he could transmit a request to the Danish police to look into this.

On his way back to the Godshus police station, James stopped at the Dypthav restaurant. The maître d', who had just arrived to prepare the restaurant for dinner, confirmed the statements of the doctors about how last night's Julebord proceeded. He also produced a credit card receipt of the payment Dr. Boisen-Jensen made for the Julebord, which showed a time of 21:23. In addition, he affirmed that he saw Dr. Boisen-Jensen getting on his bike and cycling away.

The whole bicycling thing about Dr. Boisen-Jensen still felt a bit out of place to James. Cycling in the middle of winter—in Norway. But it was one of the things the doctors in the conference room had told him when he talked to them.

It was pitch-dark outside already by the time he parked the white Volkswagen Passat station wagon at the Godshus police station.

He then called the number of the national crime investigation unit in Oslo.

"Sorry for bothering you just before Christmas, but I would need you to look into some data for me."

"Sure. What can we help with?"

"I'm trying to figure out if there is any localization info you can find on a man who was found dead this morning. So far the

1 Ældrecentret Lundgårdends – Demensby – *Danish*: Lundgårdends Elderly Center – Dementia 'town'.

last thing I have on him is that he left a restaurant a little after twenty past nine last night. Could you check if there are any additional transactions on his credit card and also any pings from his cell phone?"

"No problem. We'll start working on this."

When his young colleague Maria Michelson arrived, she was still almost as upset as he had left her on the beach earlier that morning.

James felt bad for her. Betrayed just before Christmas. Scandinavians and their out-of-control sex drives at a Julebord. He decided not to tell her what he had learnt at the hospital—that her now ex-boyfriend had left the restaurant quite inebriated together with a young female colleague of his.

The forensic team had recovered several items from Dr. Boisen-Jensen's pockets: a wallet containing just the usual, an iPhone which was no longer operational, and three Pasante King condoms in their yellow packaging. Of course, it was unclear if there had been anything in the left pocket of his black pants as that part of his wardrobe would never be found.

The moment the analog watch on the wrist of Dr. Boisen-Jensen had stopped was at 21:38.

They would have to send his iPhone to the 'mobile device forensic unit' in Oslo. Given that it had likely been submerged in the salty ocean water for quite some time, James doubted that they would be able to retrieve anything.

After spending some time and unsuccessfully trying—in a fatherly way—to mend Maria's heart, which had been shattered into a million pieces, he went home.

It had started snowing heavily by the time he made it home. NRK Lørdagsrevyen, which he watched that evening, was filled with a variety of news stories: An interview with the mother of a 28-year-old Norwegian woman who had been murdered in the Atlas Mountains of Morocco a year earlier by a group of men linked to ISIS. A report about the growing disagreement between the United States and Europe—but especially Germany—over the Nord Stream 2 Pipeline on the bottom of the Baltic sea, which would allow Russia to bypass the Ukraine when supplying gas to Europe. Footage about two cruise ships colliding in Mexico and a story that one would no longer have to pay an entrance fee to visit Nordkapplatået.[1]

After waking up on Sunday, he drove back to the police station. It had snowed heavily overnight and walking to his car through the still pitch dark morning he estimated that at least thirty centimeters of fresh snow had covered the ground.

At the police station, an e-mail from the national crime investigation unit confirmed what he had suspected: Dr. Boisen-Jensen's credit card was last used at 21:23 at the Dypthav restaurant, and a cell phone tower standing on top of a small coastal hill received the last ping from his iPhone. The timestamp of the last ping was 21:36. Overlying the coverage of the cell phone tower with the local map placed the last known location of Dr. Boisen-Jensen's cell phone in the area of a dead-end road leading from the Dypthav restaurant to the home listed as Dr. Boisen-Jensen's address in the National driver's license database. The map showed that the road leading up the hill curved back and forth seven times just prior to where the cell phone tower coverage started.

As soon as it had become light outside, James drove to the location from where the last phone ping came from. It was no longer snowing and like the day before it was an unusually clear day, with only a few thin, high clouds. The faint sun was just barely rising above the glittering of the glacier peaks in the distance, illuminating the fresh snow. His black Norwegian police officer uniform contrasted with all the white, blue, and grey that surrounded him.

It took him about three minutes to drive up the seven serpentines. James estimated that Dr. Boisen-Jensen would have been able to cover the same distance in about ten minutes on his bike. He briefly stopped at the top of the hill next to the cell phone tower. From here the single-lane road now led more gently straight down the hill until it reached a trough and then started going uphill

---

1 **Nordkapplatået** – *Norwegian*: Large flat plateau on top of the 307-metre-high North Cape cliff.

again, towards several houses which he saw in the distance. The coastline—initially quite at a distance from the road—gradually approached the road until it almost hugged it from the left side where the trough was. No road guardrail was to be found in any section along this small country road. James drove down to the trough. The freshly fallen snow would have covered any tracks, but at this point, the road was only about one meter away from the cliff face. James got out of the car, waded through the snow, and looked down.

He took a deep breath in through his nose.

The smell of freshly brewed coffee filling the Godshus police station interrupted the memories of the bluish-grey waves crashing onto the occasional boulders sticking out of the ocean below him. However, the instinctive feeling of suddenly knowing what had happened, when he was standing on top of the cliff, persisted. He got up and poured some fresh coffee into his cup and then sat down to finish his work for the day.

It was getting late. He would need to begin driving to the airport soon.

James pulled up his electronic report in the National Police Database and scrolled down to: 'death clearly accidental—no further investigation needed'. Of course, finding the bike at the bottom of the cliff would have been the needed conclusive evidence. But there was no way James would risk the life of a diver to try to find it between crashing waves, boulders, and ice-cold water of an unclear depth. Besides, the ocean current had likely carried Dr. Boisen-Jensen's bike away somewhere already by now.

He clicked the check box.

How sad and tragic. On a Friday night just before Christmas, the chief physician of a small hospital at the end of a fjord in Norway had fallen to his death off a cliff when he veered off a single lane road while bicycling home from a Julebord. The doctor's watch had stopped at 21:38. His body must have been floating around in the grey-blue, ice-cold water of the North Sea for almost exactly twelve hours before it made a young Swedish colleague of his fall off a surfboard.

A pop-up menu appeared on the screen, and—as James would always do—he selected 'likely', as a response to the obligatory 'Did alcohol consumption contribute to the accident?' question.

Then he clicked the 'save and close investigation' button.

There was one more thing James needed to do before he could leave. He did not want to be late. He would feel bad if he wasn't at the airport on time to greet his daughter Keira. She was coming to Godshus from New York City for the holidays. He had never got used to the emptiness of the house—especially during the holidays—since Eva's death. Occasionally, it still felt unusual for him that the child he'd thought of as a son was the daughter he had always wished for. James remembered that, at a time when he still called his child Kevin, she had been such a Harry Potter fan. Of course, that name and her fascination with wizards was a matter of the past, and had no place either in the present or in the future. Keira loved reading Rick Riordan's books and James would still have to gift-wrap *The Hammer of Thor* for her—it had finally been translated into Norwegian. The thought of hugging his child soon made James smile. For now, he was still tied to Norway to become eligible for his pension, but in a couple of years, he would move back to New York City to be close to her.

James opened the e-mail program and found the message from the Godshus General Hospital Management Team. He pushed reply and started typing:

Dear Godshus General Hospital Management Team,

Thank you for your email and for letting me know who took over as chief physician of the medical department of Godshus General Hospital.

Regarding the investigation into the passing of Dr. Boisen-Jensen: The case is now closed, and I think there will be no need to talk to any of the doctors again.

If you could get this message to Dr. Andersen, that would be great.

Please also congratulate her on becoming the new chief physician. It is always great to have dedicated doctors like her remain in our small community.

We need them.

I feel so sorry for her that she had to cancel her holiday in Thailand. Gledelig Jul!

Yours sincerely,

James W. Redding
Chief Investigator—Godshus Police Department

After hitting the send button, James got up, put on his winter coat and left the warmth of the police station, and walked out to his car.

He would still need to briefly stop by the supermarket to buy some lettuce. Otherwise, he had everything at home to make the meatloaf, peas, and mashed potatoes for tonight's dinner.

James decided to put on Eva's and his song for the drive.

It was the melody they had danced their first dance to as a married couple—just a little more than a year after they had met.

The car audio system started playing: *We Are the World*.

He was looking forward to celebrating Kwanzaa[1] with his daughter in Norway this year.

---

1 **Kwanzaa** – Celebration of African-American culture held every year from December 26th until January 1st. The holiday culminates in gift-giving and a feast of faith called 'Karama Ya Imani'. It was created by *Maulana Karenga* and first celebrated in 1966.

This is our World.

In winter.

—At
— — the
— — — very

B—E—G—I—N—N—I—N—G

— — of
— winter.

A

COLD

D
A
R
K

unforgiving

winter.

L—O—N—G,

but

n —
— o
— — t

without an

END. ?

Forty Selected Dates

May 17th, 1814
The Constitution of Norway is signed in Eidsvoll. May 17th since then has been celebrated as Norway's National Day.

April 5th, 1905
The Italian Parliament passes a law uniting all parts of southern Somalia into an area called 'Somalia Italiana'.

October 26th, 1905
King Oscar II of Sweden (1829-1907) renounces his claim to the Norwegian throne, which means the peaceful dissolution of the United Kingdoms of Sweden and Norway.

March 8th, 1914
International Women's Day was held for the first time on March 8th in Germany. It had been celebrated on other days of the year previously and afterwards, but following the October Revolution, the date was made an official holiday in the Soviet Union.

August 5th, 1915
The 'Hiroshima Prefectural Commercial Exhibition Hall' designed by Czech architect Jan Letzel (1880-1925) is officially opened to the public. It is destroyed thirty years and a day later when the Enola Gay drops the 'Little Boy' atomic bomb and its ruins since then have been transformed into 'The Hiroshima Peace Memorial' (Genbaku Dome).

461

September 30th, 1938
Nazi Germany, the United Kingdom, the French Third Republic, and the Kingdom of Italy conclude an agreement in Munich, which results in the cession to Germany of the Sudeten German territory of Czechoslovakia. The members of the Czechoslovak delegation are kept waiting in a nearby hotel and are handed the signed document. Upon returning to London, the British Prime Minister Neville Chamberlain (1869-1940) delivers a speech which is known as 'Peace for our time'. He ends his speech with: 'Go home and get a nice quiet sleep.'

April 9th, 1940
Following the invasion of Norway by Nazi Germany, the Storting (the Norwegian parliament), which had been evacuated to the town of Elverum from Oslo, allows the Norwegian executive branch to temporarily assert absolute authority in the so-called Elverum Authorization (Elverumsfullmakta). The meeting takes place in the building of the Elverum folkehøgskole. Two days later, on April 11th, Elverum is reduced to ashes by the German Luftwaffe.

November 24th, 1941
The first Jewish deportees arrive in Theresienstadt.

February 20th, 1944
Norwegian resistance fighters sink the railway ferry SF Hydro to prevent Nazi Germany from receiving heavy water.

June 23rd, 1944
An official Swiss/Danish delegation by the International Committee of the Red Cross (ICRC) visits the Theresienstadt concentration camp.

April 15th, 1945

The so-called 'White Buses' organized by the Swedish Red Cross and the Danish government arrive in Theresienstadt and evacuate 423 Danish jews.

May 11th, 1945

Soviet medical units arrive in Theresienstadt and take charge. Due to a typhoid epidemic, strict quarantine measures are imposed. Over 1500 prisoners and 43 nurses and doctors die around this time.

October 10th, 1945

The Palmach (special forces unit of the Haganah) break into the Atlit detainee camp, which had been established by the authorities of the British Mandate for Palestine to prevent Jewish refugees from entering Palestine. About 200 detainees—some of them Holocaust survivors—escape. Yitzak Rabin (1922-1995) had been part of planning the operation.

November 30th, 1947

The day after the United Nations General Assembly adopts the Partition Plan for Palestine as Resolution 181 (II) a bus carrying Jewish passengers is ambushed near Kfar Sirkin and five passengers are killed.

February 25th, 1948

The Czechoslovak President Eduard Beneš (1884-1948) accepts the resignation of the non-Communist ministers of the Czechoslovak government and appoints a new government in accordance with the demands of the Communist Party of Czechoslovakia. This concludes the so-called 1948 Czechoslovak coup d'état.

April 1st, 1950

The 'Trust Territory of Somaliland under Italian Administration' is established by the United Nations in present-day northeastern, central and southern Somalia. A little over ten years later on

July 1st, 1960 the Somali Republic [Jamhuuriyadda Soomaaliyeed] is established by unifying the Trust Territory with the State of Somaliland (the former British Somaliland).

August 20th, 1968
The armies of four Warsaw Pact countries—the Soviet Union, Bulgaria, Poland, and Hungary—start the invasion of Czechoslovakia.

April 20th, 1972
The Norwegian Parliament repeals section 213 of the penal code, decriminalizing homosexuality in Norway.

October 6th, 1973
Around 14:00 local time, the Egyptian military launches Operation Badr marking the start of the Yom Kippur War.

January 6th, 1977
The text of the 'Charta 77', which is criticizing the government of the Czechoslovak Socialist Republic for its failure to implement human rights, is published with the names of its first 242 signatories. Václav Havel (1936-2011), who later becomes the last Czechoslovak President, together with Ludvík Vaculík (writer and journalist, 1926-2015) and Pavel Landovsky (actor, playwright, and director, 1936-2014) are detained in Prague when they try to deliver a copy of the document to the Czechoslovak parliament, the Czechoslovak government and the Czechoslovak Press Agency.

October 13th, 1977
Four members of the Popular Front for the Liberation of Palestine hijack Lufthansa flight 181—a Boing 737-230C jet named 'Landshut'—en route from Palma de Mallorca to Frankfurt. The aircraft is stormed in Mogadishu, Somalia on October 18th, 1977 by the West German counter-terrorism group GSG 9.

May 30th, 1978
The Norwegian Parliament passes a law which allows for abortion on request in the first twelve weeks of pregnancy. The law passes with a one-vote majority.

November 20th, 1979
Around five in the morning, close to 500 fundamentalists led by Juhayman al-Otaybi (1936-1980) begin the seizure of Islam's holiest site the Masjid al-Haram (the Great Mosque with the sacred Kaaba in its heart) in Mecca, Saudi Arabia. The date of the attack corresponds to the first day of the year 1400 according to the Islamic calendar and the extremists used the popular tradition of the 'mujaddid' that refers to a person who appears at the turn of every century of the Islamic calendar to revive Islam by cleansing it of extraneous elements and purifying it. The extremists' goal was to restore theocracy and accused the Al-Saud dynasty that is ruling Saudi Arabia of having betrayed Islamic principles because of the aggressive policy of Westernization. Some of the extremists were former military officials of the Saudi National Guard, giving the group access to automatic weapons and ammunition. The stand-off lasts for two weeks until the mosque is recaptured with a total death toll of more than 230 people. Sixty-three of the surviving Grand Mosque militants were subsequently beheaded by sword on January 9th, 1980 in the public squares of eight Saudi cities. At the time of the attack, renovations of the Great Mosque were still ongoing with the 'Saudi Bin Laden Group' being one of the most important contractors—a company led by the father of Osama bin Laden (1957-2011). As a response to the attack, Saudi King Khaled (1913-1982) chose not to crack down on religious puritans in general, but ended up increasing the influence of religious conservatives, believing that 'more religion' would be the correct solution to the religious upheaval.

February 28th, 1984
Scandinavian Airlines System Flight 901 from Stockholm Arlanda Airport with a stopover in Oslo overruns the runway at JFK International Airport in New York City. All 177 passengers and crew members on board survive.

March 2nd, 1985
Abbott Laboratories of Chicago, Illinois receives approval for a blood test to screen blood for exposure to the AIDS virus.

February 28th, 1986
The Prime Minister of Sweden Sven Olof Joachim Palme (1927-1986) is shot on his way home from the Grand Cinema in Stockholm at 23:21. He is pronounced dead 45 minutes later.

June 4th, 1989
In the early morning hours, the Chinese People's Liberation Army starts liberating Tiananmen Square in central Beijing from protesting students.

July 9th, 1989
Bishop Pietro Salvatore Colombo (1922-1989), who was appointed as the first Bishop in Mogadishu in 1975, is murdered in the city's cathedral. He had served the people of Somalia since 1946.

October 15th, 1990
Mikhail Gorbachev (1931-2022) is awarded the Nobel Peace Prize. Later that year in December he is unable to travel to Oslo to accept the award in person and sends first deputy foreign minister, Andrei Kovalyov, to accept the award in his stead.

November 4th, 1995
Yigal Amir—a right-wing extremist who opposed the signing of the Oslo Accords, kills 1994 Nobel Peace Prize laureate Yitzhak Rabin (1922-1995) in Tel Aviv with two shots.

June 30th, 2000
Nine people are crushed to death at the Roskilde festival while Pearl Jam is performing on the Orange stage.

September 28th, 2000
The Israeli politician Ariel Sharon (1928-2014) walks onto the Temple Mount in Jerusalem, surrounded by hundreds of Israeli riot police. He had been asked repeatedly not to visit the site due to the multiple controversies surrounding his persona. The subsequent escalation of violence is referred to as 'Second Intifada' or also as the 'Al-Aqsa Intifada'.

December 27th, 2008
After several years of rocket attacks launched by Palestinian groups from Gaza, Israel launches 'Operation Cast Lead'. Initial airstrikes eliminate around 100 pre-planned targets in the Gaza strip within about three and a half minutes. Until the end of hostilities on January 18th, 2009, a total of between 1166 to 1417 people are killed on the Palestinian side. On the Israeli side, 13 people are killed—including four Israeli Defense Forces' soldiers, who are killed by friendly fire, while defending Israel on Gaza soil.

December 17th, 2010
The twenty-six-year-old street vendor Tarek el-Tayeb Mohamed Bouazizi (1984-2011) sets himself on fire in the Tunisian city of Sidi Bouzid as a response to the harassment from a corrupt municipal official. He dies from his extensive burns on January 4th, 2011, and his act of self-immolation is considered the catalyst of the so-called 'Arab Spring' against the autocratic regimes in North Africa and the Middle East.

July 22nd, 2011
Anders Behring Breivik—a lone wolf domestic far-right terrorist—launches two sequential terror attacks in Norway. The first attack is a car bomb explosion within the executive government quarter in

the center of Oslo killing eight people. The second attack is a mass shooting at a youth summer camp on the island of Utøya, where sixty-nine people are killed. As of now, the shooting on Utøya remains the deadliest mass shooting by a lone perpetrator in recorded history.

November 12th, 2015

After accepting over 150,000 refugees since January 1st, 2015 Sweden suspends the Schengen Agreement and introduces border controls. These prove to be especially difficult to implement on the Øresundbron bridge between Copenhagen and Malmö, as it lacks the needed facilities. It was planned and constructed relying on very relaxed custom checks and opened to traffic on July 1st, 2000.

April 4th, 2018

A decommissioned cruise ship named Ocean Gala 1, which was initially launched on October 16th, 1981 as the cruiseferry MS Scandinavia (and subsequently was also named Stardancer, Viking Serenade, Island Escape, and Ocean Gala) is beached for scrapping in Alang in the Indian state of Gujarat.

May 25th, 2019

All WHO (World Health Organization) members endorse the eleventh revision of the International Classification of Diseases (ICD-11). 'Parental Alienation Syndrome', which has been first named by Columbia University child psychiatrist Dr. Richard A. Gardner (1931-2003) in 1985, is for the first time included under ICD-11 code QE52.0 using the term 'caregiver-child relationship problem'. 'Parental alienation' and 'parental estragement' are initially approved and included as index terms for QE52.0. The WHO ultimately removes these two index terms after receiving a multitude of commentaries including—among others—a document called 'Collective Memo of Concern to: World Health Organization' dated July 10th, 2019 from '352 Concerned Family Law Academics,

Family Violence Experts, Family Violence Research Institutes, Child Development and Child Abuse Experts, Children's Rights Networks and Associations and 764 concerned individuals'. The overwhelming majority of the individuals supporting the memo have feminine given names.

July 12th, 2019
Forty-two-year-old Somali-Canadian social activist and media executive Hodan Naalaye (1976-2019) is killed together with her husband during a terrorist attack on the hotel they were staying at in Kismayo, Somalia. The couple leaves behind two sons.

December 31st, 2019
The Municipal Health Commission of the city of Wuhan in Central China's Hubei province informs the public about a viral pneumonia outbreak.

Trademark and Copyright
Acknowledgement:

| Migrationsverket | Swedish Migration Agency | Viking Serenade | Google | World Surf League Men's Championship Tour | Aker Sykehus | Vinmonopolet | Folkebibliotek | Sparebanken Vest | DNB | One Desire | Dolce&Gabbana | Facebook | *Verdens Gang* | European Commission | Bang&Olufsen | AirPods | Ginger Organic | Danish Foreign Ministry | International Red Cross | Frederiksberg Hospital | Nokia 5110 | FADL | Rigshospitalets Kollegium | South America on a shoestring | Lonely Planet| SOS Alarm | Novo Nordisk | IRONMAN | Våpenkort | It's a small world | Garmin Forerunner 945 | Mr. Sweden | Bispebjerg Hospital | Kildeskovshallen pool | Dyrehavsbakken | ÖTILÖ | Bodil Award | Serie 7/Model 3107 chair | PK55™ | Legemiddelverk | PAN Pharma Ltd. | Glock P80 | krteček | Czechoslovac Radio | Antonov | Malmö Bultofta Airport | Grand Mosque in Mecca | Indiana Jones | *Bergens Tidende* | *British Journal of Obstetrics and Gynecology* | *Neues Deutschland* | Handelsbygningen | CNN | United Nations | Starbucks | Stratosphere Tower | Disneyland | Democratic National Convention | The Jewish Agency | World Pro Surf team | World Zionist Organization | Rabin Medical Center | Global Week for Future | Wright-Geimsa | Pipe Masters | Vans Pro | Hawaiian Pro | Corona Open Gold Coast | Manolo Blahnik Butina pumps | Škoda Octavia | Google Maps | BeoPlay | Pasante King condoms | Air France | Tango Festival y Mundial | European Society of Cardiology | Politiken e-avisen | Christian Louboutin | Sydvestjysk Sygehus | nature | Sycamore | DSB | World Trade Organization | Netflix | la casa de papel | Ole Mathiesen Classic 1962 | United States Space Force | Hangar 6 | Joint Base Andrews | Havforskningsinstituttet | Ambu | Siri | Ældrecentret Lundgårdends | Lørdagsrevyen | Nord Stream 2 Pipeline | The Hammer of Thor

Music Cited:

Billie Jean (Written by: Michael Jackson; ATV Music Publishing)

Englishman In New York (Written by: Sting; Sony / ATV Music Publishing)

I Shot The Sheriff (Written by: Bob Marley; Kobalt Music Publishing)

Fernando (Written by: Benny Andersson, Björn Ulvaeus; Sony / ATV Music Publishing / Universal Music Publishing Group)

Rehab (Written by: Amy Winehouse; Sony / ATV Music Publishing)

Fairytale (Written by: Alexander Rybak, Kim Bergseth; Sony / ATV Music Publishing)

Satellite (Written by: Julie Frost, John Gordon; Emi April Music)

Por Una Cabeza (Carlos Gardel; Lyrics by Alfredo Le Pera)

The Nutcracker (Pyotr Ilyich Tchaikovsky)

It's The End Of The World As We Know It (And I Feel Fine) (Written by: John Michael Stipe, Michael Mills, Peter Lawrence Buck, William Thomas Berry; Universal Music Publishing Group)

Macarena (Written by: Dalmo Medeiros, Antonio Romero Monge, Rafael Ruiz Perdigones; Sony / ATV Music Publishing / Werner Chappell Music)

Corduroy (Written by: David Abbruzzese, Eddie Vedder, Jeff Ament, Mike Mccready, Stone Gossard; Universal Music Publishing Group)

Oops! ... I Did It Again (Written by: Martin Max, Rami Yacoub; Universal Music Publishing Group / Kobalt Music Publishing)

Rise Like A Phoenix (Written by: Alexander Zuckowski, Charlie Mason, Joey Patulka, Julian Maas; Universal Music Publishing Group / Kobalt Music Publishing)

It's A Small World (After All) (Written by: Richard M. Sherman, Robert B. Sherman; Disney / UNICEF)

I Will Survive (Written by: Dino Fekaris, Frederikk J. Perren; Universal Music Publishing Group)

Boléro (Maurice Ravel)

Piano Quartet In A Minor, Op. 66 (Charles Marie Widor)

Swan Lake (Pyotr Ilyich Tchaikovsky)

Concerto For Orchestra Bb 123 (Béla Bartók)

Arcade (Written by: William Douglas Burr Knox, Duncan De Moor, Joel Nils Anders Sjoo; Spark Records / Universal Music)

Bella Ciao (Italian Folk Song)

We Are The World (Written by: Michael Jackson, Lionel Richie; Sony / ATV Music Publishing)

What Is Truly Scandinavian? (Created by '&Co.' and produced by 'New Land' for SAS—Scandinavian Airlines System)

Two Insomnias (Jalāl ad-Dīn Muhammad Rūmī—aka 'Rumi')

Friendship (Alexander Sergeyevich Pushkin)

Personal Acknowledgements

This story would never have been told without the selfless guidance and incredible support of Hanka and Alex, who are its godparents, as well as Noëmi, who is Faiza's guardian angel.

Special thanks to Alexander, Belinda, Connie, Devin, Dia, Henry, Hyunmee, Joanne, Karen, Laura, LP, Maryam, Riley, Sara, Silvia, Tom, Victoria, and Xeni for all their feedback, input, and advice.

Thanks to Teryl for all the help selecting Pia's cocktails.

Last but not least, special thanks to Kate G. and Megan Badilla for all their professional help with the editing and cover design—I met both of them through the "Books for Palestine" auction held from June 1st until June 4th, 2021 and our collaboration benefited the "Middle East Children's Alliance [MECA]"—www.mecafor-peace.org .

Correlations Trilogy

BOOK III: A Story about the Future—'One Day in the Life of WJ0-two-zero-eight-four'

It would be the brightest day; as every thirty-three days. Although day means something different here and it's not clear why Earth conventions are still used. As if Earth is the center of the universe. But all this doesn't really matter anymore, as it's the day you now know, you will die.

* * *

BOOK I: A Story about the Past —'Folios from an Epistle written on a Steamer'

Epilogue becomes Prologue
Borgo a Buggiano – Italy – Wednesday May 27th, 2020

"Dr. Gianetti?"
"Yes, Shewit. I'm upstairs together with Charlotte, Tore and Erik."

instagram.com/correlations_trilogy

Printed by Imprimerie Gauvin
Gatineau, Québec